REASONS
for Avoiding
Friends

MEGAN LEAVELL

REASONS
for Avoiding
Friends

MEGAN LEAVELL

Cedar House Press

This is a work of fiction. Names, characters, businesses, places, events and incidents are either the products of the author's imagination or used in a fictitious manner. Any resemblance to actual persons, living or dead, or actual events is purely coincidental.

ISBN 978-0-578-88685-5

REASONS FOR AVOIDING FRIENDS

Cover art illustration © kmeds7 / Shutterstock
Author photo © AGL

FIRST EDITION

For Hal

REASONS
for Avoiding
Friends

1

GWEN

SEASON'S GREETINGS, FRIENDS and family, and a Happy New Year!

Would it be a happy new year? Gwen wasn't so sure about that. She set her pen down on the kitchen table, her lips pinching when she noticed a fresh marker stain near Bea's chair. Purple, of course. A worse offender than grape juice. It would never come out now. She could spend the next twenty minutes scrubbing and cursing and regretting a string of life choices that had brought her to this moment, or she could close her eyes and take a calming breath like her "books" (yes, they were of the self-help variety) suggested. She decided to do neither. Instead, she did something her books would never support and walked to the fridge, pulled the wine from the inside door, and refilled her glass, savoring the sweet sense of rebellion.

She took a long, steadying sip before topping the glass off and returning to the table. Still, the words were there. *Happy New Year.*

Well, no need to dwell on that.

REASONS FOR AVOIDING FRIENDS

It's been a wonderful twelve months in the Riley household.

She chewed the cap of the ballpoint. *Wonderful* was such a broad term. She could think of a few more fitting adjectives to describe their year, *disastrous* being at the top of her list. But no one needed to know about all of *that*, so she gripped her pen and persevered.

Beatrice, our "baby," is now seven, and absolutely thriving in first grade. She's made oodles of adorable little friends, and I'm fortunate enough to volunteer in her classroom at least once a month to observe her zest for learning.

More like pluck the straw wrappers from juice boxes as the noise grew to a fever pitch and the teacher, six months out from collecting her pension, sat at her desk with a glazed look in her eyes, her attention fixed on some random object in the corner, refusing to take control, while Gwen fought off a migraine. But no need to overshare...

While she's been busy with ballet, ceramics, and gymnastics, her love for tap dancing simply shines nearly as much as her thriving artistic talents.

Gwen's gaze drifted to the purple marker stain. She reached for her wineglass again. There was no sense in mentioning that Bea was unable to do a somersault, something that had made Gwen feel like a failure of a parent when it was brought to her attention that first, miserable day of gymnastics class, which also turned out to be their last. Olga, a Russian instructor in her mid-sixties who appeared more like a twenty-something blonde from behind and who probably looked better in a bikini than Gwen ever had (make that *certainly*, not *probably*), gave Gwen an icy stare at the end of class, saying in a thick accent, "She cannot do a somersault."

Bea had stood at her side, sniffling, her eyes red from crying, and Gwen had been too stunned to even rebuff the accusation. Instead, she had turned to Bea and said, "You don't know how to do a somersault?" Gwen had naïvely assumed they taught this in school. As a child, she'd spent hours doing cartwheels in the backyard, even if she'd never been good.

"I don't know how. And...I'm scared," Bea said in that small voice of hers, and Olga's right eyebrow gave a judgmental lift. But no need to mention that.

Declan, almost ten, tickled the ivories at the annual Christmas concert, and nearly brought down the house with applause.

Now that was a stretch. The poor kid had barely pushed through "Jingle Bells," stumbling on every note and going back to the beginning out of frustration not once but twice, leaving the audience all but tortured for the entire five minutes until finally he lifted his fingers from the keys and turned to give them all a hesitant smile.

From pure relief, the audience of the Westlake Music Academy had clapped more fiercely than it had for even Victor Smythe, who had played some complicated piece by Mozart, even while propped on a phone book. His mother, Caroline, had leaned eagerly forward in her chair for the entire performance, practically mouthing the notes, her anxiety so overwhelming, Gwen couldn't peel her eyes from her next-door neighbor until the piece was over and a victorious smirk filled Caroline's face, followed by a less-than-subtle fist pump.

Gwen sighed at the memory. Declan and Victor had started piano lessons the same day, three years ago this February, just a few short months after Caroline had taken occupancy next door, sparking the trend of newcomers to Elmwood Lane after

Westlake was officially branded the best suburb for young families in the state of Wisconsin, and the small downtown erupted with chic boutiques and yoga studios and manicured housewives pushing double strollers, lattes in hand. Declan had been seven; Victor had been two and a half. Gwen had assumed that based on their age discrepancy, just for once, one of her children might have an edge on the two neighboring Smythe children, who had proven within weeks of their arrival that they were more gifted in every possible way.

Gwen was starting to suspect that Caroline wasn't being completely honest when she claimed that Victor only took a thirty-minute piano lesson each week. She vowed to sit down with her only son once a week and put her rusty musical skills to the test. It would be one of her New Year's resolutions. Along with dropping the fifteen pounds she'd put on since moving out of the city and back to her hometown eight years ago, less than one hundred miles from Chicago but another world entirely.

Make that twenty pounds. Oh, who was she kidding? Twenty-five.

Gwen felt the familiar tug of nostalgia, followed by the heavy heart that always accompanied it. She looked around the kitchen—big and bright, with white cabinets that soared to the ceiling. In the city, they had a galley kitchen. You couldn't open the fridge and oven doors at the same time. Even Declan's high chair had been stuck in the dining room, which doubled as a playroom.

It was the right choice to move back here, she told herself for the umpteenth time. Her life was better here. Her life was wonderful.

She looked back at the letter.

Norah is now a thriving high school freshman. It's a rigorous program—and she's choosing to completely devote herself to her studies for the moment. Perhaps cheerleading or the drama club are still in her future, but for now, she's keeping her head in the books.

Crap. This reminded Gwen that she had to deal with another parent-teacher conference in February. It snuck up on her each year when she'd only just recovered from November's meeting. Miss Sweeney was barely out of high school herself, and sometimes Gwen didn't know which was worse: dealing with a know-it-all teenager or her know-it-all teacher. Maybe Michael could go in her place. He still owed her for that last time, when, after Gwen had hit every red light on Main and shown up twelve minutes into their fifteen-minute slot, Miss Sweeney had dared to ask her why she seemed so stressed, and rather than let it go, Gwen had taken the bait, gone through a laundry list of everything she was dealing with, from Bea wetting her pants in ballet class, to Declan breaking a window above the garage with a basketball, to the endless stream of perceived domestic inequalities that seemed to have defined her marriage for the last fifteen years, the latest of which was an argument right before the conference about who took out the trash more often. Miss Sweeney's sweet, unlined face had faded from its oddly condescending smile to one of confusion and then pity.

Gwen didn't need pity. She needed some help.

Really, she needed a vacation.

Gwen narrowed her eyes at her Christmas letter. Michael. She would have to mention him in the letter. But what to write? *Michael is STILL unemployed.* Or maybe, *Michael has now taken to disappearing from the house for long periods of time, without bothering to mention where he's going. I'd offer a reward for any tips, but seeing as we might lose the house soon, I'm belly-up at the moment.*

She chuckled into her glass, even if there was nothing funny about her situation. She'd come back to Michael later.

As for me, I'm happy to report that after a nearly fifteen-year sabbatical, I have finally returned to the workforce! While it's certainly a challenge to balance domestic life with my new role in sales and marketing, it's definitely not without its perks.

Sales and marketing. Yes, that's what she called it. It had been odd at first, a little foreign as the words rolled over her tongue, but the more she said it the more natural it felt. She wasn't just a mom anymore; she was in sales and marketing! A businesswoman, taking charge of her life and her future, making something of herself.

Smiling at the thought, she was just bringing her wineglass to her mouth for one last sip when Bea started her tap dancing on the laundry room floor, and Bailey, who had been asleep on his favorite bed near the back door, let out a bark so loud that Gwen gave a little jump and smacked the glass against her teeth instead of gliding it between her lips.

She darted into the powder room and flicked on the light. Her reflection these days always gave her a little startle. Sometimes she'd pass a mirror and she wouldn't even recognize herself. Other times, she'd positively gape and wonder, when did *that* happen?

Gwen thought back on her younger, thinner, cuter self and felt something awfully close to jealousy. But could you even be jealous of yourself? You could, once you had gray roots every three weeks and it had been four since your last seven-buck home-coloring job.

There were frown lines around her mouth from worry and hollow circles under her eyes from lack of sleep.

"Gwendolyn, the problem with you is that you wear every emotion," her mother had said to her when she was eighteen and anxious about meeting her college roommate and going to the freshman orientation alone. "I can tell everything you are thinking just by looking at you."

Like so many conversations with her mother, Gwen hadn't been sure if that remark had been a compliment or an insult, and she had spent the entire party obsessing over how she appeared to her new classmates. That and hiding in the bathroom.

She practiced her tight-lipped, *see, it's all going to be fine* smile in the mirror. But God, it took effort. And really, what did she have to smile about? She'd just slapped a wineglass to her teeth and...

Well, fabulous. She'd chipped her front tooth. On a *wineglass*. Not by much, but it was there, and it couldn't be undone.

She closed her eyes, just for one moment, daring to hope that when she opened them again she might see a different reflection staring back at her. Not just an almost-forty-year-old woman with an intact tooth, but the woman she used to be. The woman with a freshly cut bob that bounced when she walked. A woman who only had to color her hair for variety, not from necessity. A woman who didn't have saddlebags and a bit (okay, not exactly a bit, if the ripped camisole tops that used to slide over her torso said anything) of a muffin top that wouldn't go away, no matter how many mornings she choked down a kale smoothie.

Gwen went back into the kitchen and dumped what remained in her wineglass down the sink, resisting the urge to funnel it back into the bottle to save a few bucks, then wiped the crumbs from the counter (frozen pizza—she wasn't proud, but it was quick and easy and kept all three kids happy). On the magnetic notepad stuck to the fridge, buried among Bea's drawings, some holiday cards, and the school's K-12 calendar, she made a note to call the dentist first thing Monday morning. The tooth would have to be sanded down, and the other one as well, to match. The price would be a few hundred at least. Perfect timing, when the credit card bill from Christmas purchases was expected any day.

She checked the clock on the microwave. Eight twenty-one. She fluttered her lashes, mustering up all the willpower she had, and began the long trek up the stairs to Norah's room.

Upstairs, it was quiet; only the muffled sounds of Bea's tapping could be heard from below. Meaning that Norah had either followed her orders when Gwen had sent her upstairs in the middle of dinner, or she was wearing earbuds.

She didn't bother to knock but instead reached for the handle, only to find that the knob didn't turn.

It had started. Her daughter was locking her out. Of her bedroom. Of her life. Gwen's heart began to ache when she thought back on that little girl who would flash her a smile full of baby teeth and reach up to hold her hand when they got out of the car.

Wait. What was she saying? That was Bea, not Norah. Norah had always yanked her hand away in defiance, even at the age of eighteen months, and Gwen had been forced to hold her by the wrist, clenching her teeth in frustration against the wiggling child who even then seemed to want nothing more than to get away from her.

She knocked on the door. Hard. Nothing.

She sighed, knocked again. This time she heard the rustling of bedding. A word—no doubt a curse—muttered under Norah's breath, and the pop of metal as the glass knob twisted under her palm and the door opened in front of her.

Norah stood in her plaid flannel pajamas. Her light brown hair was pulled off her face in a topknot. She was wearing a bright green face mask that made the whites of her eyes look a little sallow.

So this was how she'd spent her hour and half of solitary confinement. Performing beauty treatments. Maybe someone should send Gwen to her room for an hour. Imagine the luxury! She could take a hot bath without the threat of someone pounding on the door, needing something. Or she could paint her nails—something she really should do before the next Forevermore Beauty meeting, she thought, glad that she had remembered.

She knew she should probably remind Norah that being sent to her room meant she was supposed to lie on her bed and stare at the ceiling, not indulge in a spa routine. She glanced at the bed, where one of the romance novels Norah had started reading (and which Gwen had also forbidden) was splayed facedown on the dark purple duvet cover.

Once this room had been a sunny pale yellow, with pink-and-yellow-striped roman-style curtains that billowed at the bottom. There'd been a small round table in the corner with two pink chairs where Norah would sit and draw pictures, scribbling "Mommy, I love you!" at the top. God, how she'd taken it for granted. Cherished each one, but assumed they would never stop coming. She looked away, at the window seat. A heap of clothes was dumped where sweet little stuffed animals had once sat in a row. Teddy Bear. One-armed Rabbit. Lady Goose.

Gwen tried not to let the disappointment register on her face as she studied the newest addition to the room—Norah's posters of pop stars and teen idols, which replaced the precious pink-framed prints of little girls engaging in simple pleasures such as skipping rope or holding a balloon. She worked on maintaining a closed-mouth, *see, I'm perfectly pleasant* smile.

"What are you smiling about?" Norah immediately accused her.

"Nothing." There was nothing to smile about in this situation. Not only had the room been taken over by teenage angst, but the little girl who had once lived in the sunny yellow and pink bedroom, first door on the left at the top of the stairs, with the window seat that lent a view of the tall oak in the front yard, was gone. And in her place was a scowling teenager.

Maybe she wasn't scowling, Gwen reconsidered. Maybe her face was just tight from the mask.

She looked into her daughter's angry gray eyes. No. She was definitely scowling.

"You know you're not supposed to be reading those!" Gwen grabbed the book from Norah's bed, tsking at the cover of the man and woman engaged in rapture against the side of an office desk, and decided to give it a read next week when the kids were (finally!) back in school.

"Then why do you keep buying them?" Norah asked evenly.

"I don't keep—" Except she did. But not for the reasons her daughter believed. She bought them because her mother bought them. Because it was something to talk about when there was nothing else to talk about, other than a new line on Gwen's face or the sad fact that she had inherited her father's sisters' thighs after all. "This is Grandma's book. She left it here last week."

Norah didn't look convinced.

"Fine." Gwen tossed the book back onto the bed. "But skip the naughty parts."

Naughty parts. Had she really just said that? That's what her mother called those scenes, even though she clearly enjoyed them, not that she'd ever admit it. She curled her lip, realizing her error too late.

"What's wrong with your tooth?" Norah blurted, her eyes growing wide in alarm.

"Nothing." Gwen clamped her mouth shut.

"But there's something!" Norah was pushing toward her, but Gwen pulled back.

"It's nothing," she replied through partially closed lips. She could tell by the lift of Norah's eyebrow that her daughter wasn't convinced. Pulling in a breath, she turned back to parenting mode, and the issue at hand.

She moved to sit next to Norah on her unmade bed, but then, remembering the tooth, thought better of it and took the desk chair a safe five feet from Norah instead.

"You know why I sent you to your room."

Norah flopped onto her bed and rolled her eyes dramatically to the ceiling. "It was no big deal!"

"Skipping fifth period to go to the mall in a car of an up-perclassman is a big deal. And I'm just finding out about this now? Three weeks after it happened? From another parent?"

It had been so humiliating, bumping into Lucy's mom like that at the cheese counter today. It had been bad enough that she'd been caught by the size-two woman reaching for a hunk of double-cream brie, but then to find out that both their children had broken school rules!

"Lucy's mom doesn't care," Norah huffed.

"Oh, I know she doesn't care!" Gwen's voice rose. Lucy's mom seemed to find it amusing, seemed tickled at the thought of their girls being popular with an older crowd. "So you lied to me, on top of it all."

Where was Michael? If Michael were here, Norah would be sitting in rod-straight silence, not daring to speak so much as roll her eyes. It wasn't that Michael was the disciplinarian—no, that job had fallen neatly into Gwen's lap, because someone had to take it. But because Michael never—okay, rarely—played Bad Cop, when he did, he got results.

Whereas Gwen got face masks and eye rolls.

"It was just gym!" Norah replied.

Gwen fought hard not to agree with her here. Gym class every day did seem excessive, especially when they were constantly threatening to cut funding for the arts, which were much more interesting.

See, if she could only bring herself to attend a PTA meeting, she might have an opportunity to voice her opinion. But the thought of attending one of those… She practically shivered. She'd sooner enroll in high school all over again.

"I understand it was gym, but it still counts as skipping a class. And leaving school grounds."

"We were just going to lunch!"

Such a reasonable argument, the human side of Gwen thought. The mom side, however, was forced to stick to the rules at hand, which had been broken. "If it happens again, they could suspend you."

She could just picture how that would go over with the other moms. It was bad enough that every semester, the school's honor rolls were posted in the *Westlake Current* and that none of her children had ever hit it.

Yet.

With the tutor she'd found for a whopping sixty bucks an hour, there was newfound hope. Bea was still on the "satisfactory/exceeds grade expectation" system. Declan had one year to go before real grades kicked in. Maybe he'd surprise her.

"Lucy's nice to me," Norah said in a low voice, and something in Gwen softened. She knew that Norah had lost some of her middle school friends over the summer. She knew what it was like to just want to fit in.

"Promise me you won't do it again," Gwen said.

"Can you at least write a note to get me out of gym sometimes?" Norah's eyes drooped at the corners, the way they used to when she was little and helpless and needed her mommy to help her. And damn it if the trick didn't work.

Gwen could still remember those miserable middle and high school days, back when gym was only twice a week, not five. All the other girls would casually disrobe in the locker room, and there would be Gwen, cramming herself into a stall, squeezing her nylon shorts between her knees as she wiggled out of her too-tight jeans, hoping an article of clothing didn't slip into the toilet. Then there was the tyrannical Miss B (Gwen wasn't sure she ever did know the woman's full name), with her stocky build and her whistle hanging around her neck at all times, who would bark out orders and only showed a human side the one day that Romy—always a little awkward, that girl—had thrown a basketball right at Gwen's nose when Gwen was standing less than two feet away. The tears had flowed hot and fast, and Gwen had waited for the name-calling, the beratement that was sure to come following any whiff of weakness in Miss B's gymnasium. Instead, Miss B had declared her tears to be an "unavoidable reaction" to the location of the injury and sent her off to the school nurse, where Gwen had spent a glorious forty minutes lying on her back with an ice pack on her face, fantasizing about kissing Joe Cassidy from her math class.

It was no wonder that the day she graduated from high school, she never exercised again. And why now she relied on compression leggings to smooth her paunch. Thank you, Miss B!

"I'll write you a note," Gwen said, with mixed feelings. She hesitated. "Just don't tell your father."

Mother of the year. Yet again, mother of the year. It was becoming a theme, from the day her first child was born and she and Michael had read in some ridiculous parenting manual that the only way to keep an infant from ruining your life was to essentially train them like a dog. To show them that you were in charge, and that life ran on a schedule, and that you would not cater to their every demand. And so, not knowing any better, they had attempted to train their infant through psychological mind games of teaching her that they would not come when she cried unless it was for a valid reason, like when a diaper needed changing or when she was due to be fed (on schedule!). Gwen had cracked after two days and was still waiting to forgive herself. Now, more than fourteen years later, she looked back on that first night at home with Norah and the shame filled her so deeply that she was willing to do anything and everything to make it up to the poor child. And if that meant writing her a few notes to avoid a hundred sit-ups and some pull-ups on the very bar that Gwen herself would dangle from, while kids giggled in the background and Miss B barked out "Fight through the pain!" and eventually "You have no muscles!"—well, then, so be it.

She'd left her one-week-old infant to cry it out in the crib, alone, for God's sake. The least she could do was save her now.

"Can I be excused now, Mom? This face mask is starting to harden and I need to wash it off before it ruins my skin."

Gwen sighed. There was no point telling Norah that she had beautiful, flawless skin that neither makeup nor facial treatments needed to fix. There was no point in saying anything, she feared.

"Sure."

Norah grinned, her teeth a flash of white through the avocado-green mask that indeed did seem to crack a bit at the effort. "You're the best, Mom."

Gwen savored those words. She tried not to think of what Michael would say if he found out about this anti-gym class conspiracy. Michael was probably at the gym right now, if his membership hadn't already been revoked.

15

She pushed that thought aside for a moment. She was a mother, above all, and right now, she was the best. Nothing would spoil this moment.

From downstairs, her phone started to ring.

About time, she thought. There were days when Michael used to check in all the time, call just to say hi. Then, later, it was usually her calling, to discuss dinner plans, to remind him about Declan's soccer game, like they were coworkers tasked with an endless list of shared responsibilities that didn't stop until they passed out from exhaustion, only to have it all start up again the very next morning. Now Michael was home most days, job searching, and when he wasn't home, he was "networking." Sometimes going to the gym fell under that category. When he didn't call by six, she knew that they'd be eating dinner without him.

She took her exit from Norah's lair and hurried down the stairs and toward the back of the house. She lifted the phone from the kitchen table and frowned at the screen.

Eileen Warner.

Her mother.

Gwen experienced the same internal debate she always did when her mother called, which she did at least once a day, even though she never seemed to particularly enjoy the conversation.

Regretting not finishing her glass of wine, Gwen only then remembered her tooth. She'd have to get it fixed before her mother saw her. She'd never hear the end of it otherwise.

The phone rang again, possibly for the last time. Decision time.

If she didn't answer, her mother would just start to text. There was no avoiding her.

Gwen swiped her screen, closed her eyes, and pressed the phone to her ear. "Hello?"

"What is that dreadful noise?" came the greeting. "Are you letting that child tap dance inside the house again? She'll ruin your floors, you know."

Gwen walked to the adjacent laundry room and, after giving Bea a wink, closed the door. "Hello, Mother," she said wearily, wishing she had taken the text route after all.

"Is everything all right?" her mother replied, her tone accusatory, implying quite clearly that she did not believe everything was all right in the least.

"Yes. Why do you ask?" *Now, don't get defensive, Gwen. She just asked you if everything was all right, for Chrissake. It's not like the time she asked you if you were feeling constipated.*

"The way you answered… You sound so tired!"

And cue the insult. "I am tired, Mom."

"Why?" Her mother posed the question as if it were the most preposterous thing Gwen could have said, other than, say, she'd decided to shave her head and get her nose pierced.

Gwen refrained from pointing out the obvious, like the fact that she had three kids who were all helpless in their own special way. She thought of Michael. Make that four kids these days.

Bailey slapped his empty water bowl, causing it to thump against the floor. Five. Five dependents who needed something of her from morning to night. She was tired. Tired enough to be going gray before the age of forty. Something else she'd inherited from her father's sisters, her mother had been sure to point out.

Gwen picked up the ceramic water bowl before Bailey could slap it again and turned on the tap, running her hand under it until the water turned cold. She was projecting again, letting a small thing her mother said bother her in a very big way. She was looking for the problem, assuming the worst. Her cup was already full, the self-help books explained. And all it took was one was more drop to send things spilling over the edge.

The important thing was to take a sip from that cup every once in a while, replenish the relationship so to speak. Give credit where it was due.

On Christmas Eve her mother had completely abstained from commenting on the food Gwen had cooked, instead choosing to only slide it around on her plate, even if everyone else seemed to enjoy it.

Gwen softened. Okay. The glass wasn't overflowing just yet.

"Well, speaking of tired, you'll never guess whose picture I saw in one of those celebrity magazines today," her mother said.

Gwen carefully set the water bowl back on the floor. Bailey sniffed it and then walked away to curl up in his bed.

"Since when do you read those kinds of magazines?" Her mother was more of a *Reader's Digest* type. Or so she liked people to think.

"Why shouldn't I read those kinds of magazines? What are you implying?" Eileen sniffed.

Her mother was fishing for a compliment again. Or picking a fight. Gwen didn't have the energy for either. "Am I going to guess?" she asked, sinking onto a counter stool that gave a view of the dirty dishes.

"It was Iris," her mother replied, her tone laced with satisfaction.

Iris. Gwen's heart beat a little faster. Sure, not a day went by where she didn't think of her childhood best friend, especially since moving back to Westlake, and she kept tabs on her current life through social media, too. But it had been a long time since she had talked about Iris. Even longer since she'd spoken to her. "Iris Winarski?"

"Iris Drake," Eileen corrected. "You remember she married that wealthy man years ago. Didn't invite any of us to the wedding, of course."

"I think they eloped," Gwen explained, and by then Gwen had three young kids and a dog and responsibilities that would have made any sort of travel nigh to impossible, but nonetheless, she'd been a little stung.

"Iris always did aim high," Gwen's mother was saying. If there was more implication to that statement, Gwen didn't press. It was true, after all. Iris had always planned for a big, exciting life, whereas Gwen... She'd just wanted this.

Or a better version of it.

"I haven't talked to Iris in years." Gwen still felt sad about that. They'd gone to different colleges, ended up in different cities, drifted apart the way people did. Only it wasn't that simple, was it? Not really. They were technically still "friends" on Facebook—Iris had been the first person that Gwen had "friended" when she started her account back before Declan was born, back when they still communicated at least monthly through text or email or the occasional phone call. But then, there were lots of "friends" like that, and Iris rarely posted anything aside from a snapshot of a particularly gorgeous plate of food at a restaurant that Gwen could only dream of dining at, or a posed photo from a charity event. Gwen tended to analyze those for quite some time: the hair, the makeup, the dress, the shoes. The jewelry.

"Well, I saved the clipping. She's still pretty." Of course. "Finally got those teeth fixed, not that it mattered with her looks."

Gwen remembered the slight buck teeth, the wide grin that Iris would flash her that was both exciting and reassuring at the same time. It was the very smile she'd given her that first day they'd met, in first grade, when Gwen was feeling shy and nervous and all of the other girls seemed to snicker at the filly lace pink dress her mother had made her wear when everyone else was in jeans or T-shirts.

The prettiest girl in the room had marched right over to Gwen at recess, where she sat on the swings by herself, wishing she could fit in, wishing she could hide.

At first, she'd been nervous as Iris approached, but as the purpose in her eyes turned into that big smile, Gwen had relaxed.

"I wish I had that dress," was the first thing Iris had ever said to her. "I'd do anything for a dress that pretty."

Gwen smiled now, thinking of how her life had changed that day.

"Iris was always the most beautiful girl in town," Gwen mused. And she'd chosen Gwen out of everyone to be her closest friend.

"Even more beautiful now!" Eileen went on. "But so thin!"

Gwen sighed. This morning she had realized that she could no longer remove her wedding rings. And it was winter!

"She sure got the life she wanted, didn't she? Married to a rich man. Living in New York City!" Eileen mused. "It was always about glamour with that girl. She never would have been satisfied in Westlake."

"No," Gwen admitted. "Probably not."

Certainly even less satisfied than Gwen was. If such a thing were possible.

"Well, I should probably go. I want to get these holiday cards out in the morning post." As soon as Gwen said it, she wished she thought of a better excuse, like Bea slipping in her tap shoes and needing stitches.

Sure enough, her mother cried, "You're just sending them out *now?*"

In her mother's defense, it was December 30. Still...

"The holidays are a busy time," Gwen replied.

"Couldn't you have just done a little each day?"

Deep breaths, Gwen reminded herself. She willed one of her children to interrupt her, need her, call out to her. She looked desperately at the laundry room door. Bea was still tapping with full force.

"You could have done them in front of the TV."

"I was busy wrapping presents in front of the TV."

"But when you were done wrapping."

"I didn't finish wrapping until eleven o'clock on Christmas Eve!" Gwen all but shouted.

"Oh my." Eileen sounded very put out. "When you were little, I had everything wrapped and waiting in the closet by the twentieth, that way I could enjoy my holidays. But then, I had to be organized. Your father was a busy man, just like Michael."

Gwen had long ago stopped explaining how busy it could be to take care of three kids, a dog, and a house.

"Well, I should go."

"Don't forget our brunch on Monday."

Gwen had indeed forgotten the brunch. Now she closed her eyes. The kids had been off school for nearly two weeks. She'd been counting down the days until this coming Monday since five minutes after the school bus drove away.

"I have a hair appointment that day," she said, immediately vowing to make one. "Does the following Monday work?" It was her thirty-ninth birthday, and brunch with her mother was not how she wanted to spend it, but this was nothing new.

"I thought I would come over for cake that night."

Gwen frowned, trying to remember if she'd made a promise she hadn't intended to keep, and then realized that Eileen had developed this notion all on her own.

"If you want to celebrate with everyone, then a weekend brunch would be better. You know how school nights are with the kids."

"But your birthday is on Monday, and it's my special day!" Eileen cried.

Technically it was her special day, Gwen wanted to point out, but as her father used to say, "You know how she is, Gwen."

Eileen dragged out a long sigh. "I don't suppose my opinion matters anyway. I'll just have to accept the scraps I'm given."

Taking that as a yes, Gwen ended the call. She added the brunch to her calendar, just in case she did forget, even though her mother would no doubt send her a text to remind her. Just in case.

And then, because she couldn't resist, she pulled up Iris's Facebook account on her phone and scanned for any recent posts she might have missed as they came through her feed. There was one of Iris on a jog, looking carefree and happy with Central Park in the background, a fur ear wrap keeping her warm, wearing black workout clothes and a coat that might have cost more than everything currently hanging in Gwen's closet. She didn't look like she would break a sweat.

She looked happy, content, completely at peace with the world. Gwen pushed back the nostalgia that always crept in with the envy when she saw these photos and moved back to the kitchen table, where the draft of her letter still waited, pen poised, for her to finish it. She scanned her mailing list and crossed Caroline's name out—she'd never buy the bit about Declan, and she'd never given Gwen the impression that she thought of Gwen as much of a friend, either. Her mother's card could be given in person, but Eileen would feel slighted if she didn't receive it officially.

There was one name that wasn't on the list. One that must have been cut years ago. Iris.

They were friends, after all. They'd been as close as sisters. Once. You couldn't erase that kind of history, couldn't undo it.

Gwen added Iris's name to the bottom, knowing she could dig up her address somewhere. She ordered Bea to brush her teeth, and Declan the same, and when all three children's bedrooms were silent, only the light still drifting from under Norah's door, she returned to her spot at the kitchen table, Bailey settling at her feet. He was still wearing a Christmas sweater because there was a draft in the house and, well, she'd forgotten to take it off him. He looked particularly cute, with his big brown eyes and a hint of a grin on his mouth. She snapped a picture—but not before angling the camera so she wouldn't pick up any of the dirty dishes in the sink and the clutter on the counter—and uploaded it to her profile, grinning when the first "like" popped up.

So she didn't have size zero workout clothes folded neatly in her drawers. She had the world's cutest dog. And what Iris didn't know wouldn't hurt her. It wouldn't hurt anyone.

Feeling better, she began typing, omitting the part about her new career, because she couldn't even fool herself with that one.

Let them all believe every word in this perfect letter. Because that's what her life was. Just perfect.

2

IRIS

AT FIRST, IRIS had dreaded coming to these meetings, but she did, every Friday at noon when she could be having lunch at Saks.

She didn't come by choice. She came because, like so many other things in life, there was no choice. Fridays at noon. Every Friday; that was the deal, and so help her, she would hold up her end of it.

The unspoken agreement was that by coming here once a week, she and Julian would get back on good terms, back to the way they used to be when they were first married, when life felt exciting and full of possibility. Back when she felt special. Wanted.

So far, that hadn't happened.

As she did every Friday, she walked straight to the folding table at the back of the room, next to the plastic bins of Christmas decorations that were stacked there, since this room was otherwise used for extra storage. The meeting didn't officially start for another eight minutes, but already the box of donuts was empty, save for a sad maple cream that was always left for Kathy. No last name. Just Kathy.

Here she was Just Iris. Iris with the blond ponytail and puffer vest and black leggings, because she told everyone in her real world that she was going for a run and that she'd be back in a little over an hour. But here, in this sterile room in the basement of an Upper West Side church rec center, with overhead lighting that left no room for secrets or disguise, she was Just Iris. No expectations. No assumptions. No pretending.

She used to dread that. Now, it was the most relaxed she felt all week.

She reached for a paper cup and filled it with the watered-down coffee that Nick—the ringleader—always brewed after he stopped to pick up the donuts. The coffee was terrible. She wouldn't drink it, but preparing the cup gave her something to do. Kathy always brought her knitting along. She literally sat and knitted, as if this were some ladies knitting circle and not an AA meeting! The first time Iris had seen Kathy whip out her blue metal needles and set to work on a gender-neutral baby blanket, her eyes had darted to Nick, waiting in heart-thumping anticipation for him to say something. But this wasn't school. And Nick wasn't the teacher. They were all adults. There were no rules. Well, not really.

"Oh, a maple cream!"

Kathy had arrived. As always, she seemed surprised by the discovery of one last maple cream donut sitting in the box. Her meaty hand greedily reached for it and then stopped roughly an eighth of an inch from the orange-hued frosting that coated its surface. She glanced up at Iris, her doe eyes round behind her thick glasses. "Unless... Do you want to split it?"

Iris shook her head. She hadn't lived on salads and white wine for nearly two decades to ruin her figure with a maple cream donut. Especially now. "It's all yours," she said.

Kathy's shoulders did a little dance. "Lucky me!"

Iris watched her consume half the donut in one bite, thinking that Nick really was a good man. No one liked those donuts. He bought them just for Kathy. It was quite possibly the highlight of her week.

Sadly, it was becoming the highlight of Iris's, too.

She took her seat—across from Kathy, two spots down from Nick, and next to Walter, who was now four years clean after falling off the wagon on his fiftieth birthday, buying a sports car with his daughter's college savings fund, and driving it up to Yonkers, where he crashed it through the window of a convenience store a mere forty minutes after driving it off the lot. Once in a while, a new addition was made, and a chair would be dragged over, randomly dividing and expanding their circle. Eventually, their stories were shared. Eventually, they evolved. Sometimes people disappeared. That wasn't an option for her.

She held the coffee cup in her hand, letting the heat warm her fingers. She tried not to think of her to-do list when she was in these meetings. She tried not to let her mind wander to all the things that made her need a drink in the first place. Things like her lunch with Stephanie Clay.

Some might think that was mean of her. Technically, Stephanie was her best friend in New York. They'd known each other since their modeling days, back when Iris was scouted her freshman year of college and did some catalog work to pad her otherwise empty bank account and fix her teeth—even though some in the industry found her smile unique. They'd seen each other through marriages, and, in Stephanie's case, divorce. They were as close as two women could be…technically. They shared everything, after all.

Iris's lips curled. Yep. Everything.

Except this. Stephanie didn't know about her Friday meetings, and Iris intended to keep it that way.

Stephanie wouldn't understand anyway. Back in the day, when the city was still new, she and Stephanie hit all the clubs, all the bars, and somehow managed to wrangle reservations at the hottest restaurants. And it was Stephanie who had been the one to insist on another round that weekend last summer at Iris's country house in Connecticut. In the city, it wouldn't matter—but in the suburbs, where driving was required, it did, and all it took was one missed stop sign on an empty road to cause the police to pull her over, ask her to step out of the car, and determine that she had been driving under the influence.

So really, she had Stephanie to thank for sitting here today. Clutching a paper cup of rapidly cooling bad coffee. Being leered at by Jimmy.

Iris looked away. Jimmy hadn't been around in two weeks, and she'd gotten rather used to it. Speculations had flown, of course. When you missed a meeting, people assumed the worst. The rumor was that Jimmy had gone back to Jack—his favorite brand of whiskey. Jimmy loved to joke about all the fun times he had with Jack, his cloudy blue eyes always turning a little wistful when he described those days, as if he were describing an old friend.

Iris understood. Chardonnay had been the only thing she could depend on for years. Not her husband. Not Stephanie.

There was no security, and the wine had become her one sure thing.

She should just cancel. For a million reasons, she really should. But then Stephanie might get the impression that Iris was avoiding her, and Iris couldn't have that.

Nick took his chair, a signal that the coffee break was over and it was time to get down to business. They started and ended with the Serenity Prayer, the part of each meeting that Iris dreaded the most. It made her feel uneasy. Helpless. Like she wasn't in control of her own life but needed a higher power to get her through the day.

It made her think of Julian. And she didn't like thinking about Julian Drake. Divorce attorney extraordinaire. A real shark in the courtroom, Stephanie murmured to her that first night they'd been introduced, at a charity event for underprivileged youth's art education. Julian had represented Stephanie in her divorce from her first husband, Tony, a man she had married in the heat of the moment before she learned about his gambling habit.

Right. No thinking about Julian, or the way his hand had lingered when they were introduced, or how he'd offered to buy her a drink, then a second, then suggested they get a nightcap somewhere. No thinking about how thrilling the following weeks and months were, how different he had seemed than all the men before him, enough to make her dare to think that finally, her life was settled. That he loved her.

No thinking about him at all. Not here. Not now. This was the one hour per week she was not allowed to think about Julian. Even if he was the reason she was here.

Kathy was up first. Her hand always shot up, but she never stood. She preferred to sit, to share, and sometimes, at first to Iris's horror, to cry. Now, when Kathy cried, a part of Iris died, too. If anyone deserved a drink in this room, it was Kathy.

"Esther Rose isn't doing well," Kathy said tearfully. She kept her eyes on her knitting, her fingers working quickly.

A collective wave of compassion went up in the group. Kathy had spent her entire adult life caring for her ailing and verbally abusive mother, leaving her with no time for romance, no opportunity for children; her joy only to be found in accessible pleasures, like the liquor cabinet and in her sweet gray cat.

When Kathy's mother passed away last year, Kathy had felt empowered to start living her life, and cold turkey, she'd tossed every bottle in the house in the trash and started coming to Saint A's morning meetup. She started knitting again, to keep her hands busy, making baby blankets that turned out to be for Esther Rose, who got cold easily, she explained.

Now Esther Rose was in the vet once a week. Things weren't looking good. For the cat. Or for Kathy.

Kathy started to speak and then shut her mouth, swallowing hard, her lips a thin, pinched line. Her metal knitting needles clicked at a rapid pace. A single tear dripped onto the blanket.

Iris glanced at Nick, thinking again about that stupid donut. A good man. There weren't many of them, she knew all too well.

Next, it was Jimmy. Turned out Jimmy had a visit with Jack on Christmas, which lasted straight through to New Year's Eve. "It was the family pressure," he explained, gritting his teeth at Nick. "All those damn casseroles and all those elderly aunts wanting to know why I haven't settled down yet."

"The holidays are a trying time," was all Nick said. Even Iris was nodding. Christmas was always a hellish experience in the Drake household, thanks to Delilah and Katrina, Julian's daughters from a previous marriage. Not his first marriage. But his second. When Iris married him she'd been naïve enough to think they'd spend holidays vacationing somewhere warm. Instead, she was playing hostess to his former family. People who had never warmed to her. People who wished she wasn't there. Oh, how she had eyed that drinks cart, the eggnog bowl, the champagne... But she had survived not just a torturous few hours with Julian's insufferable ex, Nance (not Nancy; just Nance), but the snide and nasty remarks Delilah and Kat had made over the gifts she'd so carefully chosen for them (French perfume for Kat that was deemed to be for "dried-up middle-aged women" and a Tiffany charm bracelet for Delilah that Iris had secretly wanted for herself, even if Delilah had called it "costume jewelry"). She hadn't broken. Hadn't caved. And didn't that prove that all this was an overreaction? That she didn't need to be here at all? She'd made a foolish error and had the bad luck of being caught.

Really, she should be sitting beside Julian with a couples counselor, not fidgeting against the hard back of a folding chair in an AA meeting. She didn't have a drinking problem. She had a shaky marriage. And so help her, she would save it.

She had to. Without Julian... She couldn't even think about it without her stomach twisting so hard that she felt like she might be sick.

She brought a trembling hand up to her mouth, and then, remembering her manicure, dropped it. Tonight she'd suggest something fun. A vacation. They hadn't taken one in a while.

Work kept Julian too busy. She'd offer it up. For his birthday. Just the two of them.

"Today is New Year's Eve. A night that most of us used as an excuse to drink excessively in the past." Nick looked around the room as people murmured their consent. "It's important that you have a plan in place for tonight. Something constructive. Something that doesn't trigger you."

Would a party at the Rosens' count as a trigger? They were Julian's friends, really, and it was an annual event. Iris knew from experience that the champagne would be flowing, likely from a fountain. She couldn't exactly pass up the chance to have a toast for the New Year, could she? Julian had never told her to stop drinking, not completely. He'd just told her to get it under control. *Or else* was the unspoken threat.

Or else what, she wanted to know, feeling angry and agitated and suddenly in serious need of a drink more than ever. As if Julian Drake was in any position to threaten *her*. It should be the other way around. Julian was the one who had stopped sending her flowers just for the heck of it. Julian was the one who had stopped whisking her off on trips to the Bahamas when the cold weather hit the city. Julian was the one who had started working later and later.

And she kept up her end of the arrangement. She'd given up her career, devoted herself to being the perfect society wife. She kept herself in shape. She didn't complain. And lately, there was plenty to complain about.

"Does anyone else want to open up today?" Nick was asking.

Iris stayed quiet. She wasn't ready to share. Not yet. Sharing would mean telling, admitting, and she wasn't there yet. She needed a sponsor, Nick told her, offering his services. With great reluctance, she'd exchanged numbers with him, but coming to the meetings and having a sponsor were two very different things.

Her feelings were mixed when Nick stood, signaling that their hour was up. Another day she'd gotten by unscathed, her secrets still safe. But lunch with Stephanie was looming.

"Want to grab a coffee?" Jimmy asked. His breath was hot on her face as she folded her chair and stacked it against the others.

"Sorry, but I've got lunch plans with a friend," she said with a forced smile.

Because that's what it was, right? Lunch with a friend.

Stephanie was already waiting for her at a window table of Hugo's when Iris arrived, ten minutes late and not even sorry for it. Six months ago, she would have called or texted to say she was running behind, trouble with a cab, go on, order a drink without her, but things were different now. If it had been up to her, they would have met on the Upper East Side, or even the Upper West—she could have batched trips. AA with a dry lunch. She could think of nothing better.

But Stephanie had insisted, as she always did, that they meet on her turf. She'd purchased an art gallery with her most recent divorce settlement money, a job that allowed her to pursue her passion and meet suitable men.

At least that's how she'd described it when she invited Iris to walk through the space with her a year ago. Iris had been thrilled for her friend then, happy to see that Stephanie was bouncing back, finding purpose, after her second husband,

33

Richard, had run off with their interior decorator and then sued her for custody of their labradoodle. How many bottles of wine had they devoured during that custody battle? Iris knew all the details, not just from Stephanie firsthand, but from Julian, who had represented her, of course.

"I've seen some crazy shit in my days, but a custody fight over a dog is a new one," Julian had said after the first deposition.

They were in his study at the time. She'd followed him back there, as she often did when he rolled in from the office at nine or ten, loosening his tie and walking straight to the bar at the far back wall.

He poured her a glass of wine. A scotch for himself. She settled into a leather club chair and curled her legs up underneath her, settling in.

"She's not going to lose that dog," Julian assured her, as if Iris ever doubted his ability to win a fight, get his way. It was one of the things she loved most about him, ironically. "But how much is she willing to spend to keep it?"

Julian billed eight fifty an hour. A grand for court time. Their fortune was fueled by the desperation of others. Their dreams were built on others' setbacks.

"Promise me this will never be us," Iris had sighed, leaning her head against the leather chairback.

Julian's lips had curved that wolfish grin that used to make her heart flutter with excitement but now made her experience a strange mix of attraction and apprehension. Julian was calm, cool, and in control. He had an ego that was as big as his bank account. Julian always got what Julian wanted.

Now, Iris wasn't so sure what Julian wanted. And that...that made her stomach go all funny again.

"Relax, honey," he'd said, and then, just when she started to let her defenses down: "Why do you think I never wanted a dog?"

Or more kids. Or a new apartment that he hadn't lived in with his former wife. Or anything else that would be shared between them.

In the end, Stephanie was given primary custody of the dog, Richard was given visitation rights, which he rarely exercised, and Stephanie got the funds for her gallery—a win the three of them had toasted with champagne and caviar.

Today Stephanie was wearing dark sunglasses even though the sun hadn't peeked through the clouds since the second week of December. When Iris approached, she slid them off and folded them into the leather handbag that was resting on the seat beside her. Her big blue eyes were her best feature; Iris never understood how she could hide them. Stephanie got everything she wanted with those eyes. All she had to do was open them a tad wider than normal and bat her lashes a few times, and just like that, the world was hers. The first time Iris had seen Stephanie use this power, she'd run back to her dorm room, flicked on the bathroom light, and practiced in the mirror of the rusting medicine cabinet.

But it wasn't just the eyes. Stephanie had a laugh—a peal— that was infectious. Even when you were mad at Stephanie, even when you actually sort of hated her, a part of you (a part of you that you loathed) couldn't help but want to be near her.

The waiter took their orders (two Caesar salads with dressing on the side, sparkling water for Iris, another glass of chardonnay for Stephanie) and set a breadbasket on the center of the table that would remain untouched, in one of those strangely rewarding, self-disciplined ways. Iris hadn't tasted bread in twenty years, not since Stephanie had invited her out to lunch after a photo shoot and balked when Iris ordered a sandwich. She was nineteen, on an academic scholarship at NYU, and anything she ate outside of her meal plan felt like a huge splurge and had to last. From that day forward, Stephanie took her under her wing, introducing her to all the right people she'd met growing up in Manhattan, eventually helping her to secure her first job at a major cosmetics company.

"No wine?" Stephanie pouted. "You know I don't like drinking alone. Besides, it's New Year's Eve! We're meant to be celebrating." And there went the eyes. She could even seduce women with them if she tried. But Iris would not be swayed; besides, what was she celebrating?

Who knew what the next year would bring?

She stared at the breadbasket in the middle of the table. Her stomach turned over with nerves.

Aware that Stephanie was watching her, Iris gave a smile she hoped passed for casual. "I'm trying to fit into that dress for next Saturday." A bald-faced lie, considering the dress was a forgiving cut and wine had never interfered with her dieting plans in the past, but it moved the conversation in another direction.

"That's right! Julian's fiftieth!"

Julian's fiftieth. A party she had been planning for three months. A party that was the root of every last ounce of hope that remained in her. It was her chance to shine. To remind

Julian of what they had. Why he had married her. Why he should stay married to her.

"Remember, it's a surprise."

"Of course." Stephanie eyed her over the rim of her wineglass. "You know you can trust me to keep a secret."

Yes, Iris supposed she could. After all, Stephanie was very good at keeping secrets.

"I'm going shopping right after this for something special to wear," Stephanie continued, and Iris just stared at her, wondering how she should respond to that. Under normal circumstances, she might tag along, or hint about eligible men on the invitation list that might be a good match for her friend. But Stephanie was hardly a friend anymore. The Rosens' party was a convenient excuse. She had an appointment booked at the salon at three.

Her heart was beginning to beat faster when she thought of Julian's party and how important this night was. How crucial it was that everything went perfectly. But now all she could think about was the dress she'd chosen for the night, and if Stephanie would top it. She watched Stephanie take another sip of her wine, and her mouth watered. It would take away that anxiety. It would make her feel better.

She looked away. Quickly.

She shouldn't have come today. She should have made up an excuse—a dentist appointment or something equally boring.

Nick would claim she liked to punish herself. Addicts did, apparently. But she wasn't an addict. She was no different than Stephanie or Lucia or the handful of women who constituted her social circle, the difference being that she, unlike them, had been caught in a weak moment, at her worst, by the one person whose opinion had come to matter most.

The salads arrived, but Iris had lost her appetite. She picked up her fork and poked at the lettuce leaves, dragging them around her plate, forgoing the dressing. Stephanie was telling a story about some tourists who had stopped into the gallery last week, commenting on her latest collection by an up-and-coming artist.

Sometimes when Stephanie talked about her gallery, Iris felt her old inferiority complex surge, until she reminded herself that while she might have given up her own aspirations, she was married to Julian Drake and the life they had was everything she had ever wanted.

"I could hear them talking. Claiming their seven-year-old daughter could paint just as well!" Stephanie scoffed. "They clearly had no appreciation. Midwesterners, no doubt. Probably from somewhere like Iowa or Wisconsin."

"I'm from Wisconsin," Iris said mildly. Normally, she didn't draw attention to this fact—or her past—but today she wanted to watch Stephanie squirm.

"Yes, but you're different! You're, you're..." Stephanie blinked rapidly, while Iris waited patiently, having no intention to help her out of this situation. "You're married to Julian Drake!"

Yes. She was married to Julian Drake. Her biggest achievement yet. She didn't have a career, or a child, or even a dog. She had nothing of her own. But she had Julian.

For now.

"That I am!" She gave her most dazzling smile, even if it was forced. She eyed Stephanie over their undressed salads, wondering if she should finally call the woman's bluff once and for all. If she should come right out and say that she knew everything. Or if instead she should just give Stephanie a little scare, see if she might come out and admit it on her own.

Iris took another sip of her water. She needed to cool her head. Remember what was important. If she admitted what she knew, or even half of it, her dignity would never be salvaged. And her lifestyle, the life she lived and loved, would be over. And then what?

Julian had insisted, in his lawyerly way, that she sign an airtight prenup that she knew deep down benefited him and only him.

So no, no, as much as she'd love to tell Stephanie that just last week she had discovered a red lace G-string that most definitely didn't belong to her wedged under the club chair seat cushion in Julian's office, she would refrain. Just like she would refrain from going home and pouring a glass of wine. Just like she would refrain from saying anything to Julian.

Sure, it would be rewarding to watch Stephanie shift in her chair, her cheeks no doubt turning pink as her wide blue eyes did their innocent blink, hoping no doubt that Iris was too stupid to remember their pre-Christmas shopping trip, when Iris had bought an ivory silk nightgown and Stephanie had opted for something a little smaller, a little redder, a little lacier.

With a sigh, Iris pulled the napkin from the table and freed it from the ring, setting it on her lap. She went to set the ring on the table, off to the side where it wouldn't interfere with the water glass or utensils, but something about it made her pause.

The napkin ring was heavy in a reassuring way. Round, pewter, with an etched pattern around the rim. Iris held it in her palm, squeezing it until the metal warmed against her skin.

And then, reaching for her sparkling water with her free hand, she extended her other to the empty seat beside her and casually dropped it into her handbag.

3

GWEN

THE FIRST FRIDAY of every month was meeting day at Forevermore Beauty. Gwen had already added the meetings to her new annual planner, one she had chosen with great care when she was Christmas shopping with her mother and Norah. She'd gone with a desk planner in a vibrant turquoise blue—Forevermore Beauty's signature color. One with a spiral binding that detailed not just the month but also the days of the week. A big, fat book that reeked of a busy schedule that didn't solely revolve around after-school activities and meal planning. Her mother had encouraged her to go for a slimmer option, one she could keep in her bag, but Gwen had an image of herself at her desk (okay, the kitchen table, but still...), poring over invoices with a warm cup of coffee at her side, her week perfectly laid out in front of her, her days filled with purpose.

The first night she brought it home, she waited until the house was quiet and everyone was in bed for the night, then she pulled out a beautiful pen in a matching shade of blue, an elegant color, she thought, and certainly more interesting than black, and began filling in her meetings. She planned all the way out, through December, only pausing when she realized that by then, she'd be perilously close to forty. Each time she flipped a page to write "Monthly Meeting," she was filled with fresh hope and a delicious sense of possibility. By March, she may just meet those sales goals Susan had heavily suggested to her batch of recruits. By May, she hoped to set herself apart by doubling that effort. And by August, she hoped to earn a spot in the Silver Circle.

Technically, today marked Gwen's second First Friday, and the new-girl butterflies had kept her awake most of the night. She'd tried to distract herself, first with the thought of watching a movie on the iPad, but Bea had drained the battery and not bothered to tell her, and the charger was all the way downstairs in the kitchen, and if she got up, then Bailey would get up, and then he'd need to go out, and the whole thing just wasn't worth it. She could have read, but that would require turning on a light, admitting that no sleep would come, and accepting the fact that she would look like hell the next morning.

Instead, she'd lain in bed and waited. Waited for the dawn to come, for the darkness to soften to gray, for the sound of life in the house again.

There were so many times when all she longed for was the stillness that could only come when her children were finally asleep. But that was a long time ago. Now, this kind of quiet gave rise to restlessness. And boredom. And the depressing inspection of her own life and all its shortcomings.

And worry. So much worry that sleep became impossible. Would Michael find a job? What happened if he didn't? What would happen to the house? What if her mother found out?

What if someone else found out and then it got back to her mother?

Her mind would go around and around until she felt dizzy and couldn't think straight and she would forget things, like the one item she was supposed to buy at the grocery store, or the check for the piano teacher.

No, best to keep busy with other things, positive things. Best to feel proactive, even if she still didn't feel in control at all. Forevermore Beauty could offer all that. She was an entrepreneur, managing her own business. She alone was in control of her future, and it was, at least according to Susan, limitless.

Of course, she couldn't deny the thrill she'd felt when Susan Sharp had extended the invitation to her open house with the promise of warm cookies, a free makeover, and lots of wine. Wink, wink. Gwen had been walking Bailey, stooping to pick up dog poop (though she liked to omit that part from the memory) at the base of Susan's freshly brick-paved driveway. Since moving onto Elmwood Lane last summer, Susan had made many home improvements, not that Gwen had ever found much wrong with the large white Colonial. Nonetheless, the yard was fertilized, the front door repainted deep gray-blue, evergreen shrubs replaced with blossoming hydrangea bushes, and fading black shutters swapped out with blue to match the door, of course. Gwen had regarded her own plain black front door with a critical eye ever since.

So there Gwen was, picking up Bailey's business, when the front screen door (Susan's newest addition) had suddenly opened, and Susan appeared, blue eyes bright if not a bit manic, smile broad and eager.

Gwen resisted the urge to flee. She'd always liked the way Elmwood Lane was quiet. Neighbors waved, but they didn't randomly knock on your door or stand around chitchatting too long at the mailboxes. Susan was wearing some kind of yoga outfit, her blond hair in a perky ponytail as she jogged—yes, jogged—from her front stoop to the base of her drive, where the plastic dog waste bag hung limply in Gwen's hand.

"I was wondering," Susan said, not even slightly breathlessly, "if you're free this Friday morning? I'm having an open house for some of the ladies on the street."

Gwen's mind immediately raced with what she would wear and whether she had time to shed ten pounds in forty-eight hours.

"It's just a little get-together. I'll have snacks out. Wine of course." There was the wink. "The door will be open from ten until one. Drop by when you can!"

And then she was off. On the first of her twice-daily jogs, her hair bouncing against the nape of her neck as she disappeared down the street and took a left at the playground on Wesley Boulevard. It was late October, and the leaves were at their peak, and for the first time since Gwen had moved back to Westlake, she felt the thrill of endless possibility.

For the open house, she agonized over wearing her jeans or pants, or a skirt, which seemed far too formal. If only it was still summer, she could wear a casual-ish sundress and not have to worry about underdressing or trying too hard. Which was worse? She couldn't decide.

In the end, out of legitimate fear that she might pop the zipper of her jeans if she sat down, she wore black leggings and a gray tunic sweater her mother had bought for her on her last birthday. One that hid the bum, as her mother had pointed out, making Gwen consider this every time she pulled it over her head.

She showed up to Susan's house with some sunflowers from the grocery store, making sure to tear the plastic wrapping and price tag from the bundle, thinking that a bottle of wine at ten fifteen in the morning wasn't exactly sending the right message.

Susan was already halfway through a glass of rosé when Gwen walked in, immediately regretting her attire. Susan's long, reed-thin legs were covered in jeans—the expensive kind that Norah kept nagging Gwen to buy her for Christmas—and on top, she wore the softest, creamiest cashmere sweater Gwen had ever seen and could never hope to own. She was chatting with another, equally thin woman that Gwen vaguely recognized from the school drop-off, but she stopped when she spotted Gwen.

"Flowers!" she exclaimed. If there was a thank-you, Gwen didn't hear it, and she never did see where the flowers went either. She was being ushered by the shoulders into the living room, a soft, calming room that made Gwen immediately want to dispose of every furnishing in her home. She dropped onto a white slipcovered sofa that would last about four and a half minutes in her house before Bea scribbled on it or Declan spilled juice or Bailey lifted his leg, and, before she knew what she was doing, she guzzled half a glass of wine from the tray on the coffee table, because, why not? Her kids were in school, they'd be taking the bus home, there were no activities this afternoon to shuttle them to, she didn't have a job, and she was an adult, damn it. If she wanted to have a glass of wine before noon, she would.

Maybe it was the wine, or maybe it was the thrill of holding the glass—at a quarter to eleven(!), when she was usually still in flannel pajama pants and greasy hair from morning drop-off since they never did seem to make it to the bus on time, a load of laundry in the washer, another in the dryer, and another pile still to go, the desire to strap on a bra at all that day lessening by the second—but when Susan Sharp tapped her glass and opened her rose-gold-plated display case and called Gwen up to have her "complimentary" makeover, she fell for it. Hook, line, and sinker. Sitting on Susan's tufted beige ottoman while her newest neighbor swept a large brush over her cheeks and another over her eyelids and then finally held up a mirror and triumphantly cried, "And there you have it!" to the group, who then cheered, Gwen felt like she was living another woman's life. A life she preferred. A life she wanted.

A life closer to Susan's life.

Here was a woman living very much the same existence as herself, after all. A house on the same block. A husband supporting the family. Kids in the same school. But she was doing it all better.

All this, she was told, as Susan's eyes held hers in rapture, could be hers. It could be all of theirs. They could be hosting their very own open houses. (Not that Gwen thought she'd be offering wine at ten in the morning. A mimosa, perhaps, but even then, coffee seemed more her style.) They too could have their very own gilded case etched with their initials. They could be part of Susan's team. Her dream team, because with her, their dreams were in reach.

Gwen hadn't belonged to a team since high school field hockey, when Iris insisted it would help their college applications, and half the time she'd been benched. But this was her second chance; an opportunity was being handed to her as casually as the mini avocado toasts on Susan's sterling silver platter.

Gwen wanted silver platters and white slipcovered sofas. Walls that didn't have oily handprints on them. Rugs that didn't smell faintly of dog urine. Cashmere sweaters and even a modest thigh gap.

By the time she left Susan Sharp's meticulous home, she had agreed to become a Forevermore Beauty consultant, and Susan's personal protégée. She'd smiled the whole walk home, swaying only a little, and fell into bed until her alarm went off at three, dreaming of silver platters and morning cocktail parties. When she woke up, Ravishing Rose lipstick (Gwen's signature color, Susan had said, slipping it into her palm with another wink) was smeared all over her white pillowcase.

For her first official First Friday in December Gwen hadn't slept, so great were her nerves. Determined to get things off to a strong start, she'd decided on a sweater in a soft shade of camel, a color that she remembered Iris telling her should be part of her palette, back when she was finally allowed to start picking out her own clothes for school. She wore her hair back in a low ponytail and swiped on Ravishing Rose. Her notebook was tucked into her black leather tote, which she'd freed of old receipts and gum wrappers and a half-eaten apple that Bea must have tucked in there at some point in the somewhat distant past. Everyone had sat in silence while Susan stood at the whiteboard she'd propped next to her fireplace and scribbled goals and went over lingo and made them role-play approaching unsuspecting female strangers between the ages of twenty-five and fifty in "target centers" (gyms, department stores, grocery store checkout lines, and even elementary school class parties).

The key, Susan had stressed, was to look friendly. To give a big smile and open your eyes wide. She demonstrated, looking only slightly demonic. Or drugged. Gwen couldn't be sure.

When it was Gwen's turn to pretend to accost someone—by then, in her more sober state, she realized that's what it was—she strongly considered blurting out that she'd found another job and could no longer be one of Susan's protégées. Drama class had never been her safe place—she preferred the library, where she could sit quietly and fade into the background—and the thought of acting out a scene in front of these women was as horrifying as the thought of giving birth in front of ten first-year medical residents. Which she'd done. Twice. By the time Bea came along, she'd learned she actually had rights and could refuse that sort of thing. But by then, her dignity had been lost. Forever.

Gwen sucked in her stomach and moved slowly to the front of the room, standing next to Susan's elaborate stone hearth, and picked her target. Sarah Tucker. Sarah, like Gwen, was one of the few people left in town that had grown up here. Most went on to Chicago or even Milwaukee or Madison, and some, like Iris, to LA or New York City.

Sarah was nice enough, and always friendly, but not quite a friend. She'd married her high school sweetheart, moved into a rambling farmhouse near the playground, and breastfed her five children until they had a mouthful of teeth, whereas all of

Gwen's brood had ended up on formula for various reasons. Sarah was rosy-cheeked, raised her own chickens for eggs, and still wore her hair in a long braid down her back, just as she had back in school. She didn't seem to yearn for anything, not even Susan's approval.

Gwen secretly wondered why she was even here.

Gwen bet Sarah's husband sat down to dinner every night at six. Asked about her day, listened with interest while she told him about all her homemaking duties. And now he'd ask about Forevermore Beauty, encourage her along, while Michael had only given her a look of amusement when she'd told him about her new venture, rather than the enthusiasm she'd hoped for.

She narrowed her eyes. Well, she'd show him. She'd show all of them! She'd be the best damn Forevermore Beauty consultant this side of Lake Michigan. And it started with wooing Sarah Tucker.

"Where are you?" Susan quizzed from her perch on the ottoman.

Gwen thought fast. "At the playground."

A tired mom. A soft target. Gwen saw the flicker of approval in Susan's eyes and felt her confidence lift.

As instructed, Sarah stood and pretended to push one of her five children on the imaginary swing.

Gwen, feeling like a real ass at this point, stepped beside her and did the same. "Is he your first?" she asked in that friendly but slightly restrained manner one typically reserved for the playground.

"My fifth," Sarah replied, as Gwen knew she would. The others were too big to be pushed on the swings. Technically Bea was too, but then, this was make-believe. Her eyelids fluttered. She was standing in the middle of Susan Sharp's exquisitely furnished living room, stone sober, pantomiming. If Michael saw her now, he'd never let her live this down. He'd probably laugh until he cried, and once, she would have too.

She pursed her lips. No sense getting off track. "It's not easy being home with the kids all day."

Sarah blew out a breath. Man, she was good. "Nope. But there's nothing I'd rather be doing."

Gwen narrowed her eyes slightly. Was this true, or was she aiming for a hard sell?

Gwen decided that it was probably true, that Sarah was perfectly content with her life and her choices, that she didn't yearn for anything. Blinking back the guilt that rose, Gwen pressed on. "Ever think about going back to work?"

Sarah shook her head. "Day care costs a fortune, and with school runs and activities, I couldn't even commit to something part-time. Besides, my husband has a good job."

The air seemed to come out of the room and Gwen froze, momentarily forgetting her mission, forgetting that she was pretending, that none of this was real. But it was real. She felt every eye in the room on her and wondered if they knew. About Michael. About the state of her marriage. About the fact that they probably wouldn't be able to give the kids the kind of Christmas they'd hoped. That they weren't taking a vacation for spring break like everyone else. That she lay awake at night wondering if the bank was going to repossess the house. If her mother would find out. And how much it would annoy Michael if he knew how much she cared if her mother found out.

Susan was watching Gwen very carefully now. From the looks of it, she might even be holding her breath.

Gwen shook away the cobwebs. They didn't know. If they knew, they would have spoken up—Susan wouldn't have been able to help herself. There would have been more funny looks. She probably wouldn't have been invited into this group.

"Let me give you my card." Gwen stopped pushing the imaginary swing and reached into her pocket to pull out an invisible business card. She handed it to Sarah, who did a killer job of studying it, her brow now wrinkled in suspicion.

"Forevermore Beauty? I don't have time to wear makeup these days." Sarah gave an apologetic little smile and then, the traitor, started pretend-lifting her child from the swing as if it were time to go.

"Don't let her get away!" Susan cut in, her tone laced with warning.

Gwen's heart was racing. She'd always had a fear of being in trouble, and something told her that Susan's bad side was not a place she wanted to be. "Oh, I wasn't talking about wearing makeup," she rushed to say. "I was talking about selling it."

Sarah, mercifully, hesitated. "Selling it? Oh, I don't think I'd be good at that."

Gwen shrugged. "You can work around your kids' schedules, from the comfort of your own home. No boss. No office hours. And it gives you the chance to make new friends while earning a little extra cash on the side." Was this nonsense actually coming out of her mouth? It was. It was! She was pulling it off!

"Well, when you put it like that…" Now Sarah and Susan were both smiling.

Gwen felt a swell of satisfaction rise in her chest. "What have you got to lose?" she asked.

Exactly, Gwen thought. What did she have to lose?

Today, Gwen had to lose ten pounds. However, with the meeting now fourteen minutes away, that wasn't possible. Her hair was freshly colored with a new shade. Maybe a little too freshly colored, she thought, turning her head from side to side. She picked up the box again, the one that promised "natural" auburn highlights and a "healthy" shine. One that she had envisioned would give her a little something special, a richness to her drab brown, not just cover the gray hairs that her tweezers could no longer keep up with.

Was it just her or were her ends darker than her roots? She could use a trim. More like an actual cut, one that would frame her face and not just remove the split ends. But who had the time?

Well, Susan did. She'd gleaned that from Susan's social media pages. The same ones that boasted her spring break trip to Italy, her elaborate dinners out, her flawless Christmas decorations, and a backyard housewarming party last summer that the Rileys hadn't been invited to.

Sighing, Gwen added an extra swipe of blush, carefully applied her Ravishing Rose lipstick, and opened her mouth to practice her smile, giving herself a start.

Damn it! She'd forgotten the chip. Now it was all she could see. No time to fix the tooth, obviously. She'd just practice her pleasant smile and keep conversation to a minimum.

Gwen caught her frown in the mirror. She rearranged her face accordingly and turned off the bathroom light before she could think any more about it.

For Christmas, her mother had given her a soft pink cashmere scarf, and she wore this with a black top and her best jeans, even if they were, as suspected, popping a bit at the zipper and digging rather hard into her hip bones.

Still, it was only for two hours, and then she could slip back into her pajama pants until school pickup.

She checked her phone. A text from her mother, confirming Monday's brunch, and a reminder that since her birthday was coming up, she needed to remember to go to the DMV to renew her license.

Gwen bit back a wave of impatience. Every year, her birthday gift from her mother was a string of emails, texts, and phone calls, reminding her to renew her license. Because she was twelve, not almost thirty-nine.

Thirty-nine. And she was getting fatter by the year.

Well, no time to dwell. She dropped her phone into her bag and braved a smile.

Grabbing her food offering—a boxed-mix coffee cake that she'd been bringing to every school event since Norah was three—she slipped into her boots, opened the door, and gave Bailey a brave smile. "Wish me luck," she said, catching the nervous trill in her voice.

She'd have to work on that before she arrived. Luckily she had two houses to walk by and a street to cross before that happened.

She took her time walking down the driveway, which Declan had done a poor job of shoveling before school. She walked by Caroline's house, which rarely showed any sign of life. The kids weren't allowed to play outside due to allergy and risk of injury—instead, their time was spent reading, practicing for the annual math bee, and, of course, playing the piano. Despite seeing each other every Tuesday at the music academy, Gwen's conversations with Caroline were brief and a little stilted, and their social interactions over the years had been kept to a wave over the short hedge that divided their property lines.

As she walked by Maggie Simmons's blue Cape, the cherry red front door opened and Maggie emerged, clutching a fruit platter, a bright green scarf wrapped loosely at her neck.

Maggie was a fellow townie, born and raised in Westlake and still here, only Maggie had always been popular back in school, protected by a large group of friends that remained in her close circle to this day. She'd lived on the street longer than Gwen had, with twin boys who were closer in age to Norah and not interested in hanging out with Declan, but she'd welcomed Gwen back with a basket of freshly baked cookies and an invitation to stop by for coffee sometime. Now, all these years later, Gwen had never made good on that invite. Sometimes she wondered what might have happened if she had. If she hadn't let her middle school social status bother her to this day.

Gwen opened her mouth in greeting and then, remembering the chip, quickly clamped it shut again. She buried her chin in her scarf, even though it was a mild winter morning, one of those rare, sunny January days that made you almost not mind the snow. She was supposed to have remembered to call the dentist on Monday when the kids were back in school, but the week had slipped away, and there was so much to do with packing up the Christmas decorations and preparing for today's meeting, not to mention the afternoon struggle to run every kid all over town. Now, she wished she had prioritized the tooth.

She'd call today and hope to get in first thing Monday, before brunch with her mother. Her stomach clenched in the familiar knot it did every time a get-together was looming.

"How was your month?" Maggie asked as they crossed the street.

Gwen hated to admit that the only sales she'd made were to herself—gifts that she'd given to her mother, who'd wrinkled her nose and then set them to the side, and, in total desperation, Norah, who was too young to even be wearing makeup yet, at least according to Michael.

Gwen sighed. "The holidays were a bit of a hiccup," was all she could say.

Maggie's brows shot up. "Really? I sold out my inventory and even had to place three orders from corporate."

Corporate. Gwen was yet to be in contact with corporate—a mysterious office housed in Nebraska, but whose very name just reeked of glamour nonetheless. Susan was in contact with corporate for them. But every spring, the top one hundred sellers from each state were invited to an annual conference held in New York City. As soon as she heard about it, Gwen had started dog-earing the catalogs that were always arriving in the mail, planning her wardrobe.

Gwen frowned, wondering where Maggie was finding these people, and then remembered that Maggie was one of four sisters and that she had a handful of teenage nieces, too. They all still lived in Westlake.

An unpleasant thought made her almost want to turn around and run home. "Have you recruited any of your sisters?" She and Michael were both only children. His parents lived in Florida. There weren't even any cousins. No built-in network.

As protégées, their main goal was not just to sell products, but to recruit new consultants. Recruiting one to two members elevated your status to Pewter. Three to five made you a Bronze. And six to ten earned you a place in the Silver Circle, like Susan.

With her immediate family alone, Maggie could quickly jump the ranks from protégée to Silver, or maybe even…Gold. Even Susan was yet to reach Gold, but it was her mission, and she wasn't shy in saying so.

"My sisters?" Maggie's peal of laughter caught the attention of Courtney Hayworth and Teresa Leahy, who were coming up the street together, dodging icy puddles in their weather-inappropriate boots. "God, no."

Now Gwen was curious. "Why not?"

"Well, for starters, Linda's a doctor. And Nicole is way too busy with her committees to be bothered with another project. You know she's head of PTA now?"

Yes. Gwen knew. Nicole was also the class mom of all four children's rooms, in charge of the annual fundraising committee, the annual bake sale, and the winter coat drive, and was suspiciously cheerful. She smiled and held hands with her husband in public for extended periods of time. And he didn't seem to even flinch. They were probably one of those couples who ordered two entrées and two plates. The ones who split a sandwich down the middle, each taking one half.

Michael would never split an entree with her. For starters, his appetite was too big. But they just didn't operate that way.

They were two distinct identities, with their own tastes and patterns and routines. And over the years, instead of coming together, they'd drifted further apart, slowly but steadily, and it had only been worse since the layoff last winter.

"And Addie doesn't wear makeup."

Gwen was going to remind Maggie of Susan's line about one not needing to wear makeup to sell makeup, but then decided to let it drop. There was something in Maggie's reaction, something about the amusement she found in Gwen's question that made Gwen start to feel uneasy.

"Why are you doing it, by the way?"

"Because Susan begged me to," Maggie replied. She rolled her eyes as they approached Susan's walkway. "I probably won't sell anything else until next Christmas."

Saying nothing, Gwen followed Maggie into Susan's front hall, hung her coat in the perfectly organized closet next to Maggie's, set her boots on the mat, and maintained her pleasant face as she walked into the living room, where she deposited her coffee cake next to the fruit platter on the coffee table.

"Carbs!" Susan's eyes bulged as she studied the offerings, as if Gwen had set down a plate of pot brownies. She set a hand on her flat belly. "I suppose my winter cleanse can wait until tomorrow."

"It works well for a crowd," Gwen said through a tight-lipped smile, wishing she was home folding laundry in front of the television instead.

What was she doing even thinking about going to the national convention, fantasizing about getting off the plane, sliding into a cab, pulling up to a hotel, where she'd have a room all to herself? She hadn't sold a single product, hadn't even worked up the nerve to approach any of the moms at dance or school. She shouldn't even be thinking about standing at a cocktail party, drink in hand, nibbling passed hors d'oeuvres and then going back to her hotel room, where in the bliss of silence she could spread out on the high-thread-count sheets, order room service the next morning, and not even have to worry about making the bed, knowing instead it would be made for her.

The temptation of just two nights of mercy from the cooking and the cleaning and the straightening up, with no one calling her name over and over until she finally responded, and no one needing something from her, was enough to make her show up today, pretending that she wasn't dreading every second of it.

She added some fruit to her plate. Talked to Sarah Tucker about her holidays. Eased herself onto Susan's crisp white sofa. Pretended to check imaginary texts on her phone.

When Susan dropped onto the seat beside her and set a hand on her knee, she nearly jumped.

"Would Bea like to have a playdate with Taffy one day soon?" she asked sweetly.

For a moment, Gwen was so stricken she almost didn't dare respond for fear she had misheard Susan's question. Despite Bea and Taffy being classmates, Susan had never extended a hint of encouragement that the children should play together, and the one time Gwen had encouraged Bea to join the Sharp girls on the front lawn, where they were playing in a pile of leaves, Susan had swiftly opened the front door and called her children in for a snack. The one solace Gwen had about buying in the neighborhood was that her children would have the simple thrill of neighborhood friends, a chance to hop on their bikes or run next door, and it hadn't happened yet for Bea, much to her disappointment. But now...

"Bea would love that." While Bea got along well enough with the other girls at school and the dance studio, Gwen longed for her to find a friend in the neighborhood, or even within bike-riding distance. When Bea hadn't been invited to Taffy's birthday party in the fall under the excuse of it being for the classroom only, and Bea was in room three, not room four, Gwen had been offended and angered on Bea's tearful behalf when she looked out the window and saw the balloons tethered to the Sharps' mailbox. But maybe she'd been wrong about Susan Sharp. Maybe she was a nice person. Yes, those ice-blue eyes were a tad crazy, the way they held your stare a little too long and the way seconds could pass before the woman ever blinked. But once you got past that, and the strange little smile, and the baby voice that really did set Gwen's teeth on edge, there was, perhaps, a normal person underneath.

"Good! Let's do Monday after school. And one more thing." Susan smiled. Gwen held her breath. "Keep working on Caroline. Your son takes piano with her toddler, right?"

Gwen felt her eyes hood. "I think he's actually in kindergarten, but...yes."

"Work on her."

Gwen nodded, even though she knew she would do no such thing. She had half a mind to ask Susan why she hadn't recruited Caroline herself, but then she remembered that Caroline had snapped at Susan in October when Susan had let her two girls run over to Caroline's yard to take as many of the leaves that had fallen from the trees as they wanted for their pile. "My girls wanted them!" was all Susan would say when Caroline threatened to call the police.

Gwen, who was miffed over the birthday party by then, had gleefully watched this particular neighborly exchange as she ever so slowly collected the mail and made her way back up the front path, had purposefully stayed out of it, and had secretly been disappointed when Caroline didn't make good on her threat. Maybe there was a friend to be found in Caroline after all, she mused, and added a note to her phone to chat with her next-door neighbor soon.

Now Susan stood and took her place near the hearth, signaling that party time was over and it was time to get down to business. First up: monthly sales. "Let's go around the room and report our success!"

Oh, kill me know. Gwen darted her eyes to the hallway. There were two options: the front door or the bathroom. She stared at her phone, which she was gripping in a sweat-slicked hand, willing it to ring with news of a sick child in urgent need of being picked up from school.

How could she say that she had sold nothing, only bought from her own stash, under the guise of giving gifts?

She could make up an excuse, claim she'd been out of town, or that she had been sick, but everyone would have seen her shoveling that damn driveway half the days of winter break, or walking Bailey around the block.

"Gwen?" Susan's smile was expectant. Gwen had to make a choice.

"Seventy percent sold," she blurted, her heart pounding so hard she could feel it pressing against her ribcage. More like ten percent, and to herself, but she'd figure out that mess later.

"Seventy!" Susan whooped and put a little happy face next to her name on the whiteboard. "Looks like you'll need to re-stock! I'll get that order processed for you pronto!"

Well, crap. More money out of her pocket. Meaning she'd have to sell more than planned this month, and to whom?

She wrung her hands in panic, breathing only slightly easier as the attention shifted onto Sally Bernard, who had the unfortunate experience of selling only four tubes of lipstick and three hand creams last month, which was far better than Gwen had fared, in truth.

"Oh." Susan clucked her tongue and drew a sad face next to Sally's name. "Better luck this month," she said, and Gwen could have sworn her eyes narrowed a notch.

Gwen glanced at Sally, who fidgeted in her seat, a deep frown line appearing between her eyebrows as she stared at the sad face next to her name. Gwen stared at it, too, thinking of how easily that could have been her instead.

Worst case scenario, she'd have to buy out her inventory. A small fortune, yes, but she wouldn't have to go shopping for makeup for herself for another two to three years. It wouldn't be a complete waste. It would be…an investment.

Still, her stomach was starting to hurt. Now was the time to be watching their bank account. Saving. Pinching. Not spending on things like nail polish and lipstick and moisturizer that gave the false promise of making you look ten years younger.

"And now, let's discuss strategy." Susan set down her dry erase marker and waited until everyone had plucked the caps from their pens.

The Forevermore Beauty line was limited, and this, Susan explained, was because the real ticket was the monthly specials.

Sure, you had your staples: fifteen shades of lipstick, nail polish, blush, eye shadow, along with the typical foundation products, but every month, a series of special colors was released, replaced exactly thirty days later, perhaps never to be seen again. You like the holiday nail polish in that exact shade of cherry red? Better stock up… And you love putting that vibrant shade of pink on your toes every summer? Take six bottles. You'll never run out.

The monthly specials, Susan pressed, were the money makers. Without them, you'd only make a few sales a year. After all, how many tubes of lipstick does one woman go through in a year? Two at best? No, urgency was key. "Play on their fears of missing out," Susan stressed. Because they all knew, deep down, that no woman wanted to feel like they had missed out. On marriage, children, a career. Women wanted it all.

And Gwen wanted it all too.

4

IRIS

IRIS HAD A guilty pleasure that no one could ever find out about. Every day, she read Delilah's blog. She hated herself for doing it, wondering why she cared, and she'd tried to quit, several times, but each time a morbid curiosity that she couldn't shake took over, and it became all she could think about until her agitation became so strong that she had to pull out her phone or run to her tablet to type in the web address.

She'd at least unflagged it from her favorites. That was some progress.

Today's post hadn't popped up yet. She checked first thing every morning, once Julian had left for the day and the only people in the apartment were the maids, who still judged her. She was a trophy wife, of course, even if she and Julian were only ten and a half years apart, but chances were they'd taken bets the day she'd walked through the doors. Five years? Ten? They were coming up on their seven-year itch.

Who would win? Ernie, the sweet doorman who hailed her cab every morning? Would he be the last to usher her out? Or

Sofia, the housekeeper who took an hour-long break to watch her favorite talk show every afternoon and knew that if it was ever her word against Iris's, she would win.

Just like Katrina and Delilah always won. Not that it was a contest. Iris had never set out to make it that way. But she wasn't welcome here by Julian's daughters. And not by Sofia, either.

"It's Nance's birthday!" Sofia would announce every March fifteenth. "I'll order some flowers from you, okay?" After Julian had mumbled a distracted agreement, Sofia would give Iris the side-eye as she walked out of the breakfast room, a victorious smirk on her face.

Once, Iris had dared to question the need to have Sofia in the household, offering to do the housework herself instead, a desperate act, hardly what she had signed on for, and certainly an unsettling reminder that she was willing to do anything, anything at all, to make this work. Even clean a forty-eight-hundred-square-foot apartment. That had been early into the marriage, but soon enough for her to sense the hostility with the older woman and question the entire arrangement.

"We can't fire Sofia! She's been with Kat and Delilah since they were infants! She's *family*."

And what did that make her, Iris often wondered. The third wife. The third wife who was perilously closing in on forty.

Now, sitting on the velvet ottoman in her walk-in closet, where she'd been hiding since ten minutes into Julian's party, she tapped on her iPad and pulled up Delilah's blog. It had started as a beauty blog, and then grew into product reviews, something that enabled her to get free stuff and claim she had a job. Of course Julian didn't care that the job didn't pay enough for her menthol cigarette habit, something she hid so well that even when Iris had mentioned it to Julian, he'd snapped at her, "Why would you say something like that about my daughter?" He was proud of Delilah for having a job. And New York was expensive for young people, he insisted, as he forked over her rent money each month and tossed in some extra for "fun."

Iris watched it all with silent judgment, wishing she could give Julian a little perspective, tell him that plenty of girls Delilah's age found a way to make it on their own, struggling in the process. But doing so would mean admitting that she'd been one of them, and by the time she'd met Julian, she was already settled in a promising career with a good salary, and an expensive wardrobe, thanks to samples from her modeling side job.

Lately, though, Delilah's blog had taken a turn. Instead of selfies in the hottest restaurants or dramatic poses in the latest styles, she spiced up her articles with juicy society gossip. Last week she'd slandered her best friend since middle school, calling her out on her eating disorder and highlighting her breakup with Teddy Thompson, a boy that Iris was well aware had been on her radar since high school.

No one was safe when it came to Delilah's posts, not even Katrina, who was outed for not having influenza but rather being suspended from boarding school last month due to "sexual misconduct" with the field hockey coach. Since she was eighteen, charges had not been pressed, and Iris was fairly sure that despite the coach being reassigned to boy's lacrosse, nothing good was happening at the New England prep school where three generations of Drakes had attended, but Julian had made a substantial donation to the school's library expansion, so she was allowed to stay on and graduate.

Delilah's blog was now getting hundreds of comments a day, and no doubt the spike in traffic was stemming from the malicious gossip that everyone wanted to read and no one wanted to admit.

The party was in full swing behind the doors. Iris could hear the piano player belting out some old Billy Joel song—one of Julian's many favorites that she'd added to the playlist. Her heart was banging, and she felt the pressure to go out there, to greet the guests with a frozen smile, to mingle, offer them drinks, play the happy wife as she had done since the day she'd married him.

The party tonight was just one of many events that Iris oversaw. She slipped easily into charity work and women's leagues, and lunches and benefits and galas. At first, it had been fun, proof that she had made it, that she wasn't the little girl with skinned knees and only a dream of a future. Now, life was full of possibilities.

Eventually—and she couldn't pinpoint when—the excitement had waned. Sure, Julian had been happy to come home from his club tonight and be greeted by a hundred of his closest friends and colleagues, champagne flowing, a live band playing, everyone in a good mood.

Except for her. Iris was not in a good mood. Julian had made a show of thanking her, but then he was pulled away, leaving her to linger behind with a bunch of people she didn't really know and couldn't connect with, no matter how hard she'd tried. Deep down, she knew she was different. That maybe she didn't belong. And then there was the matter of

Stephanie. Stephanie, who had climbed the social circles with her, the only person in all of Manhattan who knew her before she'd become who she was, back when her hair wasn't quite so blond or as long, back when she was thin but at least fifteen pounds heavier.

She'd watched the crowd mingle from a distance instead, her entire body tense, and the desire to release it so strong that she'd slipped away, just for a moment, standing with her back against the closed bedroom door trying to catch her breath. Trying to tell herself that it would all be okay. That tonight would be a turning point. Julian would see her effort. He'd appreciate it.

Everything would be okay.

She told herself this over and over, but she could not bring herself to go back to the party. Not yet. The fear of knowing that it wasn't the answer, that it wouldn't be okay, that nothing had in fact changed, was too strong.

She realized she was gripping the iPad so hard that her fingers were starting to cramp. The page finished loading and there it was. A new blog post, time stamped an hour ago, right before the party started. Subject line: *When three isn't a charm.*

And there it was, a picture of the charm bracelet that Iris had bought her for Christmas, sitting on a pile of trash—specifically, resting in the middle of a pile of half-eaten rotting takeout in a dumpster. Iris felt her anger rise in her face until her eyes scanned lower. The article wasn't about the stupid bracelet at all. It was about her, thinly disguised as "Number Three," and the implication that her days were numbered, the countdown had begun, and that a more glamorous, desirable, preferable "Number Four" had already been chosen.

Stephanie.

Iris dropped the iPad onto the bed and paced the room like a caged animal, searching within the four walls for a release, an exit, a solution. Anything.

It was too cold to go onto the terrace, but she did it anyway. The wind was like ice against her bare arms, but her skin was hot. It was on fire. She felt like she might be sick, or faint.

Finally, after a few deep breaths, her skin began to prickle, and she closed the doors behind her, alone in her room once more.

Sofia must have brought the mail in earlier, or Julian, when he'd come in to dress. Whereas the bills were set on Julian's desk in his office, Iris's personal mail was set on the brass tray on her nightstand. She sighed now, thinking heavily of the lunches and charity events that she'd have to sit through, the smile she'd have to wear, pretending that everything was just fine when most of the women in the room would probably know by now that it wasn't.

She flicked through the stack, her hand pausing when she saw the unmistakable Westlake return address, her heart beginning to hammer when she wondered if Sofia had noticed it, read into it. As far as everyone knew, she had no ties left to her hometown.

She looked closer at the handwriting, blinking at the name she hadn't seen in a very long time. Gwen Riley had sent her a Christmas card. She didn't even know she had her address! But then, of course, back when she and Julian were first engaged, she'd been so delirious, so thrilled at the notion of coming into this sprawling apartment and becoming his wife, that she'd sent an announcement card to everyone she'd known.

Even those who weren't invited to the wedding.

A strange feeling twisted in her stomach, as it always did when she thought of her hometown. She turned the envelope over in her hands, thinking of the last time she'd seen Gwen. It was right after Gwen had Norah. She was living in Chicago then, a vintage apartment that was huge by New York City standards, and Iris had flown in when the baby was only weeks old, in awe that her friend was now a mother. A real grown-up. That she had already achieved everything she'd wanted in life when she was only twenty-four years old! Iris, meanwhile, was still working her way up the corporate ladder at a slower pace than she'd hoped, despite the hours she was clocking and the extra effort she had made. No, she didn't want a baby. She'd seen firsthand how burdened her mother had been by two children. But she'd wanted that glow that Gwen had. That look of sheer and utter contentment.

It was the first note of strain in their friendship, and an unsettling feeling had come over her that she and Gwen weren't on the same path anymore, that she couldn't relate to Gwen's need to talk about her baby every chance she had any more than Gwen seemed to understand Iris's desire to get the upcoming promotion she'd wanted so badly.

Eventually, things had settled down. They'd still talked on the phone. Gwen had been the first person Iris called when she did get the promotion, and Iris was the first person Gwen called when she found out she was pregnant with Declan. But then Gwen really became busy with motherhood, and Iris's career was taking off, and at some point, the phone calls stopped altogether.

Iris opened the envelope to reveal one of those holiday letters that she didn't think people actually sent, complete with a photo of three beautiful children and a golden retriever wearing a plaid bow tie, all standing in front of a large tree that appeared to be decorated with homemade ornaments, unlike the generic oversized bulbs that filled the tree the decorator set up for her every December.

Iris scanned the letter before dropping onto the edge of her bed and reading it again, slower, absorbing every word, every detail of Gwen's picture-perfect life.

And there, on the back, a handwritten note. Just one line: "Would love to see you again next time you're in town."

Town. She hadn't been back to that town since she'd left it at age eighteen. She'd said goodbye to that life. Goodbye to the people in it. But Gwen... She'd never said goodbye to Gwen and never intended to, either. Gwen was the one good thing that had come out of her childhood.

Gwen was the reason why Iris had dared to dream that life could be much different than what it was once. Gwen was the reason why Iris was sitting here today.

She folded the letter back into the envelope and set it inside the drawer, under a magazine. Then she walked to the full-length mirror and took a close look at the crow's feet around her eyes that she hadn't yet hit with Botox, but she would have to next time. She smoothed the skirt of her dusty-rose-colored designer silk dress, thinking that once upon a time, she would have done anything to wear a dress like this. And she had, hadn't she? It hadn't been easy. The Iris from Westlake, Wisconsin, wasn't the girl that Julian had fallen in love with. He'd fallen in love with the new Iris, the tall, extra-lean blonde who had done catalog work through college and still maintained top grades, who kept her eye on the prize, who kept moving forward. Who never looked back. He didn't know the Iris who rode her secondhand bike to the gas station for her mother's cigarettes and smoked a few on the way home, whose best friend was anything but cool or sleek but was funny and kind and generous.

Who had the life Iris could only dream of—a big, clean house, with full-length curtains on all the windows, a closetful of frilly dresses, vacations each summer, and family dinner around an actual table.

Iris walked back into her closet for her shoes, but her mind wandered to something else as she fastened the clasps on her heels. Her eyes darted in case Julian or Sofia or even Stephanie came into the room looking for her, and she quickly rummaged through a collection of scarves, sighing in relief when she uncovered her hidden bottle of vodka.

She took a shot, and then another, measuring each by the mouthful. Once she was satisfied that the evidence was securely tucked away and out of sight, she went into the white marble bathroom, brushed her teeth, reapplied her lipstick, and practiced her best smile in the mirror. And then, because she couldn't stall any longer, and because she was Mrs. Julian Drake, she walked through the bedroom and into the hallway.

The buzz of the party immediately hit her, causing her heart rate to spike and her blood pressure to rise, and she grabbed a glass of champagne from a tray being passed around by a waiter, drinking it back in one long sip before reaching for another.

71

She wound her way through the groups of faces she barely recognized, smiling politely, nodding and murmuring her greetings. At the back of the living room, near the crackling fireplace, Stephanie was at Julian's side, laughing at something he was saying, a hand on his elbow. A proprietary hand.

Iris finished her champagne and handed it to a waiter, nearly catching her footing on the edge of an area rug. That was one thing she'd learned early: expensive shoes didn't always mean they were comfortable.

"Are you okay, miss?" the waiter asked, and she smiled demurely as she reached for another flute, hating the way her hand nearly knocked another off the tray.

She looked up, catching Julian's eye. There was a buzz in her ears, a sound that she couldn't identify, and she felt like she was swimming through the crowd, her body was weightless, her surroundings murky. She saw the alarm pass through Stephanie's eyes before she gave a nervous laugh.

"I think it's time for a toast," Stephanie said gaily, and Iris just stared at her, daring her to admit it, to come clean and be honest.

Iris cleared her throat, but no one heard her over the noise. A few people frowned in her direction, as if they were aware that trouble was brewing.

She looked for a spoon, or a knife, or something to tap against her glass, finally resorting to the metal objet d'art in a shape of a snake that Iris had purchased from Stephanie's gallery. Quite fitting really.

As she slapped it against the side of her crystal glass, she tried to read Stephanie's reaction. Was that horror because she knew what was about to unfold? Or because the artist of this particular piece (a thirty-something eccentric with no eyebrows and a thing for ripped jeans) was in the crowd?

Frankly, Iris didn't care. She didn't give a damn about the artist, the stupid metal snake, or Stephanie. But she cared about Julian.

The room went silent, and it was then that she saw Kat and Delilah at the center of the room. Their eyes were alive with glee, and their smiles were mocking and mean.

For a moment, she had a flashback to another time, another place. Westlake girls, always sure to point out that she was different—worse, an outsider in their otherwise bucolic suburb.

But she wasn't in Westlake, and hadn't been in half a lifetime.

She was exactly where she always wanted to be.

The entire room seemed electric with anticipation. Julian's jaw was clenched. Stephanie looked downright scared. An undeniable current of family drama was present, and the guests were eager for a front-row seat.

There were things she'd planned to say, of course, but she couldn't remember any of that now.

That champagne had gone straight to her head, and she'd forgotten to eat today. She'd been too busy having her nails done, her hair done, her makeup perfectly applied.

"A toast," she managed, lifting her glass. Her fingertips were numb and she feared she might drop it. Her arm swung up, higher than she'd wanted. Her voice felt thick. Her tongue felt heavy in her mouth. Her voice was loud in her ears.

"To Julian," she said. There was a pause as Delilah and Katrina glanced at each other and burst into laughter. Iris bit back the urge to push through the crowd and slap them both.

"And Stephanie," she said, looking at the woman she had once considered a friend.

Her heart was banging in her chest and she knew she should walk away now before things got worse, but she didn't know how to. She couldn't think straight.

The room seemed to tilt and she felt warm, too warm, and her heart was beating too fast, and she shifted the weight on her feet, trying to think, and her ankle buckled in those ridiculous heels, and the next thing she was aware of, a man was standing over her, patting her face and asking if she knew what day it was, and Iris had the very uneasy feeling that she'd messed things up. Badly.

5

GWEN

THIRTY-NINE. NOT yet forty; one more year to get her life on track, and another reminder that time was passing quickly and she didn't know where it had gone or if she'd spent it wisely. That everything she'd dreamed and hoped and planned for had already come and gone and now it was up to her to make the most of it, before it was all over. When did birthdays become depressing?

Still, she did manage to smile when Bea presented her with a birthday card first thing Monday that read "You're sweet. You're kind. Congratulations, you're twenty-nine!"

"What's this about?" Michael had asked, frowning when he turned it over.

Gwen had nearly forgotten that three years ago when Bea had first taken an interest in her age, she'd shaved off ten years.

"One year to thirty, Mom!" Bea declared as Gwen wrapped a pink scarf around her youngest's neck and plopped her unicorn hat on her head.

"Imagine that," she said wistfully. "Before you know it, I'll be completely gray."

"I like your hair, Mommy," Bea said, tugging on her mittens.

Gwen blinked. A random compliment. At her age?

"It's like…pumpkin spice!" Bea beamed, and Gwen felt her smile falter. Sure, the color had faded a bit, but at least it had evened out.

"It's called acorn," she explained.

But Bea just grinned. "It's pumpkin spice."

There's no use arguing with a child, Gwen told herself. Still, she'd been tempted. "Well. Off you go. Have a good day, and behave!" Not that she ever needed to tell Bea that, or even Declan, for that matter.

Now, determined to savor what remained of her youth, Gwen was dressed in her slimming black pants because it was time to admit that the jeans no longer fit and she'd be damned if she spent money on a bigger size, especially when she lived in some form of pajamas most days anyway. Her "pumpkin spice" hair was combed and shiny. Her Forevermore Beauty makeup perfectly applied. Her speech about her monthly plan prepared just in case Susan asked, and she might, because she was sort of Gwen's superior in that way.

Norah was assigned to babysit Declan, even though in an argument before school that morning she'd negotiated an hourly rate of seventeen fifty, coming down from twenty when Gwen pointed out that Declan would just sit in his room and play video games the entire time anyway. But seventeen fifty was her final offer. She wasn't budging. And Gwen was desperate.

The phone rang as she was walking out the door to meet her mother, and she tensed when she saw the school number pop up on the screen. January was always the worst time for colds. No sooner did the kids go back to school than they were off again, one after the other, taking up the entire sofa while cartoons danced across the screen.

"Hello?" She squeezed her eyes shut. She couldn't cancel this playdate. Bea was looking so forward to it. And admittedly, so was Gwen, in a strange, confusing way that she couldn't quite identify.

"Mrs. Riley? This is Paula Manning. I'm the school guidance counselor at..."

Gwen didn't even hear the rest of the introduction. Her blood was boiling and her heart felt like it could pound right out of her chest, and all she could think was, *What has Norah done now?* It wasn't always this way. Norah had never given her problems with school before. Even middle school had been a relative breeze, aside from a few mean girl episodes and of course the awkward onset of puberty. But then high school hit, and even though Norah was technically only in a different wing of the same school she had attended since they'd moved here when she was starting first grade, everything was suddenly different. Now Norah dressed differently. Now she even laughed differently. Now she had some new friends that Gwen didn't particularly approve of. And now Norah was almost failing two classes.

"I was hoping you could come in for a meeting," Paula continued.

Gwen felt weary. "Do you mind me asking what this is about?"

"I'd prefer to speak about this in person. Will tomorrow work? Say...ten?"

Gwen mentally ran through her calendar, even though she knew she was free. Still, she pulled out her new agenda just the same, cursing when she saw the note to call the dentist before her brunch today.

"What was that?" Paula's tone was sharp.

"Nothing," Gwen said quickly. "Tomorrow will be just fine."

She disconnected the call and brought her finger to her tooth. Well, happy birthday to her.

The parking lot of the Main Street Café was full, thanks to some jackass who was parked down the center line of two perfectly good spots. With a flicker of annoyance, Gwen realized that the car belonged to her mother.

She tightened her grip on the steering wheel, already arguing with her mother before she was even in front of her, and forced three calming breaths as she looped around the block and finally saw a car pulling out of a spot on the street. So she'd have to feed the meter. She'd only put in an hour's worth. Ninety minutes, tops. It would give her an excuse to leave early.

She dug her phone from her bag to check the time as she deposited the change from her coat pockets into the meter. Sure enough, a text from her mother, sent three minutes ago, five minutes before their agreed-upon meeting time, informing Gwen of her arrival and asking if Gwen was still coming.

Deep breaths. Calming breaths.

Her mother was sitting near the window, her eyes darting around the room in that anxious way that made Gwen's blood pressure skyrocket as she approached the table.

"There you are!" Eileen's tone was accusatory.

Gwen stifled a sigh. She didn't have it in her to point out that she wasn't late. In fact, she was exactly on time. But saying so would just lead to an argument. Semantics. Watch checking and insistence on her mother's part that she was right, Gwen was wrong, and Gwen was late. When she was not late. But then Gwen would say nothing because that's what she always did. That was their relationship. Even now, at the age of thirty-nine.

So it made sense just to stifle the sigh now and cut out all that other BS.

"I couldn't find a parking spot," she said.

Her mother frowned. "Really? I had no trouble at all."

"Well, the lot was full when I got here."

Her mother's expression turned smug. "I always arrive everywhere ten minutes early to allow for parking. When I got here, there were two open spots."

"And you parked between both of them." Gwen forced herself not to glare at her mother.

But Eileen didn't seem fazed by the accusation at all. She shrugged and said with a little sniff, "I can't have anyone opening their door into the side of my Lexus!"

"This is Westlake," Gwen said, unable to hide her frustration. "Everyone has a nice car in Westlake."

Her mother raised a single eyebrow. After a less than subtle pause, she said, "Not everyone."

And there it was. Gwen had fallen right into the trap. She knew it shouldn't hurt. After all, she liked her Honda. It was comfortable, like an old sweater that you could just slide right into, without having to worry about any adjustments. It worked just fine, it got her where she needed to go, she didn't have to twitch when Bea spilled her crackers and then stepped on them as she was getting out, and best of all, it was paid off.

She pulled off her hat and set it on the table. She was already mentally ticking off the minutes until the meter ran out.

"Oh my!" Eileen set a hand to her chest. "What did you do to your hair?"

Gwen froze. Bea's comment echoed, clear and loud. "Nothing. I just tried a new color."

"At home?" Eileen tsked. "You can always spot a box dye job. Still, at least it's not streaky. Just oranger than I'm used to. What color do you call that?"

"It's called acorn," Gwen said evenly, ignoring her mother's critical squint.

"That's a nice coat," her mother said, sizing her up in a way that Gwen couldn't quite be sure was a compliment or not. "Is it new?"

"It is." She didn't elaborate that it was an after-Christmas sale, marked down fifty percent and then an extra twenty percent off that, whatever that amounted to. She'd save that in case her mother accused her of it looking too expensive.

"My, Michael must have had a nice bonus!"

Gwen said nothing as she unbuttoned her coat and set it on the back of her chair. They'd never tell her mother about Michael losing his job. Eileen knowing that Michael was unemployed would just lead to...trouble.

"And a new outfit!" Eileen's eyes lit up. "Look! Twins!"

She stood, turning side to side like she was on the Milan runway, her eyes flicking over the room, looking for an audience, for recognition or approval. Sure, enough, there it was. The black pants. The boatneck sweater that Gwen had found so chic and, let's face it, forgiving when she'd tried it on at the mall over the weekend. Her special outfit. Her redemption outfit. Her cool-kid outfit.

Her playdate outfit. Her attempt to be friends with Susan Sharp outfit.

Holy shit. She'd started dressing like her mother.

"What are you all dressed up for?" Eileen asked as she sat down.

"What are *you* dressed up for?" Gwen asked in response. They were, after all, twins. God help her, right down to the string of faux pearls at her neck.

"Oh, these are my everyday clothes," Eileen said with a dismissive wave. "You never know who you might run into. But I know you don't care about those things."

Gwen opened the menu and studied it. She had eaten before she'd come, so she could just have a yogurt parfait and forego judgment, but now her eyes were drifting to the French toast. The stuffed French toast. With cream cheese. And berries. And whipped cream. She needed to find some enjoyment in this birthday brunch.

"I just thought I'd take your advice."

"Well." Eileen looked pleased. "It's nice to see you making an effort. I see these women wearing leggings everywhere! Even to work! In my day, you dressed up for work. And school."

And plane rides. Yes, Gwen knew. On their last family vacation (Gwen was horrified to realize that it had been three years ago, already), Eileen had called the day before to ask what Gwen intended to wear on the plane. She'd planned to wear leggings, a T-shirt that covered her butt, and flip-flops that could easily slide off and on again as she passed through security. She'd taken a calming breath and told her mother that she was wearing jeans and a blouse and her ballet flats, hoping that this would satisfy and she could get back to packing. Instead, Eileen had said, "Jeans? On a plane!" And then, of course, came the tsk.

Nothing set Gwen on edge more than that tsk.

"I have plans after this," Gwen finally said, wishing she hadn't, because it would only lead to an interrogation, and each explanation would then lead to further need for detail.

"Oh? An appointment?" Eileen's eyes went wide as they drifted to Gwen's abdomen.

Gwen frowned. If her mother was implying she was pregnant, she could think again. "No. Not an appointment."

"I just went to the dentist yesterday. Every six months, on the dot! There's nothing more wonderful than a fresh, clean mouth, is there? I love the feeling of running my tongue over my teeth. It feels soooo clean." To drive this home, she did just that.

In a moment of panic, Gwen wondered if her mother had noticed the chip on her tooth, but she quickly calmed herself with the knowledge that if she had, she would have said something outright. No, it was just the usual comment she received every six months. "Actually, Bea has a playdate after school," Gwen said as she closed her menu.

"And here I thought I might come over after this. But...no, no, it makes sense that she would want to play with other kids instead of spend time with her grandmother." Eileen fell silent as she sipped her water. "Well, your choice. I've grown used to being alone since your father died."

Gwen didn't wait for the waitress to ask for her order when she finally approached the table. "I'll have the stuffed French toast and a side of the hash browns," she said. "And a Diet Coke."

She could feel her mother glaring at her across the table.

"Just a poached egg for me and one slice of rye toast, dry."

"That's all you're eating?" Gwen frowned at her as the waitress walked away.

Eileen puffed out her cheeks and set a hand to her stomach. "I ate a banana for breakfast. *So* filling."

"Well, I didn't have breakfast," Gwen said, which wasn't true. She'd had half a stale bagel, three cups of coffee, and a handful of Goldfish crackers. Make that two handfuls. Okay, make that three. "And it is my birthday," she added, feeling the need to explain herself and hating the fact that she felt she had to.

"How could I forget?" There was a pause. And here it came. "I've been thinking about it all day. What I went through." Eileen shook her head miserably. "*Forty-two* hours of labor. Back then they didn't induce." She shuddered.

"Well—"

"Then I started thinking, thirty-nine! You are nearly *forty*! How can I be the mother of an almost *forty*-year-old woman? Do you know how *old* that makes me feel?" She narrowed her eyes at Gwen as if this were somehow Gwen's fault.

"Anyway," Eileen said, grimacing. "Tough day."

Yes, it was shaping up that way. And it had started so hopeful. Gwen sighed as the waitress arrived with her Diet Coke.

"I can't believe you drink that poison," her mother said.

Gwen took a long sip. It was delicious.

"It ruins your teeth, you know. And it leads to weight gain."

"It's sugar-free!" Gwen said, but her pulse flicked, damn it.

Her mother tossed her hands in the air, as if to tell everyone in the restaurant that, well, she'd tried.

"I'm thinking of trying a Pilates class in the spring," Gwen said defensively, hating herself for feeding into this conversation.

"Why wait?" Eileen remarked.

"I'm busy getting my business off the ground."

"Oh for heaven's sake!" Her mother's eyes rolled. "Are you really earning any money?"

"There's potential to earn money." And she certainly needed it. "It's like any job in sales—"

But Eileen was in a huff. "I don't understand why you would take this on. Three children and a successful husband who can afford to give you a comfortable lifestyle. If you have that kind of free time, I don't see why you won't come to the mall with me. Or lunch more often. But then I guess that's your choice…"

"Free time?" *Think about the whipped cream*, Gwen told herself firmly. *Think of bringing the spoon to your mouth, feeling the cold, creamy sweetness coat your tongue.* "I can assure you that I'm extremely busy."

"So you said," her mother murmured. "Well, someday I'll be gone. You'll have to live with that."

Gwen balled her napkin in her lap.

When it was clear that she wasn't going to get a response, Eileen said, "I still haven't received your Christmas card, by the way."

"I mailed them last week. You'll probably get it by tomorrow."

"In the middle of January. Such a pity." Eileen shook her head gravely. "Why, when I hosted my bridge club two weeks ago, everyone was asking why I didn't have a card from my daughter on display. I had to tell them that it was upstairs in my bedroom, on my nightstand where it can be the first thing I see every morning and each evening, and then quickly change the subject before they asked me to go get it."

"Why didn't you just tell them the truth? I'm sure they wouldn't have cared."

Eileen didn't look convinced, but then, her mother didn't understand that other people didn't hold everyone to such incredibly high standards, either.

"Anyway," Gwen said sharply. "Ballet has started back up for Bea and—"

"I would have loved ballet lessons as a child," her mother said wistfully. "But then, no money. Six brothers and sisters. I didn't have the opportunity for piano lessons, ballet, private tutors." In other words, all the things Gwen's children had. Gwen waited for it. "Michael's such a hard worker."

The implication, of course, was that Gwen, who was the primary caregiver for three kids, was not.

Oh, thank God. The French toast had arrived.

Avoiding her mother's eye, she doused it in maple syrup and cut into it with the side of her fork.

"He does work hard," she said, even if these days he was working hard at finding a job. "Most nights he falls asleep on the sofa watching television."

The moment she said it she wished she could take it back. Eileen's eyes widened, and this time not over Gwen's dietary indiscretions. "You know what they say," she said, shaking her head.

No, Gwen didn't know what "they" said, but she had a feeling she would soon be told nonetheless.

"If he isn't sleeping with you, he's sleeping with somebody else," her mother said glibly.

Gwen was aware that her breath had turned heavy. She was staring at her mother, who proceeded to poke at her food as if she hadn't just delivered the most cutting of words. Gwen wanted to laugh, wanted to say that she was being ridiculous, that of course Michael wasn't having an *affair*, but she also knew there was no point in arguing with her mother. It would just make her more upset, and she wasn't sure that was possible.

Michael *was* leaving the house for long periods, and unlike before, when she knew he was at the office, now she wasn't exactly sure where he was. She'd never thought she needed to check up on him, didn't think there was cause for true suspicion.

But no, Michael did sleep on the sofa—downstairs or in his home office. Either way, he was home.

"Your father never once fell asleep on the sofa," Eileen continued. "He wanted to be next to me all night long."

Gwen's chest ached when she thought of her father, his kind, sweet face, his ever-patient way of sitting back, letting Eileen shine. He was Gwen's biggest ally. Her only ally. The only one who understood what it was like to live under such a critical eye.

Michael's answer to Eileen was avoidance, and he'd suggested Gwen do the same every time she complained. "You have your own family now," he pointed out. "You're a grown woman."

But somehow, being in the company of her mother again, she was a child.

"Don't let it bother you," her father used to say affably, but it wasn't so easy for Gwen, never had been. When she tried to tell him that, he'd say, "You know how she is. Just slough it off."

That's what she should do, she knew. But she couldn't help it, it hurt. And she was tired of not showing her hurt.

Her eyes wandered to a table at the other end of the restaurant, where another mother and daughter were sitting, each with coffee in their hands. The daughter was younger than Gwen, mid- to late-twenties, just coming into adulthood. She was chatting, telling a story, and the mother was leaning forward across the table, her head tipped a bit to the side, listening intently. The daughter said something and the mother hooted with laughter, and then reached over and squeezed the daughter's hand, gave her a smile so warm that something deep inside Gwen, a part of her she didn't even know existed until moments like this, felt like it might break.

She looked away. At least if her father were here she could tell him about her plans for Forevermore Beauty. She could tell him about Michael, too. About the bills and the house. Voice her fears.

Gwen scraped the last of her French toast from her plate and brought it to her mouth. Once, she could have told Iris everything too. Found some humor in it. Or at least some escape. But now, it was all on her.

Gwen had every intention of changing her clothes before her playdate with Susan—make that Bea's playdate with Taffy—but an inventory of her closet left her with no other options unless she wanted to wear a sweater that made her look like a marshmallow. At least that's what Eileen had said when she wore it at Christmas, with a smile on her face, as if it was meant to be a compliment, or so Gwen perhaps couldn't complain that it wasn't one.

Finally, in a fit of exasperation, Gwen turned off her closet light and admitted defeat. Susan would have no way of knowing that she was playing twins with her mother today. Besides, time was running out. They were meant to leave in—Oh, God.

"Bea! Time to go!"

Bea flung open her bedroom door and ran past her, down the stairs to the hallway.

Gwen pulled in a breath and blew it out. This was it. A playdate at the Sharp house. A neighborhood friend for Bea. Joining Forevermore Beauty was finally paying off.

"No asking for food," she instructed as she bundled Bea into her coat. She'd been sure to supply her with an afterschool snack. "And no running inside the house either!"

Bea nodded solemnly.

"And pick up any mess you make," she said as she opened the front door and they stepped outside.

"But what if Taffy makes a mess?" Bea asked.

"Then you still help clean it up," Gwen said. She eyed the Sharp house. Her heart started to race. Redemption was within reach.

"But that doesn't seem fair," Bea pouted. "Why should I have to clean up a mess that I didn't make?"

"Because you want to be invited back? Right?" *Yes, Bea, you want to be invited back.* Even if she didn't know it yet.

They walked the rest of the way in silence, Bea's hand in hers, their pace quick and determined. When they reached the door, Bea buzzed the bell, and then, dammit, she pressed it again.

"Just once!" Gwen hissed. The last thing she needed was to look eager. Susan may run the block but Gwen had been here first. Gwen was from Westlake. This was her home base.

Somehow that little pep talk fell short.

Through the frosted glass door panel, she saw Susan's figure appear. "You'll have fun, honey. You can play, just remember to—"

"Pick up. I know." Bea groaned.

The door flung open and there she was, blond hair pulled back in a sleek low ponytail, her eyes unnaturally bright. A smile on her face that didn't quite meet her eyes.

"Hiiiiiiiiii!" said Susan.

"Hiiiiiiiiii!" said Gwen.

Bea mumbled something under her breath. Gwen pushed back the familiar swell of insecurity. She missed the ease of a real friend. She missed the ease of being herself. But this is what it took, it seemed. To connect with other mothers. To not be an outcast on her own block. To ensure that Bea had a neighborhood friend.

"Come on in, Bea. Taffy and Clementine are upstairs in the playroom."

"Thanks so much for having us over to play," Gwen said, stepping inside. The space between Susan's brow pinched, but she didn't say anything. Bea was quick to kick off her boots and shed her coat. Gwen gave Susan an amused smile as Bea ran up the stairs.

Yes, ran.

Calming breath.

"Well." Susan bared a smile at her. She blinked a few times. "Come in."

Gwen unzipped her boots and set them neatly next to Bea's. Susan was already moving toward the kitchen at the back of the house. Gwen felt warm in her coat, but Susan made no mention of hanging it up for her. Gwen shifted uneasily around the center island.

"This is a beautiful kitchen," she said, and it was. Larger than her own, with new, high-end appliances that Gwen doubted Forevermore Beauty earnings had paid for.

"Thanks," Susan said with a hint of a genuine smile. She began unpacking a grocery bag: three containers of hummus, a large tub of guacamole, some pita chips. A party perhaps?

Gwen stood uncomfortably near the edge of the island as Susan reached for another bag: fresh linguine, baby kale, and some other green vegetables that Gwen was ashamed she didn't even recognize. Growing up, her mother had been a fan of frozen vegetables, and well, Gwen was guilty of cooking separate meals for the kids all these years.

She had become everything she had promised not to be. A microwave mommy.

"What are you making?" Gwen asked, thinking that maybe she'd get some ideas for child-friendly dinner fare.

"Linguine with lobster and snow peas in a light cream sauce and a kale Caesar salad. Of course, I only use a splash of cream," she added.

"Of course." Gwen's mouth went dry. There was nothing more to contribute to that conversation. "Celebrating something?"

Susan looked at her quizzically. "Just...dinner."

"Of course." Gwen sucked in a breath and looked around the kitchen, to the backyard, where there was a trampoline, a playscape nearly as big as the one at Bea's old preschool, a tree house that put the Swiss family Robinson to shame, a playhouse that was a miniature model of the actual house, and a giant pink tent that probably belonged in a circus.

Susan walked to the fridge and studied the contents.

"I have some calls to make, but if you want to hang around, you're welcome to go down to the basement and watch television there. Stay as long as you want!"

The *basement?* Gwen felt her cheeks flush with fresh humiliation as she tried to gracefully grasp the upper hand. Her mouth opened and closed, and she had the sickening sensation that she was gaping like Bea's pet fish, which, like this playdate, had lasted about five minutes.

Perhaps to underscore her point, Susan made a grand show of picking up her cell phone and scrolling through it, not even casting another glance in Gwen's direction. Gwen watched her through narrowed eyes. She didn't even like Susan! Didn't want to hang out here, in her ridiculous kitchen with its double ovens and secret freezer drawers. She was only here because Susan had invited her in. And because she couldn't think of an excuse to leave quick enough.

And now she had the fortune of finally explaining why she really did have to be on her way, only to have it look like a lame excuse.

"Oh, no, I have to run to get a start on dinner tonight. Maybe I'll do lobster, too!" *Too much, Gwen. Too much!*

She was already walking toward the hall, but Susan stayed behind in the kitchen. "Pick her up at five?" was all she had to say.

Gwen didn't like the tone Susan was using. Not earlier. Not now. As if she were the boss and Gwen was some eager puppy, all too happy to jump on command.

"Quarter to five is better for me. See you then." Gwen managed a tight-lipped smile as she walked out of the kitchen, down the long hallway, and slid into her boots, which were still cold. She let herself out the door. She could already hear Susan's peal of laughter somewhere in the distance behind her as she took the steps and hurried across the brick pavers to the driveway.

She wanted more than anything to cut across the lawn, but she couldn't mess up the perfect blanket of snow.

She made it home before the tears could fall, and she was already staring into the contents of her processed-food-filled pantry before Norah's bedroom door could be heard opening at the top of the stairs, the music belting from the room a sure sign.

"Hey! You said you'd be gone for two hours!" she cried.

"Change of plans," Gwen muttered, vowing to go all organic next time she was at the store, the way she'd always planned, before life got in the way. She stared at the clock over her modest range. The thought of going back to the Sharp house filled her with dread so deep, she almost considered offering to pay Norah to go instead.

But Norah couldn't be trusted not to do something even more embarrassing than Gwen had done.

She checked the garage, happy to see Michael's sedan parked next to the minivan, her decision made.

She wasn't going to pick up Bea at quarter to five. Michael was. It was, she thought, the least he could do for her, considering that it was her birthday.

With Bailey at her heels, she went into her bedroom, quickly changed into her daytime pajamas of leggings and a loose sweatshirt, and climbed onto the unmade bed.

"I hate that bitch Susan Sharp," she sniffed into Bailey's sandy hair, loving the way he smelled, even if he did probably need a bath. He didn't speak or tell her it would all be okay or that Susan was a horrible person and he was happy he had shat on her lawn that one day, but she knew he was thinking it, because he loved her, and God, did she love him.

She smiled, because just looking into Bailey's warm brown eyes made her smile, and stroked his fur for a few minutes until her heart felt full again.

It was already growing dark, and the room was quiet and still. She could have stayed here all night, but she had two other children and still the issue of Bea's pickup to deal with.

She wiped the tears from her eyes and made a promise to herself that the next time she saw Susan Sharp she would be ten pounds thinner, wearing a trendier outfit (though, just like in her youth, this seemed more impossible somehow than losing more than two-point-five pounds per week between now and the next First Friday meeting), and she'd have doubled her sales goals for the month. For once, she'd have the upper hand.

The room above the garage had a separate entrance, built with exterior stairs. An afterthought and, now, a convenience. It wasn't just Michael's home office. It was his home away from home.

If she was being honest with herself, it was more than that. It was Michael's home these days. The pullout sofa had become his bed, because he often fell asleep watching television, and she didn't see a reason to wake him. The only perk to this arrangement was that she had the master bathroom all to herself. She wasn't complaining.

Gwen would like to think that there was a time in her life when she could turn to Michael. When she had the comfort of knowing that no matter how bad the day was, the sun would suddenly come out the moment his key turned in the door. That all he had to do was smile, reach out, and take her hand, or just give her a look, and everything would be right again.

But she couldn't say any of those things. Truth was, she couldn't be sure when she'd stopped. It had happened slowly, so gradually she didn't even see the warnings, and somewhere in the midst of changing diapers and signing school forms and making sure someone didn't break an arm or light a match, she and Michael had drifted apart.

She left Bailey in the kitchen, outdated as it now seemed, slipped on her snow boots, and took the back door around to the stairs that led to the annex above the garage, realizing that it had been a long time since she had come up here.

Michael looked confused when he answered the door. They rarely had time as a couple anymore, just a few stolen moments that were spent in practical ways, like shoving presents under the tree or arguing over bills. He could have taken her in his arms and had a nooner, but it didn't even seem to cross his mind. Or hers, really.

Her mother's earlier comment haunted her as she looked up at him.

"Is everything okay?" he asked.

Everything was so far from okay that she wanted to scream and shout and even cry. It wasn't supposed to be like this. None of it. She was supposed to still be in Chicago. She was supposed to have three children who behaved themselves. A husband who had a secure job. A good sex life. A cute figure. A group of friends that she met for coffee or book club once a month. Family dinners where everyone laughed and where the magazine-worthy kitchen was always clean and she wasn't the one cleaning it. But she couldn't say all that. And maybe Michael even knew all that. Maybe he felt just as disappointed as she did. Maybe that's why they'd drifted so far apart.

She reached for the most obvious issue and walked inside the warm room, aided by the assistance of a space heater that ran up their electricity bill at an alarming rate. "No, everything is not okay. I got a call from the school guidance counselor today. They want a meeting."

Michael closed the door. The office was a mess. It looked like a frat boy's bedroom. The desk was strewn with papers, and there were empty soda cans next to crumbled chip bags. When Michael was stressed, he ate. The grocery bills had never been higher than now, when they should really be watching their spending. There was no evidence of an affair. If anything, it just proved how much time Michael spent in this room.

"What happened now?" Michael tried to shove the papers around, but it was no use. A folder slid to the floor. His laptop was open. A cover letter was lit up on the screen. She resisted the urge to ask if he had a lead, which company he was targeting, but this was delicate territory, and she had enough to deal with at the moment.

Gwen tossed up her hands. "I don't know. She didn't say. She said we would discuss it in the meeting tomorrow."

Michael's mouth was pinched. "Well, let me know what they say."

Gwen straightened her shoulders. "Can you take this one? I'm trying to build up my sales numbers, and I did sit through the parent-teacher conferences alone."

"I'm trying to find a job, Gwen!" Michael ground out. He looked at her like she was crazy. "I can't do that if I'm playing Mister Mom!"

"I'm not asking you to be the mom. I'm the mom. You're the dad. I'm just asking for a little help around here." A long silence filled the room.

"Fine." Michael eventually said. "What can I do to help?"

Funny he should ask. "I need you to pick up Bea from a playdate at four forty-five. It's just down the street."

Michael glanced at the clock on his laptop. "I'm trying to get this cover letter out by close of business, Gwen."

Gwen wavered. He had a point. She considered her load, weighing the most bearable to the least.

"Fine. I will help you with the cover letter, and I'll go to the meeting with the guidance conference if you pick up Bea. Five minutes of your time." She'd do just about anything if he would just go pick up Bea. Clean this sty. Cook his favorite meal. Anything.

"Why are you so determined not to pick her up?" he asked, looking at her suspiciously. "Whose house is she at?"

"Susan Sharp's," Gwen said, avoiding eye contact.

Michael chuckled under his breath. "The lady from your pyramid scheme?"

Gwen chose not to react to that common misunderstanding. "My leader from Forevermore Beauty. Yes."

"Your *leader*?" Michael gave her a strange look. "What is this? The neighborhood cult?"

"It's not funny," Gwen said, even though under other circumstances, she might have thought it was.

"Are you sure you want to do this? You don't even wear makeup half the time. I'm going to get a job, Gwen."

He said that with such conviction that she wavered. The truth was that she wasn't so sure she wanted to do this, but she also saw it as a chance to maybe fit in. She'd toyed with going back to work this fall when Bea was in full-day school, but Michael insisted he would have a new job any day, and who would run the kids around, who would take a day off when they had school vacations and summer break or caught a cold? Then there was the glaring fact that she hadn't been in the workforce for over fourteen years and her resume was brief, considering she was only two years out of college when Norah was born. And then Forevermore Beauty came along, with the promise of infinite potential and flexible hours. She wasn't a dummy. She knew it was probably too good to be true. But it was…something.

And she could never admit it to Michael, but she didn't believe that he was going to get a job any day. She didn't even know the last time he had an interview.

"We're not talking about Forevermore Beauty right now. Susan made me feel very unwelcome in her house when I dropped Bea off." She felt the back of her eyes begin to sting. She couldn't cry. Not over this.

"Well, I'm sorry that Susan hurt your feelings," Michael said, giving her a small smile. "I don't know why you let women like that make you feel bad about yourself."

"I just want to fit in," Gwen finished, looking down at her nails.

Michael went back to the desk chair. It swiveled a little when he sat. "You grew up in Westlake. I find it hard to believe you don't know anyone else here."

Gwen sighed. "I know them, but I wasn't friends with them. Iris was my closest friend here. And now…" Now she was back to being the overdressed kid on the swing, all by herself. Only this time, there was no Iris to come along and sit beside her.

"Please, Michael," she begged. "I wouldn't ask if it didn't matter. This can be my birthday present."

He looked at her sheepishly. "I haven't had time to go to the store yet."

She gave him a long look, knowing that if she made a big deal out of it that he would run out after picking up Bea, get a card, maybe even some flowers.

She'd rather him just pick up Bea. Face Susan. Save her the misery. And the money.

"This can be my present."

He lifted an eyebrow. "If it means that much to you, I'll go. The white Colonial, right?"

The white, pristine Colonial with the playroom and the crisp white furniture and the oversized fridge bursting with organic food and lobster. "Yes," she said.

Gwen resisted the urge to close the distance between them and fling her arms around her husband's neck, to sink against his chest, to thank him for taking this burden off her. But what would Michael do if she were to spontaneously hug him like that? She didn't know, and right now, she wasn't exactly sure she wanted to find out.

There'd been enough disappointment for one birthday.

But there was cake, at least. She'd bought it herself last time she went to the store, and stuffed it in the freezer, knowing that Michael probably wouldn't remember to pick one up this year and not even really taking it to heart—at least, not too much. But still, it was there. And God knew she deserved it.

6

IRIS

REHAB. IRIS WASN'T going to rehab; at least, that's what she'd said.

Yet here she was. In Upstate New York. Sharing a room with a fifty-year-old woman named Hilda who slept with three teddy bears on her bed. "Daddy issues" was Hilda's go-to response for anything.

A cop-out, Iris thought. After all, where had her father ever been? Her mother never mentioned him, said he didn't stick around long enough to even find out she was pregnant, and whenever Iris had asked for his name (once for a family tree, another time for genetic history when she was undergoing a rhinoplasty for a "deviated septum") her mother always made up an excuse to get off the phone.

She could say she had daddy issues too. Or maybe she couldn't. Maybe you actually needed a daddy to claim "issues."

Hilda's "daddy issues" were vague at best. She was much more eager to discuss the other people on the floor, something the art therapist referred to as "deflecting."

"You're deflecting again, Hilda!" Marcia would bark from the table at the front of the room, where she was building a birdfeeder out of Popsicle sticks, when she heard Hilda give a recap of every person who came through the door: Ricky, a middle-aged bachelor with a red face and a round belly had told his sixteen-year-old niece she was "foxy" after one too many, prompting his sister to file a restraining order; Carl had diabetes, but that didn't stop him from enjoying his gin; and Sari, who looked like the kind of grandmother who crocheted baby blankets and made chocolate-chip cookies every Sunday, was on her fourth visit here, and had driven her car through the garage door one night, after taking down two portions of the fence and the mailbox.

Hilda didn't bat an eyelash when Marcia yelled at her. Instead, she picked up a pair of safety scissors and grabbed a stack of construction paper.

"Aren't you making anything?" She seemed baffled as she stared at Iris across the table.

Iris wished she had a cup of coffee right now, but stimulants were strictly banned. No uppers. No downers. No alcohol. No sharps.

Hilda struggled to cut the paper nearly as much as she struggled to get her hands through the child-sized loops on the handles of the scissors.

"I hate art," Iris blurted, and she wasn't even sure why she'd said that. But then it occurred to her. Of course. Art made her think of Stephanie, her so-called friend, who was probably sleeping in her California king right now, her head on Iris's pillow, Julian's hand on Stephanie's ass.

She felt like she might be sick.

"I love crafts," Hilda said. "Better than group."

Group was the worst, Iris was quick to discover. Actually, the "recovery sessions" were the worst, because in those sessions you had no one to hide behind, no one to take center stage. It was you and your assigned counselor. And you were held accountable.

That was a word they liked a lot around here. *Accountable. Responsible. Honest.* Big words. Big subjects. As if Iris were hiding some horrible secret that she didn't want anyone to share. As if she was in denial. This morning, she had sat across a small gray table in a small gray room with Patty, who had been in recovery for twenty-three years. "Every day is a journey," she said with a knowing smile.

Iris held up a hand. "Look. There's been a mistake. I'm not...I'm a social drinker."

"I see." Patty's expression remained blank.

"And I have an active social life. Charity events, parties... My husband is on the board of a few museums."

Patty didn't flinch.

"I go to lunches. With friends. We order wine. Everyone is drinking, not just me. I see no reason to be singled out."

"Your husband thinks you have a problem," Patty finally offered.

"Well, my husband is sleeping with my best friend," Iris replied with a strange sense of satisfaction. It was the first time she'd told anyone, and it felt good to be honest, not that she'd be slipping again.

"So you've been self-soothing with alcohol." Patty gave a knowing head tilt.

Iris shook her head. "There is nothing wrong with me."

"Are you happy?" Patty had asked, and this was the first time Iris felt her defenses waver. When was the last time anyone had asked her that? When had she ever asked herself that or dared to consider the answer?

"I'm living the life I always wanted," she said firmly.

Patty let out a sigh. "We'll try again tomorrow."

But there would be no tomorrow. There couldn't be. Iris fumed the entire way to art, sat and watched as Hilda cut her paper and Marcia glued her birdhouse together, and then followed Hilda to the recreation room, where a circle of ten chairs was gathered near the fireplace. Ricky and Carl and the sweet-looking grandmother were there, and a few others that Iris might have seen in the television room last night, but that was vague, and yesterday was a long, bad day that felt like half a lifetime ago, not a mere matter of hours.

She'd awoken with a headache. Champagne always did that to her. Red wine, too, not that she bothered with that much. Turned your teeth and lips purple and it stained. Julian was usually gone for the office by the time she awoke or, on Sundays, out for a jog at Central Park that usually turned into brunch at his club. Now Iris suspected that brunch was with Stephanie in the apartment he had ensured would remain hers in the divorce settlement.

But yesterday morning, Julian was not at the office or the gym or the park or in Stephanie's bed. Yesterday, he stood at the foot of their bed, the sunlight pouring in from the French doors behind him, suitcases at his feet.

Her entire body had gone cold with panic. He was actually doing it. He was leaving her. And then she realized that the suitcases weren't Julian's at all.

"What is this?" She knew better than to think it was a spontaneous vacation.

"You're going upstate," Julian had replied. "To Andover. It's a rehab center."

He had officially silenced her. That place was the real deal. She knew three wives in their social circle who had spent twenty-eight days there in the last two years. Pills. "You've got to be kidding me."

He didn't say anything as he began opening her suitcases, then her drawers.

Iris quickly tossed back the duvet. "Julian, come on! It was a party. Everyone was drinking."

He gave her a look she'd never seen before, one he probably reserved for his courtroom time. "Not everyone was falling-down drunk, Iris."

He couldn't make her, she wanted to say, but she closed her mouth because she knew he could. Not going meant it would be over. The apartment. The dinners. The vacations. The wardrobe. Julian.

The dream.

Because what was the alternative? Westlake? Her mother's house? She'd left that life and sworn she'd never return. That her future would be bright. That there was more for her out there.

And there was.

"Fine. I'll go," she told him then. She was still wearing her dress from the party. No doubt her makeup too. She had slipped, lost herself, lost the person that Julian had married.

She walked to the shower, bathed and dressed, and then, because she didn't want any more trouble, and because she couldn't bear to see the look in her husband's eyes, she put on her warmest winter coat, her biggest sunglasses, and took her bags to the elevator, a part of her thinking that maybe, if she went without a scene or a fight, he'd feel bad, about everything.

She made it all the way to the black town car before the hope started to fade. He hadn't come after her. She stared out the window the entire ride upstate, the bare branches of the trees whirring past her, making her head spin.

And then she'd signed the papers. Checked herself in. Waited for a phone call. Waited for him to see that she was trying, that she was doing her share, unfair as it may be, because maybe if she stayed here, then he would meet her halfway too. And maybe, when she got out of here, they could start over.

Her heart began to speed up as they sat in the circle waiting for group to start. She turned to Hilda, who looked radiantly happy as she swung her legs and greeted every single person who entered the room with a compliment that seemed insincere at best.

"Love that pink shirt, Sari!" she told the grandma who had flattened her three-year-old grandson's new bike with her car. "It really brings out the color of your eyes!"

"You look so well rested today, Ricky!" she told the man who had hit on his niece. "I can tell you've been taking yoga seriously."

"I love the birdfeeder you made in art therapy today, Carl," she told the man with diabetes. "Maybe tomorrow you can show me how you get the base so even!"

What would Hilda have said about her? That her manicure was still intact, and so were her highlights? That it was a good thing her last Botox appointment was only three weeks ago since she was stuck here for four weeks?

"Is there a place we can get internet access?" Iris asked Hilda. Cell phones, tablets, any connection to the outside world had been seized. But she had to know what was going on. Surely Delilah wouldn't be able to hold back. Maybe there was some insight on her blog. Something, anything, that could give a window into what was happening back in the city.

"Oh, noooo. No internet!" Hilda started to laugh, too loudly, making Iris regret saying anything.

She shoved her hands between her knees and stared at the center of the room. No internet access meant no reading Delilah's blog, no finding out what mention of last night was shared across her Upper East Side readership. It meant no access to Facebook, where she could see if Stephanie's posts correlated with Julian's schedule. It meant she was completely cut off.

She felt like she couldn't breathe. Like she was being strangled. Like she might do something really foolish, like cry. Her heart was pounding and her mouth was dry and there was only one thing she could think of that would ease this agitation, numb her feelings, and make everything good enough again.

Wine wasn't an option. She scanned the room, looking for another distraction.

There were no donuts. No watered-down coffee with powdered creamer. No familiar faces other than Hilda's joyous expression as she now gazed out the windows overlooking a huge, dead lawn that led to the big gates that met the road that led to freedom, to Manhattan, to her life.

As soon as the meeting was over, she went to the patient phone and picked up the receiver. She would just call him;

maybe she'd suggest that vacation that she'd been thinking about.

She wouldn't blame him or provoke him or even ask about Stephanie. Maybe when things got better, Stephanie would just go away.

She was breathing deeply into the receiver, and a line was forming behind her. Someone swore, loudly, telling her to hurry it up in not so nice of words, but she couldn't move, couldn't think. She had to be clear-headed. There was too much at stake and nothing was for certain.

Well, except for one thing. If she went back now, without giving this a real chance, Julian would probably divorce her.

She couldn't go back to New York. But she couldn't stay either. If she used a credit card to fly to a resort or check into a hotel, Julian would know. Of course, he might always call, check on her after all. It was a risk.

And she was a betting woman.

She saw no choice. She'd have to call her mother.

She set a hand on her stomach. She could practically taste the wine in her mouth. It would all be okay. It had to be okay.

Every Sunday night while Julian sat in his study enjoying a cigar, she called her mother. She knew the number by heart, without the assistance of the stored files in her phone. Lois answered on the third ring.

"Hi, Ma," Iris said, keeping her voice light.

"What's wrong?" Lois asked suspiciously. She could hear the flick of a lighter, the crackle of paper. The hiss of a breath.

"Nothing's wrong." Iris covered the receiver as she steadied herself. Nothing was wrong. This was just a little drama, a little misunderstanding. It would blow over. It had to. "I missed our call last night so, I'm calling now…" She stared at the bulletin board above the payphones. Construction cutouts with positive messages had been made by the patients, and Hilda's was front and center. A giant sun with a smile that was nearly as wide as the crudely cut circle. "I was thinking of coming home for a visit for a few weeks."

There was a long silence, followed by a rumble of laughter, followed by a hacking cough. When she'd finally recovered, Lois said, "What made you finally decide to come back? Something going on with Julian? Is he dead?"

Iris rolled her eyes. "He's not dead, Ma."

"Trouble in paradise then?"

If anyone understood disappointment when it came to men, it was her mother. Admitting that Iris's marriage was on the rocks would just lead to a string of *told you so*s, though.

"He's got a big case. It's a good time for me to get away."

"It's not a good time for me," her mother replied. "I've just started seeing Wayne."

Of course. There was always a new relationship.

"Don't worry. I won't stay with you. I just need you to…pay for my ticket. I have the cash to reimburse you when I see you," she added quickly, hoping her tone seemed light and convincing. She needed her mother's help. It was a natural instinct. She had never asked for anything before. Never expected much, either. She wasn't sure why she thought today would be different.

"Pay for your ticket?" Lois's voice rose. "I knew something was wrong! You telling me you lost all your money?"

Lois was a sharp one. Iris's heart began to pound. She was close to having nothing. No husband. No money. No so-called friends.

"We're having a problem with our credit cards. A fraud thing..." She mentally calculated how much she'd thought to cram into her handbag. She'd emptied her travel bag. She had at least two thousand in cash and a couple hundred in traveler's checks. Enough to get there and back. "I have the cash. I'll give it to you as soon as I see you."

"Don't be getting any notions about flying first-class," her mother said, blowing out what could only be cigarette smoke. "When are you coming?"

Iris's pulse skipped a beat. The sooner the better. But she didn't want to spark suspicion. "Wednesday?"

"Okay." Lois didn't sound pleased, but at least she'd agreed to it.

"I'll call you back tomorrow morning with the details then," Iris said before her mother could back out of the deal.

"But you can't stay with me," Lois reminded her. "Who you gonna stay with?"

Iris thought fast. She didn't have enough money for a hotel, not if she wanted to purchase a return ticket to New York. There was only one other person in Westlake she knew. One other person who had recently reached out, who must still care.

Would love to see you next time you're in town.

Gwen had always been the answer to her troubles, always there to offer a hand or open a door or a seat at her dinner table.

If there was anyone in this world she could turn to right now, it was Gwen.

7

GWEN

AS A CHILD, Gwen had made herself sick to her stomach on the eve of parent-teacher conferences, incapable of focusing on the facts that she was a good student who never got in trouble. Somehow none of that mattered, and all she could do was twist herself into knots about what the teachers would say to her mother, and what her mother would, in turn, say to her. She'd sit in her room, brushing the hair of her dolls over and over, her mind going to dark places, imagining the slamming of the door when her mother returned, her name being shouted out to come downstairs (first and middle name—always a very, very bad sign), unable to even think about the prospect of a cool teenage babysitter downstairs. When she finally heard the usual sounds of car doors opening and closing, she'd brace herself, her hands balled into fists that left nail marks embedded in her palms, her breath stuck in her lungs.

Once she was a teenager, she and Iris would study together every night and every weekend—Gwen was motivated by sheer terror, and Iris knew that her only chance at college was an academic scholarship. Still, she never could focus on the fact that she tried her best.

Trying your best wasn't enough for Eileen. You had to *be* the best.

Now, at the age of thirty-nine, she sat in the car of the very school she had attended, her heart feeling like it was going to pound right out of her chest, her breath tight and her hands shaky.

Wasn't this supposed to stop by now? Wasn't the fear of being in trouble with authority supposed to end at some point in adulthood, other than, say, fear of arrest or a tax audit?

She rang the bell outside the building, waving up at the security camera that she knew Betty, the school receptionist, monitored closely, feigning a cheerful smile and a wave as if her stomach wasn't in knots.

The door buzzed and she pushed it open with dread.

"Volunteering today?" Betty asked.

If only. Gwen tried a breezy smile, but she had the sense it came off a little manic. "Room three fourteen, actually."

A knowing look transformed Betty's face. She nodded. "The guidance counselor."

Really, could she have said it any louder? Eager to get things over with, Gwen pushed out of the administration office and smack into the chest of...

"Joe Cassidy?" High school football captain. Garage band leader. Object of her teenage fantasy.

"Gwen Warner." It was Gwen Riley now, but she didn't bother to correct him. He leaned down and hugged her, and oh, if her knees didn't go a little soft. How many times had she dreamt of this moment, lying on her frilly lavender bed, imagining how it might feel to have Joe Cassidy touch her? And now he had, as if they'd always greeted each other this way.

What would fourteen-year-old Gwen have said if she knew that, yes, dreams did come true and that one day Joe Cassidy would, in fact, hug her?

She'd have to think that fourteen-year-old Gwen would be pretty damn thrilled. She would be equally horrified to know that she would be thirty-nine, a mom of three, and married to another man when it finally happened.

"What…what are you doing here?" *Please don't say you're here for one of your kids*, she thought. Last she knew, Joe was single, after a short-lived marriage in his late twenties that prompted him to move a few towns over for a fresh start. (Gwen's mother had always been eager to keep her up to date on Wisconsin gossip when Gwen was still living in Chicago, and when it came to updates on Joe Cassidy, Gwen had been all too happy to listen.)

"I'm the music director," he said, holding her gaze so intensely that she almost felt the need to look away. Joe Cassidy, with his hundred-watt smile and deep-set brown eyes was talking to her. Back in high school, the closest she got to a conversation with him was the time they'd been paired up over the Bunsen burner in science class, and then she'd been forced to wear those embarrassing goggles, which shadowed the entire experience and, she liked to think, her only chance.

Deep down, though, she knew she never stood a chance with Joe. He was too athletic, too popular, too friendly to everyone. And when she and Iris walked down the hall, it was clear that his eyes were only for Iris. Still, Gwen had relished that connection, even if it was only a reflection of being Iris's best friend.

"How didn't I know that you worked here?" she asked, because really, how did that one slip through the gossip mill that seemed to percolate at every school event or lunch with her mother?

"I just transferred over this fall. From Colter Day."

"Ohhh." Gwen nodded knowingly. Colter Day was the private day school about twenty minutes north. Gwen's next-door neighbor growing up, a tedious girl named Katie, had gone to Colter for the last two years of high school, recruited for her athletic abilities, not that her 4.0 GPA hurt matters, and Eileen had never let Gwen forget it, even though Gwen had been relieved. No Katie meant no more comparisons. "What grade did Katie get?" Eileen would always ask when Gwen handed over her recent math test. It didn't matter if it was an A or an A minus; if Katie got an A plus, Eileen would fall silent, her mouth pinched in naked disappointment. Looking back, Gwen wondered if she and Katie might have been friends if she hadn't learned to view her as the enemy. But then she would think about the pushy way Katie would march through the halls, the aggressive way she would get the ball to the goal in field hockey, showing no mercy to anyone's shins and happy to cheat when the ref wasn't looking, and, of course, the way her parents always wrote her student council speeches for her, guaranteeing a win.

Iris, on the other hand, was no threat to Eileen. Sure, she was thinner and prettier than Gwen, but she was also polite and hardworking and gave Gwen's mother a chance to try to "help the poor child," a saying that could be heard nearly every time Iris left their house to return to her own.

"Can you believe it's been almost twenty-one years since we left this place?" Joe said.

Twenty-one *years*. The thought was downright horrifying. Once, she couldn't wait to turn twenty-one, to be legally allowed to drink, to be an adult. To be free. Now, twenty-one years had passed in the blink of an eye. And what did she have to show for it? Oh, yeah, she had three kids, one who might get suspended in about ten minutes, and an unemployed husband who was more like a roommate, and she was still afraid of parent-teacher meetings, even though she was the parent.

Oops. Gwen looked up the clock over the door to the gymnasium, feeling her anxiety rise.

"Well, I don't want to be late for my meeting. Teenagers." She rolled her eyes, and Joe gave a polite laugh in return. She gave a smile she no longer felt, and the flutter in her stomach came back in full force.

"You'll be fine," Joe said, giving her a wink that made all her worries disappear for one glorious, magical moment.

Joe Cassidy, she thought as she strode through the familiar halls. She swallowed back what now felt like excitement as she approached room 314 and raised a hand to knock on the door. But there, taped to the door was a note saying that Ms. Manning had left for the day due to a migraine.

If only Gwen had thought of that excuse sooner, she might have saved herself this entire trip and all its anxiety, but then, she wouldn't have seen Joe...

Gwen looked down at her phone and pulled up her email. Sure enough, a note from Paula Manning, asking to reschedule for later in the week.

Gwen let out a breath she hadn't even known she'd been holding and sank her head back against the door. She closed her eyes for just one moment, daring to imagine that twenty-one years hadn't passed and that she was still the same girl that she always had been, and that life felt full of possibility, and that Joe Cassidy had just hugged her.

Gwen daydreamed as she folded laundry, for once not even remembering what had happened on her favorite soap opera that played in the background—Iris had turned her onto it when they were just kids, and she'd never given it up. She smiled as she walked the dog around the block, not even tensing up when she strolled past Susan's house. After all, had Joe Cassidy just hugged Susan? She thought not.

She gazed serenely out the living room window as the school bus deposited the children, and only lost her footing when she noticed that Susan had already replaced her Christmas decorations with an elegant Valentine's wreath on the front door. Back when they'd first moved into this house, Gwen had taken such pride in the furnishing and the gardening, always keeping her planters updated and blooming. Then Bea had come along. And then Gwen's father died. And then, well, life, as they say.

Life, however, didn't seem to stand in Susan's way, and she changed her planters like clockwork with the turn of every season. Gwen could have sworn she'd put up her fall décor in the dead of night, on August 31 to boot, beating everyone else to the punch.

"We have to out-cute them," Bea said, narrowing her eyes as she followed Gwen's stare, and she quickly got to work with a stack of pink construction paper.

Still, Gwen smiled all the way to the library to drop off Norah for her tutor, then Declan at piano, and last, Bea at ballet. She practically floated down the aisles at the grocery store, even stopping by the lobster tank to consider an alternate universe where she, too, whipped up gourmet meals on random weeknights and presented it to her happy family.

By the time she got to the studio an hour later to pick up Bea, the only thing she could think of was how she might run into Joe again when she went back for the actual conference in room 314, what she should wear, and how she might drop fifteen pounds by then.

"Mom?" Bea was frowning at her as she climbed into the backseat, as if Gwen had done something truly crazy like dye her hair pink or get a tattoo on her arm, or something else unexpected of a suburban mom of three.

Something like fantasizing about a man who wasn't her husband.

Gwen started. "Oh, hi, honey. How was ballet class today?"

"Boring," Bea replied as she fastened her seat belt.

Gwen looked at her sharply. This wasn't like Bea. She loved ballet! It was the only reason that Gwen had registered her for the second session, even though she'd strongly encouraged (sometimes through the offer of a piece of candy or a trip to the toy store with a crisp ten-dollar bill) Bea to take a break from it. It wasn't that she was opposed to ballet. Heck, back when Norah had been born, she'd held her in her arms in the hospital and actually visualized her a few years down the road, dressed in pink tights and leotard, a little hand holding hers as they walked to class... She'd had those days; the thrill had been fleeting and Michael had been quick to voice her shared sentiments that ballet was a little boring. When Bea came along, Gwen hoped her youngest might take an interest in something new and fresh, like gymnastics. So much for that.

"What was so boring about it?" she decided to ask.

"All the other kids got to dance. And I had to sit and watch!"

Gwen blinked at her child. Bea had been subjected to this once before—when the traffic was bad and Bea was subsequently six minutes late to Tiny Toes. Extreme, yes, but it was in the rules, the ones she had signed off on at Miss Bambi's Dance Studio. Where, contrary to what one might assume, strict ballet instruction, rather than pole dancing, was the attraction.

"You weren't late!" Gwen was sure of it. She had checked the clock when they'd pulled away from the library, pleased that they were early for a change, that she was the mom she always set out to be—organized, calm, and utterly content. She hadn't even flinched when they hit that red light on Thornton. Hadn't even cut through the gas station on the corner of McLane and Foster to shave off forty seconds. Yet Bea had spent the last hour sitting in a corner watching other girls dance, while Gwen had been grocery shopping, none the wiser.

"Did you act up?" As soon as she saw the hurt in Bea's eyes, she regretted asking the question. Bea never acted up. She was as sweet as Norah was stubborn. "I'm sorry, honey. I'm just angry, that's all."

And of course, now Bea had started to cry.

Gwen sighed and checked the time on her phone. Caroline had offered to bring Declan home from the piano studio. The boys were no longer at the same level, but both still took lessons on Tuesdays. (And Victor was probably there five other days, too.) She had eleven minutes to get to the library to pick up Norah. But she was fourteen. If she had to wait, she could wait.

Gwen swerved into the nearest parking spot and exited the van. Grabbing Bea's hand, she turned and walked back into the dance studio and straight to the office. She'd hoped to talk to a receptionist, or maybe Miss Jill, Bea's friendly tap teacher instead, but as luck would have it, Miss Bambi herself was bent over the desk, adjusting her leg warmers.

Gwen eyed her calves greedily. Miss Bambi had to be sixty-five and then some. And Gwen was jealous of a senior citizen's toned body.

"Miss Bambi?"

Oh, God. There was that dark, penetrating gaze. The no-nonsense set of her jaw.

Gwen struggled to swallow. If this were about her, she would make up an excuse and flee. A lost ballet slipper, a question about the spring recital. Time to fetch Norah! But this wasn't about her. This was about Bea. Sweet, good, precious little Bea. The only one of her children who happily bounded up the stairs when Gwen asked the kids to clean their rooms.

"Bea mentioned that she had to sit out today's class?"

Miss Bambi's expression never changed. "She wasn't properly attired."

Gwen glanced at her pink-clad child. Shoes, leotard, tights, all accounted for. "Excuse me?"

"Her bun was not up to studio standards," Miss Bambi clipped.

Gwen was now staring at the back of Bea's head, where the bun she'd administered in the downstairs bathroom a mere hour and twenty minutes ago was still intact, more or less.

"She has loose hairs. Perhaps you didn't read our instruction manual on how to do a bun?"

No, Gwen hadn't read the manual. She'd tossed it in the trash, instead. She knew how to make buns. She's been making them for over a decade.

"I'm sorry, but I don't see what the problem is," she said, feeling the heat rise in her face.

"Our studio guidelines strictly state that hair must be worn in a bun."

"And her hair is in a bun."

"Her hair is a mess," Miss Bambi said.

By now, Gwen was aware of the hush that had fallen over the lobby, and the audience behind her. She counted to three and sweetly asked Bea to take a picture book from the shelf on the wall and have a seat near the window.

"I don't want to," Bea pouted.

Gwen gave her daughter a look—*that look*—the look she'd never thought she'd use back when she was pregnant with Norah. The look that said she was the boss, and so help her, they had better know it. "Please, Bea."

"No."

She looked right, then left. Several mothers skirted their eyes. Some, like Miss Bambi, brazenly stared.

Gwen wrestled with herself. Finally, she cupped her hand over her mouth and whispered directly into Bea's ear, "Go sit near the window and I will buy you a Happy Meal on the way home. And don't tell anyone I just said that or I won't buy it."

Bea nodded happily, biting her lip to hide her bursting smile, and skipped off to grab a book.

Gwen sighed. One crisis handled. Now, for the next.

She set her hands on the desk and tipped her head. Miss Bambi dealt with children. She probably had a few of her own once. Surely she could understand.

"I know how to make a bun. I am an expert at making a bun. But when I'm dropping my three kids off at three different activities in under fifteen minutes across town, I just don't have time to put the same effort into Bea's bun for a class as I would for a recital."

"Then Beatrice will have to sit out the class."

Gwen's heart was pounding. "Then I'd like my money back."

Now Bea's voice cut across the room, shrill and loud. "No, Mommy! I love ballet!"

Gwen looked at Miss Bambi. Miss Bambi looked at Gwen.

"There are other dance studios, Bea," Gwen said tightly, but now Bea's face was creased in concern. "*Better* dance studios."

Off the top of her head, she couldn't think of any, and certainly none as convenient as this, but there must be other places, of course there were.

"But I like it here!"

And there it was, the part of motherhood they didn't warn you about. When they said you had to pick your battles, they didn't mean a simple squabble over eating carrots or getting to bed on time. No, they meant this, the real shit: other parents, teachers, the adults that you were forced to deal with to advocate for your child.

"I would like a make-up class for today's situation," Gwen said hoping to come out of this with a shred of dignity. She didn't know what she would say if Miss Bambi refused.

"Will her hair be properly arranged?" Miss Bambi arched a single eyebrow.

Gwen pinched her mouth, feeling exhausted at the mere thought of the pins and hairnet. "Yes."

"She can come to Saturday's class this week, then, as a make-up for today."

Gwen turned, grabbed a smiling Bea's hand, and marched out the door, her chin high, her shoulders back, unsure if she should feel triumphant or mortified. She was exhausted by motherhood, by conflict, by the sinking knowledge that no one had ever fought for her the way she fought for her kids and that it was half the reason she did it.

All fantasies of Joe Cassidy and a different life vanished. Back to reality. Back to the old minivan that had been in four fender benders and still had a dented front bumper. Back to the house where dinner would need to be made and the kitchen would need to be cleaned and then homework would need to be supervised. But first to the library, to pick up Norah.

"Do I still get my Happy Meal?" Bea asked as she climbed back into the car and buckled up.

Gwen rested her head against the seat back for a moment. Her phone pinged. No doubt a message from Norah or—

Iris?

Gwen hadn't an expected a response from her holiday card. She hadn't even known that Iris still had her phone number. That Iris would care to even be in touch.

But she did care. Enough to say hello. Enough to tell Gwen that she was coming to Westlake. Tomorrow. She was hoping to visit. Stop by for dinner… Tomorrow.

This could *not* be happening.

Memories of her holiday letter came rushing back to her. Their picture-perfect life. Her idealistic vision of domestic bliss. The house. It was a mess. And her life. It was a mess too!

She was shaking as she started to tap out a response and then deleted it quickly. What could she say? Iris had never come back to town, not once in all these years. Even if Gwen claimed she had a meeting with the school, or she was sick with the flu, it wouldn't hold up.

It wouldn't be nice.

"Mommy, if you can't do a bun, I can ask Norah to do it," Bea said sweetly from the backseat.

Jesus, she had been staring so firmly at the screen of her phone that she'd almost forgotten her surroundings.

"I know how to do a bun!" she snapped. And she did. She could make a killer bun, thanks to one of those foam donuts, a hairnet, and about fifty-six French pins, she could make the best damn bun that skinny bitch had ever seen enter her studio. It wasn't about not being able to make a bun. It was about not having the *time* to make a bun. "Sorry, honey. I didn't mean to snap. That Miss Bambi…" She didn't finish that thought.

122

Couldn't finish it. She couldn't think about anything other than Iris.

Iris was coming to town. Tomorrow. She wanted to have dinner. See the house. Meet the rest of the family. It would be fun. *Like old times.*

Another text came in, this one from Norah, wanting to know if Gwen was coming to pick her up, it was getting late, and the library was closing soon. Damn it. She started the car, lurched out of the parking lot, and took a right down the street.

"We're going the wrong way," Bea pointed out.

Were they? Crap. They were. She did a U-turn, even though she wasn't sure it was legal. She was living on the edge, and she didn't like it. It wasn't her! Gwen Riley was a stand-up citizen. She was a happily married mother of three who lived in a beautiful house with hospital corners on the beds that were always made and ate all organic food and crawled into bed with the husband who brought her nothing but sheer joy every day. Gwen Riley wore cute clothes and had a good figure for her age and her kids made the honor roll.

But Gwen Riley was none of those things.

"There's the McDonald's!" Bea cried out from the back of the car as if to remind her.

She swerved into the drive-thru lane, leaned toward the speaker, and rattled off her order on autopilot: "Six-piece nuggets, apple slices, chocolate milk. No sauce. Girl's toy." Shame filled her, and her only saving grace was the merciful anonymity of tinted windows and the lack of a recognizable vanity plate. No one had to know. No one could know. Technically, she was living the life she had always wanted. Only it was nothing like it was supposed to be.

And Iris didn't have a clue.

"Look, Mommy! You and Ronald McDonald are twins now!" Bea called happily from the backseat.

Gwen scowled as she handed the money over to the cashier and pulled up to the next window. A giant sign hung from the building, and she stared at it, seeing no resemblance.

"You both have orange hair!" Bea giggled as Gwen collected the meal and rolled up the window quickly. She glanced in the rearview mirror, gasping when she realized that by God, the child was right.

It was supposed to be acorn. A beautiful shiny, warm brown. Her hands shook as they fumbled with the Happy Meal box.

"Fine, let's have Norah do the bun next time," she said as she swung around to hand Bea her loot, and Bea's eyes lit up at the implied conspiracy.

After all, Gwen didn't have time for this crap. She had a chipped tooth to fix. Orange hair to color. A house to gut of stains and mess. An Oscar-worthy performance to master.

8

IRIS

THE FIRST THING Iris did when she arrived at LaGuardia was to hit the bar, but she didn't go for a chardonnay. No, this trip called for something stronger. She checked her funds; the bus and cab fare from the rehab center to the airport had been steep, but it was worth not having to explain to Lois why she would have preferred a flight out of Buffalo Niagara.

"What will it be, miss?" The man behind the bar asked, and for a moment, Iris got swept away. She was nearly forty, she'd just emerged from rehab, and she had a bad feeling she would live to regret giving Hilda her cell phone number. Her mind was just too crowded to think of a fake number at the time, and, after she'd jotted down the digits, Hilda had studied the paper for a long, quiet moment before asking darkly, "You didn't give me a fake number, did you?"

Yesterday, Iris had seen the way Hilda had taken that plastic bat to the blow-up doll that was supposed to be anyone or anything they wanted it to be, so long as they could release their anger. She didn't want to be that blow-up doll.

Now, like this morning, when she was trying to think of a fake number and had failed, she couldn't focus. She felt twitchy, nervous, being this close to Manhattan. It was so tempting to go back to the apartment, unpack her things, and reclaim her life.

But space would be good, she decided. It would give her a chance to think about her next step, because she always had a plan. Ever since she was young enough to know that some kids had it easier than her, she was plotting how to achieve it too.

"Surprise me," she said, giving the bartender a slow smile. She was rewarded with a cock of an eyebrow and, a few moments later, something large and pink.

Freedom had never tasted so sweet. Besides, she was going to need a buzz if she was going back to Westlake today. Talking with her mother always stirred up conflicting emotions. Seeing her would heighten them. There were common interests: soap operas being the main one. Iris could still remember sprinting from the bus stop during November sweeps so she wouldn't miss a minute of the rapidly moving plot. By first grade, she knew every character's name and history. Occasionally, Lois would look up from the ironing she took in to keep food on the table when she wasn't on the phone, head tilted to the side, device wedged in the crook of her neck, claiming to be able to predict people's futures and reconnect them with lost love ones, while she gave herself sloppy home pedicures and chain smoked.

"Close your eyes, Iris," she'd instruct when two characters wound up in bed, and Iris would do as she was told, pulling the crocheted afghan her grandmother had made up over her eyes, wondering if Lois knew she could still see through the gaps in the yarn.

She still watched those soaps now and then, the same actresses whose fashion senses had inspired her so much in her teenage years, allowing her to find her own style, eventually playing up her looks until she was no longer the girl that everyone pitied or whispered about but instead a girl they envied from a distance. It was a constant in her life, the characters, their backstories, their daily presence. There was little else so reliable.

By the time boarding was called for the flight, she'd consumed two of the pink drinks and felt considerably better than she had this morning. She pulled her compact from her bag and checked her reflection, relieved to see that rather than looking pale and sickly, a few days in rehab had almost given her skin a healthy glow—still, she'd feel better once she could properly blow out her hair, giving it the luster she was used to. For now, a ponytail would have to do.

She sloughed on her winter coat, her favorite one with the fur collar, and slid her leather gloves over her fingers after she had counted out the exact amount for the drinks, plus a twenty-percent tip.

Looking at the gap that already left in her wallet, she felt a swell of panic rise in her throat. Three and a half weeks in Westlake. Nowhere to stay. Not enough for a hotel, not if she was going to get a ticket back to New York.

She couldn't be buying twelve-dollar drinks. She'd have to be resourceful.

She watched as the couple next to her muttered something and left, abandoning half a glass of wine each, one white, one red, fighting the urge to pick them up and drain them back. Her gaze drifted to the bartender, who was now giving her a funny look and deservedly so. Finishing off other people's booze was something her mother would do, not her. Certainly not Iris Drake.

She felt like she was floating as she moved toward the gate and joined the line of travelers, mostly dressed for business. For a split second, she had a moment of panic when she thought she saw Stephanie standing three gates down. She always wore a red coat. It was flashy. Like her lace thong. But no, what would Stephanie be doing at the airport in the middle of the week?

She kept walking, her breathing becoming labored as she studied the woman closer. The drinks had gone right to her head, and she couldn't make out the woman's facial features, not clearly, at least. Her eyes darted to her gate. The line was moving slowly.

She had time, and so she stopped behind a tree, the waxy kind, with the moss at the base of the trunk. She wasn't even sure the thing was real. Wasn't even sure why she cared. All she cared about was this woman. The woman who might be Stephanie. And what she was doing here.

She was looking around, she was waiting for someone.

Iris felt her mouth go dry. Could *Julian* be here? Was this what it was all about? Had he sent her off to rehab so he could have a little fun without any interruption?

She pulled her cell phone out of her leather tote. There were two missed calls in total since the device had been confiscated: one from her trainer at the gym, wondering why she had missed her standing appointment, and the other from her manicurist, confirming Friday's appointment. Nothing from Julian. Or Stephanie.

A family with two kids and a giant stroller was blocking her view now, and she shifted deeper behind the tree, trying to get a good look at the woman.

Blond hair—not natural, obviously. Shoulder length. Stick skinny. Fake boobs. God, her heart was pounding.

"Final boarding call for flight two sixteen to Milwaukee," an announcement called out.

Final boarding. There wouldn't be another chance. Who was she waiting for? Where was Julian?

"Final boarding for flight two sixteen to Milwaukee."

Damn it! They were forcing her hand, making her choose, to defend herself against this blatant injustice or to protect herself, shield herself, to take the time she had been given. Twenty-eight days, minus the three she'd already served.

She tapped her face to see if she was wearing her sunglasses. The lights were so bright in the terminal she couldn't even be sure. But yes, good, they were on. They'd been on the entire time she'd been in the bar, she now realized, not sure what that said about her state of mind.

She glanced behind her, catching the eye of a security guard, whose eyes narrowed in suspicion.

"This is the final boarding call for flight—"

Right. Final boarding call. Time to move.

She kept her eye trained on the woman as she moved to the counter, and she was rewarded just in time to see the woman turn, as if she had felt Iris's stare, and look right at her.

It wasn't Stephanie at all. Stephanie was prettier; she hated to admit it, but even this realization couldn't bring her down.

It wasn't Stephanie. Of course it wasn't. And now a man was approaching. And a child! A little boy who took the woman's hand.

It wasn't Stephanie. It wasn't Julian.

She was losing it, unraveling, and she never unraveled. For as long as she could remember, she'd fought for what she wanted and never backed down, never let anyone hold her back or push her around. Never let anyone see the weakness because that's when they slipped in, through the cracks...

She checked herself, took a deep breath, and squared her shoulders. Adjusted her six-thousand-dollar handbag on her shoulder and handed over her ticket to the woman at the gate.

Her stride was confident and purposeful as she walked into the tunnel, and the door closed behind her along with the entire life she'd fought so hard to have.

In three hours she'd be back in Westlake, Wisconsin. Back to the life she'd run from, never looking back.

She could only pray they served wine on the flight.

She must have fallen asleep somewhere over Pennsylvania because she was awoken by a ringing of a bell and a flight attendant asking her to put her seat in the upright position. Iris blinked and looked around her, at the graying woman to her left who was still reading her paperback romance novel, at the businessman to her right who had tucked away his laptop for landing.

Iris patted her face, relieved to know her sunglasses were still there, but they did little to hide the tears that had started to fall. It wasn't a dream or even a nightmare. They were circling the Milwaukee airport. Every reminder of the life she had discarded was right there, out that window.

"Is everything okay, dear?" the woman beside her asked, looking worried.

Iris hadn't even realized that she had sniffed. Was she actually crying? Iris did a lot of things, but Iris didn't cry. She fought. Maybe it was the drinks, or maybe it was the thought of her mother somewhere, down below, probably pulling up to the terminal now, but she was suddenly exhausted. "I'm sorry. It's just that my husband is having an affair."

It was the second person she'd told, again someone she'd never have to see again, and oh, the release was good. To admit it. To hear the words on her tongue. To let her guard slip for just one second. To take off the mask.

"Is that so?" The woman's eyes were round as saucers, and she firmly tucked her bookmark into the spine of her novel, giving Iris her full attention.

"Yes." Iris's voice broke, and the woman reached down in the bag tucked under the seat in front of her and pulled out a packet of tissues.

"Are you here to catch him in the act, or did you leave him?" the woman wanted to know.

Iris held the tissue in her hand, thinking hard about that question. The truth was that she wasn't sure what she was doing here. She just knew that right now, she had no other choice.

"Well, I'm sure a pretty girl like you will have no trouble finding another man," the woman said reassuringly.

Iris gave her a watery smile. She didn't want another man. She'd made a point of never depending on any man. Not her father, whoever he was, not her brother, who floated in and out of the house like a guest, and not a boyfriend. Julian had been her weakness.

"Do you have kids?" The woman pulled a pack of gum from her bag and offered Iris a stick.

Iris accepted it, thinking it wise considering the libations she'd enjoyed, and shook her head. "No kids."

She'd never wanted kids. Never yearned for the whole picket-fence lifestyle. No, what she'd wanted was security. Success. She wanted all those people who thought they were better than her, or pitied her, to realize that they'd been wrong.

Besides, she would have made a terrible mother. Whereas Gwen...

Gwen had three kids. The thought was a dead weight in her chest. Gwen had a husband and three children and a dog. She had a family home. She had memories and photo albums and homemade ornaments on her Christmas tree.

And Iris...Iris had nothing.

She took out her phone and pulled up Gwen's Facebook page, something she only occasionally did over the years, and each time she was struck with a strange mix of wonder and disappointment. Now there were Christmas photos, of course. A dog wearing a sweater in a cozy-looking family kitchen. Another one, taken earlier, of her son standing beside a grand piano, dressed in a plaid shirt and navy pants. Another of a little girl, building a snowman. And another of a tree in a bay window, with all the trimmings.

In other words: idyllic. Gwen didn't have a care in the world. Her life was full.

Feeling more depressed than ever, Iris checked her watch, knowing Lois would raise hell if she was stuck circling the passenger pickup lane for too long, but even though she'd been trapped at the back of the plane, waiting for people to grab their overhead luggage at a glacial pace, Iris was a few minutes ahead of schedule.

Well, then, something to look forward to after all. She'd stop for happy hour in the terminal before heading back to her hometown.

Suddenly the entire day felt much more palatable.

Lois didn't get out of the car when Iris emerged from baggage claim, wheeling a trolley of luggage and clutching the largest bouquet of flowers she could find for sale. Lois rolled down the window and called out, "Trunk's unlocked" instead, like she had just seen Iris yesterday, not twenty years ago. Knowing she shouldn't have expected more, Iris loaded her luggage into the trunk, having to push aside the grocery bags that clanked so much it was clear they contained more booze than food.

Iris glanced up, meeting Lois's eye, and then reached deep inside the trunk under the pretense of rearranging her luggage so she could slip a bottle of whiskey into her leather carry-on.

Breathing easier, she closed the trunk and walked around the car to the passenger door. Here went nothing.

"Hey, Ma!" She gave a smile she didn't quite feel as she slid onto the cloth seat. The smell of cigarettes was so overwhelming that she started to cough.

"Well, roll down a window!" Lois huffed, and Iris did as she was told, pressing the button until the window was lowered halfway and the cold winter air filled the car. "I need the fresh air to get the stink of that perfume you're wearing out of my upholstery."

"It's probably the flowers," Iris replied.

"Those for me?" Lois looked at them eagerly.

Instantly, Iris saw her error. "These are for Gwen. For having me over tonight. I have something else for you in my luggage." It wasn't true, but Lois would be happy with one of the handbags that Iris had brought with her.

Lois shifted in her seat. "Let me have a look at you before airport security tells me to get moving." She dragged on her cigarette as her eyes roamed over Iris. Lois had colored her hair since the last time Iris had seen her, but then, that was a long, long time ago. It was blonder now. Dry at the ends. She was wearing a low-cut tank top, even though it was mid-January, and jeans that were designed for a teenager. Yep. All signs that a new man was in her life. For now. "My, look at you." She tutted. "You certainly got the life you wanted, didn't you?"

Iris said nothing. There was nothing to say. She swallowed hard and fibbed, "You look good, Ma. You been taking care of yourself?"

"If you mean have I been cashing those checks you send me every month, yes. Bought myself these jeans for Christmas."

Iris opened her mouth and then closed it again. Not much had changed, even after more than twenty years. She wasn't sure if this was unsettling or reassuring.

"How long are you in town for?" Lois's voice was more of a growl, revealing years of chain-smoking.

"About three and a half weeks."

"Three and a half weeks!" Lois piped. "You sure Gwen will let you stay that long?"

Iris wasn't so sure in the least. Her stomach felt funny as she looked out the window. "I can always check into a hotel." She couldn't afford that length of stay, not if she wanted a return flight home, but she'd deal with that later.

"Well, I wish you'd let me know in advance. We could have spent more time together, planned something."

Iris knew her mother didn't mean that, even if her intentions were in the right place. Lois couldn't plan for anything. She couldn't even remember to pay the bills on time.

"Wayne's awfully stressed at work these days," Lois continued. "And he's not the most social creature. When he gets home from work, he just wants a cold beer, a hot meal, and, well…" She gave a satisfied grin.

"So where'd you meet this one?" Iris sighed, even though she wasn't exactly sure she wanted to know.

"He was a regular," Lois said with a wistful smile. "Called every night at eight sharp."

"To have his cards read?" Iris was aghast. She never understood who would call even once to have their so-called tarot cards read, let alone frequently. Had Lois's "predictions" actually materialized?

Lois's eyes darted to hers as they approached a red light. "The cards weren't working out. I, uh, starting working for another company."

Iris stared at her mother, not daring to believe that what she was insinuating could be true. "You mean you take…*sex* calls?"

"It's not like that!" Lois tapped her ashes out the window. "These are *lonely* men, Iris. They're just looking for a little company. And I need the money."

"And you met one of them in person?" Iris was aware that she was yelling now, and she knew that she should stop, because the roads were slick and it was hard enough for Lois to focus on driving with one hand holding a cigarette (ironically, the same brand that Delilah smoked).

"Well, we got to know each other quite well." Lois chuckled, and Iris seethed, but then why should she be surprised. It had always been this way. Lois didn't think about the future or consequences or actions. If it hadn't been for the house they'd inherited from her grandmother, Iris wasn't sure where they would have ended up. Sometimes she thought Lois would have just put her up for adoption.

Sometimes, when she was younger, Iris would even dream of that happening.

"And how long have you been dating now?" Iris didn't exactly care. Wayne was just another cloud passing through Lois's sky.

"A few weeks," Lois said. "He got me this bracelet for Christmas, see?" She shook her wrist, and the charm bracelet jangled. It wasn't Tiffany, but Lois seemed to like it all the same.

"That's pretty, Ma." Iris felt a heavy weight of sadness. For a moment, she feared she would cry.

Her sunglasses were still on, even though it was already growing dusk. Coming up on late afternoon now. Coming up on dinnertime. She could picture Gwen in her big country kitchen, probably rolling out a pie crust while her children helped to set the table. She could still remember how out of place she'd felt all those times she'd sat at the Warners' big formal dining room table, watching Gwen carefully, only taking a bite when Gwen took a bite, stopping when Gwen stopped. As much as she loved being in the big, clean house with the formal living room with a velvet sofa that no one was allowed to sit on, it was also a reminder of how different her life was. How worse her life was.

Tonight would be no different. She was Iris Winarski again. Odd girl out.

"I have time before I told Gwen I'd be there," she offered to her mother, suddenly getting cold feet about walking into domestic bliss, sitting at a family table, bearing witness to her oldest friend's bone-deep happiness.

"Wayne's home sick today," Lois said firmly. Then, after a beat, she said, "Maybe we could get together tomorrow. Stop by while he's at work? He usually has to travel to Madison a few nights a week, too."

Iris forced a smile. "Sure, Ma."

"If I'd known you were coming…"

Iris held up a hand. There was no sense in being disappointed. She looked out the window as they approached her old school, where the kids used to taunt her, call her homeless, or worse, and then past the town library, where she and Gwen would study for hours, hoping for good grades, hoping for a better future.

She looked over at her mother, who still drove with one wrist hanging limply over the wheel, the other holding tight to that cigarette.

Nothing had changed. But she had.

She adjusted her fur collar and tucked her sunglasses into their case. "It's fine, Ma, just drop me off at Gwen's." She gave her the address that Gwen had texted to her, along with a short but friendly note about being excited to see her after all this time.

All this time. It had been over fourteen years since she'd visited Gwen in Chicago. Nearly seven since they'd lost touch outside of social media.

"Nice neighborhood" was all Lois had to say about that, and they sat in silence for the rest of the drive, Iris nursing the onset of a headache, Lois turning up the radio—a country station that she'd always listened to, but somehow Iris had forgotten about that over time.

More like chosen to forget.

Finally, Lois pulled into a driveway of a large gray Colonial and tossed her cigarette out the window before rolling it up again.

"Thanks for the ride, Ma," Iris said, but her voice felt locked in her chest and her heart was thumping and all she could think was that the last time she'd seen Gwen they couldn't connect, and what if they still couldn't? Where would she go?

"Iris?" Lois set a hand on her wrist as Iris reached for the doorknob, and for one wonderful, hope-filled moment Iris thought that maybe she'd had a change of heart, that maybe she would ask her to stay in her old room, cramped as it might be, and that she could bide her time for the next three weeks, watching daytime television and getting her life figured out before her return to New York.

But then she thought of Gwen's home, as lovely as her childhood home, and how much better she'd always felt there, how much more hopeful.

"The money? For the ticket?"

Yep, nothing had changed at all. She tried to remember how much the airline ticket had cost and failed. And then she realized, she'd never asked, she didn't know. Julian usually took care of all that. Or his assistant did.

"Make it an even six," Lois said in that gravelly voice of hers.

Six hundred for a one-way ticket to Milwaukee. Iris didn't know if that was a fair price or a cheap trick, but she wasn't going to bother with semantics. She peeled off six one-hundred-dollar bills and handed them to her mother, who counted them out before sliding them into her pocket. She'd have to be careful with what remained. Even the old motel off the interstate would eat up her current cash.

She saw no other choice. She and Gwen were friends once. Best of friends. And then, they were not. Gwen had her perfect husband, perfect house, and perfect cherub-cheeked children. And Iris could only think of what she was missing. Or maybe, what she had given up.

And she'd given up Gwen, hadn't she?

Gwen was somewhere inside that large, family home, probably filling the dog dish or overseeing homework, or taking down notes for an upcoming PTA meeting.

Gwen had a full life. And all Iris could hope for was that there was room for one more. For a little while at least.

9

GWEN

GWEN LOOKED OUT the window of her bedroom where she'd been standing for the last fifteen minutes behind the shelter of a linen drape and felt her stomach flutter.

She watched as Lois Winarski pulled out of the drive and peeled off down the street in the same navy Dodge she'd had since they were kids, leaving Iris to deal with a duffel bag, a handbag that was, frankly, enormous, the largest bouquet of flowers that Gwen had ever seen, and—wait.

Luggage?

There was surely an explanation, Gwen thought, blinking away the panic. Maybe Lois needed the trunk space for some errands. Or maybe Iris was going to ask Gwen to drop her off at a hotel in town after dinner. Yes, that was likely it. It wasn't like Lois's place offered the most comfortable accommodations. She could still remember the times she went to play there, and later, when they were older, to hang out. Lois stayed in the kitchen mostly, smoking and drinking some mysterious beverage out of her favorite mug: chocolate brown with a silhouette of the state of Minnesota on it, for reasons unknown to either Iris or Gwen. There were no invitations to stay for dinner or to drop them off at the mall, things that Gwen's mother did for them.

Gwen always felt a little sad leaving Iris at the end of the day, but Iris insisted she'd be fine—said she'd just watch television or raid her mother's change jar and bike down to the hot dog joint near the train tracks, get a burger and fries and not even tell her brother, because he never shared with her. There was no bedtime in the Winarski household. Lois didn't even nag her about showering at the end of a long, hot summer day. Iris did what she wanted to do. Even when she was just a little girl, not much older than Bea.

Thinking back on those days, Gwen felt a surge of affection for her friend—the person who knew her back before Michael or obviously the kids did. The person who knew her first kiss. The person who heard all her dreams. The person who shared all her secrets.

And who now knew none of them.

Did Iris feel the same sense of distance that she felt? The awful uncertainty that she didn't know this person anymore? Knowing Iris, probably not. And Iris probably didn't hold herself responsible for losing touch, either. Gwen had blamed Iris, felt stung and shunned over the years, but now she wondered about her part in things. Had she not tried hard enough? Had she not wanted to keep in touch?

Iris was approaching, hauling her luggage up the two steps to the awning of the front door and then—

Even though Gwen had been watching out the window, she still jumped when the doorbell rang.

She swept her eyes around the house as she ran down the stairs, Bailey at her heels, sensing the shift in her mood.

The house looked better than it had in months, thanks to her decision to clean rather than sleep last night. The floors shone. The light fixtures were dusted, throw pillows washed, and everything back in its place. And thanks to the apple pie she'd picked up at the local bakery and now had warming in the oven, it smelled heavenly, too.

Now looking around the front hall, where children's coats hung on hooks and one of Bea's art projects was framed, she felt a sting of doubt. She'd seen Iris's social media feed. She knew the parties and events and restaurants and clothes that had become part of Iris's daily routine.

And she was just a Midwestern housewife.

She checked her reflection in the hallway mirror. Her hair had been recolored with her old, usual shade, and she'd dressed up for the occasion, which was ridiculous because Iris was the only person other than Michael, her kids, and her parents who had ever seen her with an unwashed face, greasy hair, and old sweats and loved her anyway.

She clung to that. Iris had loved her. They'd loved each other. And Iris had come here. Asked to come here. Even if it was six years too late.

With a smile she didn't quite feel she opened the door, and there, in front of her, with a smile as if no time had passed, was Iris. Gwen didn't even have time to react or process her emotions. Iris and her perfectly highlighted hair and her perfume were engulfing her, squeezing her tight, the silky hair pressed against Gwen's cheek, the smell something sweet and floral and obviously expensive. Gwen made a mental note to find out the name before the night was over. She might hint around for Michael to buy it for her for Valentine's Day. Or maybe next Valentine's Day—when they were back on their feet.

"Gwennie!" Gwen had forgotten that nickname. How had she forgotten it? No one called her Gwennie. Only ever Iris, and she'd done it to make Iris feel better, because Gwen had never particularly loved her name, especially when all the other girls at school were called Jen or Melissa or Katie, and she hadn't been shy in telling that to Iris, who had been blessed with such a beautiful name by comparison. A unique name, really, and one that fit her in every possible way.

"Iris." The word came out on a breath, like the last bit of anger she was holding onto, and she sunk her face into the fur of Iris's coat collar, wondering idly if it was real. Fox? She didn't want to think about it.

Bailey barked in excitement and jumped up, setting two big paws on Iris's leather pants, making Gwen twitch with anxiety, but Iris just laughed it off, and Gwen breathed a little easier as she pulled the dog back by his collar. So Iris was still letting everything roll off her. The dog hair. And the strange gap in their friendship.

"I can't believe I'm here!" Iris blinked her big green eyes as she took in the hallway, and, feeling only slightly relieved that the attention was on the condition of her living arrangements and not on the fact that she was at least ten pounds heavier than she was the last time they'd seen each other (and that was after just having a baby), Gwen closed the door and ushered Iris toward the coat closet.

"I'll take this."

Iris shrugged out of her coat, and Gwen skirted a glance at the label as she slid it onto a hanger. Chanel. Jesus.

Iris lifted the flowers from the top of the luggage where she had set them. Gwen could feel her shoulders sink as she pulled them into her arms. "These are...beautiful!"

Why hadn't she thought to buy flowers to decorate the table, to cheer up the house? Maybe because she wasn't used to buying flowers for herself. Or receiving them, either.

"It's the least I could do," Iris said, and they exchanged a brief glance, falling silent.

"Well, thank you." Gwen shifted on her feet, feeling nervous and out of place in her own home.

"It's so quiet here," Iris said, still looking around the space. "Will it be just us tonight?"

Gwen resisted the urge to laugh out loud. She hadn't had a kid-free and husband-free night in... Well, never mind that.

Now that Bailey had calmed down, she realized with satisfaction that the house *was* quiet. And it had only cost her a hundred bucks to ensure that it was. Seventy to bribe Norah, twenty-five to bribe Declan, and five for Bea, who had only asked for two, and only because the others were raising such a stink, but her good behavior was rewarded with an extra three.

"For now. Come on into the kitchen. Dinner will be ready soon." She led Iris to the back of the house. The appliances shone like new thanks to a couple hours of elbow grease and several bottles of various cleaners. She found a dusty vase in the cabinet under the sink and quickly filled it with water, then set the flowers on the center of the kitchen table. "Can I get you a glass of wine?"

"Wine would be great. What do you have?"

Oh. Gwen wrapped her hand around the bottle of white wine she'd chilled just for this occasion, a splurge at twelve dollars when she usually opted for the three-ish-dollar kind from Trader Joe's.

"Pinot grigio okay?" she asked, reading the label.

To her relief, Iris grinned. "Excellent. I need it after the day I've had."

Did Iris really have bad days? How was that even possible?

"Traveling is exhausting." Not that Gwen would know. Right now, she'd trade a ten-hour flight by herself for just one day of running around with the kids.

"I was stuck in a middle seat at the back of the plane," Iris said, swallowing back at least half her glass in one gulp. She rolled her eyes as if it was the most horrible thing a person should be expected to endure.

Gwen gave a smile like she understood completely, even though she'd never flown first class, not even for her honeymoon. She'd just been excited to be taking her first adult vacation.

"Well, hopefully a hot meal will help you unwind." She eyed Iris's near-empty glass and picked up her own. Liquid courage. After all, dinner was her crowd pleaser, her staple, one of about eleven meals she rotated over and over because it didn't require much thought and she knew that it tasted half-decent.

"It smells delicious. What is it?" Iris reached for the wine bottle and opened her eyes wide in question.

A piece of Gwen's heart broke off, just a bit. It was the same look Iris used to give her when she'd invite her over for dinner, grateful for another seat to be filled at the table, for her mother's attention to be focused on someone other than her.

Iris's grin was hopeful, and even though her teeth were now perfectly straight and almost blindingly white, it was the very same smile that she used to give when they first saw each other, every morning before school, always meeting at the big oak tree at the corner of the block, so they could walk inside together.

Despite the distance and the years without exchanging so much as a text, there was a history there, Gwen thought. A common history that only they shared. And despite the flashy clothes and fancy lifestyle, a part of the old Iris was still there, underneath.

She hoped so at least.

"I made lasagna," Gwen said as she turned on the oven light. It was one of her best dishes, but now, thinking about Susan's comment on her coffee cake and skimming her eyes over Iris's size-two figure, she wished she'd made something like fish instead. Or lobster. "With four picky eaters, it's rare to find a meal that pleases everyone."

"Four?" Iris nearly broke the wineglass she slammed it so loud on the counter. As she went to refill her glass again, it occurred to Gwen that she should probably chill another bottle. The night was young, and her nerves were still thick. Perhaps Iris's were too, given how quickly she'd drunk that back. "I didn't know you had another one!"

Now it was Gwen's turn to laugh. "What? Oh, God, no. I meant Michael. No, no more kids."

Two was what she'd always hoped for, knowing how lonely she'd been as the only child, wanting a different dynamic for her own, new family. Three had just been a bonus.

"Oh. Whew. You had me there for a minute. But then, you do seem to have made a career out of motherhood."

Gwen plucked the cork off the wine bottle with more force than needed. At this rate, they'd go through the last bottle of white and the only bottle of red left over from the holidays before the night was through. Iris probably had an entire wine cellar at her apartment.

"How's your career?" Gwen asked, knowing how important it had been to her, enough to keep her from visiting beyond that one time after Norah was born.

"Oh! I left the cosmetics company years ago." Iris waved a hand through the air and laughed, but her eyes seemed to shift to the side when she took another sip from her glass. "I'm on a lot of committees," she added.

Gwen couldn't hide her surprise. Iris's career had once been everything, all she could talk about when she'd visited for that long weekend all those years ago. Important enough to keep her from having time for daily chats anymore, important enough to give her the financial security that she'd always craved.

But then, she was married to a wealthy man and devoting herself to good causes. She'd ended up exactly where she wanted to be in many ways. Iris had never ruled out love; it just hadn't ever been her priority.

"Where are the kids?" Iris asked now, looking around.

"Norah is upstairs in her room, studying." That sounded impressive, sure, but the truth was that she was probably up-stairs texting her friends and drowning out life with her earbuds, and falling even more behind on schoolwork than she already was.

The meeting with the guidance counselor still loomed. Gwen had received an email today about rescheduling. The thought of going back into that school made her stomach clench, but then Gwen thought of Joe and brightened.

"Declan is at an after-school program. Michael will be bringing him home. And Bea is..." Where was Bea?

Gwen's heart began to race when she remembered the last-minute trip she had made to the grocery store with Bea in tow, right after tap class. They'd made a pinkie promise for a five-minute dash, which usually meant more like fifteen, but still, it kept them focused, kept them from exploring the free samples at the cheese display, for example.

She'd gone to the car, triumphant with her time, not quite so triumphant with the price she paid for the pie at the bakery, and she'd turned on the radio, her mind spinning with thoughts of how quickly she could get everything prepped and ready.

Had Bea even been in the car with her? Her mouth went dry as her vision turned to a single black hole and for a moment she thought she might actually faint. Had she left her in the store or, worse, in the parking lot?

Wait. Wait. She *had* been in the car with her. She was chattering on and on about what she was going to buy with her five bucks (a unicorn pencil topper and a fuzzy sleeping mask with cat ears), and it had made Gwen dizzy and she couldn't think straight and she'd told her it was time for the quiet game until she said "Speak!" and Bea being Bea had simply nodded and said nothing more.

Meaning she wouldn't be saying anything now. Meaning she wouldn't have called out for help when...

Oh, Christ.

Gwen set down the glass of wine. "I just realized I left something in the car." She marched as quickly as she could without drawing too much suspicion to herself to the garage door and nearly wept with relief when she saw Bea in the backseat of the old minivan, still bundled in her coat and hat, waving enthusiastically out the window.

Mercifully, it was a heated garage. It had to be. It was the only way to ensure the room above it stayed semi-warm through the winter months.

She yanked the door open and pulled Bea free, uttering many apologies, but she still couldn't be certain that Social Services wouldn't knock on her door at any second.

"You should have gotten out of the car," she said, gripping Bea's arms. When Bea just stared at her with a sleepy smile, Gwen gritted her teeth in exasperation. The one time she didn't want one of her kids to listen to her, and they were taking it entirely too far. "Speak!"

Bea let out a sigh as if she had been holding her breath as well as biting her tongue. "I didn't want to lose the game! Do I still get my five dollars?"

"Of course you get your five dollars!" She glanced at the door to the house. "Come on. There's someone I want you to meet." Her legs were shaking as she led them back into the house, her mind racing with a plausible explanation.

"Look who I found!" she said with false cheer. Iris, she noted, had refilled her glass again in the short time she'd been gone. "Out playing in the snow."

"No, I wasn't." Bea looked up at her indignantly.

Gwen felt her eyes turn to fire, the way her mother's used to. And hadn't she sworn she would never do that? But today called for desperate measures.

"Go hang up your coat and then come wash your hands, honey. You want that apple pie, don't you?" Death stare. Bea narrowed her eyes, challenging her for a moment, but then seemed to pick up on the hint.

"Yes, Mommy." Bea did as she was told and came back from the kitchen sink, eyeing Iris. "You look like my Barbie dolls."

Iris laughed. "Is that a compliment?"

Of course it's a compliment, Gwen wanted to say, and one that she had never received and never would, and not just because her hair was brown.

She let out a long sigh as Bea ran off to her room. "Michael won't be home for a while. We can go into the living room and catch up before dinner."

It was the best room in the house, and she'd spent half the morning rearranging the photo frames and throw pillows. She used to be good at this. She used to know how to pull a room together. Used to even enjoy it. She'd subscribe to interior decorating magazines, and she'd put hours upon hours of thought into this house when they'd first moved in, promising herself she would eventually create a dream home, a cozy nest her children would want to return to when they were grown. She'd assumed when the kids went to school she would have time… But somehow that time was eaten up by things like grocery runs and endless piles of laundry and vacuuming and cleaning up the breakfast dishes, and then prepping for dinner. Sometimes she resented even having hair, considered chopping it off and getting a pixie cut, because of how much time it took just to dry it.

The only small mercy now that Michael and she were, well, distant, was that she hadn't shaved her legs in so long, it seemed the hair had stopped growing. Because really, who had time to shave every day in addition to applying makeup?

Iris did. But then Iris had chosen a different path.

"Look at this," Iris exclaimed as she wandered around the living room, stopping every few feet to pick up a framed print and study the photo inside: one of the kids dressed in Halloween costumes, back when Norah was still into that sort of thing; another of the three of them playing on the sand, Lake Michigan in the background, the sky a bright blue; and another of Bailey when he was a puppy, his paws possessively holding his favorite red ball.

"You got everything you ever wanted!" Iris said, dropping onto a sofa that faced the fireplace.

Gwen looked at the photographs that captured the perfect moments of her life, snapshots of ideal times, not the whole picture.

"We both did," she said, and for a strange moment, she thought she saw doubt creep into Iris's eyes. Or maybe they were just mirroring her own.

"So, how does it feel to be back in town?"

"Weird, in a way, but also sort of like I never left." Iris sipped her wine.

"Yeah, I felt the same when I moved back." Gwen sighed heavily. The difference in their circumstances was of course that Iris was only paying a visit.

Gwen took a seat on the armchair and adjusted the throw pillow behind her back. She wondered what could have been so big, so important, that it would bring Iris to Westlake after all this time. Surely, if it were something bad, Iris wouldn't be so...happy.

"How's your mom?" Gwen occasionally ran into her at the grocery store, but not often, and it had been a while.

Iris flicked her long, lush hair over her shoulder. Gwen could have sworn she heard it swish. She peered at Iris closely. She'd always had nice hair—thicker than Gwen's, and lighter, of course. But the highlights weren't the only thing that seemed different now. Extensions perhaps?

"About the same," Iris sighed. She met Gwen's eyes. "And yours?"

They exchanged a little smile. "About the same."

Iris shook her head. "Some things never change."

And some do, Gwen thought sadly. She could still remember riding bikes with Iris into town, stopping off for ice cream at the little shop that was tucked behind the butcher shop. Gwen hadn't even known about it, but Iris knew every spot in town, she said. She rode her bike everywhere, unsupervised, and she saved up soda cans to exchange for coins, which she then saved up for money for ice cream and penny candy. She'd grin proudly, showing off her buck teeth, when she shared her garbage bags full of soda cans. Sometimes they even went hunting for them, out around the alleys behind the shops on Main Street.

"Are you...staying with your mom?" They couldn't pretend that there wasn't five cubic feet of luggage in her front hall, after all.

Iris chewed her lip as her smile slipped for the first time since she'd come through the door. A sure sign she was nervous about something. "Lois can't let me stay with her after all."

Gwen waited to see if there was something more that Iris was going to say, like that she would need a ride to a hotel, but Iris just gave her that same hopeful look she gave when she asked about dinner, and Gwen took a big gulp of her wine as panic set in.

"Oh! Well, you can stay here if you need to!" But as the words came out, she was thinking, *Where? On the sofa?* The basement wasn't finished, and she now cursed ever buying this house, knowing full well that Michael would never let her spend the money on the construction to finish it. Not that they had the funds at the moment.

She reassured herself that she was just being polite. And in turn, Iris would be polite. She wasn't that little girl anymore who was grateful for a hot meal or a ride to the mall.

"Oh, thank you!" Iris gushed, to Gwen's horror. "Are you sure I'm not imposing?"

"Of course not!" Gwen's mind was racing. All four bedrooms upstairs were occupied. She'd have to put Iris in the guest room over the garage. "You remember all those sleepovers we used to have?" Iris looked wistful, and Gwen wished she could do the same, think back on all the whispered late-night conversations, the cookies they would sneak from the pantry and hide under the covers, and, when they were older, the face masks and makeovers and the dreams they would share. Their future was so close then, and then everything would be possible. And better.

Instead, Gwen's smile froze, and she had the uneasy sensation that her shock was still showing. She needed an end date. As in, tomorrow. "Of course. Of course. Two spoons and a pint of ice cream, remember?"

Iris probably hadn't eaten ice cream since she'd left Westlake, from the looks of her.

Meanwhile, that was all Gwen could think about right now. A nice bowl of ice cream, in bed, with a locked door and the dog at her side. No kids who would start to act up or hold their hands out for more cash. No unemployed husband who most certainly wouldn't be happy to part with his space.

She could just tell her she didn't have the room. Explain the complications of her family life.

But Iris was sitting there wearing an outfit that probably cost more than Gwen's monthly mortgage payment, her hair looking like she'd just emerged from a salon, her smile dazzling as she sipped her wine as if she didn't have a care in the world.

Iris wouldn't understand Gwen's daily responsibilities. The chaos of domestic life.

"I can make up a bed for tonight," she said instead. The dinner had been difficult enough to pull off. Could she really keep this charade going through until morning?

She was starting to sweat.

Iris's cheeks flushed, almost imperceptibly, but Gwen noticed. "I really appreciate it, Gwen. Lois is having some issues with her boyfriend. You know how she is…" She rolled her eyes.

Yes, Gwen did know Lois, and the fact that this didn't require further explanation made her stomach knot with guilt. Iris had been like a sister to her once. If she needed to stay, then she would stay.

She cornered Michael the moment he walked in through the kitchen door. "Michael? Do you have a moment?"

"Sure," he said with a shrug.

He wasn't picking up on the hint. Not the wide eyes. Not the long pause. None of it. "Declan, go say hello to my old friend Iris; she's in the living room. And here, bring another bottle of wine to her." She pulled one from the fridge. That would be the last of it. She hoped that it would last through dinner.

Michael went to the pantry and opened a bag of chips.

"Dinner is ready," she told him. "I made lasagna."

"Just a snack," Michael said, sinking his fist into the bag.

Gwen peeked around the corner to the living room, where Declan was mercifully sitting down to the piano, Iris smiling politely from the sofa where she sat with Bea now at her side, showing off the Barbie she'd received for Christmas, which she'd now dressed like a dominatrix, likely to emulate Iris's black leather and fur ensemble. With any luck, Declan would play his recital piece. Four entire minutes to drown out the sounds of Michael losing his shit when she told him about their surprise houseguest.

Sure enough, his reaction was loud. "Can't she stay with her mother? She still lives here in town, right?"

"It's not an option, apparently." Gwen wrung her hands. She hadn't even dropped the worst part of it yet, and Michael, bless him, hadn't thought about the logistics, because well, that was her territory, wasn't it? Dinner planning, kids' schedules, where people would sleep…

"So I'm going to need you to move back in."

"Move back in?" He seemed to scowl at her. "What do you mean, move back in? I live here."

She gave him a long look. "I mean, it won't work for you to fall asleep in the office every night!"

"I don't sleep there every night."

"You do," she corrected him. "Most nights." And when he wasn't passed out on the sofa in the office, she would usually find him on the sofa in the family room, the television blaring, an electric light filling the space.

"No," he stressed, his voice rising to a worrisome level. Fortunately, Declan was at the part of the music where he was really pounding it out. Normally she hated this part, it set her teeth on edge, but today, she welcomed it. *Keep going, honey!* "I fall asleep there. Because I'm tired."

Gwen stared at Michael and forced three calming breaths. She could easily turn this into a thirty-minute argument about who was more tired and why, but she didn't have thirty minutes. She had about three. "Well, that's technically the guest room, so I'm going to need to put Iris there."

"Where am I supposed to work?"

"Dining room table? There's that desk in our bedroom, Michael. The kids are gone all day in school and activities anyway. It will probably only be for tonight." She paused. Probably. "She doesn't like Westlake. Trust me, she won't be staying long."

"Can't she stay in a hotel?"

Good question, and one she didn't have an answer to just now. "She's my oldest friend, and I haven't seen her since Norah was a baby."

He raised an eyebrow and said pointedly, "And whose fault is that?"

Gwen felt the sting of his words, and the truth in them too. Then she thought of Iris's radiant smile, the energy she'd brought through the door, how genuinely happy she seemed to see Gwen. How happy Gwen was to see her, even though she hadn't even really realized she still missed her. She'd thought she'd gotten over that part.

"What was I supposed to say?"

"That she hurt your feelings and owes you an apology?" Michael stared at her, and she knew he had a point.

Gwen twisted her hands. It was only one night—probably. They hadn't seen each other in so long, and Iris was in a good mood. Why ruin it? "I mean about her asking to stay."

Michael slapped the bag of chips down. "That we don't have any room! That's what you were supposed to say!"

Gwen leaped forward, shushing him. "Can you keep your voice down? Please?"

"Oh, heaven forbid you upset your friend. What about upsetting your husband?"

"What about upsetting your wife?" Gwen shot back. She felt her eyes sting with tears, and her voice was louder than usual. Maybe it was the stress, or maybe it was the buildup. She stared at her husband, who seemed as shocked as she was. "It's just for tonight, Michael," she said, lowering her voice. She thought of all that luggage, swallowing hard. "A couple at the most. And who knows, maybe she'll see what it's like around here and decide to pack up early, go to a hotel."

"What's that supposed to mean? *See what it's like around here?*"

"Nothing," she said, picking up a dishrag and wiping down a few drops of wine that had spilled on the counter.

"Hey." He frowned. "What is that supposed to mean?"

"I mean that this is a far cry from Park Avenue." And that this life, this household, was nothing like she'd claimed it to be.

10

IRIS

DINNER WAS CHAOS. Three children, each speaking over the next. A very different picture than the strict, quiet, formal dinners that she was used to at the Warners' house all those years ago. Here the food was passed around, and the kids were allowed second helpings, but Gwen still pushed most of the food around on her plate, just like she used to do.

Her dinners with Julian were usually at restaurants, civilized affairs where they shared the highlights of their day. For a long time, this nightly ritual was a reminder of how far she'd come. But sitting at the long table in the warm house, with the dog snoring softly in the corner, all she could think of was everything she'd been missing.

"I'll get the guest room ready!" Gwen said once the plates were cleared. The kitchen counter was stacked with dishes that Gwen assured Iris she would tend to later, as if it were no big deal, even though it looked like a lot of work. But then, making a happy home for her family was all Gwen had ever wanted. A bigger family than she'd grown up in, a warm and casual environment where she would bake cookies and host holidays.

Gwen made it look easy, but Iris felt bad about imposing. She'd buy a gift, in town, if Gwen could give her a ride. Depression hit her in waves, but the wine had helped with that. But now the wine was gone, and she was here, in this perfectly cozy and idyllic house, and she had the strange feeling of never wanting to leave, just like she'd never really wanted to leave Gwen's house when they were young. The only comfort she had then was knowing she'd be back again the next day, or at least the day after that, and each time she went home she was that much more resolved to have a life like the Warners' someday. Not a life like her own.

She hadn't thought about those days in years, other than a passing memory that filled her with nostalgia. But Gwen was part of her old life. The life she'd left behind.

Now, being back, it wasn't so easy to stuff those memories away.

"Do you want to see my bedroom?" The youngest one, Bea, asked. She looked so much like Gwen that it was like looking at an old photograph, and perhaps it was why Iris took an instant liking to her, even if she was a child, and children had never really been Iris's thing.

Gwen nodded with enthusiasm. "Yes, show her your toys while I get the guest room set up!"

"Well, look at this!" Iris said when she followed Bea up the stairs and into a room at the end of the hall. "It's so…pink!" Pink walls, pink curtains, pink bedding, and pink pillows. Even a pink rug. "I would have *loved* a bedroom like this when I was little."

Gwen, she knew, would have too. It was something they'd talked about, how they wished their bedrooms could have been. Gwen's mother had insisted that lavender was more elegant. Gwen had promised, way back then, when she probably wasn't much bigger than Bea was, "When I have a little girl, her room will be all pink. It will be pink perfection."

"Pink perfection," Iris whispered, taking it all in.

"That's what Mommy calls it!" Bea said, smiling broadly.

"I know," Iris said, feeling her shoulders relax for the first time all day. Nothing had changed in Westlake, Wisconsin, and right now, she was grateful for that.

"I'm making some pink hearts for our front door. See?" Bea held up some uneven paper cutouts. "We have to beat the neighbors. They're not very nice. We had a playdate, but Taffy didn't let me touch her dolls, and when I told her mom, her mom didn't even tell her to share." She looked up at Iris with injured eyes.

"That doesn't sound very nice at all," Iris remarked. But then, it sounded all too familiar. Kids were rotten, at least in her experience. Except for Gwen. Gwen had been special. And Bea, she thought, smiling at the little girl.

"Mommy told Daddy that it's a case of assholes raising assholes." Bea's eyes popped. "Oops. I'm not supposed to say bad words."

Iris laughed loudly. It had been so, so long since she'd laughed like this, and it felt strange but good. "Don't worry. I won't tell," she whispered. She was starting to warm up to this child. Maybe Gwen would let her keep her for a summer. She could take her shopping, to the zoo. Give her the full Manhattan experience.

But then she thought of Julian, who had made it clear he already had all the children he needed. Julian. Would he even be waiting for her when she went home? Would she even still be able to live in Manhattan by the time summer came around?

Nonsense. She'd lived in Manhattan long before Julian.

"Do you have a little girl?" Bea carefully set her paper hearts back on her nightstand.

Iris shook her head. "No."

"Oh," Bea said sadly. "I'm sorry."

Iris blinked, not sure what to say to that. It had been a long time since anyone had felt sorry for her, reminding her of her true circumstances.

"Bea! Time for bed!" Gwen's voice approached, and Iris turned to look at her as she came into the doorway. Gwen gave Iris a wink. "I can see you're already popular around here."

There was a first for everything then, wasn't there? After all, they both knew they'd been the outcasts growing up, at least until high school, when Iris started to garner some attention for her looks and her attitude. But by then, she wasn't interested. She had Gwennie. She didn't need anyone else.

"She was showing me her pink bedroom." She shook her head. "Pink perfection. Just like you always wanted."

Gwen's smile looked tired. "I'd forgotten about that." Looking at Bea, she said, "It's a school night, Bea. Say good night to Auntie Iris. You can see her again tomorrow."

Bea's eyes grew wide. "Are you really my aunt?"

Iris didn't know what to say to that. Even Kat and Delilah just called her "Iris" or usually just "she" and "her." Little snots.

"Sorry. I might have overstepped," Gwen said, looking shifty. Her cheeks were a little pink as she walked over to a white dresser and pulled open a drawer. "I remember that when you visited when Norah was born, that's what we called you."

"Of course I'm Auntie Iris," Iris said, even though she had earned no such title, not really. Maybe, back when she'd visited Gwen and her firstborn, she had the potential of being that kind of fun aunt who sent toys and candy just for the heck of it, but she had a career to focus on, a promotion to attain, and money to earn if she was ever going to make it. Make it. What had she made? A mess of her life, that's what.

She looked down at Bea, who was starting to protest when Gwen pulled some pink pajamas covered with butterflies from the drawer. "You know, your mommy and I have been friends since we were about as old as you."

"How long ago was that?" Bea asked, her eyes round.

"Well, seeing as we're already thirty-nine..." She tried to do the math. The drinks were making it more difficult than it should be. With a start, she realized that Gwen's birthday was this month, and that it had come and gone. She glanced at Gwen, wondering if she had been mad, but then, they hadn't wished each other a happy birthday in years. Somehow, they'd eventually stopped. Gwen, however, looked panic-stricken.

"Thirty-nine?" Bea squawked. "Mommy's not *thirty*-nine! Tell her, Mommy! You're *twenty*-nine! Last year you were twenty-eight, and the year before you were twenty-seven. I remember when I asked you how old you were and you said you were twenty-six." Bea looked on the verge of tears, and now it was Iris's turn to feel like she had overstepped.

Bea looked at her mother, horror on her face. "Are you really thirty-nine?"

After a long hesitation, Gwen sighed. "Yes."

"That means…" Bea blinked rapidly, clutching her stuffed animal to her chest. "You're *old*!"

Now Iris and Gwen both laughed, but Jesus, the kid was right. They were old. She'd be forty in September—and where would she be then? Childless. Probably single. Starting over.

"Bea, it's not nice to call people old. Besides, look at Auntie Iris. She doesn't look a day over twenty-two."

Iris rolled her eyes, not bothering to mention that if she did, it wasn't without a little pain and a whole lot of chemicals. Still, leave it to Gwen to make her feel better about herself. She always had a knack for that.

"It's fine, Bea," Gwen insisted. "I'm still young."

This was said with a little less conviction, mirroring Iris's worries.

"Now. Time for bed. Say goodnight."

"Goodnight, Auntie Iris," Bea grumbled as she pulled her pajamas from Gwen's hands. And if Iris didn't know better, she'd say she narrowed her little eyes at Gwen when she did.

Auntie Iris.

She let that name soak in as she walked down the stairs, past the framed photos of Gwen's life captured in time. Baby photo after baby photo—it was hard to tell which child she was looking at: baby Norah or baby Bea. Declan was easy, obviously. She thought about it all the way to the back door, where Gwen handed over her coat and said, with an apologetic glance, "The guest room is technically above the garage, so you have to use a separate entrance. I hope that's okay."

It was better than okay. Her own private space for the next three and a half weeks was just what she needed. No one would bother her. No one would know. Here she could be Auntie Iris. Auntie Iris who lived a fabulous life in New York City, Aunt Iris who had a penthouse in the sky and went to charity balls at the Met and who had a closetful of designer dresses. Auntie Iris had never been to rehab. She didn't like her wine a little too much. And she certainly didn't have a husband who was sleeping with Stephanie Clay.

"Michael already took your bags up," Gwen was saying, as they both slid into their coats and Gwen opened the door. Arctic wind slapped them both in the face, and Iris was reminded how brutal the Wisconsin winters could be, especially this close to the lake. She wished she had brought her fur coat instead, but then she thought of how that might have gone over here. Lois would have liked it, would have probably made a comment about it too. And Gwen… What would Gwen have said? But then Gwen never wanted to be dressed up like a doll. All Gwen had ever wanted was to blend in with the crowd.

Iris swallowed hard. They both did.

"Michael has been using this space for his home office," Gwen explained when they reached the top of the stairs behind the garage, and she pushed open a door to reveal a large, vaulted space. Sure enough, there was a desk at one end, with a chair pulled out, and a lamp that was off-kilter. Gwen quickly set it straight.

"You can keep your clothes in here, though it's not much room, I'm afraid." She opened a drawer in the end table, revealing three plastic bags of what appeared to be human teeth.

"Holy shit, Gwen!" Iris stared in alarm. "What are you? Some kind of serial killer?"

Gwen gave her a wry look. "Even scarier. I'm a mother of three."

Iris laughed, and Gwen's cheeks went red as she pulled the three bags from the drawer and, to Iris's continued horror, shoved them into her pocket.

"You saved your children's baby teeth," Iris marveled.

"I had to hide them since they thought the tooth fairy took them. You must think I'm crazy," Gwen said.

"No," Iris said softly. "I think you're the mother I wished I had."

Gwen's eyes seemed to mist for a moment, but she recovered quickly.

"There's a bathroom next to the closet. Fresh towels on the rack, and toiletries, too. Just come downstairs if you need anything. We leave the back door unlocked. There's no crime in Westlake."

Iris still found it odd that Gwen had moved back and seemed so content being here, too. Once, there was a time she was as eager to leave as Iris had been. They'd lay side by side on Gwen's frilly bed, staring up at the canopy, imagining what their lives would be like, knowing that it all hinged on making a change.

But Iris knew why Gwen had moved back. She was responsible, a caretaker, and her father had been sick.

Iris opened her mouth, but there was too much to say and she couldn't decide on just one thing. It felt too daunting, and she was so tired. Gwen was still smiling, but she could tell

Gwen was too. How could she not be, with all those kids and that dinner and the dog and those dishes still to clean up?

"Thank you," she said instead. "For letting me stay. Maybe...maybe we could go for coffee tomorrow? Or get our nails done? My treat."

"That sounds nice." Gwen blew out a sigh. "Well. I should probably make sure the kids are all in bed. It's later than usual for them."

Of course. Iris watched her go, a part of her sad that Gwen hadn't flopped down onto the bed and launched into a chatty story, the way she used to. But then, they weren't eighteen anymore, and Gwen had a family waiting for her.

Iris tried not to let herself think about the fact that no one was waiting for her. She'd ensured that, hadn't she?

She washed her face with one of the lavender-scented soaps that Gwen had set out next to the sink, wanting to shower but feeling too drained to do so. Her tongue felt thick, and she was on the verge of a headache. Andover had confiscated her ibuprofen, she remembered as she searched through her handbag for the bottle, so she settled on a glass of water instead, because of course, Gwen had left a water glass for her on the bedside table, along with a stack of glossy home decorating magazines.

Iris pulled in a breath, grabbed her phone, and pulled up Facebook. She checked Delilah's account first, bracing herself for the nastiness, but there was nothing newsworthy other than a terrible photo of her at Julian's party. Kat was next, but she wasn't as into Facebook, claiming it was for "old people," a bucket that Iris must have fallen into.

Julian didn't do Facebook either, also claiming it was for "young people," so this was her stab at a connection to her former life. Her real life. The life that felt so far away now that it seemed to not exist at all.

Or maybe it never had existed at all. She had no idea when the affair had started, or if it was even the first one. Maybe her life had been just as big a lie as the person she was pretending to be here in Westlake. Maybe the person she was lying to was herself.

That left Stephanie's page.

Her hands were shaking as the page loaded, but the only new post was some painting at the gallery. No mention of the party. Or any hint of Julian. It was all still a secret.

Well, she had her own secret, she thought, looking around the room that Gwen had set up for her. And no one—not Gwen, not her mother, and certainly not Julian—could ever find out about it.

She'd bide her time. Get through the next few weeks. Forget about this little blip in the otherwise smooth road, and then, she'd go back to her life, and everything would be okay.

It had to be.

11

GWEN

GWEN WAS UP at four, even if she had been awake since about two, and it was only partly due to the fact that Michael was snoring so loudly beside her. She'd forgotten about that when she'd insisted that he couldn't fall asleep watching television again, because what if Iris came into the kitchen in the middle of the night, needing something to eat?

"Have you seen how skinny she is?" was all Michael could say to that, which stung, badly, but at eleven that night he flicked off the television and came to bed.

Still, Gwen was anxious thinking of how her real life paled next to her social media posts and holiday letter. At least the dinner had gone off without too much of a hitch. And the food had been good, too. And Michael had only given her a funny look when Iris praised the homemade pie.

True to her word, the first thing Iris suggested in the morning after letting herself in through the back door was a trip into town. "I'm feeling like mimosas and nails," she said, her eyes gleaming much the same way they did when she used to manage to shove one of Lois's half-empty vodka bottles into her backpack, not that Gwen was ever willing to try any.

Meanwhile, Gwen was fielding texts from her mother and cleaning up the cereal that Bea had spilled as she bolted to the school bus, tears shining in her eyes over having to leave Gwen's side.

"But it's only for a few hours," Gwen had reassured her, puzzled by this sudden protest.

"But...you're *old*! You're going to die soon!"

"I'm actually quite a bit younger than the other mommies at school," she said rather proudly, and it was true. She'd gotten an early start, after all. "You know Taffy's mommy? Mrs. Sharp? She's at *least* forty-five." She beamed, and Bea did too.

Now it was already nine, Gwen had been up for hours, and Iris looked like she had just rolled out of bed. And sadly, even then, she looked far more pulled together than Gwen, who was already wearing lip gloss.

She couldn't remember the last time she'd done something as simple but self-serving as getting a manicure. Michael's holiday party last year, perhaps? Right before the big lay-off? She had planned to use the day to sit with her planner, work out a punch list for the week, a plan of attack for bringing in more business, but that was before she knew she had a houseguest.

"I have coffee," Gwen said, suddenly remembering the pot she had made, especially for Iris, though given the hour, it had probably gone cold by now.

"Let's grab one in town. I'll take a quick shower and meet you down here in thirty?" Iris asked, and Gwen nodded, it would give her just enough time to finish perfecting the house, hiding any further evidence of troubled teens—or a disgruntled husband, who was currently hunched over the laptop at the dining room table. When she ran the vacuum while the kids were eating breakfast, Michael complained that he was trying to work. Ditto when Bailey barked.

"Do you have a coffee meeting?" Gwen asked hopefully, once Iris had left, but Michael just shook his head and started muttering to himself as he stared at the screen. There had been a few of those—coffee meetings—at the beginning. Old coworkers and friends eager to offer up advice or pass on a good word. But those offers had dried up months ago, and now networking was more along the lines of working at a café or sweating out his frustrations in the gym.

Forty-eight minutes later, Iris appeared at the back door, her hair sleek and shiny, wearing oversized black sunglasses and black leggings tucked into knee-high boots that were anything but practical with their three-inch heel, and she'd tossed a bright pink scarf over her coat.

She looked like a movie star. She looked like Barbie.

Gwen considered her mother's comments about her car when she popped the garage door and unlocked the van, wishing she'd thought to ask Michael for the keys to his corporate-friendly sedan. She should have had the van washed. Why hadn't she thought of that?

Oh, right. Because she'd thought Iris was only coming to dinner.

If Iris had any opinions on the vehicle, she kept them to herself as she casually pushed the banana peel off the seat before she climbed in.

"Oh!" Heat rose in Gwen's cheeks as she hurried to grab the slimy object from Iris's hands. Her eyes cut to the backseat, where the crackers that Bea had spilled yesterday were now ground firmly into the seats and a paper that Norah had received back, boasting a C minus in big red ink, was strewn on the floor. "Let me take that. Kids." She gulped, unable to meet Iris's gaze, but she couldn't have, even if she'd tried, because of those sunglasses!

She walked to the trash can, her heart racing, and tossed the banana inside. Three breaths for courage. She'd have a coffee. A manicure. It would be *fun*. Just as Iris had said it would be.

And then, it would be over. Iris would go back to her glamorous life, and Gwen would go back to her ordinary life. The same feeling of disappointment hung over her as it did all those years ago when Iris would leave her house, and as it did when Iris eventually left for college in another city and every other time Iris had left, until she'd eventually just faded away.

Gwen forced a smile as she went back to the car and slid into the driver's seat. "Three kids!" she said again. "They treat this car like a dorm room."

"Don't worry about it. I got a lift from the airport in my mother's car, remember?" Iris's mouth crooked into a smile, and Gwen all at once felt better.

Iris flicked on the radio, seeming satisfied with the first station. "It all looks the same! Do you notice that?" she marveled as they wound through the streets into town.

"Yes," Gwen sighed. "I noticed." When they'd first moved back to Westlake, it hadn't bothered her as it did now. She knew what to expect here. What she could offer her children. Her father was sick, and she was close enough to help. She hadn't even looked back at Chicago. Hadn't even considered what she had given up. The city had been too stressful with a double stroller in a walk-up. And the cost of living had made functional living almost impossible. When Michael was offered the job in Milwaukee, it was a no-brainer.

"Where's a good place for a drink these days?" Iris asked as the center of town appeared in the distance. Back when they were in high school, they used to hit the diner off route 32, drinking cup after cup of sweetened coffee to delay returning home.

For a moment, Gwen thought of suggesting it, for old times' sake, but quickly changed her mind. The place was a greasy spoon back then, and Iris had clearly moved on from all that.

"There's a new coffeehouse near the nail salon." Gwen pulled into the nearest parking spot. She didn't dare admit to Iris that she rarely—make that never—went out for coffee, and other than brunch or lunch with her mother, she was too busy doing laundry, running errands, and, lately, thinking about how to build a cosmetic empire and not lose their house.

Iris wrinkled her nose. "I need something stronger."

So she hadn't been joking. Feeling uptight and wishing that she could call Michael to deal with the kids this afternoon, Gwen said, "Well, I have to drive."

Even if Michael could handle the school pickup, it would be too much work to explain all the after-school activities.

"So? One won't kill you." No, but one day drink was how she'd gotten roped into Susan Sharp's pyramid scheme, wasn't it?

"Driving makes me tired," she explained, thinking quickly. "I'm going through a tank a week running the kids around."

Iris looked at her blankly. She couldn't understand. How could she? Gwen was a housewife. A wannabe entrepreneur. She was a mother. Iris probably never had to fold a load of laundry, much less three a day.

"I should probably just stick with the coffee anyway," Iris said with a shrug.

Now Gwen regretted being such a drag. Here she was, thirty-nine years old, with a rare occasion to have a little fun, and she was too busy thinking about everything she had to do before she climbed into bed tonight.

She was going to say, *What the hell*, they could go down to the pub and order a round of mimosas, but Iris seemed distracted, craning her neck, looking up and down Main Street. "Same as always. A bunch of yuppies," she said with a bitter undertone.

For one fleeting second, they were bonded again. She smiled as she got out of the car and went into the coffee shop.

"Do you remember those afternoons at the diner?" Gwen said once they settled into a seat near the window, a coffee in each of their hands: black for Iris, and full cream and sweetener for her.

Iris pulled a face of pure horror. "Yes! I mean, I didn't until now, but yes. Wow. That's hard to believe it was us. We were so…"

"Laid back," Gwen said at the same moment Iris said, "Desperate."

Gwen blinked, struck by Iris's assessment of a fond memory.

Iris was still wearing her sunglasses, even though they were indoors and the sky outside was overcast. She looked out the window, her lips pinching. "Neither one of us wanted to go home. We couldn't wait to get out of this town."

Gwen felt uneasy. It was true; they couldn't wait to get out. And Iris had succeeded.

"It's not so bad now." It was a good place to raise kids, sure, and the downtown area had become quite trendy and upscale since they were kids, but she had longed for distance. She just hadn't tried hard enough to maintain it. There were so many other things to worry about that coming back to a life she knew felt like a relief.

"I still couldn't believe it when you told me you were moving back," Iris said.

Gwen sighed. "It was the right decision, for Michael's job, for the kids…for my parents." She paused, not sure if she wanted to say what came next. "My father died a few years ago. I'm not sure if you know."

Iris looked down at the table. "Lois told me. I should have called. Or written."

"It's okay," Gwen said, even though it wasn't okay, and she'd been hurt by the omission. They'd been communicating only through text or email by then, but still, when the flowers and cards had started to pour in, she'd opened each one, hoping it was from Iris, even though she'd never told her what happened, not directly. She'd been too stung, she supposed, to have not been invited to Iris's recent wedding. Normally, her best friend would have been the first person she would have called, crying, seeking comfort and understanding, but by then, she was no longer sure she would find what she needed if she picked up the phone.

"I wasn't sure if you would want to hear from me," Iris surprised her by saying.

"Of course I would have wanted to hear from you!" What she didn't say, because she didn't want to argue here in the center of Main Street, where half the moms from school seemed to gather every day, was that she had been waiting to hear from Iris. It would have been the perfect opportunity for Iris to reach out, smooth things over, apologize for not inviting her to the wedding, because she didn't believe the part about Iris eloping; she knew Iris too well to see through that lie.

"Well." Iris seemed to hesitate. "That's good to know."

They sipped their coffee in silence, but Gwen stole a few glances at Iris every few moments, waiting to see if she would open up, say more. What had happened in New York? And what was happening now? Iris hadn't visited since she'd left. Why come back now?

"How's your husband?" she asked.

She thought she saw Iris's jaw clench, just for one brief second. She glanced at the rock on Iris's finger; it was even bigger than she'd expected, and she had the strange urge to ask if she could try it on, just for a minute.

"Oh, work, work, work. You know how it is with husbands," Iris said gaily, and Gwen decided it was time to drop the subject of husbands at that point.

"Well, what do you say we go get our nails done?"

They walked the few blocks, despite the freezing temperature, and Gwen was feeling downright happy as she walked into the salon and saw the rack of jewel-toned colors, until she looked up and saw Susan Sharp sitting on a massage chair, laughing with Colleen Whitt—her "best bestie," as she was overheard telling people loudly at the fall craft fair, where Susan and Colleen had made a small fortune with their homemade wreaths.

"Oh, shit," she hissed, turning her back before one of them spotted her.

"What is it?" Iris asked, looking at her with concern.

"That woman over there. The blonde? I...don't like her." There. She'd said it. Clear as crystal. She did not like Susan Sharp. Not one bit.

"Why? What happened?" Even though Iris was still hiding her eyes behind her sunglasses, Gwen could tell by the movement of her other facial fixtures that her eyes were positively gleaming. She bit back a smile. Iris had always loved a fair bit of drama. It thrilled her. No doubt she got it from all those soap operas she grew up watching.

Whereas Gwen... Well, it made her nervous. Life was much easier when it was predictable and safe.

Under normal circumstances, Gwen would have turned on her heel and walked out the door, hurried to her car, and gone home without a manicure. But Iris was here. And Iris would never let her get away with that.

Hadn't it been Iris who pushed her forward, so hard that she nearly tripped, so she could ask Todd McAlister to the Sadie Hawkins dance sophomore year? He'd turned her down (politely, another date), but the next day he'd smiled at her in the hallway, and Iris had lifted an eyebrow and said, "See?"

Gwen lifted a bottle of nail polish from the wall and studied the name for the sheer relief of having something else to focus on, and then set it back where she found it. There were many reasons not to like Susan, but listing them now felt petty. She settled on the best descriptive, short and to the point. "She's sort of a power mom."

"*Power* mom?" Iris hooted.

"You know, the type who runs all the bake sales and puts out a list of approved ingredients beforehand, and who oversees the block party and again dictates who can bring what, and of course, she not only sits on the PTA but also serves as the class mom to both of her kids' classrooms."

"Jesus," Iris said, shaking her head. "I suppose I should be happy that I'm not a mother. It sounds like middle school all over again!"

Should be happy? Did that mean that Iris wanted kids? She sloughed off the comment. "It is middle school. Only worse. Because now it's multi-tiered. Now you have to protect your kids and yourself. You have to worry about advocating for your kids to be given certain advantages, and you can only do that by getting in good with the other moms."

"That sounds like hell," Iris said bluntly.

It is, Gwen thought. But she couldn't admit it, could she? This was what she'd wanted. What she'd chosen. She glanced over at Susan, who laughed shrilly at something Colleen had said.

But then, Susan wasn't worrying about the mortgage or her husband's job or just how big that credit card statement from the holidays would be, and when exactly it would hit the mailbox.

"They're leaving," Iris whispered, and Gwen felt herself stiffen.

"Gwen!" Susan cooed as she approached. Her eyes immediately drifted from Gwen to Iris, whom she looked up and down. Was that surprise Gwen thought she saw register on her face?

"Hello, Susan." Gwen managed to maintain a pleasant tone. "Hi, Colleen."

Colleen gave an imperceptible smile, even though her son and Declan were in the same class for the third year in a row.

Gwen expected Susan to leave then, but instead, she said, "I didn't know you came here. And who's your friend?"

Of course. Her manners. It wasn't for lack of them that she hadn't introduced Iris, obviously. It was because she didn't see a reason to drag out this fake exchange or pretend that she and Susan were friends when they were not.

But, they were neighbors. And their children were friends—sort of. And they would be classmates for another decade. And adulting was really difficult sometimes, wasn't it?

"This is Iris. Iris, this is Susan. She lives just up the street from me."

"Susan Sharp." Susan's eyes widened a notch, into that crazy calculated look that tended to be reserved for right about the time she was about to pounce on someone at a Friday meeting, or in the shoe department of Nordstrom, where she targeted new recruits. (She'd made it very clear this was her territory. In other words: stay away.)

Iris, bless her, gave a visibly limp handshake in return and said with the faintest of smiles, "We don't want to miss our appointment."

They didn't even have an appointment, but that didn't stop Iris. Nothing did.

"No!" Susan looked alarmed as she stepped back. "Wouldn't want that! I look so forward to my *weekly* appointments here. Do you usually have Cheryl?" The question was targeted at Gwen, but this time, Gwen wasn't taking the bait. Susan knew damn straight that Gwen didn't know Cheryl from Adam and that her visits to the salon were...annual.

"I'm surprised you don't use the Forevermore Beauty nail polish, Susan." She tilted her head and gave a patient smile, enjoying the flash of anger in Susan's eyes. Gwen felt a jolt of surprise. Where did that come from? She didn't say things like that!

But she had Iris beside her again.

"What was that about?" Iris asked, when Susan and Colleen finally left, claiming an important "birthday lunch" to which Gwen was clearly not invited.

"I told you. She's a power mom," Gwen said, not wanting to get into the hot mess that was her standing in the Forevermore Beauty franchise. She plucked a medium shade of red from the display rack, wondering if she might be able to keep her nails in decent condition until Valentine's Day, and then wondered who she was kidding; with the dishes alone they'd be chipped by tomorrow morning.

"Do you have time for a pedicure too?" Iris asked. She chose something darker, browner, something that Gwen would have never considered and now wished she had.

It seemed a little frivolous to get a pedicure in the dead of winter, but then, Susan just had, padding out of here with those paper flip-flops that were no doubt soaked through before she even got to her car.

Besides, Iris was probably used to the entire package, and it did sound nice. And those massage chairs would do miracles for the knots in her upper back.

They settled into their chairs, with a stash of magazines and a cup of water, and Gwen looked over at Iris, who was poring over an article in *Vogue*. She always read her magazines cover to cover, Gwen now remembered her saying when they were teenagers, sunbathing at the town pool, or in the Winarskis' overgrown backyard, Iris in her string bikini and Gwen in her modest one-piece, a sarong wrapped tightly at the waist.

Gwen still just flicked through the pages, occasionally stopping. But Iris. She was invested.

"Why didn't we ever do this before?" Gwen asked when they finally emerged from the salon and padded to the car in their paper flip-flops, gingerly holding their boots by the tops.

"Because we had no money for it!" Iris exclaimed. "At least, I didn't."

And look at her now, Gwen thought.

"Anything on the agenda for the rest of the day?" she eventually asked Iris, as they carefully walked down the sidewalk. Already she was thinking of everything she had to do: Norah needed to go to the library to see the tutor, and Bea needed more pins for her bun for Saturday's make-up ballet class, and since there was no normal food left in their house, she should probably pick up some frozen chicken nuggets at some point.

"I told my mom I'd stop by today," Iris said, giving her a long look that made Gwen feel like the past twenty years never existed and that they were still Iris and Gwen, best friends, sisters at heart, kindred spirits. "You can drop me off after this if you don't mind. I'll Uber it back after dinner. I think I'll grab a bottle of wine for her while we're here. And some for us, too!"

Gwen was aware that no sound was coming out of her mouth. That she was probably gaping, like some sort of fish, that she was wearing her emotions on her face, just as her mother always accused her of doing. That she wasn't hiding her shock. That she couldn't.

Iris reached out and squeezed her hand. "It'll be fun!"

Fun. Gwen swallowed the panic that was building in her chest and watched as Iris pushed ahead, as best she could, in her paper shoes.

She gestured to the small market a block down. "Mind if we pop in?"

What could she say? *No, I do not want to go grocery shopping with you because I can't have you see me buying chicken nuggets and processed frozen fries in the shape of a happy face for my junk-food-eating children? No, I do not want you spending another night at my house because I actually can't take another night of Michael's snoring and the thought of cooking another meal and then praying to every saint I can remember from Sunday school that it tastes good and that my kids don't complain is enough to make me run away from home?*

"Sure," she said instead, because it was her way. The easy way.

Iris's eyes lit up in a way that wasn't usually reserved for grocery shopping.

Gwen took a small cart, feeling silly in her paper flip-flops. "It says no shoes, no service," she whispered to Iris, her eyes darting toward the cash registers to see if an employee had noticed.

"You are wearing shoes," Iris said. "They're just made of paper."

Gwen's stomach knotted. She could just see being asked to leave. Iris would laugh, just like she'd laugh all those times she'd brazenly double-dipped at the movie theater. Gwen pushed the cart purposefully into the produce section, trying to focus on what she should make for dinner, but she couldn't think about anything other than the fact that Iris was spending another night.

And would tonight even be the last night? It had to be. Surely Iris had to get back to New York.

She'd just ask. Michael would ask. He would expect her to ask.

Her mouth went all dry, but she managed an "Iris?"

But Iris had darted off, her paper flip-flops sticking to the soles of her feet, leaving Gwen alone with her anxiety, wondering which of them would be caught by security first.

It would be her; of course it would be her. Iris could talk herself out of anything, and into anything too. Gwen supposed it shouldn't be a surprise that Iris had turned out as she had. She didn't let anything or anyone stand in her way.

Gwen was already at the cash register when Iris appeared with what appeared to be a case of wine.

"May as well," she said with a grin. "My treat!"

Gwen said nothing. She was too eager to get out of the store. Besides, Iris had consumed several bottles of wine last night. She was probably just repaying the favor.

"Those will last us your entire visit!" she remarked, and Iris just gave her a funny look. Didn't get the hint. Didn't give an end date.

Norah would be expecting payment again. Sensing Gwen's desperation, she might even up her fee.

They made it back to the car without interference from security, even though Gwen had already been mentally hatching a few desperate excuses, even though none felt plausible. Gwen felt positively gleeful, a rush that she hadn't felt in years, not since they were teenagers and she'd snuck off to the cemetery beside their school to take her first and last three swigs from the water bottle full of vodka that Iris had stashed in her backpack. She'd later thrown up in the bathroom, and she'd had to go home sick before science class. Iris, on the other hand, seemed perfectly at ease, carried on through the day, and even managed to climb to the top of the rope in gym class.

Gwen took the opposite route out of town, but Lois's house was close, and soon they were pulling up to it. It was once white, but the paint was chipping, and even though it was winter, it was obvious that the landscaping had been ignored.

"Jesus," Iris muttered under her breath.

"Good luck," Gwen said, giving her a sympathetic look, and just like yesterday, and all the times before it, she felt glad that Iris would be spending another night in her home. That even now, with Iris looking like she'd just stepped off the pages of one of those magazines she used to devour, Gwen could still offer her something.

IRIS

IRIS'S MOTHER USED to say that so long as they had a roof over their heads, everything would be fine. Iris had never agreed with that theory.

The house had been falling apart when Lois inherited it, at age twenty-six, when her mother died right after she'd gotten pregnant with Iris's brother, Steve. Steve was named after his father, a man neither Iris nor Steve had ever met. Whom Iris was named after, she'd never know. A flower, she liked to think. Something beautiful in the world.

"Don't go putting on airs," Lois used to warn when Iris announced this theory. But even though she'd never spoken it, she liked to think, and even believe, that somehow she was special, different, and maybe even better than the card she had been dealt.

And course, she was pretty. There was no denying that. People told her so all the time, for as long as she could remember. Even when she was a baby, people would comment on Iris's big green eyes, her small nose, and her wide smile, prompting

Lois to enroll her in some baby beauty pageants when she still had the time, but then the roof started leaking and she had to take on a second job, and that was the end of that. By the time she was a teenager, Iris noticed the way the guys looked at her, the way the attention turned from mean jabs about her home life to comments on her appearance, revering her from the distance she had always kept, if not always by choice.

But looks weren't everything. After all, Gwen had two parents who lived under the same roof. She knew her father's name. He called her Princess and was her go-to guy. Sure, her mother drove her crazy, but she also made dinner every night and bought Gwen a four-piece bedding set from Marshall Field's. Gwen's room was lavender, and she hated it, but Iris's room was no color at all. She supposed it had been white once, but the walls had grown discolored over time, scratched from furniture being moved, and she slept on the same twin mattress her mother had slept on as a girl before moving into the master bedroom, where Iris's grandparents had once slept. Steve was in the room off the kitchen downstairs, which suited him fine. He came and went as he pleased, and with their five-year age gap, they'd never been close. Gwen had curtains hanging from her two big windows. With ruffles. Iris had plastic blinds that were bent from the midpoint down. Not much had changed, Iris thought, as she stared up at 15 Sycamore Lane. Even the porch swing was still there, the one she and Gwen used to sit on as kids when Gwen came over and Lois was busy making her calls and needed the house to herself.

Iris hated having Gwen over, but Gwen loved coming, said it was more fun than being home. There were no rules at Iris's house. No order either. Iris was stealing her mother's cigarettes when she was twelve, helping herself to a splash of whatever was left in a bottle by thirteen, and tiptoeing over the mess since before she could walk. She longed for a formal meal like the ones Gwen's mother served. From her estimation, they might have even used real silver.

Not that Lois didn't have her share of treasures. Lois, after all, was a bit of a hoarder. It had developed slowly, over time, with the magazines and the clothes from her parents that she couldn't part with, the toys from her childhood, and the things she wouldn't replace, like the pillows and blankets and towels that were threadbare. She'd never met a yard sale she didn't stop for, and she loaded up the trunk, her smile radiant as she blew smoke rings at the dashboard. "Did you see those records?" she'd ask Steve and Iris excitedly.

But those records, like the old shoes and hats and dishes and salt shakers, just became dust collectors, stuffed into a closet or corner, things that Iris had come to resent when they had no money left to pay the gas bill.

Lois wore her favorite Mickey Mouse sweatshirt, which was now faded and frayed, when she answered the door. Half her hair was in a clip on the top of her head. She looked more tired than she had yesterday, and maybe a little drunk.

"Hey, Ma." Iris held up the bottle of wine.

"Sauvignon blanc!" Lois peered at the label, pronouncing it in an overly American accent that made Iris uncomfortable. "My, aren't we fancy! But then, you're probably used to it, living the high life with that fancy-pants husband of yours!"

Iris gritted her teeth. *Fancy* was a word that Lois used as an insult, to judge her choices, her way of life. It made her sound frivolous and shallow and silly.

She rose to her husband's defense, because she had chosen him and their life.

And without him…she was just Iris. Iris of the Friday meetings in the church basement. Iris of Westlake, in the house that was falling apart.

"Julian works hard, Ma. He's good at what he does." Her stomach felt queasy, knowing just how good he was and how bad it would feel to be on the opposing side.

She eyed the bottle of wine. If she knew her mother, she wouldn't wait until five to open it.

Lois said nothing as she carried the wine into the kitchen. Iris followed, her eyes skirting over the front hall and adjacent living room. Same sofa. New television. Same crocheted afghan Iris used to hide under. She hoped the thing got washed occasionally. The entire house smelled like cigarettes. She wished she could crack a window, but the snow had started to fall and the wind was fierce. "I just think it's strange that in all this time I haven't met him," Lois remarked.

And she never would.

"You know he is very busy." Iris unraveled her scarf, wondering where to set it. The kitchen table was covered in newspapers. The counters were covered with juice containers, cereal boxes, a loaf of bread, dirty dishes from today and yesterday and maybe even the day before. Milk curdled in a bowl. Orange peels littered the surface like confetti.

Iris twisted the bands on her left ring finger with the pad of her thumb. It rooted her. Calmed her. But not for long.

As much as Lois complained that she hadn't met Julian, she wouldn't like him. She'd find him fancy, to use her words. And Julian…

Iris closed her eyes. Julian could never, ever see this. Julian might not have come from big money, but his dad was a family doctor, and his mother oversaw the receptionist desk up until their retirement. They were respected in their community. They supported his education. Their house was clean. It wasn't the same at all.

"How's Wayne?" she asked, eager to get off the topic of her husband.

"Didn't work out." Lois pulled a crushed pack of cigarettes from her pocket and tapped one out. She waited until it was lit before saying, "You know how he said he was visiting his sister in Madison? Turns out it was his wife. Heard him whispering on the phone to her last night."

"I'm sorry," Iris said. She wondered now if Lois would ask her to stay here, and the thought of it depressed her. And when she thought of Gwen's lovely house, with its lavender-scented soaps and guest towels, she realized she didn't want to leave it.

"Don't be. He was bad for business anyway." Lois uncorked the wine bottle. Filled a mug to the brim and took a long slurp. "Sweet. But not bad."

Iris silently regretted not buying a case of the chardonnay instead, but she'd hoped by resisting she might be able to pace herself.

"How's Steve?" Last she knew, her brother was working at a gas station in Minnesota and ran a snow plowing business on the side.

"Don't talk to him much," Lois admitted. "You know that Misty just had another one."

Another one? Iris had lost count of how many children her brother had fathered. There was the girl in Madison, who had a son that Steve had never known. And then there were the two with his first wife, and the three with his second, who stopped speaking to him after he cheated on her with the babysitter, who was fresh out of college at the time. But now she was on baby number four with him, so maybe it was meant to be.

"That's like…a dozen children," she whispered to herself.

Lois pulled out a juice glass and filled it with the wine for her. Iris felt a flicker of guilt when she took it, not because of Julian, but because of Nick, who believed in her, believed in all of them. Yesterday she had slipped, but the occasion called for it. Tomorrow she should be at the meeting. What would they all say when she didn't show up? Would they assume the worse? Or think she was just on vacation?

A vacation. That was one way of looking at it. A vacation from her life. A life she had yearned for. A life she had achieved.

A life that was turning out to be nothing like it was supposed to be at all.

"One of my regulars usually calls around this time of day, but feel free to make yourself at home," Lois said as she picked up the phone and tapped her cigarette ashes onto a plate. "Won't take too long. This one's easy."

Iris wasn't sure what her mother meant by that, and she wasn't sure she wanted to know, either. She took the glass and wandered through the room to the stairs, wondering what had become of her childhood bedroom. She knew that Gwen's mother had turned hers into an exercise room within weeks of her leaving for college. "And then she complains that I never visit enough!" Gwen had complained over the phone back when they were still having nightly calls. "I think she did it to punish me."

But Iris's room was unchanged, exactly as it had been when she'd left after high school. She was amazed at how small it felt. The bed was against the window. No headboard or footboard. Just a metal frame. The quilt was threadbare and faded, but neat, by Lois's standards, implying that it hadn't been touched since Iris made the bed the last morning she woke up here, her bags for New York already packed, a one-way ticket resting on the chest of drawers, next to her jewelry box. The jewelry box was still there, a small, chipped thing with a ballerina inside that turned when she opened the lid. It had stopped playing music so long ago she couldn't recall the sound. It had been a flea market find, something Lois had snagged and wrapped up for Christmas, even though Iris had been with her when she bought it.

She smiled now, thinking of Lois giving her a warning look and saying, "Now, no peeking!"

She'd done the best she could. Raised two kids on her own and scrounged for every penny she earned. She was lonely. Life was hard. Iris had always known that.

And it was precisely the reason why she'd vowed to be different.

She pulled open a drawer. The knob was loose and it fell off into her hand. She set it on the dresser, feeling bad, like she'd damaged someone's property—even though it was hers, it felt like it belonged to someone else. Another little girl, with buck teeth and not a hope in the world.

Well, she'd showed them.

She looked up into the mirror, desperately in need of a cleaning, and stared into her reflection. She looked away. Quickly. She took a sip of her drink.

Most of her belongings had been put into boxes in the basement before she'd first gone to New York. There were no more mementos here, no more personal items that held any meaning. All her photos were in a box in the apartment, tucked away at the back of the closet, where Julian wouldn't see them.

She walked over to the small bedside table, where a single frame sat next to the lamp. She picked it up, frowning at what she saw. It was a picture of her and her mother. Steve must have taken it. They were at the lakefront beach, and Iris was building a sandcastle. Her mother was younger, thinner, her face half-hidden behind sunglasses, but her smile was nearly as wide as Iris's, whose eyes seemed to shine. If Iris didn't know any better, she would say she looked...happy.

"That's a nice one, isn't it?" her mother said from the doorway now.

Iris looked up. "I don't remember seeing this before."

"I found it when I was going through some stuff in the basement," Lois said. "Thought this was a nice place for it, if you ever came back."

Iris nodded and set it back in her place. "Well. Is there anything you wanted to do? Anything I can...help with?" She would clean, she decided. She wanted to clean. She wanted to do something. It would keep her mind busy. It would pass the time.

"The show's on," Lois said, referring to their soap. "You still watch?"

"Of course!" Iris was surprised her mother would even ask.

"Huh. Something in common then," Lois said and turned toward the stairs.

Iris stayed in her room a moment longer, fighting back the heaviness that had landed in her chest. The memories of a girl who used to sleep here. A reminder of the girl she used to be.

She downed the rest of her wine and went to the kitchen for a refill. When she got there her mother was on the phone, making soothing sounds to a person on the other end. She motioned to Iris to go to the other room, mouthed that she would meet her there before she gave a sudden peal of laughter. A girlish peal. A suggestive peal.

Jesus Christ.

Iris eyed a bottle of whiskey on the counter, ignored the warnings her mother had heeded over time (wine before liquor...), and poured a few inches into her juice glass. Drank it back. Felt it burn.

But it didn't do the job. She was still here, in this kitchen. Her mother was still giggling. Julian was still shagging her so-called friend.

She added another splash, telling herself that she shouldn't feel bad, that really, she deserved it. She wasn't driving. She'd take an Uber. And she'd call for one right after the show. She knew she had told Gwen that she wouldn't be there for dinner, and she wouldn't. She'd go into town, walk around. Think.

Or hit a bar, she thought. She looked over at her mother, then around the dirty, cluttered kitchen.

She walked over to the sink and poured the contents of her glass down the drain.

Without Julian, she had nothing. Nothing but that sad room upstairs. Nothing but this life she had left behind. Drinking wouldn't help her marriage. If anything, it was only helping to ruin it.

She walked back into the living room, feeling bored and restless. Delilah may have updated her blog by now. Or Stephanie might have posted something to one of her social media accounts.

She reached for her phone and then stopped herself. And so what if either of them did? It wouldn't change anything. She knew the truth. All of it. Whereas they only knew what she shared.

Iris's gaze drifted to her mother's curio cabinet, to a little figure of a small girl holding a puppy—one of her favorites as a child, because the girl seemed so happy, and the puppy had a big pink bow around its neck that made her think it had been a gift of some sort, and she used to imagine what it would be like to receive any gift that had a big bow attached, especially something as sweet as a puppy. It had a wind-up device on the bottom that she used to play, always slightly fearful that one day the motor would stop and the music would be lost forever like her jewelry box had. Her fingers went to the metal knob now, but she thought twice. She glanced over her shoulder. Lois was in the kitchen, making strange groaning noises. Besides, this house was full of tchotchkes. She wouldn't notice if one went missing.

Iris opened the cabinet door and stuffed the figurine into her coat pocket.

She already felt better.

13

GWEN

BY FRIDAY THERE was no dodging the meeting with the guidance counselor. Gwen finished packing lunches and watched from the front window as the kids walked to the bus stop at the corner, where Taffy and Clementine and some of the neighbors were already gathered, Susan holding court like she always did, while the other mothers gathered around her, laughing at whatever witty comment she made. Even at this hour, she was dressed in her athletic leisurewear and fur-trimmed parka, her blond hair bouncy, her energy high. When it rained, she held a brightly colored umbrella. Her mascara never ran. She never looked tired or puffy. She never looked like she had just had an argument with her husband over who took out the trash that week and who loaded the dishwasher. She certainly never bothered to bribe her kids into behaving. Instead, she smiled almost indulgently at them as if they were little angels, every single minute of the day, even though they were not.

Gwen turned from the window with a sigh. The house was quiet. The dog was snoring from his bed near the mudroom. The kitchen was clean. The coffee was brewed.

She hadn't seen Iris since she'd dropped her off at her mother's house yesterday, but when she'd taken Bailey for a walk last night she'd seen the light was on in the window above the garage. Michael had gone to the gym to burn off stress, saying he'd grab something to eat while he was out, and Gwen had tried not to second-guess that as she doled out leftovers to the kids and skimmed her emails while she'd washed and folded three loads of laundry.

The meeting with the guidance counselor was this morning. She had confirmed it. But she hadn't confirmed who would be attending.

Michael was upstairs in the bedroom, loading his laptop into an old backpack. "I can't think straight here with all the noise."

"The kids are gone for the next seven hours," Gwen pointed out.

"Yes, but we have a houseguest," Michael said, almost glaring at her.

"Are you saying this is my fault?" Gwen accused. "She's my oldest friend."

He lifted a single eyebrow and walked to the closet. Gwen followed him. "What's that look supposed to mean?"

Michael sighed, saying nothing as he pulled a fleece jacket off a hanger. Finally, he turned to her. "Just be careful. I remember how hurt you were when she didn't invite you to her wedding, and then again when she didn't reach out about your father."

"Well, I never told her about my father," Gwen said, but that was only partly true. Iris knew why Gwen had moved back to Westlake. She knew he was sick. "We'd lost contact by then."

"Just don't...have expectations."

Gwen knew he was right, but it still stung. What she wanted and what was reality were two very different things sometimes.

"I don't have any expectations this time. I've grown up and moved on." Well, sort of. "I just..." She couldn't explain it, at least not to Michael, not in a way he would understand. Michael was the type of guy who didn't need friends. Oh, he got along with his coworkers, was happy to make small talk at school events, but a true friend, a real confidant, someone he could bare his soul to? Michael didn't have that.

But then, Gwen supposed she didn't either.

"It's nice to have a little fun, that's all. Iris and I have history."

Michael said nothing as he grabbed his bag and walked out the door. It wasn't until she heard the door close below that she cursed to herself. She had meant to come up here and ask him if he would reconsider attending the school meeting, or at least come with her.

But then she remembered that Joe Cassidy might be there, and she decided it was for the best that she went alone.

Quickly she showered and dressed in carefully chosen control-top leggings and a sweater that only she knew was a maternity size, even though the tags had long since been snipped. With a swell of apprehension, she applied her makeup from her December Forevermore Beauty stash, finishing things with the Ravishing Rose lipstick that at least hadn't cost her anything other than her soul. She pushed in close to the mirror, inspecting her tooth. She still hadn't made it to the dentist, but it was too subtle at this point for anyone to notice, unless they got really close. Well, other than her mother.

Thinking of her mother, she checked her texts. A few more had come in since Gwen had let her know yesterday that she was out with Iris and therefore unable to meet at the mall—as if she had time for that anyway, but at least this time she had an excuse that Eileen would accept.

Now her mother wanted details on how Iris looked, how long she was staying, if Eileen would get a chance to see her, what Iris thought of her house, and of course she couldn't resist mentioning that she hoped Gwen had cleaned her toilets.

When she came downstairs, Iris was leaning against the kitchen counter, eating an apple, her hair and makeup looking as if she'd just stepped out of a salon.

"So, what's the plan for the day?" There was a sense of expectation about her, as if she couldn't wait for the day to start.

Gwen hated to break it to her that things were rather ordinary in the Riley household. You had your laundry; you had your dinner prep. You had walks with the dogs and the bills that needed to be paid and the beds that needed to be made and then the kids and their activities. And then it all started over again.

Gwen wondered how Iris usually spent her Fridays. Probably getting spa treatments and drinking mimosas. She vowed to have just one day like that if she could earn that trip to the Forevermore Beauty annual convention.

"I have a meeting at the school," she said, pouring another mug of coffee.

"At our old school?" Iris's interest was piqued. Gwen felt uneasy. "I can keep you company if you want."

Gwen tensed. "Oh...I might be a while." There was absolutely no way Iris would be coming with her to a meeting with the guidance counselor.

The old Iris might have laughed, thought it was funny, actually, that Goody Two-Shoes Gwen had a delinquent for a daughter. But thinking back on her conversation with Michael, Gwen forced herself to remember that old Iris was gone. And she'd been gone for a long time.

Iris shrugged. "I'll stay in the car. It will get me out of the house. Besides, I have nothing else to do."

Nothing else to do. And really, did Gwen need her hanging around here, unsupervised? What if she opened one of the junk drawers (because there were several), or went into Gwen's closet and saw the size on her discount clothing? Once, Gwen wouldn't have cared what Iris saw or knew, but that was back when Iris was still Iris Winarski, not Iris Drake.

Besides, Iris had nothing else to do.

Gwen thought about that statement all the way to the coat closet, where she put on her coat and scarf and slipped into her best boots. Not the ones she wore to walk Bailey around the block while she was still in her flannels. No, the date night kind. The "in case I run into Joe Cassidy" kind. She pulled her gloves from the shelf and, looking at her manicure, thought again.

Her wedding band seemed to blink back at her, the tiny diamond of her engagement ring catching the light, as if to mock her, and say it was onto her, and really, who did she think she was? She was a married mother of three. And Joe knew it. But she was an unhappily married mother of three. And she just hadn't been able to admit that until now.

Nothing else to do. Imagine that! Gwen had a huge list of things to do, and she'd already achieved a few for the day, including making sure lunches were packed and homework was, indeed, finished, that Declan remembered the permission slip for his field trip next week and that Bea had a special object for show and tell (one that hadn't come in a Happy Meal box), and that Norah wasn't wearing a skirt that went against dress code, and yes, Gwen did stare at her teenager's figure and wonder if she had ever looked that good, and the answer, she knew, as she loaded the dishwasher after breakfast, was that she hadn't. Norah favored Michael's physique. Long and lanky. Whereas Gwen...Eileen still liked to joke how "Thunder Thighs" had been her nickname for Gwen when she was young.

Nothing else to do. She thought about that as she pulled the car out of the garage, Iris fumbling with the radio stations without even asking for permission, which might have felt all nice and comfortable, like old times, if it wasn't for the fact that all Gwen could think about was that Iris had nothing else to do and that she had entirely too much to do! She still had to buy Michael a card for their wedding anniversary, and then there was the matter of the conference today. And she still hadn't recruited a single person to her team at Forevermore Beauty, much less sold a single tube of lipstick. She'd have to fudge the numbers again. She'd be in the red until she sold everything she claimed to have sold and then some. And how was she supposed to sell anything when she was busy entertaining a houseguest who still hadn't said when she planned on leaving!

She glanced at Iris. A savvier woman might try to hit her up for a few sales, but Gwen had never been wired that way. Iris—Iris was wired that way.

It was why Iris had sailed straight to the top, and now she had nothing to do!

"I don't know how long this will take," Gwen said when she finally reached Westlake Community School and pulled, rather abruptly, into a spot at the back of the lot.

"I'll leave the motor running so you don't get cold."

Iris just smiled good-naturedly and said, "No rush!" She cranked up the radio a notch and leaned back against the seat, pulling out her phone, like a teenage girl. Like Norah, Gwen realized.

No rush. Another concept that Gwen couldn't wrap her head around. When wasn't she rushing around? When wasn't she busy picking up one mess only to be told about another? There were times in her marriage that she would legitimately lose her shit when the dog would be barking to go out and Norah would be having a tantrum over a lost toy and Declan would need his diaper changed, because he wasn't potty trained until he was four, and yes, she did hold herself responsible, and Bea would be turning purple in her carrier on the counter, desperate for a bottle, her screams so violent that Bailey would only bark louder, and then Gwen felt like she would erupt, and then things did erupt, because then Bailey would have an accident on the floor, and then Norah would slip in it, and then she would need a bath, and then Declan would need a bath, and then Gwen would oversee it all while feeding Bea her bottle, tears streaming down her face.

Everything in her life was a rush. The rush to school. The rush after school. How did women like Susan Sharp manage to look so good before eight in the morning, and how in the hell did they manage to spend school hours pampering themselves?

She still needed to make that appointment for her tooth, damn it.

With a heavy tread, Gwen moved toward the doors of the school, feeling like she was just here yesterday, when at the same time that visit felt like half a lifetime ago, before Iris, before this spontaneous visit. Maybe her life wasn't as routine as she thought. Maybe that was a good thing.

She pressed the button to be allowed inside. She smiled her brave smile, only this time her nerves were less about Norah and more about seeing Joe Cassidy again.

She signed in, again confirming the room number for the guidance counselor, and walked through the halls, her eyes scanning for the music room, for a hint of broad shoulders and nut-brown hair and dark eyes that crinkled at the corners. By the time she made it to room 314, she had to admit defeat or risk being late for her appointment while she circled the building, pretending to be lost. It had—sadly—crossed her mind.

The guidance counselor was a middle-aged woman with a stiff handshake and weary eyes. Gwen suppressed a sigh as she took a seat opposite the desk. Another joy of parenting. Another requirement of the job. She'd foolishly thought when she grew up and got married that she would call the shots, that she wouldn't have to be under anyone's control anymore, but so far nothing had changed. She still felt powerless. She still had to show up, do things she didn't want to do, like sit in this chair and be reprimanded.

"Thank you for seeing me today," the woman said. She shuffled papers around on her desk as if Norah were perhaps just one of a handful of problem children around here and not forefront on her mind. Gwen took comfort in that. Norah had always been a good kid. She was just having a rough transition with high school. Surely this couldn't be all that abnormal?

She decided to beat Ms. Manning to the punch. Taking a deep breath, she leaned forward. "I want to assure you that my husband and I are fully aware of Norah's troubles in school. We've pulled her off the cheerleading team until she gets her grades under control. Academics are very important to us."

Ms. Manning's brow furrowed. "That's good to hear, Mrs. Riley, but the reason I asked you to meet with me wasn't to discuss Norah."

Gwen stared at the woman, trying to process what she could be saying. If she wasn't here to discuss Norah, then who was she here to discuss?

Oh, God, was *she* in trouble? It was possible. More than once, when she went to pick the kids up, she pushed a few miles over the speed limit in the school zone to get there in time, lest Declan be late for piano and she not have time to do an adequate bun for Bea's ballet class. And then there was that time where she caved and let the kids take six pieces of Halloween candy each in their lunch. Was it finally coming back to haunt her? Had they been keeping tabs? Was she a...problem mom?

"I'd actually like to discuss Beatrice."

"Bea?" Gwen almost burst out laughing. What could they possibly have to discuss about Bea? Suddenly, a horrible thought took hold, and she felt like her entire chest was seizing up. "She's not being bullied, is she? Because we live across from the Sharp family, and we didn't have a good experience at a recent playdate."

Her eyes narrowed at the memory.

"I can assure you that Bea is not being bullied," Ms. Manning said. She set the papers down and folded her hands on the desk. There was a pause. A long one. Gwen shifted in her chair. "I'm not sure if you're aware, but we had an incident with Bea last week."

Gwen frowned. Her heart felt like it was going to beat right out of her chest. "An incident?"

"Bea tried to smuggle a chapter book from the classroom," Ms. Manning said.

"Smuggle?" Gwen felt her jaw slacken. A nervous laugh escaped. "You make her sound like some sort of...of...criminal." It couldn't be. They had the wrong child.

"Okay, then. Bea tried to *steal* a book from her classroom," Ms. Manning said flatly. "Mrs. Williams saw her put it in her backpack and questioned her about it."

"Well, now, I am sure she just wanted to borrow it." Gwen's cheeks burned. She was in a sweat. She wanted to take off her coat but she also wanted to leave. Like, now.

"There is a policy that the only books that are to be removed from the premises are library books. The children are fully aware of this. It seems that Bea was quite upset to be caught."

"Oh my!" Gwen realized that her entire body was shaking. She stared at the guidance counselor, waiting for her punishment. There was no doubt she was being judged.

"Mrs. Williams considered calling you herself, but for matters like this, it's best if I step in."

"Of course," Gwen muttered, wondering just what was this woman getting at? Bea was seven. She was a good girl, or at least, the best of her lot.

Up until today, she had always thought that Bea was sort of perfect.

"Is there...trouble at home?" Ms. Manning asked with a compassionate head tilt.

Gwen stiffened, feeling her cheeks flush with heat. "Of course not!"

"Hopefully, Bea learned from the lesson. She is aware that we were bringing you in to discuss this."

Gwen couldn't control her eyes from popping at that. Bea knew that this meeting was about her and she never said a word? Earlier this week, Gwen was harping at Norah about it while they were sitting down to dinner, and Bea just sipped her milk and then happily changed the subject, declaring their dinner to be "the best dinner ever!" even though it was just spaghetti with jarred sauce.

Gwen narrowed her eyes. "My husband and I will talk with her tonight. Obviously, this is very disturbing. It's not like Bea."

"We've decided to let her go with a warning this time, but as you can understand, stealing is not tolerated at Westlake."

"Of course not," Gwen said, standing up. Her chair made a grating sound against the floor. She needed to get out of here, cool her head, figure out what to say and what to do. Bea! She just couldn't believe it. "Well, thank you."

Even as she said it, she wondered, why was she thanking this woman? This woman had summoned her to the school, made Bea out to be some sort of convict, and now Gwen was trying to...to...

To please her. Because that's what she did. Because it kept the peace, it minimized the conflict, and somehow, it made her feel better.

Even though it also made her feel worse.

She blindly shook the woman's hand, even managed a smile, signaling that she was a responsible adult, that she could handle this, but inside she was still fifteen and had no clue what she was doing. She was thirty-nine and her kid was in trouble, and by default, that meant she was in trouble.

She needed to get out of this building. She rounded a bend, all hopes of running into Joe gone. He probably knew. Probably looked at her with pity. The mom with two bad apples. She'd have to pin her hopes on Declan now.

She made another turn, eager to get through the doors, outside, and then she heard the laugh. She knew that laugh. It was Iris's laugh—so distinct that you had to both love it and hate it at the same time. It was more of a peal. It was the kind of laugh that got attention. Especially from men.

No, she thought. She wouldn't.

She slowed her pace, her heart picking up speed again as she looked past a group of kindergartners who were filing out of the art studio. There, up ahead, at the end of the hall, was Iris.

And Joe.

"Gwen!" Iris waved over to her, her smile wide, her eyes positively electric. She looked beautiful, radiant, happy, and young. No responsibilities to give her a rough, haggard look. No frown lines. Nothing to frown over! "Look who I found!"

Joe grinned like a schoolboy, the very same grin that Gwen used to picture every night as she lay in her frilly childhood bedroom, the same grin that used to make her swoon, even if the grin wasn't meant for her. Of course Joe would be grinning now. Or course he would remember Iris. Everyone remembered Iris. Word was that Joe had a crush on Iris in high school, but back then she wasn't interested in "local boys," she'd told Gwen.

Even back then, this distinction had separated them. Iris had bigger goals. Gwen had been content with the ordinary.

Joe gave Gwen a friendly wave and turned back to Iris, and all at once it didn't matter that Gwen was wearing her date night boots or her fake diamond earrings or that she had a fresh manicure on her fingernails. She was the short, frumpy friend. She could never rival someone as beautiful as Iris. Not then. Not now.

"Hi, Joe," she said as she came to join the group. She hated the way her insides betrayed her, turning to gel. She knew she was staring into his eyes a little longer than she should. She pulled away, looking at Iris in confusion. "I thought you were waiting in the car?"

She glanced at Joe, wondering if he had divulged her reason for being here, that the meeting was with the guidance counselor. She'd say it was about an honors class, she decided quickly. Or college prep.

But then she saw the way Joe was looking at Iris, the way the smile carried all the way up to his eyes, and she realized that they probably hadn't mentioned her at all.

"Had to use the facilities," Iris said with a guilty smile. "And then I got carried away down memory lane," she added blithely.

"I missed seeing you at our twentieth last spring," Joe said, and Gwen couldn't help but feel the sting.

She hadn't gone to the reunion either but clearly hadn't been missed.

"Oh." Iris wrinkled her nose. "I don't get back much."

"Come back more often!" Joe said with that grin. "Right, Gwen?" Oh, God, and now he was smiling at her, and his eyes, they seemed to hold her, with an intensity that Michael rarely gave her anymore, as if he were genuinely interested in what she had to say, as if he were waiting for her to say it.

That was the thing about Joe, he was friendly to all, even the not-so-cool kids, and she had fallen into that bucket. Her claim to fame was Iris, but Iris didn't care about fitting in at Westlake. Not then, and not now, it would seem. That attitude was what set her apart—she was untouchable. She'd made sure of that over time.

"Maybe I will," Iris surprised her by saying.

Gwen felt her eyebrows pull together as she glared at Iris. She couldn't be serious. She hadn't come back to town in over twenty years! Something didn't make any sense here.

And neither, she thought, was the way that Iris was looking at Joe. It was one thing for Gwen to still get sucked up by Joe's grin—oh, that grin. But that's because she was restless and bored and unhappy.

And Iris was… Well, she was none of that. Right?

Gwen frowned. "We should get going," she said, taking Iris by the arm.

Iris's brow knit. "Do we have somewhere to be?"

Gwen felt like she did the time that she was explaining to Miss Bambi that they were late for class because they got behind an eighty-year-old man going fifteen miles an hour down Main Street and Bea corrected her by saying, "No, we didn't,

Mommy. We were late because you rear-ended the mailman and the police had to come and give you a ticket!"

And who could also forget that when the insurance adjuster had visited two days later, Susan had sat in her car in the driveway, watching the entire scene from her rearview mirror.

She sighed. From experience, she knew better than to have an argument in front of the person she was politely deceiving.

"It was great seeing you again, Joe," she said warmly.

"I'll see you at the winter concert next week? I hear Declan will be performing a piece." His expression was wide and interested, and Gwen felt her heart soar, despite the anxiety of seeing another of Declan's performances. Next week. The winter concert. She had nearly forgotten. Unlike the Music Academy's concert, Declan would shine in this setting. He'd been talking about it all break, practicing for his piece, and she had said three Hail Marys every night that he would have a better experience this time.

"I hope you'll come?" he said to Iris, and Gwen felt her smile fall. Iris looked at Gwen with an excited smile. "That sounds like fun!"

Fun? There was nothing about any of this that was fun anymore.

Fun. That was what Gwen had thought her life would be when she married Michael. It was also, she thought, her chance to get away from the clutches of her mother. Being a single girl in the city just gave Eileen more reason to hover. More reason to check in. She had to know every detail of Gwen's life: where she was applying to jobs, whom she was having dinner with, what she was eating for dinner, and, of course, whom she was dating. When there were no dates, Eileen made suggestions, passive-aggressively, about diet and behavior and fashion choices. She suggested that Gwen move back to Westlake (as if!) because people who had stayed didn't seem to have any of these troubles finding boyfriends. Gwen couldn't handle the big city, was the message. Gwen wasn't able to succeed on her own.

So on a warm summer morning when Michael strolled into the office lobby where she'd been working as a receptionist since graduating from college, pitching sales for a new antidepressant drug, Gwen had listened. She smiled and nodded because it had been too long since a handsome man of the appropriate age bracket had come through the doors of her office, and because she wasn't willing to let him go just yet. She listed politely until it seemed impolite to continue. Downright mean, really. And so, with a grimace, she interrupted him. "The psychiatrist's office is actually across the hall. We're a marketing firm."

She didn't know what kind of reaction to expect, but Michael just cocked an eyebrow and said, "And you weren't planning to tell me?"

"I just did," she pointed out.

"But why'd you let me go on and on?"

Gwen drew a big breath. She wished she could hurry up and call Iris, ask her for some advice, but Iris was in New York, at her own job—a bigger, better job, not that Gwen minded. What she minded was that Iris wasn't right here, guiding her through these social interactions as she'd done back in high school. Instead, she'd had to ask herself, *What would Iris do?*

"I liked hearing what you had to say," she said.

He frowned. "You're interested in antidepressants?"

"No." She laughed. She felt her cheeks grow warm as she glanced down at her desk. A bleak future seemed to stare back at her. "I liked the way you described it. I liked your voice."

He grinned, and she grinned back. The next night they had dinner. Six months later they were married.

To this day, whenever Gwen thought of her wedding day, she didn't think of the first dance, or the weight of the bouquet in her hands, or the look in Michael's eye as she reached the end of the aisle. She didn't think of the way her father had lifted her veil and kissed her cheek. She didn't think of her first married kiss with Michael, in front of all their friends and family, something she had dreaded, actually, something that made her feel self-conscious.

Whenever she thought of her wedding day she thought of her mother. She remembered being in the hotel room with her parents and Iris, who had flown to Chicago to be her maid of honor. The bouquets and boutonnieres had just been delivered. She was in her gown—chosen by her mother but still somehow not one that Eileen was fully satisfied by.

The flowers looked exactly as she'd planned them, with Eileen's suggestions, of course, and she and Iris practiced holding them, surprised at their weight, Gwen fighting the flurry of nerves that rippled through her stomach every time she glanced at the clock. People were probably next door at the church now, taking their seats. Maybe the piano player had even started the music. People were waiting. Michael was waiting. This was it. The day she had been waiting for. The day when her life— her own life—could finally begin.

She was aware of a rustling, an argument, a tsk from her mother across the room. It was a sound she was all too familiar with. Tension immediately flared, replacing the bubbling nerves that had been there previously. In its place was dread. The usual, prickly place where she and her father lived, tiptoeing around Eileen's moods, bracing themselves for what came next.

Her mother's flower pin, it seemed, was a problem. Eileen snapped, saying something to Gwen's father she didn't quite catch. As usual, her father tried to smooth things over rather than argue.

"Forget it. Just forget it!" her mother huffed.

The wedding planner moved forward, gingerly, and pushed the pin around until it seemed to hold in place. "There. Is that better?" Eileen gave a pouty sniff in response.

Gwen looked at Iris, who gave her a wink. The most she could offer in return was a weak smile. All that excitement, all that joy and hope seemed to have vanished. Gwen's father murmured something to placate Eileen, to smooth things over, to push it under the rug. Eileen was looking at herself in the full-length mirror now, the mirror that had been set up for Gwen to use to see her dress from every angle.

"Forget it!" she said again, and with that, she stormed out of the room.

The next time Gwen saw her mother, she was a married woman. There had been no words of advice, no shared memories or sentimental tears before Gwen walked down the aisle to join a new family. No hug, no hand squeezes.

The only person in that hotel room who had told her she looked beautiful was Iris.

Gwen vowed to be different with her children. Vowed to be open and close and to communicate. To praise them. To openly love them.

She blinked back tears as she walked up the stairs to Bea's room that evening and knocked on the door, Michael at her heels—he'd been summoned home, of course. She knew the exact speech she would give to Bea on her wedding day. She knew what she would say when she held her hands in the moments before the procession and told her how beautiful she was. But she didn't know what to say right now.

"It's not *that* big of a deal," Gwen whispered to Michael. "A book? We can't punish her for wanting to read!"

"She tried to smuggle it in her backpack," he reminded her. His mouth was a firm line. Usually, Michael was Good Cop. It seemed that today their roles had reversed.

He knocked on the door and then turned the handle without waiting to be granted entry. Unlike Norah's room, Bea's was unlocked. Bea probably didn't even know her door could lock. Really, to think of Bea having a devious mind? It didn't seem possible. She was sitting at the play table in her room, having a tea party with her stuffed animals. Catching Michael's expression, the little space between her eyebrows pulled together.

"Bea, Daddy and I have something to ask you," Gwen said gently. She watched as Bea set her plastic teacup on its saucer and looked up with wide eyes.

"Not ask. Tell." Michael flashed her a stern look. His jaw was tight.

Gwen heaved a sigh. The evidence was all there. But there must be a reasonable explanation. "Your teacher said that you tried to take a book from the classroom last week."

Bea's cheeks paled. "I just wanted to read it!"

"I understand," Gwen said, avoiding the heat of Michael's stare. "But you know you can't take anything from the classroom."

"I'm sorry," Bea said, and then promptly burst into tears.

Gwen stepped forward, but Michael grabbed her arm. "Don't you dare," he hissed. To Bea, he said, "Bea, you are getting off with a warning this time, but stealing is wrong. It won't be tolerated. The school won't tolerate it, and neither will we."

Bea barely moved. She didn't blink. She had never been in trouble until now.

A first offense! Gwen gave her a little smile to show that it was all going to be okay, that she was still loved, that she didn't need to live in fear of her parents, but Michael just said, "Don't."

"Bea, do you promise never to do that again?" Gwen asked, nodding her head until Bea did the same.

"I'll never do that again," Bea said.

"Good," Michael said and turned from the room. Gwen gave her a little smile on the way, because she knew how this felt, all too well.

"I think that went well," Gwen said, relieved.

"Because I had to do all the work!" Michael barked.

"All the work?" Gwen hated arguing in front of the kids, but she was worked up as it was, and now this? She checked that Bea's door was shut. Norah's music could be heard through the walls. Declan was playing the piano downstairs, or trying to. "Last I checked, I was the one packing their lunches, running them all around town, and overseeing their homework. I'm the bad cop, Michael. I didn't choose it, but I am."

"No, you were the good cop," he said quickly.

"Today!" She realized she had cried that out a little too loudly and dropped her voice to a whisper. A harsh one. "For once I didn't want to have to be the parent pushing on my kids. Is that so bad?"

"I could have used a little backup in there," Michael said.

Now something hit Gwen, deep inside, pulling up a hundred memories of disappointing her mother yet again, being told "Just wait until your father comes home!" and then having to sit at the table while both of them went at it, or sometimes, then, just her father, while Eileen sat with a satisfied grin on her face. All her life it is had been her versus her parents. No backup.

She'd had three kids so they wouldn't ever have to feel outnumbered. She wasn't about to start now.

"Bea is seven," she reminded Michael. "She made a mistake."

"She stole."

She chewed on that for a moment. How could they not be certain she planned to return it? "She broke the rule. No books out of the classroom. I am sure it would have been returned."

Michael closed his eyes. His shoulders sank a little. "I hate this," he said.

"I do too," she said. And she did. She hated having to play Bad Cop, ever, and somehow, more and more, that felt like all she did. And it was the one thing she never wanted to do at all.

When Norah was born she imagined all the fun they would have. Ballet lessons and little chubby toddler hands that clung to her fingers, watching recitals with sparkling dresses and going out for ice cream sundaes afterward. She didn't think about the other stuff, the day-to-day stuff, the chaos that came with two children and then three. She hadn't expected so much to be just on her, for Michael to be working. Then not working. Then looking for a job while she worried about the next mortgage payment.

She balled a fist at her side. "How's the job search?"

Michael looked startled as he edged toward their bedroom door. "Fine. Since when do you care?"

"Since I'd like some help with raising our kids, that's when." Gwen was angry, and she realized now that she had been angry for a very long time. "You can't just show up when you want to and then judge my parenting in your absence, Michael, because I'm doing a hell of a lot more than you."

"A hell of a lot? Then you go find a job if you're so great!"

"I'm trying, as you know! I can't exactly get a full-time job with three kids!"

"Other women do it," he said.

"Other families are paying for childcare," she reminded him. "As you were always sure to point out."

"Norah's fourteen," Michael said, and to that, all Gwen could do was raise an eyebrow and push past him. They both knew that Norah wasn't mature enough to babysit, at least on a daily basis.

And whose fault was that? Hers, probably.

She made it to the top of the stairs only, to her horror, to see Iris standing at the base of them, a wineglass in hand,

Declan at her side. His glasses were smudged; she could see that from here. Iris had a strange smile on her face, but her eyes were hesitant. Gwen had managed to hold it together all through dinner (roasted chicken with the works; this house-guest thing was going to be the death of her), and Iris seemed to be entertained with the kids' stories they were eager to share with the newcomer, but now the kids weren't around, and all focus was on her again.

"I was just listening to Declan play," Iris said.

Of course. The music had stopped. But at what point?

"I need to get the kids to bed," Gwen said quickly, hating the edge that crept into her tone. Iris had done nothing wrong; she had simply stumbled into a conversation she never should have overheard. And she had come to a house under the pretense that it was more of a home than it was. That all of Gwen's best intentions had somehow fallen flat.

"No problem. I was going to check on Julian tonight anyway," Iris said, baring those perfectly straight, white teeth.

Gwen nodded, wondering how much she'd heard. It wasn't until she watched Iris disappear into the kitchen and heard the back door open and close that she realized this was the first time Iris had mentioned her husband at all.

14

IRIS

IRIS SAT ON the pull-out bed and stared at her phone, her only connection to her life, her real life, not the one she'd left behind. The only phone call she'd received since her arrival was from Nick. She'd missed it yesterday when she was listening to Declan play the piano, and she still couldn't bring herself to listen to the message. Just knowing he had left a message was stressful enough. She had let him down. She had failed him.

She had slipped.

But really, who wouldn't? Iris wasn't sure how much longer this could go on. She'd spent three nights at Gwen's house. Three nights pretending that everything was fine. That she was just here for a visit. That everything was wonderful.

But then, it was more than three nights, wasn't it? She'd been playing a part much longer than that. Nearly buying into it herself half the time.

It was only eleven in the morning and she'd already had two drinks, and she'd only justified this by telling herself that it was Saturday, and that she was in Wisconsin, and that no one would ever find out. She'd woken at ten. Late, yes, but considering she hadn't fallen asleep until after one, and only with the help of countless refills of the cheap whiskey she'd snagged from her mother's trunk, and only after she had refreshed Delilah's blog and Stephanie's social media accounts over and over until she finally gave up. What did she expect to see? Proof that Stephanie was spending time with her husband? They ran in the same circles; even Stephanie was smarter than that. Still, she supposed she was looking for a hand or an arm or an article of clothing in the background that would cement her suspicion that Julian was using this time to be with her. That their affair was still going on. That she had every right to be as mad as she was. As scared as she was. Because that's what it was. Fear. And Iris was tired of being afraid, promised herself she'd never get herself into a weak position again. That she was strong, scrappy, and couldn't be bullied or laughed at anymore. Couldn't be hurt anymore.

She'd fallen asleep in the clothes she'd worn for dinner. She dreamed about sitting at a table, eating a roast chicken (Gwen was such a domestic goddess!) that Julian carved, and in her dream, Delilah and Kat were younger, sweeter, more like Bea, and they were one big happy family.

When Gwen knocked on her door and suggested a walk, Iris put on her yoga pants and cross-trainers. She'd brushed her teeth three times to mask the smell of booze. Gwen, however, was wearing more or less the same thing she had worn every day since Iris had arrived—black pants, a black sweater, that blue plaid scarf, and suede boots that probably weren't as water-resistant as she'd been promised.

Iris had the uneasy feeling that she had upset Gwen yesterday and, maybe even worse, that she was overstaying her welcome. She had hoped that taking Gwen to the nail salon and supplying the wine that she alone was mostly drinking would make up for the homemade dinners and lodging, but how could coffee and a manicure compete with a homemade apple pie?

"I'm sorry if you heard anything last night," Gwen said as soon as they were on the driveway. She held Bailey's leash tight, and it was clear that the dog was the one taking her for a walk. "Michael and I had a parenting issue to deal with."

"That's so adult of you," Iris marveled, but Gwen just gave a grumpy laugh. "Besides, couples argue. It's part of the joy of marriage, right?"

She glanced at Gwen. She didn't know Michael well, but she'd been at their wedding, and stayed at their apartment after Norah had been born, and back then she'd seen firsthand that her friend was glowing, content. In love.

She released a shaky breath, wishing she hadn't broached the topic. "They never tell you how difficult adulting will be, you know?"

Gwen gave a little snort. "Remember all those grand plans we had? We made it all so idealistic, so attainable."

Iris shrugged. "We were naïve." Still, walking up the bucolic street with its snow-covered lawns and pristine brick and wood-sided homes, each with wreaths on the doors and greenery in their planters, she felt like Gwen was selling herself a little short. "But then, look at this. I think this all fits in with your plan pretty well."

"Minus the Westlake part," Gwen reminded her. She fell silent when they reached a playground at the end of the street. She said nothing as she stopped for Bailey to sniff around a lamppost. "It's just... Do you ever feel like you want to punch something?"

Iris thought about Julian. There were times recently that she had wanted to punch him. But she'd wanted to punch Stephanie more. This was a double standard, and unfair, she knew. The two were equally wrong. But Julian was her husband. A part of her still believed he loved her. Besides, he had a history. None of this should have come entirely as a surprise.

"Something or someone?"

Gwen leveled her with a look. "Someone."

Iris looked down the street at the house that Gwen had pointed out yesterday as belonging to that obnoxious woman from the nail salon. Iris grinned slowly. As it turned out, her time in rehab hadn't all been for nothing. "I know just the thing."

Ten minutes later they were inside Gwen's garage, that salt-stained van parked in the driveway, Michael's car gone while he "ran the kids around." An inflatable Santa wobbled in front of them, plastic bats in hand, the bicycle tire pump put back in place, its job done. Iris had risked looking like a complete alcoholic by suggesting they crack open a bottle of the sauvignon blanc she grabbed from her stash in her guest room. For celebratory reasons. Gwen gave her a funny look but said, "Suit yourself." After all, Iris had bought it.

"I didn't know Declan played tee ball," Iris said as she moved the bat around in her hand. In their conversations over the years, Gwen had always given him more of an artistic slant.

But then she realized with shame that she didn't really know Gwen's children at all.

"This was Norah's," Gwen said sheepishly. She stepped forward and with all her might took a swing at Santa's head.

And missed.

Iris burst out laughing, but Gwen gritted her teeth and took another swing. And damn it if she didn't miss again.

"Call it out!" Iris said, remembering what one of the counselors had instructed Hilda to do at Andover. "It helps, I promise." Hilda had looked positively rabid by the end of her turn, calling out names and stringing together profanity in a way that was nearly poetic if it hadn't been so chilling.

Iris sat down on the steps to the door and picked up her glass of wine. She set it to the side.

"Just call it out. Who you're aiming for. Why you're mad."

Gwen looked uncertain but got in position just the same. She wound up like a golfer going in for the final tee. "This is for never telling me I looked pretty on my wedding day!" She took a swing, and this time she hit him, right in the nose. He swayed to the side and then righted himself.

She was talking about her mother. Of course. It was a problem back then, and, as Iris had learned over time, problems didn't just go away. They weren't resolved with a tidy little bow. And people...people didn't change.

Try as she might.

A memory came into focus, one she had pushed back because it had made her too uneasy. Wasn't that what even Stephanie had said to her, when Iris announced she was dating Julian, way back when? *Don't expect to change him.* Meaning Julian had been married twice already. What difference was a third divorce? He didn't even need to pay for an attorney. He could represent himself.

She picked up her bat. "I think I need a swing, too."

Gwen stepped back, looking surprised but pleased. "This one is for Nance. And...and Sofia!" She took the Santa out, sent him flying straight across the garage, even though he was weighed down by sand, meant only to bob in the winter wind. He hit a wall of garden tools hanging from hooks and then bounced back to the concrete floor.

Iris froze, hoping she hadn't killed him. She needed another swing, after all. She was just getting started.

Gwen and Iris exchanged a glance. "I think he's okay."

"Me too." She hit him again. Twice more. Good and hard. One for Delilah. The other for Kat. But she whispered their names. Gwen just wouldn't understand.

Gwen stepped forward, fire in her eyes that would have made Iris laugh if she didn't realize they were glistening with hurt. "Here's to always comparing me to Katie next door. She was a little...bitch." She struggled on the last word as she took another swing, harder this time. "And I was nice. I was *nice*!"

Harder and harder went the bat. Sometimes it hit. Sometimes it missed. And the more she missed, the more she hit.

Iris had a few good swings left in her that she had hoped to take at Julian and Stephanie, but watching Gwen attack the Santa, she decided that Gwen needed the release more than her. Besides, she had the bottle of wine to take the edge off. She took a sip now, feeling her shoulders relax like they always did. She wasn't far gone enough to know that this was bad, that she shouldn't feel this way, that she shouldn't need a crutch. That she wasn't happy.

It was all going to be okay, she told herself. For today at least. But what happened three weeks from now, when she went back? Her teeth hurt from clenching them. She couldn't think about that now. It was so much easier to hide from reality than to confront it.

Gwen beat the Santa until the air came out of him and he fell to the ground, a pile of plastic.

"I think you put a hole in your Christmas decorations." Iris realized she was slurring a little, but Gwen was too busy glaring at Santa to notice.

Gwen dropped the bat, panting. "It was worth it," she said, giving a small smile. "I never liked that thing, anyway. And my mother never stopped complaining about it either. I only kept it up for the kids, and the neighbors on this street go all out every year…"

In other words, so did Gwen. It was no different than in first grade, when Gwen wanted the jeans and character-covered T-shirts the other kids were wearing instead of the beautiful party dresses her mother insisted upon, why in high school Iris would comb through the racks at the secondhand shop, looking for the brand of jeans that were in fashion, and why Iris still felt compelled to smile wide when she sat at those stuffy committee meetings with women of an entirely different pedigree, pretending that she was one of them, even though she wasn't so sure she wanted to be, she just knew that it was easier than being an outcast.

"Can I ask you a question?" Gwen asked as she dropped onto the step beside her. "Why did you never come back to Westlake, even to visit?"

Iris gave her a funny look. "You knew I couldn't wait to leave."

"Leaving and never returning are two different things," Gwen said.

"I guess I don't like being reminded of the person I was here," Iris admitted. She took a sip of her wine. It didn't taste as good as it had just a few minutes ago.

"Hey, I liked that girl just fine," Gwen said, jabbing her with her elbow.

"I could the same about you." Iris grinned. "You were the only good thing in this town, Gwen. You still are."

Gwen blinked rapidly and looked down at her hands. "This town isn't the same without you."

Iris laughed. "Oh, well, Lois is still the same. And all these mean girls from school have just grown up into mean adults. But you've done okay. More than okay."

Gwen's expression was wry. "The difference is that I can't run away like you did."

"Run away," Iris mused. She drained her glass. "I never thought of it like that."

"I ran away in my own way," Gwen sighed. "By marrying Michael so young. But unlike you, I didn't stick with the plan."

"Oh, yes you did!" Iris said in surprise. "You always wanted a big family, and you have one. You always wanted a house that was full of laughter, not rules. You have furniture you sit on, and a piano that your child actually plays, not just something for show. And you have an inflatable Santa that you stick on your front lawn because it makes your children happy." That made her think of something. "Isn't your anniversary soon?" She couldn't remember the date, only that it was winter, after the holidays. It had snowed on the morning of Gwen's wedding day, and the entire city of Chicago felt quiet and serene. Well, except for that tantrum Eileen had thrown right before the ceremony.

Iris thought of her own wedding day, a late spring affair with enough flowers to fill two rooms in their apartment. She'd told people she'd eloped, even though 250 people she didn't recognize had attended.

Gwen had been hurt, she knew. And she still felt bad about it, even though she'd tried not to, told herself it was one of those things that had to be done, like so many other steps she'd taken to climb the social ladder. Claw at it, really.

She felt the panic overtake her, weighing down her chest and leaving her feeling helpless and angry.

"Today," Gwen said. She didn't look particularly pleased.

Sensing Gwen's eyes on hers, she straightened her shoulders, forced a smile. "Big plans?"

Gwen snorted. "Yeah, right."

Iris frowned. "You don't want to go out?" She studied Gwen, wondering if there was something going on with Michael that she wasn't revealing, but then she realized that this is what her counselor at Andover would have termed "projecting." She was displacing her suspicions and feelings about Julian onto someone else, assuming that their marriage was rocky, too. Maybe even wishing it.

It was less lonely that way, she supposed, and it wasn't until now, being here in Gwen's house, that she realized that she was lonely. Most of the time the apartment was empty, except for Sofia, whose disdain for her was obvious. Sure, back in New York she had Stephanie, who was fun to hang around with, but

Stephanie had betrayed her. Julian was never home, and when he was it was clear that something in their relationship had shifted.

"We, uh, forgot to make reservations," Gwen said. She stood to gather up the deflated Santa.

"So? Make one now!" Iris was about to point out that this was Westlake, how in-demand could the restaurants be, but stopped herself just in time.

"It's hard to be spontaneous with kids," Gwen said. She shoved the decoration into the garbage bin and closed the lid with a bang.

"How about I babysit for you while you go out?"

Gwen frowned at her and then slid her eyes to the bottle of wine.

They both knew that Gwen had been the babysitter between the two of them. She started at age twelve, and parents fought over who would get her for a Saturday night. She had regulars. The Osberg trio was the worst, but the parents paid the best, and they also loaded the fridge with junk food, and they had HBO. Gwen made it all sound so great that Iris had helped out once, but within ten minutes she had bored of playing hide and seek and had gone to the sofa to watch television instead.

"I'm not cut out for this," Iris recalled saying to Gwen at the end of the night. And Gwen had just shrugged and said, "That's okay."

But was it okay? More and more, people seemed surprised that she had no children. Julian was a convenient excuse, but still, she couldn't help but feel...judged. As if they were all part of a club that she was excluded from, even though she had never particularly wanted to join it in the first place. And with each passing year, she was all the more aware that her choices were catching up with her, that her window of opportunity was closing. That the future wasn't as wide open as she'd once thought it was.

"I have two stepdaughters," Iris pointed out. Gwen had no idea how much they hated her. "And it was only a glass of wine." It was more than that, but Gwen didn't know. Besides, it was midday. She could pull herself together by tonight. It wouldn't be the first time. And she wanted to do something nice for Gwen. To repay her. And because...because they were friends.

The best friend she'd ever had. The only person who knew her and accepted her just as she was. If there was anyone she could share the truth with, it was Gwen. But somehow, she just couldn't bring herself to admit that the sacrifices she'd made had all been for nothing.

"True," Gwen said with a sigh. "I suppose it would be nice to go out for dinner."

"You don't ever leave Norah in charge?" Iris asked.

Gwen snorted. "No. She's not as responsible as I was." She paused for a moment, studying the bat. "But that's okay. I wanted her life to be different than mine. I wanted her to find her own way, not be controlled every step of it. It's just hard to sit back and watch her make mistakes, sometimes."

"How about your mom? Does she ever babysit?" Iris asked. She eyed the bat in Gwen's hands, waiting for her to take another swing.

"She does... It's just usually more aggravation than it's worth."

"All the more reason to let me take the kids for a night and give you a break. We can get ready together, like old times?"

Gwen gave a small smile. "Like old times. Sometimes I can't even believe I was ever that person, and sometimes I feel like I'm exactly the same."

Iris nodded slowly. She couldn't agree more.

15

GWEN

GWEN COULDN'T REMEMBER the last time she and Michael had gone out on a date. When the kids were younger, they'd needed the break, but it always felt so complicated. Declan needed his asthma medicine, and Gwen's mother could never remember how to administer it. Eileen only ever wanted to watch the kids at her house, usually requesting a sleepover, even though Michael preferred the kids to sleep at home. There was never any explanation for Eileen's strong view on this, other than what Gwen suspected to be a desire for control or the fact that her mother used that opportunity to give the kids so much junk food that they often had stomach issues for days.

"I thought your mom was strict with your diet," Michael would comment with a frustrated frown.

"She was," Gwen said. Finally, after the time Eileen had fed them hot dogs for dinner, brownies, ice cream, a second helping of dessert, and a donut for breakfast, Gwen worked up the nerve to speak up.

"We don't let the kids have two helpings of dessert," she said anxiously, the next time she dropped them off.

"Oh, but this is special from Grandma!"

"Well, it's not good for them," Gwen said, feeling the anger build inside her. "You never let me eat like that."

Eileen's eyes had dramatically drifted to Gwen's hips. "Gwen. Those children take after Michael. They don't have to worry about their weight."

"This isn't about weight," Gwen had said. "It's about their health. Last time they had a hot dog, two bowls of ice cream, and two brownies, and today they had a donut for breakfast."

"They also had some broccoli," Eileen said simply.

Gwen was furious, but she knew better than to show it. "No more donuts for breakfast."

"Fine" was all Eileen had to say to that.

The next time Eileen came to pick them up, Bea reported that she had taken them directly to the bakery, where they could each pick out their donut. Bea ate hers right after her hot dog dinner.

"You told me no donuts for breakfast," Eileen said innocently when Gwen asked her about it. "That was dessert!"

After that, the date nights stopped. They could have called a sitter, but Norah would have squawked. Besides, they couldn't exactly afford a sitter these days.

Now, sitting beside Michael in the car, she wasn't even sure she knew how to be alone with him like this. It felt awkward and too quiet. She was used to the kids being in the back of the car. She was used to Michael holed up in his office, hunched over his laptop, or at the gym.

She flicked on the radio, even though the restaurant was just up ahead. Commercials played on every station they had programmed. She flicked it off again.

"This is nice," she said, settling back against her seat.

"You sure we can trust Iris with the kids?" Michael hadn't commented much on Iris since she arrived, but then again, he'd also been leaving the house for longer periods of time since he said he couldn't think straight at the dining room table, and he was back to falling asleep on the sofa with the television blaring all night, something she'd decided she would laugh off if Iris were to notice. But Iris slept late, so the worry was unfounded.

Must be nice, she thought.

Still, was Michael going to sleep on the family room or the office sofa forever? It had been going on for so long that it had started to feel normal, but it wasn't normal, and because she was afraid of what it meant, Gwen had said nothing.

Sometimes it was easier to say nothing at all. What would it change? They had three kids. A dog. A mortgage they could barely pay. Bills from Christmas that were slowly rolling in. Arguing over a dry patch in their marriage felt frivolous.

But keeping their problems a secret—that felt depressing. Susan and her husband went jogging every Sunday together while the girls were at their gifted program. And suddenly a dinner with her own husband was becoming a huge event.

"I'm sure it's fine. She has two stepdaughters," Gwen pointed out. She frowned, thinking it was strange that Iris barely mentioned them, but then again, they were older. One in high school, one already out of college. Or had she never gone to college? That part was hazy. She made a mental note to ask more about them tomorrow. It was rude of her not to have done so before. Just because Gwen's children were her own didn't mean she should minimize Iris's role.

"Is this the place?" Michael frowned as he drove by the restaurant that had opened last summer. "Looks pricey. They have valet parking."

"It's our anniversary," Gwen said, hurt. It was bad enough that she had to make the reservations herself.

Grumbling, Michael found a parking spot a few blocks down. Gwen said nothing as she slid out of the car. She was wearing an outfit that Iris had pulled together—some basics from Gwen's closet and probably the lone article Iris had that would even fit Gwen.

Still, she was happy to share the cashmere poncho with a fur collar (most definitely real fur, but Gwen didn't like thinking about that), which made Gwen realize just how long it had been since she'd had a true friend in her life. Most of her friends now were other parents, acquaintances, really, and conversation topics centered on what little Zoe or Chloe was up to, not what people were wearing to dinner.

She adjusted the poncho as she followed the waitress to the table. She scanned the room: mostly couples, some she recognized from school, but right beside the table where the hostess paused and smiled was a group of women. Women who looked familiar. And then she saw Susan.

Damn it.

She tried to scoot to the other side of the table, where her back would be to the group, and where she could pretend to not notice them, but Michael never had been quick on picking up on her nonverbal clues, and so he just frowned at her and said, "What are you doing?" Loudly.

Gwen glared at him and then—because by now they had of course caught the attention of Susan Sharp and her clique—she forced her sweetest smile and faked surprise. "Susan? Hi."

"Gwen? I didn't know you came here."

Gwen tried not to let that comment hit her any harder than she had the first time Susan had said it the other day at the nail salon. Did Susan think she owned the town? Or that Gwen never left the house? Because she was implying something, and whatever it was, it wasn't good.

"I didn't know you did, either," she said, catching herself by surprise. Sure, it wasn't quite as punchy as she'd hoped it could be, but it was better than just nodding and smiling and admitting that it was her first time and asking what was good on the menu. All her life, she'd been terrible at comebacks, never being able to think in the moment, never able to rise to her own defense. Instead, she'd gone through life in her father's footsteps, turning the other cheek, being the bigger person, trusting that would make it all easier for her, that she'd be happier that way, better off somehow, because he was the only parent offering any sensible advice, even if now she wasn't so sure he had been right.

"Oh, we come here all the time for girls' night," Susan said with a little smile. She glanced around the group of women, who sipped their white wine. "But I think this is our last time. It's gone downhill recently."

Gwen couldn't reply to that one if she tried. Instead, she forced a smile and said, "Well, enjoy your dinner."

She was shaking when she pulled out her chair and faced Michael, just like she had thirty years ago, when no matter how hard she tried she always seemed to get it wrong with the other girls. She couldn't ease into their conversations, didn't dress the right way or say the right things.

But just like thirty years ago, she had a best friend in her life. That, she supposed, was something.

Behind her, she heard Susan's peal of laughter. It was more like a cackle.

She opened the menu, grateful for something to look at, even though what she really wanted to do was tear into that breadbasket. The butter was a large, thick slab on its own plate. But she'd be damned if she would be the big girl stuffing her face with bread while all the skinnies sipped their drinks.

Michael, however, had no reservations. He tore into the baguette. "This is good. You should try some."

Gwen shook her head, and something in Michael's expression softened. He leaned forward, giving her a boyish smile, a hint of his former self. "I think you look nice, just the way you are."

"You have to say that," she said, flicking the page in her menu. Gwen blinked at the prices, wishing she had checked the website beforehand. But this was their anniversary, she told herself. And didn't one nice meal even out when it was such a rare occurrence?

Maybe, she thought, as her eyes roamed to the dessert section, she'd even have a slice of the flourless chocolate cake.

She thought of the four women sitting behind her. A good ol' girls club. Exclusive membership.

Maybe not.

She looked around the room, at the other couples, who seemed to be enjoying their time. The ones who laughed, who looked into each other's eyes, who seemed genuinely engaged in the conversation.

"Maybe we could split a bottle of wine," she said, noticing that other tables had bottles chilling in chillers, or anchoring the table, drawing out the meal.

"Did you see the price?" Michael asked. "I'll do a glass of the house red," he told the waitress when she approached.

Gwen stiffened, wondering if Susan had overheard, and quietly said, "I'll do the same."

They studied the menu in silence until the wine came. Gwen took a small sip and said, "So...did you get the cover letter sent out?"

As soon as the words slipped from her mouth, she connected it all. Michael's mood tonight matched his expression. "It's not a fit."

She had run out of things to say to this. At first, she was encouraging, hopeful, but now that felt flippant, inappropriate. "I'm sorry," she said.

They shouldn't have come. She thought it again after they placed their orders: fish for Michael, and the cheapest thing Gwen could find (pasta with pesto) for herself, even though she'd been eyeing the salmon that a nearby table had ordered.

She sipped her wine, watching Michael slather another chunk of the baguette with his knife. Her stomach grumbled. This was her anniversary. It was supposed to be special. She was supposed to have fun.

To hell with it! She grabbed the bread, feeling her heart race with anticipation, and slowly spread the butter over it. It nearly melted when she brought it to her mouth.

"Oh my! That looks decadent!" a voice suddenly said.

On reflex, Gwen dropped the bread. Her heart was pounding, and even though she knew it wasn't her mother's voice, she could feel her presence, sense her disappointment. Her appetite was lost.

Gwen looked up to see Susan standing beside the table, smiling wickedly down at her. She swallowed the bread that was currently stuffed in her cheek. She hadn't chewed enough, and it barely went down. Her eyes now watering, she reached for her water glass and took a small sip. "Special occasion," she said with a tight smile.

Susan's eyes widened a notch, even though Gwen hadn't thought that physically possible. "Well, enjoy. Oh! I see you already ordered a glass of wine. Too bad. I would have suggested the bottle we always order. It's heavenly."

It was also eighty-five dollars. Gwen had already checked.

"She seems friendly enough," Michael said when the group of women left, the other three barely acknowledging them, perhaps not even knowing who Gwen was, even though they'd seen each other at school activities for as long as Gwen had been back in Westlake.

"She is not friendly," Gwen said. "She's mean."

She eyed the breadbasket, feeling her appetite wane. "I've been thinking..."

Michael glanced up, showing he was listening, and Gwen pulled in a breath. It was so seldom that they found the time to connect like this, to really talk, that she wasn't sure if she should spoil the night with hot topics or use it for the opportunity.

"Maybe you should expand your job search out of state," she blurted.

He frowned. "You want to move?"

She hadn't actively given the thought consideration until now, when all she could think of was that she'd wished they'd never come into this restaurant, wished that for once she could walk out the door or into her kids' school without feeling like she was walking into middle school again, without the prying eyes of other women who didn't seem to accept her, no matter how hard she tried.

"We were happy in Chicago," she said slowly, but Michael was already shaking his head.

"You have ·a selective memory. Our apartment was too small and the parking was a nightmare and it was impossible to raise two kids there, much less three."

"They're older now," Gwen pointed out.

"And they're settled into their school and activities. You don't really want to uproot them." He studied her across the table. "Is this about your problem with those women?"

Gwen snatched another piece of bread from the basket. "It was just an idea. An opportunity to…start over."

Gwen scooped up more butter and spread a thick layer onto a piece of focaccia that had been hiding under the baguette, hating herself, but finding comfort in it all the same.

"Something is going to turn up now that we're past the holidays. This will all just be a rough patch in our distant future soon enough," Michael said softly, and Gwen gave him a small smile.

With the bread in her stomach and the wine in her hand, Gwen was able to relax into the meal, and Michael seemed happier than he'd been in months, all talk of their problems set aside for now. He even extended the evening by suggesting they split a dessert.

She wanted to ask if they could afford it. She'd nursed that glass of wine all through the meal. She'd forgone the Caesar salad that was tossed at the table and looked, as Susan would say, heavenly.

"I'm glad we did this," Michael said as they finished their coffees and set the empty mugs on the saucer.

Gwen felt a twinge of sadness over how much they had drifted apart in recent months. But it was further back than that. Back to before they'd even moved to Westlake, when the stress of city life with two young kids was wearing them down.

Maybe Michael was right. Maybe she did have a selective memory. Maybe she was so caught up in Iris's picture-perfect life that her own felt pale in comparison.

She opened her mouth, wanting to say something, anything, that would take them back to a place where they used to laugh together, and they had, not so long ago.

I'm sorry, that's what she wanted to say. But it was what she always said. She said it even when the fault wasn't hers, took responsibility when the other party wouldn't, brushed away the things that had been said and done, buried the hurt. But it was still there. It was always there.

The waitress approached the table, stopping her before she could speak.

The woman's face was ruddy as she handed over the leather-bound folio containing the bill. "I'm very sorry, sir, but this card was declined."

Gwen's heart hammered. She stared at Michael, who was frowning, deeply.

"No problem," he said, quickly tucking it back inside his wallet and retrieving another one, a card she'd never seen before. "Try this one."

Gwen stared at Michael, her chest pounding, the blood rushing in her ears. "What's going on?"

"I forgot to pay the bill. It's not a big deal," he said.

She wanted to argue, but knew that this was not the place for it. It was a big deal.

She waited until they were in the car to say something. "Where did that card come from?" It was the least of their problems—or maybe the source of them. But it was the easiest question to ask in this moment. Her mind was spinning. How bad was it? What wasn't Michael telling her?

"I opened it a while ago." Michael was going ten miles over the speed limit. Gwen highly doubted they could afford a ticket on top of everything else, but she said nothing. His jaw was set, and he hadn't looked in her direction since the waitress had approached their table.

Their moment was lost. The anniversary spoiled.

"You maxed out the Visa," he suddenly accused her when he pulled onto their street.

"What choice did I have? We have to eat! I had to pay the dance studio for the winter semester, and the piano lessons are a monthly charge."

"You didn't need to go so overboard at Christmas," Michael said.

"The kids deserved a nice Christmas!" Gwen felt tears prickle the backs of her eyes. She shouldn't have bought that new outfit, even if it was on sale. She shouldn't have lied about how much she'd sold at Forevermore Beauty and then eaten the cost. She vowed to sell more now, to make up for the loss.

"The kids would have understood," Michael said, but there was sadness in his eyes, a pull at his mouth that she'd never seen before. She felt a sudden urge, to reach over, take his hand, and tell him that they would get through this, together, somehow.

It had just been so long since they'd touched like that. It faded slowly, over time, when the hand she held was replaced with Norah's, then Declan's. When they no longer did things together but tag-teamed. He would be off at tee ball with Norah; she was home feeding Declan. There was no time for affection, and eventually, no desire.

She reached out, her finger was inches from his hand, but she jerked it away when he said, "Shit. Is that your mother's car?"

Gwen stared at their driveway up ahead, where sure enough Eileen's silver Lexus sat.

"Did you invite her over?" Michael asked.

"Why would I do that?" Gwen asked, giving him a long look. Seriously, how did he not get it by now? Seeing her mother was not a willing choice. It was an obligation. And tonight she had thought she was off the cuff.

"Maybe Iris invited her. Or one of the kids?" Michael pulled to a stop next to Eileen's car. She was blocking the entrance to his side of the garage.

Maybe Michael was right. Maybe something had happened.

The lights were on. There was no sound of screaming. Still, Gwen was quick to release her seat belt and power-walked to the door on shaking knees.

Her eyes were wide as she pushed open into the hall and hurried to the kitchen, where five guilty faces looked up at her, towering brownie sundaes in front of them. Make that three guilty faces, Gwen calculated again. Eileen was incapable of feeling bad about anything she said or did, and Bea was too young to suppress her joy.

Two of her teeth were blacked out from the chocolate.

Gwen glared at her mother. "Did you bring these?"

"Grandma made us brownies!" Bea said with a big smile. "I got three servings."

"We talked about this!" Gwen realized she was shaking in an effort to control her voice, to not say something that would only make this whole evening worse, to not say what she wanted to say, which was that this was her house, her children, and that Eileen had overstepped. That in this house, Gwen was in charge. Instead, she took a calming breath and said, "What are you doing here?"

Eileen looked dramatically affronted. "This is how you talk to your mother? I came by to visit my grandchildren. Then I saw that I had been replaced by a new babysitter." Her lip curled subtly, but there was a gleam in her eye that Gwen had seen before, when she knew something Gwen didn't, or when she was about to get her way. "It's just too bad I got here too late."

Gwen frowned. "Too late?"

Before she could answer, Bea chirped happily, "Look at Norah's ears, Mommy! Iris pierced them. I got to hold the ice!"

"What?" boomed Michael's voice behind her, causing Bailey to bark in alarm.

Norah glared at Gwen with naked defiance. Her ears, Gwen now noticed, were hidden by her hair, which was usually pulled back in a ponytail.

"You know how your father feels about this, Norah—"

She caught the look Michael gave her and suppressed a sigh. They had been going around this argument ever since Norah started asking to pierce her ears four years ago. Gwen didn't see the big deal, but Michael was adamant. Not until she was sixteen.

"Do you know how dangerous this is?" Michael said. "What did you use? A needle? Did you even sterilize it?"

"They got it from your sewing box, Mommy," Bea was happy to share. She scooped up some more of her sundae. She had chocolate sauce on her cheeks.

Declan's eyes shifted from side to side. Gwen decided to put him out of his misery. "Declan, you have had enough treats. Bea, you too. Please bring your bowls to the counter and go get ready for bed." It was well past their bedtime, after all. She'd pay for this tomorrow, especially with Bea, who would sleep late and then struggle to get to bed later that night, making it then hard to drag her out for school come Monday morning.

The kids groaned as they set their spoons into the dishes. Eileen, Gwen noticed, gave them a conspiratorial wink as they passed by her chair.

Gwen gritted her teeth. "Norah, you know that we had not given you permission to pierce your ears."

Eileen clucked her tongue and then gravely shook her head.

Gwen felt her temper stir, but she had bigger issues at hand. She looked at Iris. The adult. The one who should have known better. The one who should have at least checked with Gwen first. "How could you do this?"

Iris opened her eyes wide to underscore her innocence. It was a look Gwen knew all too well. "She was admiring my earrings, and I noticed hers weren't pierced. I suggested we go to the mall, but we didn't have a car, and I didn't know how you would feel about me putting them in an Uber."

Gwen laughed, but she was far from amused. "So you were concerned about putting my kids in a taxi but not about sticking a needle through their ears?"

"That's how my ears were pierced back in the day," Eileen commented. "Infected, of course. But they didn't have these modern contraptions like those guns they use now. So I just balled my fist and closed my eyes. I was strong. I was so strong." She nodded her head over and over, her eyes closed at some distant memory.

Normally, Gwen and Iris would have shared a glance about this type of behavior, would have had a secret understanding. But not tonight.

"Norah, go to your room. I will speak to you tomorrow."

Norah skulked out of the room, leaving her bowl of ice cream on the table, melting.

Eileen frowned deeply. "She didn't even tell me goodbye!" she demanded, looking around the room indignantly. "She didn't even tell me goodbye!"

"Three servings of brownies, Mom?" Gwen said. "Three?"

"It wasn't three." Eileen pursed her lips.

"Even seconds is too much! There's no need for that! You never would have let me have a second helping of dessert!"

"The children enjoy what I bake for them, and they have the physique to be able to handle it." Her mother took a step forward, her brow knitting as she squinted at Gwen. "Did you color your hair again?" Gwen's hand shot to her hair, which indeed had been colored a "milk chocolate" in anticipation of Iris's visit. Eileen stood close until she was practically sniffing. "An improvement. That other color was so *brassy*." She shuddered and threw a glance at Iris. "Did you see the other color?"

Iris looked from Eileen to Gwen, visibly confused by this shift in conversation. "No."

"Good." Eileen gave a little chuckle.

Gwen stared at her mother. "We're not talking about my hair. We're talking about my children."

"Oh, pfft." Eileen brushed a hand through the air. "You're always so *sensitive*."

Tears burned in the back of Gwen's eyes, but she refused to let them fall. "I'm going to bed," she said, backing out of the room.

"I don't even get a thank-you?" Eileen was aghast.

"I asked you not to give the kids so many sweets, Mom," Gwen pleaded, hoping that once, just once, she would connect with her mother, that she would get it, that she might even apologize.

Instead, Eileen's eyes flew wide and she put a hand on her chest as if she had just had a huge shock. "I gave up *my* Saturday night to bake brownies for *your* children, Gwen. For all of you. I did it as a surprise for your wedding anniversary. How was I to know that you had decided to go out instead? That you had asked Iris to watch the children instead of me? I'm their *grandmother!*" She narrowed her eyes, glaring at Gwen, and then walked over to the counter and began fumbling for the cake pan of brownies, or what remained of them. "You know, forget it. I'll leave. I'll just leave! I can tell I'm not welcome here."

"Mom." Gwen felt her shoulders sink. She could practically feel her father's voice in her ear, low and deep. *Just be the bigger person, Gwen. Let it go.*

Her mother grabbed her handbag. Swung it over her shoulder. "I'll go," she said quietly. "I'll go." She hung her head, her shoulders were hunched. She made no true attempt to move. She was waiting for Gwen to do what she had always done. To make it all right. To give her a pass. To apologize.

"Mom. Stop," she said wearily. She heard Michael sigh heavily. "I didn't say you had to leave." Gwen rubbed her forehead. She hated this. She hated herself. And right now she hated her mother too.

Eileen sniffed. Her nose inched upward. When she met Gwen's eyes, her own dropped to the floor again.

"I didn't mean to hurt your feelings," Gwen said, which was the truth. She didn't want to even be having this conversation. She didn't want her mother here. She didn't want her feeding her kids junk. She didn't want her mind games. "I just don't want my kids getting stomachaches."

"They only had a small serving, Gwen," Eileen said patiently. Gwen eyed her mother, wondering if she could believe her, knowing she shouldn't, but wanting to all the same. It was the same cycle as always, where she looked for the best and dared to hope that someday their relationship would be everything she had wanted it to be. But it never was. And the older she grew and the worse it became, the more she feared it never would be.

She nodded. "Thank you, then. For thinking of us tonight on our anniversary."

"Thank you for saying *thank you*!" Eileen sniffed again, and Gwen looked around the silent room, at Michael, who was stone-faced in the doorway; at Iris, who had one hand on the back door, no doubt eager to leave.

"I'm going to check on the kids," Gwen said, needing to get away. The conflict in the air was thick, and she had the uneasy sensation that she had contributed to it, even though deep down she knew she had only reacted to it. Still, the outcome was all the same. Things were tense, they would need smoothing over, or they would sit and fester, and either way, the night was ruined.

Her friend had just pierced her daughter's ears and her mother had yet again undermined her parenting. And yet somehow she was the one feeling guilty.

When she reached the top landing and saw Norah's closed door, she knew she couldn't wait until tomorrow to confront her. She tried the handle, still disturbed as she always was to find that it was locked, and knocked on the door. Norah opened it without a word and then walked back to her bed. Her eyes were red, and Gwen realized that she must have been crying.

Remorse? Or pain?

Her money was on the latter.

"Why would you talk Iris into piercing your ears?" she demanded. "The one night I go out, and this is what happens?"

"She's cool," Norah said, and the insinuation was clear: Gwen was not cool. She never had been.

But Iris was, even if she was different. Iris could take her secondhand clothes and turn them into something fashionable. She had no high school boyfriend, despite many guys showing an interest. She was poor, and her mother was considered eccentric at best—the rumors were fierce in a town this small and, even though Iris would never let them see it, hurtful. But still, Iris was tall and thin and pretty and above all else, Iris didn't give a shit—or at least, she didn't let them think she did. Iris was cool. And Gwen was her sidekick. Her confidant. Her polar opposite in many ways.

A familiar feeling of envy filled her then. The wish to be more like Iris, just for a moment, to have the luxury to be Norah's friend, to break the rules, to have some fun.

But that wasn't her role. And because she loved her, she wouldn't go that far. She owed Norah far more than fun. She owed her structure and responsibility and accountability. More than anything, she had to take these moments and show that despite everything, Norah was loved.

"I'm not mad that you pierced your ears," she admitted, and Norah blinked up at her in surprise. "You know that I've been trying to convince your father to let you do it sooner. I just wish that you had come to me. That you could feel like you could talk to me. Believe it or not, I'm on your side, Norah. Even when I'm mad at you. Even when I have to give you consequences for your actions, I'm doing this for your own good."

Norah shook her head, a single tear slipped down her face. When her hair rustled, Gwen could see that her ears were a deep red.

"Am I in trouble?" Norah asked.

"Of course you're in trouble!" Gwen cried. Michael would no doubt dole out some punishment, or ask Gwen to take care of it.

Gwen's breathing was heavy. It was late. She saw her mother's headlights in the driveway out the window. She heard the back door close. It was just them now. The family. The picture-perfect family that was starting to reveal its cracks.

And she didn't even care anymore.

"You need some ice for those ears," Gwen said. "And some hydrogen peroxide." She went to Norah's bathroom, which was Jack-and-Jill style, shared with Bea, and began pulling open drawers.

"Please tell me she sterilized that needle, Norah." Her stomach felt sour when she came back into the room.

"Of course." Norah rolled her eyes.

Thank God for that, at least. "Do you want me to help with this, or do you want to take care of it yourself?"

"I can do it," Norah grumbled.

"Okay then." Gwen set the items on the bed. The cotton balls. The cold washcloth. It would soak the duvet if Norah didn't take her up on the offer, but that was the least of her worries. "I'm going to bed now."

"Hey, Mom?"

Gwen paused when she reached the door. "Yes?"

"We did have three servings of ice cream and brownies. I mean, Bea and Declan did. Iris seems too vain to eat like that, and you know I'm trying to stay in shape because I want to get back on the cheerleading team soon. And the brownies were huge. Like as big as the ones at the bakery."

Gwen pursed her lips. Of course.

"And Mom?

There was more? "Yes?"

"I liked having Iris babysit us. I mean, not just because she's cool, but when we go to Grandma's she has, like, that entire shrine to Bea. It's creepy."

Gwen dropped her hand from the knob. There were photos of Bea all over the living room of her mother's house, and all over the fridge too. Gwen had tried to balance it out, offer up a few photos of Declan at Halloween and Norah at cheerleading, but those contributions were still outweighed. It bothered her. She just hadn't realized that it bothered her children, too.

"I know that Bea's her favorite—"

"Stop. Don't say that." Gwen's tone was sharper than intended, but her heart was pounding. What Norah probably didn't remember was that Eileen used to bask in Norah's glow at one point too, her first grandchild. She was doted on and spoiled, and Eileen was always quick to pull her off Gwen's hip and onto her own, always quick to carry her into another room. She was "Grammie's girl" just like Bea was now "Grammie's girl."

"But it's true. She likes that she can dress her up and parade her around, like some pretty doll."

"Bea is pretty," Gwen said. "But so are you."

"All moms say that," Norah said.

"No, they don't," Gwen said, knowing that Eileen had never felt the need to say it to her. She gave Norah a smile. "I said it because it's true. Now good night, honey."

"Mom?" Gwen turned once more. "I'm happy you're my mom."

Gwen didn't know whether to cry or smile. "And I'm happy that you're my daughter," she said. "But you're still in trouble."

Norah gave a small grin. "I know."

Gwen went into the bedroom, changed out of the borrowed outfit, and washed her face. Bailey was already on the bed, watching her, waiting, and she snuggled into bed next to him and flicked off the light, even though she wasn't tired and even though she should march downstairs right this minute and ask Michael if he intended to watch television all night.

But he was probably already asleep on the sofa.

She needed to put today to rest. And she needed to think about what to do about tomorrow. And the day after that. Because somewhere along the way, she'd lost sight of what she'd wanted out of life, and what and who mattered most.

16

IRIS

IRIS WAS ABLE to avoid Gwen all day Sunday by staying in her room and cyberstalking Julian, Stephanie, Delilah, and Kat. The weekend was passing quickly. There was nothing noticeable, nothing that made her feel connected to her life in New York at all.

Iris's hands shook as she poured a drink from the bottle she'd snagged from Lois's trunk. She was only slightly concerned to see that it was more than two-thirds gone. She wondered if she could sneak in the back door of Gwen's kitchen and grab a couple of bottles of the wine she had purchased the other day without anyone noticing—the ones she'd kept in her room were long gone, after all. Surely they had to leave the house sometime? She could always take an Uber into town, load up on some important items, like food, which she also didn't have in the guest room, but the snow was falling down in big flakes outside the window, and the wind was picking up. Still, the thought of a nice bottle of chardonnay might be worth the trip. She pondered that for a moment but then went back to more important matters at hand.

She had to know what was going on. But who could she trust? All of the other wives she'd met through her various committees were acquaintances at best, and even the couples she and Julian boated with in the summer and dined with in the winter were more his friends than hers, and the deepest conversations got was minor trouble with kids, which was glossed over with a laugh and a change of subject.

After a few moments of going through the names of everyone she knew, she reached the sad conclusion that she couldn't trust anyone.

Once, she would have said Gwen. But she'd blown it. Just like she was blowing her marriage.

She took another sip of the whiskey, wishing she had ice, but not willing to go downstairs to the main house. It felt wrong somehow to let herself in after what happened with Norah, and if they were home, she wasn't so sure that she would be welcome.

And then what? She reached for her wallet and spread the cash out on the unmade bed, certain that if Gwen saw the state of her guest room, Iris would be in trouble for that, too.

Between the bus and cab from rehab to the city, the drinks at the airport, airfare, more drinks, and the case of wine she hadn't exactly scrimped on, not to mention the coffee and manicures and the Uber back from her mother's house, half her stash was gone.

And another three weeks to go. And a return ticket to buy.

A return to a life in New York that no longer seemed to exist. And maybe, she realized, staring at the screen blankly, never had.

She had to make it up to Gwen. Apologize. Something. Buy her flowers. But flowers weren't cheap unless they were the kind that Lois's boyfriends brought to her, the kind that made the water in the vases turn the color of the petals.

She smiled, remembering a time in high school when all the kids were exchanging roses for Valentine's Day, from secret admirers. Gwen wanted one desperately, and as much as she'd never admitted it to anyone but Gwen, Iris had, too, even though she was fairly certain that some of the guys on the football team would be sending them her way. The same, she knew, probably wouldn't happen for Gwen, so she hatched a plan: They'd buy each other roses. They'd be each other's secret admirers. Then no one would have to know.

She could still remember how surprised they'd acted when the roses were delivered in homeroom period. She could still remember how Gwen proudly displayed hers on the corner of her desk, and how good it felt to make her smile.

She must have fallen asleep thinking about that because the next time she opened her eyes, it was already dark outside and the bedside table clock said it was half past nine.

Her stomach twisted and turned and the whiskey bottle was empty and it was too late to go downstairs and try to make anything right, but she had to, because she didn't like feeling this way.

She'd lost Gwen once before, and she didn't want to lose her again. Especially not now, when she was already on the verge of losing so much.

*

Gwen was sitting at the kitchen counter, a pen poised over an official-looking notebook, when Iris knocked on the back door at ten o'clock on Monday morning. A large box sat at her feet, opened, and a few bottles of what appeared to be nail polish were displayed on the counter, in a tidy row. Gwen looked up from her task, seemed to hesitate, and then, after what felt like a long consideration, gathered up the nail polishes and stuffed them into the box before walking to the back door.

"It was unlocked," she said when she opened it.

"I wasn't sure you would let me in," Iris admitted.

Gwen sighed and walked to the counter near the sink, where she dropped a paper filter into the coffee machine. "You're my guest. I'm not going to lock you out." She began scooping coffee grounds with a large metal spoon. Angry scoops, Iris noted. And too many. The coffee would be bitter.

She decided not to comment. She had a raging headache that was always a reminder of a day that got away from her. Some strong brew would do her some good.

"I wasn't sure you still wanted me here," she said.

Gwen, unfortunately, said nothing to that.

"I'm sorry, Gwennie," she said.

"It's Gwen now, okay? Just Gwen." Gwen's tone was harsh but her eyes, when she met Iris's, seemed sad and dejected. Maybe she really was upset about Norah's ears, or maybe she was upset at Eileen for those brownies, which was over the top, even to Iris, who knew nothing about kids, as so clearly demonstrated on Saturday night.

Or maybe there was more to it.

"I'm sorry, Gwen. I should have asked your permission. Norah didn't tell me you would have a problem with it, and she seemed nervous about those piercing guns they use at the mall, and really, can you even trust one of those preteen joints at those stores to center the holes correctly? I mean, the girls working there aren't much older than Norah."

Gwen's shoulders seemed to sink a little. "Michael felt very strongly about her not piercing her ears until she was sixteen."

They exchanged a look, and Iris could tell that Gwen was fighting to keep up her defense. "He's struggling to watch her grow up. They don't tell you that this is the hard part. The diaper changing is easy."

Iris cringed, but Gwen was busy pressing buttons on the machine and didn't notice. Iris had never changed a diaper in her life, and never would at this rate.

"I was trying to bond with Norah," she explained, dropping onto a counter stool. She had the uneasy feeling that she might get sick. She hadn't eaten since Saturday night and her stomach felt raw. "I like her. She reminds me a little of me at that age."

Gwen's eyes widened and Iris knew what she was thinking, that this was precisely what concerned her. Gwen would be able to handle a mini Gwen. Little Gwen had been a goody-goody. She wouldn't even double-dip at the movies, even when no one was standing at the door to check tickets, for fear of being escorted out of the building.

For fear of her mother finding out.

"It was fun, hanging out with her," Iris said. "She's a good kid."

"She's not your friend, Iris. We're not fourteen anymore." Gwen's voice inched up a notch as she leaned back against the counter. Behind her, the coffeemaker began to steam.

"I'm just saying, she's a nice kid to be around, and the truth of the matter is that Delilah and Katrina don't like me very much." There. It was out.

To her surprise, Gwen didn't look fazed. "They're teenagers. You remember how that was."

"No, Gwen. This isn't some teenage mood stuff going on. They seriously don't like me. I try everything with those girls. I offer to take them shopping. I buy them gifts. I ask them about school."

"It's the same with Norah and me." Gwen opened a cabinet and reached for two mugs.

Iris knew she could leave it at that, bond over their mutual struggles with adolescent girls. But it wasn't the same situation, and she couldn't go on pretending that it was.

"They threw away the gifts that I bought them for Christmas. They posted photos. A Tiffany bracelet sitting on a pile of rotting food. Believe me, if Delilah could have shown a rat nibbling on it, she would have."

Gwen burst out laughing, and despite herself, Iris managed a small laugh. "They smoke. They lie. Kat got kicked out of boarding school for have sexual relations with her twenty-two-year-old teacher, but Julian wrote a check and they let her back in. They make Julian go on family vacations with them."

Gwen looked hesitant. "That part sounds…nice."

"With Nance." Iris lifted an eyebrow. "With their mother."

"You mean…?" Gwen blinked a few times.

Iris nodded. Gwen knew exactly what she meant. "I'm not invited."

"He goes on vacation with his ex-wife and not you?" Gwen looked so satisfyingly astonished that Iris almost blurted out everything else.

But she couldn't bring herself to say it. Saying it would mean admitting it. Owning it. And it would mean she would have to do something about it. And she just didn't know what to do.

"Those girls are wicked," Iris said, and Gwen laughed again.

"They're teenagers. They are all wicked," she said casually. She went back to filling their mugs.

"They won't call me by my name," she went on. Man, this was therapeutic. When was the last time she had dared to speak like this? Not to Stephanie. God no! Not to the AA group. Not even to Nick. Not even, she realized, to Julian. "They refer to me like I'm not in the room. *She. Her.* They have the maid tied in with this, too."

Iris saw Gwen's expression shift.

"I wanted to get rid of her, but Julian said she is family," Iris was quick to add. They were all family. The whole lot of them. All of them but Iris.

"Wow." Gwen seemed to digest this as she added sugar to her coffee and stirred it in. She didn't bother to ask Iris how she took it; she'd known that since they were hanging out in the diner twenty-five years ago. Cream and sugar for Gwen. Black for Iris. It was cooler that way, then. It was also how Lois took it. With a splash of liquor, of course.

"Do you want me to leave?" It had been bursting inside her all morning, and she had to know, just like she had to know if

Julian had spent every night last week with Stephanie, even if sometimes knowing was more painful than not.

She could go to Lois's, unless Wayne had been replaced already, which was entirely within the realm of possibility, but the thought of going now felt permanent and depressing. It wasn't even about the situation with her mother's house. It was about giving up on Gwen, just when she'd found her again.

"No," Gwen said. "Unless you want to go. It was pretty tense here the other night. I'm sorry that you had to witness that bit of family drama."

"Is your mom still mad at you?" After Gwen had gone upstairs, Eileen had given a speech, the audience of which was unclear. Iris had been relieved in a way, happy to have the silence filled, the focus taken off of her for a minute, especially because she wasn't sure if Michael intended to say something to her about the whole ear-piercing thing or if he felt Gwen had said enough.

"I give, give, give, and this is the thanks I get!" Eileen had puffed, and Iris was quite impressed with the way Michael politely nodded his head, wrapped up what remained of the tray of brownies, and helped Eileen into her coat without a word. Iris had used the time to hop out the back door.

"My mother is always mad at me," Gwen said, her lips thinning as she clutched her mug in both hands.

"Can I admit something to you?" Iris asked, forcing herself to take a sip of the coffee. Her head was pounding, and she knew she should probably eat something. That tray of brownies would have been perfect. "When we were younger, I was sometimes jealous of the attention your mother gave you."

"Jealous?" Gwen cried. "But it was all negative attention! All she ever did was pick at me. All that mattered was that my bow wasn't crooked and my dress was clean and that I didn't say or do anything that wasn't perfect in her eyes. And I failed. Every time. No one can live up to those expectations."

"But she gave you attention," Iris said, leaning forward. "Lois barely noticed when I came home from school half the time."

"And I envied that," Gwen said eagerly, dropping onto the stool beside her. "You had freedom! You still do!"

Iris frowned. It was an odd comment to make, considering they were both approaching forty and had been adults for some time. She was financially dependent on her husband. And unless you counted fundraising and charity efforts as resume builders, she was at a loss for how to explain her large gap in employment, considering she didn't even have a child. She had about four hundred bucks in cash left to her name if she intended to buy a return flight for New York. Less if she factored in the cab fare from LaGuardia to the Upper East Side. She didn't call that freedom.

And looking around the tidy kitchen, where the dog slept in the corner, thinking back on the chaos of Saturday night and the fact that Gwen hadn't been on a date with her husband in over a year, she started to think that maybe she wasn't alone in that department after all.

"What were you working on when I interrupted?" Iris asked, glancing over at the open notebook. It was an agenda, she realized. And there was a folder with an official-looking logo next to it.

She frowned down at the box. In addition to nail polish, there appeared to be tubes of hand cream, and lipstick too.

"Oh." Gwen shot out of her seat, but now Iris's curiosity was piqued. "It's something some of the women in the neighborhood do. Michael calls it a pyramid scheme, but it's just...a social thing."

Iris's eyes flitted over the papers. Marketing materials. Strategies for selling. Catalogs for buying. Party ideas.

If there was one thing Iris knew how to do, it was to plan a kick-ass party.

"And you can make money doing this?" She flipped through the catalog. Cosmetics, lotions, nail polishes. She chewed her bottom lip. Maybe it was the coffee, or maybe it was hope, but her mind suddenly felt clearer.

"Some people do..." Gwen set down her coffee. "That woman we saw at the nail salon?"

Iris looked at her sharply. "The bitchy one?"

Gwen grinned. "She's sort of the top of the pyramid."

"Why can't you be at the top of the pyramid?" Iris asked, turning back to the materials.

"It doesn't work that way. She brought me in. This neighborhood is her territory."

"Her *territory*? What is she, a mob boss?" Iris snorted.

"It feels like that sometimes," Gwen said with a little smile.

Iris set the catalog to the side. She clutched her coffee mug, leveled with Gwen, eye to eye. "But she only earns a portion of what you sell, right? What if you bring in more people?"

"Well...maybe..." Gwen's gaze skirted to the side. "But it's hard to find people. It's easier to sell the products than to bring in a new salesperson."

"You just brought me in. How hard was that?"

Gwen's eyes shot open, but she couldn't fight the smile that was forming on her mouth. "You don't have to do this."

She did, actually. She was down to petty cash, and she didn't have a return ticket to New York. When she got there, she didn't know if she would be met with open arms or served with divorce papers. Julian was supposed to be security: financially and emotionally. But she'd learned her lesson long before he'd come along, long before Gwen, long before she even knew what lesson she was learning. She must have been only three. Lois was passed out on the sofa after one too many. Iris hadn't been fed, it was dark outside, and the snow had been coming down all day. She tried to shake her mother awake, tried to tell her that she loved her, tried to ask for some milk, some dinner.

Finally, she went to the kitchen and opened the fridge, but she couldn't make sense of any of the items. The only thing she saw was a potato. She liked potatoes. She took it back to the living room, and she ate it, raw.

She was fed. She fell asleep, and in the morning she woke to the sound of Lois on the phone again, helping one of her regulars connect with someone "on the other side."

You couldn't depend on anyone else to take care of you in this world. And yet that was just what she'd gone and done by marrying Julian and giving up her job.

All her life, she'd been so determined not to fall into her mother's trap, refusing to let the weight of her circumstances hold her back, telling herself she could move forward. That she could only rely on herself.

But she'd been wrong. She had relied on someone else. Someone who had always stood by her and still did.

She could always count on Gwen.

17

GWEN

THERE WAS ONE thing that Gwen had never forgotten about Iris in their years apart: When Iris set her mind to something, she saw it through—she'd gotten a full academic scholarship to college with that determination, and now her attention was turned to Forevermore Beauty.

The plan was to sell everything in the box before the next meeting, including everything leftover from December. That was upfront cash, something that Iris seemed strangely focused on.

"We're going to have a party," Iris said on Thursday morning. "Next Saturday should give us plenty of time to plan."

"Are you sure about this?" Gwen asked as she made a fresh pot of coffee. The kids were at school, and Iris had been sitting at the kitchen table since they'd left for the bus, the latest installments of the Forevermore Beauty catalogs spread out around her.

"Of course I'm sure about this," Iris said. And then, giving the only explanation she was yet to give: "This will be fun!"

Fun. Gwen was detecting a theme here.

"What we need to do is expand our circle," Iris said, studying a spreadsheet. "It's clear that Susan Sharp has this neighborhood covered."

"Well, except for Caroline," Gwen muttered as she filled her mug.

"Who's that?"

"Next-door neighbor," Gwen explained as she handed Iris her mug. "I've been working up the nerve to sell her a few lipsticks."

"You should," Iris said emphatically. "It would be good practice for you. Plus, at twenty bucks a pop, that's sixty dollars."

"Minus Susan's cut."

"Right." Iris's eyes narrowed. "That's the part of this I don't like. Still. Do it."

Gwen cringed. She hadn't admitted to Iris that she actually hadn't yet sold anything to anyone.

"Don't go making that face," Iris scolded. "Do you want to do this or not?"

"I want to do it," Gwen said without much conviction. She *had* to do it. If she could sell out her newest supply, then it would at least make up for the loss she'd suffered over the holidays, and it might lead to some regular customers, too. She flicked through the seasonal brochure. The specials. She had to focus on the specials.

Besides, it really would be wonderful to go into the next First Friday meeting and be able to say, honestly, that she had sold out her supply, had a string of new customers and...a recruit!

"I'll talk to Caroline next time I see her." When Iris cocked an eyebrow at her, showing she wasn't convinced, Gwen crossed her fingers like she had when they were twelve and said, "I promise. Next time I see her."

"And when is that?" Iris was holding her to it. She was sharp, Iris. Always was.

"Tonight," Gwen realized with sudden dread.

"Oh! The concert!" Iris's eyes gleamed. "This will be fun."

Would it? A week ago, Gwen had thought so, but now Iris was coming, and her mother too. And then there was the fact that she and Michael weren't exactly on the best of terms these days, and it was becoming harder to pretend nothing was wrong in front of people. Especially when he had asked her no less than six times this morning when Iris was going back home. Gwen had run out of excuses, and it was becoming more and more difficult not to worry that she might never leave.

"Have you talked to Julian lately?" she asked, studying Iris carefully.

Iris just tucked a strand of hair behind her ears and flipped to another page in her notebook. "Of course! Hey, I have another assignment for you, before tonight," Iris said, handing her a pad of paper and a pen. "I want you to write down the names of every woman in this town that Susan Sharp wouldn't deign to engage with. Those are the women we are going to target. They're the untapped potential. I'll spend the afternoon coming up with a flyer. Do you have a printer I can use?"

"Here, use my laptop. The printer is in the dining room for now. Michael——" She stopped herself. What excuse could she even give? Most of these days, Michael was "networking" or job searching from a coffee shop or the library, but she couldn't hide the evidence of his unemployment indefinitely. Iris wasn't a child. She wouldn't buy the excuse that they'd given the kids that Daddy had more "free time" now.

"Michael moved in there since he's usually in the home office." She saw a chance to segue back the nagging question in her mind. Iris hadn't made any mention of going back to New York anytime soon, and now they were planning a party nearly ten days away. "The guest room?"

But Iris didn't take the bait. Instead, she licked her lower lip in a way that made Gwen feel suspicious. She tapped excitedly at the keyboard.

"It's good that you got into this, Gwen," she suddenly said, looking up. "It's something all your own, well, minus the nasty neighbor part. But it's important for a woman to have something to fall back on."

Gwen studied her friend, wondering if she was picking up on the marital discord in this house, but then Iris said, "Look at Lois. I always promised myself I'd be self-sufficient, never ending up like her."

Gwen barked out a laugh. "You are nothing like your mother, Iris."

A shadow seemed to fall over Iris's face. "I jumped from the corporate ladder to the social ladder."

"You have your charity work," Gwen pointed out.

Iris didn't look very convinced. "True. I have the parties. The events. But that's all because of Julian. But this is different. I'm proud of you, Gwen."

Gwen didn't quite know what to say. It had been a long time since anyone had said those words to her.

"Well, I only joined so I could play nice with the neighbors. Sometimes this feels like high school all over again," Gwen admitted as she began writing down the names of the women who weren't part of Susan's cool club: Caroline scared Susan, so she was on the list, as were some of the less popular kids' moms at school.

"That's because it is," Iris said simply. And tonight they were going back in, literally, in all their glory.

They arrived at the school that night on a mission. Iris was in charge of handing out the invitations, and Gwen was happy to let her. With her skills of persuasion, she was sure to spark more interest than Gwen would on her own. Besides, she had to make sure all three kids were where they needed to be. And poor Declan was nearly green with nerves over his solo.

"Listen to me," she said, crouching down and gripping his arms.

"If you say to think of everyone in the audience naked, I'm really going to puke," he said miserably.

Gwen bit back a smile. "I was going to say that you need to remember that you have two cheerleaders out there, minus the pom-poms. Dad and I are proud of you, no matter what happens. But I know you can do this. Or do I need to get up there and play myself?"

"Mo-om!" But Declan was smiling now. After all, he too had been witness to her painful attempt at "Silent Night" over Christmas.

"Hey! I thought I was pretty good," she said, elbowing him lightly. "But I guess you're the expert."

"The expert," she heard him mutter through a little smile.

Still, as she sat in the audience, wedged between Michael and Iris, her mother intentionally at the end of their foursome so she wouldn't whisper to her the entire time the way she had all through Declan's last concert and Bea's spring recital before that, dissecting every child's performance without considering that the parents might be within earshot.

The class songs were first: Norah was clearly moving her mouth but not singing along, while Bea belted it out, loud enough to make even Michael's eyebrows shoot up. By the time the soloists were up, Gwen felt like she might be the one to get sick when Declan emerged from behind the curtain and took a seat at the piano. The entire room fell quiet, and if she didn't know better, she'd say she heard her mother cluck her tongue. Finally, after what felt like minutes but was probably only seconds, he began to play. He stumbled over a few notes, paused a little longer than he should to turn the page, but by the time he pushed through to the final note, his face was spread in a big wide grin of redemption, and Gwen had to resist the urge to give him a standing ovation.

"Better than the last time, at least," Eileen leaned across Iris and stage-whispered to Gwen through clenched teeth, out of the side of her mouth.

Gwen fought back a swell of anger. She glared at her mother, who just batted her eyes innocently in return.

At the end of the concert, Michael pulled Gwen aside. "This is the last show I want your mother to attend."

"What am I supposed to say? I don't even invite her! She looks up the school calendar and just assumes she is coming."

"These are our kids, and these are our experiences, and we deserve to enjoy them," Michael said.

"I know." Gwen's face felt hot as she shuffled out of the aisle. Iris was up ahead with Eileen, lost in the crowd that was pushing out of the auditorium doors. "I don't want her here either!" She had ruined every event, with her loud whispering and commentary, and the way she had to be the one to run backstage and greet the kids first, one time elbowing past Michael to be the first to pose for pictures with Bea. When she was first married, Gwen had dreamed of these family moments, waited for them, and each time, she stood back and let her mother overshadow it, the resentment grew.

"Then why do you let her come?" Michael stared at her, hard. "It's not fair to me, Gwen. And it's not fair to you, either. She had her chance. This is our turn now. We're the parents. These are our kids."

He was right, of course. He was echoing every thought she felt, but he was putting her in an impossible position: to be in trouble with her husband, or to be in trouble with her mother.

"I couldn't exactly not invite my mother when Iris was coming," she pointed out, and immediately regretted it when she saw the way Michael's interest piqued.

"And about that. How much longer?"

"I don't know," Gwen said, pinching her lips. But she had a bad feeling it wasn't anytime soon, not if Iris was already making plans for a Forevermore Beauty party. Next weekend. She shook her head. "I have to find the kids."

Eileen was already holding Bea's hand when Michael and Gwen made it into the hall. Declan was still beaming. Norah announced she was going into the cafeteria for the refreshments that were being offered.

And Iris...Iris was down at the far end of the hallway, talking to Joe Cassidy.

Gwen felt instantly more depressed than she already was. And she shouldn't be. Michael was right. This should have been a happy night. A special night. But it wasn't.

"Of course our Bea stood out," Eileen beamed. Lowering her voice only for show, she said from the corner of her mouth, "Did you see some of those other kids? It looked like they didn't even have their hair brushed!"

"Mom." Gwen's heart began to pound with panic.

"I'm just saying!" Eileen cried with feigned innocence. "Our Bea is the prettiest in her class, that's for sure."

Gwen's eyes darted, hoping that none of the parents were overhearing this conversation. Mercifully, most of them had already gone into the cafeteria or were on their way in for punch and cookies.

"You did a very good job tonight," she told Bea. "You, too, Declan. I'm proud of you, getting up there all on your own."

She put her arm around her son and pulled him close, but he just said, "Mo-om." Still, there was a pleased smile on his face as he scuffed his shoe against the linoleum floor.

"Oh, a wonderful job, Declan," Eileen crooned. "It can't be easy following a tough act like that boy who went before you. He must have been in kindergarten! But then the poor thing..." She winced and, in a mock whisper, hissed from the side of her mouth. "Not much in the looks department. At least he has something going for him."

Now Gwen's mouth had gone dry and all she could hear was the pounding of her own heart. She stared at her mother, knowing that the easiest path would be to say nothing, bid her goodnight with false cheer, promise to see her soon, gather up the kids, go home, and pour a fat glass of wine. Wait about a week to stop fuming.

But these were her children. This was her school. And this? This was too much.

"Do not drag me into your judgments of people," she said firmly. It was one of the few times in her life she had dared to speak up to her mother, and her heart was pounding out of her chest, waiting for the counterattack.

Eileen's eyes flashed and then narrowed on Gwen. Michael scurried the children away, and even though she was grateful for it, she wished he was at her side.

Her mother's eyes were two mean slits, her mouth pinched in fury. She looked as if she could slap Gwen, and Gwen knew she wanted to. But slapping would be too obvious, too harsh. No, her mother preferred the hard squeeze of her hands; she preferred to dig her nails deep into Gwen's skin, wherever they'd grabbed her, where no one could see.

Gwen shook her head and walked away on shaking knees, to her husband, to her children, to the life she'd thought would be her happy ending. She turned, halfway to the door to the cafeteria. Her mother was still standing, rooted to the spot, and when she met Gwen's eye she stuck out her tongue.

Now something surged in Gwen. Anger that she rarely dared to feel, a sensation that she had learned to suppress. One that was dangerous, because it meant she couldn't hold back, couldn't look the other way, couldn't be the bigger person anymore.

"You owe me an apology!" she ground out as she stormed back to her mother.

But Eileen just closed her eyes and gave a little shrug as her nose went into the air. "I have no idea what you're talking about."

Gwen felt hot tears sting the back of her eyes, and she was brought back to another time, after Norah was born, and her mother tsked at her when she reached for the breadbasket. Gwen had been hurt and told her father so the moment she could get him alone. But he'd just frowned and said, "I didn't hear her do that." It was what he always said when he didn't want to rock the boat, when he didn't want to make things worse. When he just wanted her to let it go and be the bigger person.

She couldn't let this go. "You owe me an apology," she said again, firmly.

"Lower your voice!" Eileen hissed. She flicked her eyes to the sides.

"I'm telling you how I feel, and you're telling me to lower my voice?"

"People will hear you!" Eileen accused her.

The hallway was all but empty, but Gwen realized that she didn't care what strangers thought. She cared what her mother thought. She cared that she couldn't get through to her.

She was thirty-nine years old. A mother. A wife. She needed to get back to her family. She wanted to join them in the cafeteria, laugh and smile and enjoy this moment—these moments she had longed for, all her life.

"Ready to go soon?" Michael was back at her side, and in that moment, she felt she had never loved him more.

"No celebration?" Eileen blinked. "But I was looking so forward to it! I thought we'd go get some ice cream."

"The kids are grabbing some refreshments in the cafeteria with their friends. It's a school night," Gwen explained, not sure why she had to. It was after eight. Bea should already be in bed. Declan, too. And of course, Norah would still have homework to finish, even if she'd never admit it.

"But it's a special occasion," Eileen insisted. "Don't they want to celebrate with their *grandmother*?"

"The kids need to get to bed," Gwen said again, but she felt herself wavering, knowing how much worse her mother made things when she didn't get her way.

"Fine, fine." Eileen's voice took on an edge of hurt, and she kept her eyes downcast. "I'll just go home and make a cup of tea. Play some solitaire. I'm used to being alone, after all."

Gwen's fists balled at her side as she opened her mouth, but one look at Michael silenced her.

"It's late. You ready, Gwen?"

Gwen nodded and looked around for Iris, who was still standing near Joe, her body language suggestive as she leaned into him, her eyes locked on his as if she were hanging on his every word.

"You coming, Iris?" she called out, forcing a smile.

Iris barely glanced over. "I offered to help Joe clean up."

"I'll give her a ride," Joe said, his voice loud and clear down the length of the hall.

Gwen's mother wasted no time in sharing her opinion of that exchange. They were barely into the hallway before she raised her eyebrows skywards and declared, "That girl was always trouble if you ask me."

Gwen stopped walking. "How can you say that? She was my best friend!"

Eileen gave a little mew. Her chin jutted and her nose remained in the air.

"She was my best friend all through childhood. You always treated her like you liked her, and now you're telling me you didn't?"

"I tried to help her," Eileen insisted. "Look at how that poor child grew up! It was because of me that she saw what a normal, healthy family should look like!"

Gwen's breath felt ragged, and there was a lot she wanted to say, but Bea took her hand. She was rubbing her eyes with the other. It was late. Maybe too late for this conversation, too.

"Where's your car, Eileen?" Michael asked when they stepped outside. The temperature had dropped, and there was a dusting of snow on the hoods of the cars that hadn't been there when they had first arrived.

"To the left," Eileen said. "I guess I'll be okay walking there myself. Of course, you never know what can happen in the dark…"

Gwen met Michael's eye. "Michael, can you walk my mother to her car?"

Eileen lit up like a Christmas tree. "Oh, what a gentleman! Thank you. Honestly, Gwen, you're so lucky to have a man in your life. I hope she lets you know just how lucky she is, Michael."

Gwen clenched her teeth and started to lead the kids toward the minivan, but Eileen wasn't finished yet.

"Oh! Goodbye, my girl!" Eileen swooped in for a hug with Bea after giving the older two children a perfunctory squeeze. Bea did what she did best, cuddle and beam, and Eileen, as usual, showed no signs of releasing her. "I just love my girl!"

"I love you, Grandma," Bea said in her sweet little voice.

"Time for bed, Bea. Go with your mother." Michael glanced at Gwen, his annoyance showing in his face.

"Oh, I'm going to miss my girl!" Eileen jutted her lower lip in a dramatic pout. "I don't know when I'm going to see you again!"

"We see each other all the time, Grandma!" Bea chirped.

Eileen's eyes darted to Gwen and back to Bea. "Is that what your mother tells you?"

Gwen and Michael exchanged a long look. "Time for bed, Bea," Michael said tightly. Still, Eileen showed no signs of releasing her.

"Come on, Bea," Gwen said.

"I love you!" Eileen cried out as Gwen freed Bea from Eileen's arms. "I miss you already!"

"I miss you, Grandma!" Bea said, but even her smile seemed strained.

"What's wrong with her?" Norah asked once they were out of earshot.

"She's lonely," Gwen said, realizing as she said it that it was the excuse she was giving her, not the one she truly believed. It was partly true, of course. Her father had been the center of Eileen's world, and Gwen...Gwen had just been a giant disappointment, and clearly, still was.

"Was she like that with you when you were little?" Declan asked as they crossed the lot to the car.

"No," Gwen said, with more emotion than she'd meant to show.

She glanced behind her. Michael was running toward them. She envied how briskly he could handle her mother, and there were fewer people filtering through the doors now. Iris was still inside, no doubt, laughing with Joe Cassidy and his slow grin.

"Time for bed, honey," she said, looking at Bea, who seemed half-asleep already.

She fumed the entire way to the car, Michael now silent at her side. Of course Iris would find a way to hitch a ride with Joe Cassidy, and of course Joe Cassidy would oblige. Iris was blond and thin and beautiful. And Gwen was married with three children.

But it wasn't the married part that was on her mind. Or the kids' part. It was the fact that no matter how hard she tried or what she'd accomplished, she would never have the breezy success that seemed to follow Iris wherever she went.

It was late, and the overhead light flicked on, illuminating a sprinkle of objects on the crumb-covered floor of the van.

"What is all this?" Gwen asked, looking down. She picked a coin and studied it closely. "Is this a Japanese coin?"

Michael frowned at the object when she held it up to him.

"But wait, there's more!" There, on the floor of the backseat, was a leather rope bracelet, a polished purple rock, and an arrowhead. "An arrowhead!"

She gathered the objects into her palm and presented them to Michael, her heart beginning to race with panic. "Do you think someone broke into our car?" None of this stuff belonged to them. She blinked, trying to process if they'd accidentally opened the door to the wrong vehicle—a crime in itself, quite possibly, even if it was done by accident—but there was Bea's purple unicorn toy on the seat.

And of course, Michael had unlocked the door with his key fob.

She looked at the objects in her hand, trying to make sense of the situation, and then turned to her husband, hoping he could figure this out for her.

Michael's jaw was set, his eyes stony, and he grabbed Bea by the arms. "What are you doing?" Gwen cried in alarm.

Without a word, he pushed his hands into Bea's coat pockets, looking Gwen deep in the eyes as he pulled out three more foreign coins and a laminated four-leaf clover.

"What? What is all this?" Gwen blinked at the objects and back at Michael, whose expression was hard. "Where did you get all these, Bea?"

"She stole it," Michael ground out.

Gwen felt numb. No. Not Bea. She wouldn't have. Couldn't have. The chapter book had been a misunderstanding, truly, but this...

She flashed her eyes on her youngest, willing this all to be a mistake, willing her first instinct to be correct, that someone had broken into their beat-up Honda Odyssey while they were quasi-enjoying the winter music concert and... And what? Spilled their pockets? Forgot their Japanese yen and Indian rupees in their quick getaway?

Bea stared at the ground. She didn't deny it. She didn't even cry. If this had been Gwen, she would have been crying, howling, begging for forgiveness. But of course, this never would have been Gwen. Gwen lived in too much fear to ever do anything that would invite trouble like this.

And Bea...Bea didn't. And right now, Gwen wasn't exactly sure which was worse.

"Get in the car!" Michael barked out, making Gwen jump. "Everyone!"

Even Gwen did as she was told, her eyes darting the parking lot for anyone who might have witnessed their family drama, particularly her mother, who would never let her forget it. She was shaking, she realized, more like vibrating, from her head to toe, and the children were so quiet in the backseat that for a moment she couldn't even be sure they'd all gotten into the car before Michael had peeled away. They drove in silence, the entire eight minutes home, no radio, just the sound of her heart beating to keep her company.

There was no excuse, not really. She had failed as a parent. She had one mission, one goal her entire life, and she had messed it up.

Declan and Norah dashed upstairs as soon as they all got inside the house. Even Bailey knew better than to greet them with his usual playful joy.

"Where did you get these items?" Michael said as he spread them out on the kitchen island. Gwen's stomach turned just looking at them. Thinking of Bea selecting each one, stuffing them in the pocket of the down coat Gwen had picked up for her last fall, the one with room to grow, the coat that everyone complimented because of the little ruffle at the bottom. Didn't she have enough? Wasn't she loved?

"It was treasure day at school."

Gwen closed her eyes. This was even worse than she'd feared. "And you stole your classmates' treasures?"

She imagined the pride these children felt presenting those items to the classroom, wanting to share them, expecting to get them back! She looked at Michael. She had never seen him look so disappointed. It hurt to see, and she had to look away.

Bea's mouth drooped.

"You stole from your friends, Bea." Gwen shook her head. "You told us you wouldn't do that again. You weren't honest."

"Neither were you!" Bea said, bursting into tears. "You said you were twenty-nine! And you're thirty-nine! You're an old lady! And I don't want you to die!"

Gwen managed to stifle a smile as Bea flung herself at her waist. She caught Michael's eye. He was far from amused. "What I did was wrong," Gwen said. "I...shouldn't have said that. It was a silly thing to do. But it's different than taking something that doesn't belong to you."

Bea said nothing.

"Bea, I need you to promise me that you are not going to steal again. From school. From anyone. Do you understand?"

Bea's face was red when Gwen pulled her back to arm's reach. "Okay."

"Go to bed," Michael said wearily. "We'll discuss your punishment tomorrow."

Bea did as she was told, and Michael left the room without a word. A few moments later, she heard Bea's door close, followed by the master bedroom door. Bea probably hadn't brushed her teeth. Normally, this was something that Gwen would check on, but tonight she didn't have it in her, and she didn't trust herself either. She was oscillating between wanting to berate her child and wanting to take her into her arms, hug her, and tell her that she loved her no matter what, even if she was a little thief.

A thief!

The dog was starting to whine, and with a start, Gwen realized he had been waiting to go out. "I'm sorry, guy," she murmured, giving him a scratch behind the ears. Since she still had her coat and shoes on, she decided to take him on a short walk rather than let him into the backyard. He'd enjoy it, and she needed to clear her head, get out of the house. She hooked his leash to his collar and led him to the front door. The neighborhood was dark except for the streetlamps.

Even though she didn't want to, Gwen looked up at the window above the garage and saw that the light was out, just as she knew it would be, and ironically, she decided that it was for the best that Iris had decided to get a ride from Joe Cassidy.

18

IRIS

IRIS WOKE UP with a pounding headache and the hazy reminder of how much alcohol she had consumed the night before. Regret filled her like it always did on mornings like this, and she groaned as she rolled onto her back. Quickly, she assessed the situation. The room wasn't spinning, which was a good sign. And she and Joe had only split a bottle of red. But then, that was following the two drinks at the bar, and merlot had never been her friend, especially when it chased scotch.

She fumbled to the bathroom and drank three glasses of water, cursing the rehab staff for confiscating her ibuprofen and not returning it. Just in case she'd missed something, she rifled through her cosmetic bag, but all she found there were her usual products, and the Ruby Red nail polish that she'd snagged from Gwen's Forevermore Beauty box yesterday. A sample, she'd told herself. Still, she slipped it into her suitcase, next to the figurine she'd taken from her mother's house.

By the time she had finished showering, she felt almost okay, or at least comforted with the knowledge that she would be, by about noon. She sat down at the edge of the bed and reached into her handbag for her phone. Her heart was thumping, just like it always did when she saw the flashing blue light. Had Julian tried to reach her? Indiscretions from the night before filled her with shame, even though she knew that she had really done nothing wrong. A few drinks, a few laughs. It wasn't like they'd kissed. Joe knew she was a married woman. But now he also knew that she was an unhappily married woman.

She'd said it. Out loud. And now, she wondered if it was the plain and simple truth.

She checked the text. It was from her mother. She had promised her last week that she'd stop by this week to help clean out the basement. Was it already Friday?

Two weeks since her last AA meeting. A second week where her chair would be empty. Last week they might have thought she was sick, but Nick had called anyway. By now, speculation would fly. No one missed two meetings without someone assuming the worst.

Two weeks. Nearly two weeks since the party. The party that was supposed to change everything.

But not like this.

She felt like she might be sick, and this time she knew it wasn't from the hangover. With a shaking hand, she combed her wet hair, took a swig from the dregs of the empty bottles in the closet left in her possession, plucked a piece of gum in her mouth, and called an Uber. She dressed quickly while she waited for it. She checked her cash situation: not good. She'd paid for the wine at the bar. It would send the wrong signal otherwise. And of course, she'd gone for the best bottle. And she'd Ubered it back to the house last night, not liking the idea of Joe driving her, not sure what kind of message that would send to Joe, or to Gwen.

No, better to make a clean break at the bar, and that's what they'd done. A hug, a peck on the cheek, an offer to talk. Joe was divorced himself, he'd reminded her, as she slid into the back of the car, suddenly thinking that she didn't like the sound of that. That she didn't want to be part of that club. That it wasn't some common ground he was grasping at.

She fingered her rings now. A four-carat oval-cut diamond rested above the pave eternity band. Eternity, that's what she had been promised.

But then hadn't Nance? And the one before her? Vicki? The sweet girl from back in Julian's hometown in Jersey? The one who didn't fit into his Manhattan lifestyle?

The Uber arrived, and she bolted down the back stairs, her coat unbuttoned, her eyes scanning for Gwen as she rounded the house. She was probably at school drop-off. Or did the kids take the bus? She wanted to talk to her, to at least share the good news that she'd managed to pass out every last invitation in the cafeteria last night, even to the mom of that musical prodigy who lived next door.

Maybe, just maybe, it would offset the fact that she'd gone for drinks with Joe.

Her mother was sitting on the front porch, smoking, when Iris stepped out of the car ten minutes later.

"You'll get cold sitting outside like that," Iris scolded her. She wasn't even wearing a coat, just a blanket draped over her shoulders. Her coffee mug was in her free hand. It was no longer steaming.

But then, maybe it didn't contain coffee.

"I could say the same for you," Lois said, giving her a once-over.

"Please. You always sent me out of the house with wet hair," Iris said, coming to sit next to her on the old swing.

"That's because you never liked to get out of bed, and we were always running late."

Iris considered that. She did enjoy her sleep, the luxury of sinking into bed and folding the covers over her. Of course, her bed at home was nothing compared to the accommodations she had with Julian. California king. Egyptian cotton sheets. A duvet that could have qualified as a cloud. And that mattress.

She loved that mattress. But did she love Julian?

"So," she said, forcing her thoughts away from all that. "You wanted some help cleaning out the basement? I think I took any of the stuff I wanted when I moved out." It hadn't been much.

Lois looked at her for a moment. "It's not your old stuff. I sold that off a long time ago."

Iris frowned. Sure, she hadn't wanted any of it, but she hadn't expected Lois to get rid of it, either. Still, her mother had kept the jewelry box. Her room at least was intact.

Why, she wondered, did she suddenly care?

"I'm thinking of moving," Lois surprised her by saying.

"Moving?" Iris repeated. In all her life, her mother has never even suggested such a desire. She wondered if a new man was already in the picture. "Where?"

Lois shrugged. "Somewhere warm. You know I love a good tan."

Iris laughed. They'd both spent many summer afternoons spread out on towels in the backyard, lemon juice in their hair, baby oil on their skin—it had thrilled Gwen, whose mother would never have allowed such a thing. She shook her head, but a pang squeezed her chest. It hadn't been all bad.

"I can help you. Get you set up."

Lois waved her hand. "I don't need anything fancy. I was never like you, Iris."

Iris swallowed the lump in her throat. It was a true statement. But it hurt all the same. "Well, I can definitely help you get the house ready." Who knew what it would sell for. She didn't want to think about how the inspection would go.

She realized with a heavy heart that it was probably going to be a teardown. Someone would buy it for the land and build a McMansion. It was the practical thing to do, the realistic thing, but something about it depressed her just the same. This was her home, her childhood, and even though she'd turned her back on it, walked away, and never returned, she'd always taken some level of comfort in knowing it was still there.

Try as she might to have denied it at all.

They spent the better half of the afternoon cleaning out the basement, which was mostly old junk that should have been tossed years ago. She left with a promise to be back to tackle the living room and had the Uber bring her into town. Her head was pounding and her mouth still felt dry. Lois didn't have any clean dishes in the house, and besides, she had to make calls in her kitchen. Iris stopped at the café in town for a coffee and then stood on the corner, eyeing the liquor store at the end of the next block. Gwen was probably mad at her again. Her mother was selling what was left of her personal history, meaning she could finally officially deny it ever existed. And her husband was having an affair with Stephanie Clay.

She deserved to self-medicate.

She pressed the button for the crosswalk and waited, just as a familiar figure climbed out of a black SUV and walked over to feed the meter.

"Joe!"

He looked so genuinely happy to see her that for a moment she was taken aback. Julian didn't even look up when she walked entered the room half the time anymore. One time, she calculated how long it would take him to look at her after he came home from work. It was twenty-six minutes. They were already seated at the dining room table, midway through the second course. And then she could only be sure he had looked up because she had dropped her fork so loudly that he probably worried she had chipped his china.

His china. That was half the problem. It should be their china. Really, it felt like Nance's china. Julian had simply secured it in his divorce. The very next day she'd booked an appointment for fillers. Clearly, Botox alone wasn't cutting it.

Iris decided that she was happy to see Joe. It would be a good opportunity to clear the air. "About last night." She was eager to get it out. "I feel like I might have sent the wrong message. My marriage...it's not over."

Joe's eyebrows pulled together but his expression was otherwise unchanged. "Marriage is complicated. I understand."

Iris gave a little smile, even though he couldn't understand. If only it were just about her marriage, maybe she could think more clearly.

"I was just going over to the pub for a burger, if you're up for it?" His eyes were kind, and he hadn't put any moves on her last night, only listened, with compassion and kindness that she hadn't found in all her time in Manhattan. No, the crowd she ran in was far too self-absorbed to want to get deep.

She wavered, but only for a moment. She'd texted Gwen earlier to let her know she was at her mother's. No response to that. Gwen wasn't expecting her back any time soon. She'd probably made dinner plans for her family. And it was getting late. Already coming up on five.

And…she liked Joe. Liked his company. Liked the way he looked at her when she talked, and the way he made her laugh. "Okay, then."

He added some extra change to the meter and led the way to the pub—not the one they'd gone to last night, but a different one, new to town since she'd moved away, which wasn't saying much, considering that was more than half a lifetime ago.

The realization of this calculation settled heavily in her stomach as she climbed onto a barstool. No wonder Lois was making a change. Her children had fled the nest. She never had found love in this town. And Iris had been away for longer than she'd lived here.

Mission accomplished, she thought bitterly. She wasn't Iris Winarski anymore.

Beside her, Joe grinned. He was sweet. Attractive. Maybe even safe. She could lean on him if she wanted to, just like she'd leaned on Julian. It would be easy, but it wouldn't be right.

And Iris Winarski had never leaned on anyone. Except for Gwen. And even that hadn't lasted.

"I'll be right back," she said to Joe as she slid off the stool. She made her way to the restrooms and locked herself in the largest stall.

What was that code they used to press when they were teenagers and they would call boys, wanting to save face if they lost their nerve when someone answered? Gwen was the worst, always chickening out at the last moment, always worried that they would be repulsed that she had called at all, or that they would have nothing to say, and then Iris would huff out a sigh and show her how it was done. She'd take the phone, sometimes not even bothering with the code, and call one of the boys on their list, stroke their ego a bit, the way she'd seen her mother do it a hundred times, and then say that she was going to be at the mall later, and maybe she'd see them there, hint, hint. She'd turn to Gwen and grin. "See? Couldn't be easier."

But Gwen would just shake her head, blinking back tears of frustration, and say, "Easy for you."

Iris stared at the phone in her hand, putting herself back in that moment, with her faded jeans and J.Crew T-shirt she'd found at a rummage sale, a real score. She smiled as she remembered the code. Three buttons, followed by the number saved in her contacts list.

She'd call Julian. Hear his voice. And then what?

She took a deep breath, then pulled up a different number instead. A missed call number. Not a sponsor, she told herself. But maybe...a friend.

Nick answered on the second ring. "Hello?"

She swallowed hard, wondering if she should hang up now, if she could really go through with it. It was the second Friday she had missed. People would think the worst about her. She could set them straight. Say she was on a last-minute vacation, which is what she would of course tell all her so-called friends when she got back to the city.

But she couldn't lie to Nick. Nick bought maple cream do-nuts just for Kathy.

Nick was worried about her. It had been a long time, maybe never, since anyone had worried about her. She'd never given anyone the impression that they needed to.

"Nick? It's Iris."

"Iris!" She could hear the surprise in his voice. Maybe even the relief. There was noise in the background, and it was an hour later in New York. Maybe he was at a restaurant. Maybe he was on a date. He wasn't a bad-looking guy, now that she thought about it. She'd just never thought of him that way.

"We've missed you in our meeting," he said, and Iris was surprised to find that tears stung the back of her eyes. She'd missed them too. The whole, sad lot of them. Even Jimmy.

"I'll be back," she said, and she would. "I just... Well, it's sort of a long story."

"I have time," came the response.

She hesitated, wanting to tell him every single thing that had transpired since the Friday before the party just as much as she couldn't bear to relive it. But that would take time, and Joe was waiting for her. And he was at the bar, with a drink. And she didn't want to drink right now. It hadn't solved her problems, just like it hadn't solved Lois's problems.

"I'm visiting my mother," she explained. "I just wanted to...check in."

He understood, just as she thought he might. "That's what I'm here for."

"Thank you," she said through the tightness in her throat. "I didn't want you to assume the worst."

The worst. Like the fact that she'd slipped, ended up in rehab, and then checked herself out. That instead of facing her problems, she was running from them. Again.

"You doing okay?"

She thought about it for a moment, realizing that in many ways, she'd felt better than she had in a long time. More hopeful, at least. Less panicked about losing everything because, in many ways, she already had.

"I'm getting there," she said honestly.

"Hang in there, Iris," Nick said.

She swallowed hard. "I'll try."

And she had tried. So, so hard. Tried to get out of this town. Tried to better her circumstances. Tried to find the stability that she was lacking.

She disconnected the call and waited a few minutes for her heart rate to slow down and the tears in her eyes to dry. She looked at her reflection in the mirror, at the woman with the long, silky hair made possible with the help of extensions, expensive products, and a colorist who was in such demand that she had to book six months out. Her lips were plumper from filler, her eyes greener from the clever attention to shading, her brows thicker from microblading, her body trimmer from dieting, her clothes a symbol of her status in life.

Maybe she had everyone else fooled, but she saw through it all. And it didn't feel good. She could dress up all she wanted, but it was still just pretend.

She wiped the last of her tears away, dabbed her face dry, touched up her makeup, and then went back to the bar, to sweet Joe Cassidy who was still perched on his stool, waiting for her with a patient smile, who liked her now just as he had way back when. And just for a fleeting moment, she wondered if she wanted to go back to New York at all.

19

GWEN

IRIS DIDN'T MAKE another appearance in the house until Monday morning, once the bus had come to take the kids to school and Michael had already left for the gym and the sofa cushions from where he'd slept the night before had been plumped with the back of Gwen's fist.

Gwen had been wondering when she would finally show up. She'd seen her text on Friday, known that she was helping her mother with the house, which would no doubt be an undertaking, but she knew that wasn't the real reason Iris had stayed away.

Iris never came home Friday night. And there was no way she had slept at Lois's.

Gwen was cleaning the breakfast dishes when Iris walked into the kitchen, wearing oversized sunglasses and a black turtleneck and looking nothing short of ridiculous for nine in the morning in Westlake, Wisconsin.

"You don't need to wear the sunglasses, you know," Gwen said. "You can't hide from me forever."

"Who said I'm hiding?" Iris pushed the sunglasses up onto her head. She wasn't wearing very much makeup, but even still, she was beautiful. "You're mad," she observed, flatly.

"Why would I be mad?" Gwen asked, even though her heart was starting to pound. Damn straight she was mad! But she wasn't just mad about Iris and Joe—that wasn't fair, not really. That just touched a nerve. The hurt went so much deeper.

She put the cereal boxes back in the pantry and gave Bailey a treat while she was there. He ate it and pawed for another. She gave in, just like she always did.

"You're mad at me about Joe, aren't you?" Iris said, coming around to the other side of the island.

"It's not my business what you do, Iris," Gwen said.

"So you're saying you don't care that I've been spending time with Joe." It was a statement, not a question, and Gwen struggled to control her expression. Of course it bothered her. It bothered her deeply. But it shouldn't.

"You didn't come home Friday night," she said. "Did you?"

Iris hesitated, looking her in the eye as if wondering if she should call her bluff or lie. "No."

"Were you at your mother's house?" Gwen asked. It wasn't her business, any more than what was going on in her own life was Iris's business, but Iris's business used to be her business. When did they go from telling each other everything to sharing nothing?

"I was with my mother," Iris surprised her by saying. "But then…"

Of course. "You spent the night with Joe Cassidy?"

Iris looked chagrined. "Nothing happened. I…fell asleep."

Gwen raised an eyebrow. "What's that supposed to mean?" Iris snapped. Her eyes were furious, and Gwen couldn't remember ever seeing her so mad, not even the time the mean girls at school called her a bastard. Gwen had needed to hold her back that time. She saw Iris's fist tighten, the way it did when her brother Steve would steal her soda cans for cigarette money.

"Why do you even care if I slept with Joe or not?" Iris said, giving her a hard look. "You're a happily married woman!"

Gwen felt her defenses rise. "And so are you!"

"Look." Iris's tone had softened. "I know you used to have a...thing for Joe."

"That was more than twenty years ago!" Gwen said. She gave Iris a look that said she was crazy, even though she wasn't. Gwen was the crazy one. To think that she stood a chance against Iris. To even be thinking of another man when her husband was looking for a job to provide for his family.

Something she'd denied. Something she'd hidden. Because she was scared.

And because maybe she was ashamed.

"My life isn't the picket-fence lifestyle you think it is," Gwen said slowly. "I wanted it to be. I still want it to be. But...it's all a mess. Everything I do goes wrong."

"You have three children and a husband who loves you," Iris pointed out. Bailey looked up from his bed in the corner and let out a bark. Iris laughed. "And a dog. I can't even keep a houseplant alive."

Gwen shook her head. "That's how it appears, sure. But Norah hates me half the time—"

"She's a teenager, like you said," Iris insisted. "She'll get past it."

"Will she?" Gwen wasn't so sure. "It scares me, this distance I have with her. It was everything I feared would happen, everything I tried to stop. I don't want to end up like my mother."

Iris laughed. "Please. You couldn't be more different than your mother."

Gwen chewed her lip, nodding. "Maybe. But maybe I should have been more like her. Norah is on academic probation because she skips classes and fails to finish her homework assignments. She had to quit the cheerleading team, and she was so proud to earn a spot. And Declan…I don't even know what to say about him. He has no athletic capabilities, no matter how many activities we've tried to get him into, and you heard my mother! Even the five-year-old next door has surpassed him with piano. And Bea…" She swallowed hard. "Bea has become a kleptomaniac."

Iris barked out a laugh of surprise. "What?"

Gwen jutted her chin. "She takes things. Little things, from school, but still. I couldn't peel my eyes off her when we were in the drugstore picking up a prescription yesterday! I don't trust her anymore. I don't…know her anymore." Her voice broke and Iris walked over and put her arms around her.

"Listen, you need to get a grip," Iris said, once they'd pulled apart. "Bea is going through a phase. She's testing the waters. She's little. She's testing right from wrong. Norah will figure things out. Look at me. Well, bad example." She gave a wry smile. "And Declan just has to find his niche. So he's not going to be captain of the football team. No offense, Gwen, but I bet Michael never was, either."

Gwen laughed and brushed away a tear. Michael was tall and lanky and smart, but it stopped there. "True. But Michael is smart and caring and—" And she was a terrible person to even be looking at Joe, much less wishing for another life.

"He's a good guy. Better than most. And believe me, I know."

Gwen frowned, wondering if Iris was referring to her mother's revolving door of ne'er-do-wells, or something else.

"For someone without kids you seem to know an awful lot about them," Gwen said, feeling better.

Iris looked her in the eye. She wasn't smiling. She looked like she wanted to say something and wasn't sure if she should. "I take things too, Gwen."

That wasn't what Gwen had been expecting. Some revelation about Joe, sure. But this? "I don't understand."

"I take things," Iris said again. "That's what I do. I see things I want, and I take them." She hesitated for a moment. "Julian was still married when I met him."

Gwen tried to keep her expression neutral, but she wasn't sure she was succeeding. "You never told me that."

"Well, I wasn't proud, obviously," Iris said. "He said he was unhappy. He was planning to leave her. I saw what I wanted to see." She jutted her lower lip. "Maybe I still do."

"You could have told me. We used to tell each other those things."

"I felt bad. About all of it. About the wedding, and not inviting you." Iris glanced up, and even now, all these years later, Gwen still felt the sting of that rejection.

"So you didn't elope?" Gwen suspected this, but she needed to hear it.

"I didn't invite my mother, Gwen, so how could I invite you? I was ashamed. Of where I came from. Of who I was. I wanted a fresh start. I wanted to shed Iris Winarski. I wanted to be everything Julian wanted me to be and thought that I was. I guess I didn't think he would love me otherwise."

Gwen knew she could stay strong, say that yes, Iris had hurt her, badly, that it had been unforgivable that she hadn't been included in the wedding, much less invited. But the truth was that they'd drifted apart. It happened to the best of friends. It had happened to them. And now she had a decision to make. Did they go their separate ways again? Or did they give it another try? Had life brought them together this time, instead of tearing them apart?

"Who couldn't love you? You're Iris Winarski with the big smile and the *I don't give a shit* attitude. You're unstoppable."

Iris blinked back tears. "I'm not just here for a visit, Gwennie."

Iris splayed her fingers on the table. Her rings caught the light; her manicure was starting to chip. Gwen was surprised that she hadn't already gone for another.

"Julian...well, he thinks I'm in rehab."

"*Rehab?*" Gwen gasped.

"And I was," Iris said. "I lasted less than a week and then I came here. And Julian...Julian is probably in bed with Stephanie."

Gwen knew that name. She'd heard a lot about Stephanie over the years, felt resentment towards the unknown woman, even jealousy. Stephanie was the New York friend, the glamorous replacement.

Iris brushed away a tear, and Gwen, being the mom that she now was, ran over to her handbag and pulled out a travel-sized pack of tissues. Iris laughed as she took one, but the tears fell harder as she brought one to her cheek.

"I've known about it for a while. I can't say it's the reason why I sometimes overserve myself, but it certainly didn't help matters. I guess I didn't want to admit to myself how unhappy I was." Her eyes filled with tears, and even in her expensive clothing and jewelry, she seemed just as lost and scared as the little girl who had to make it home on her own after dark all those summer nights, even though she had to pedal over the train tracks, and even though they would scare each other with talks of boogeymen and wolves hiding in the woods, and at that moment, Gwen couldn't understand how anyone could walk away from Iris. Not even her.

"I didn't sleep with Joe, if you want to know."

Gwen gave a little smile. "He's a nice guy. He always had a thing for you."

Iris's grin was rueful, but Gwen could see that she was pleased to hear it.

"So Julian doesn't know you're here?"

Iris shook her head. "He would never think to look for me here. He...he doesn't think I have any reason to come back. That I have anyone here."

Gwen nodded, telling herself not to feel insulted or brushed aside. But she couldn't let it go, not this time. "I've always been here, Iris."

"I know that now." She hesitated. "I'm sorry, Gwen. For everything. You were always there for me, and I let you down. And I never wanted to let you down. I just...lost my way."

Gwen pulled in a shaky breath. "That's all I needed to hear." She leaned forward, gave Iris a hug like the ones they'd used to have all those years ago, not like the one that had felt so forced and foreign when Iris showed up on her doorstep.

"You're welcome to stay for as long as you need to," Gwen said.

"Another week?" Iris winced. "And a half?"

In other words, what probably added up to twenty-eight days. Gwen should be mad. Maybe she should even feel used. But if her house, her home, was giving Iris the peace she needed right now, then maybe she should simply feel flattered.

And maybe, a little grateful. The area rugs might have stains from juice and chocolate milk that no amount of steam cleaning had ever fully gotten out, and she didn't have white sofas like Susan and her coffee table was nicked. But it was loved.

Gwen walked over to the cabinet, where the remaining bottles of wine that Iris had purchased were stored. There weren't many left, and she suspected that more had been purchased. "I'm not sure what we should do with these, but I don't think I want to keep them around."

A devilish smile played at Iris's mouth, and Gwen felt a mixture of apprehension and excitement, just like she always did when Iris got one of her ideas. "Don't dump it. We're going to serve it. At the party."

"The party?" Gwen had nearly forgotten that whole scheme. She closed the pantry door. She may as well come clean. "I never got a chance to talk to Caroline—"

"That's okay. I did." Iris beamed, her smile radiant, even though she still had mascara stains under her eyes. "I tracked her down at the refreshment table in the cafeteria after the concert. I recognized her because she was with that little kid of hers. And I passed out all the other invites, too. We're already up to thirty responses."

At first, Gwen couldn't even react, but then her shoulders started shaking. First, she thought she was laughing, but then she realized she was crying. Now it was Iris's turn to look completely stunned.

"Sorry, I'm sorry, it's just..." She pulled in a shaky breath, and she smiled, a smile that came straight from the heart, where a smile hadn't come from in a very long time. "Now I know why you wanted to do this party. But why don't I tell you why I need to."

"Sounds like this calls for coffee," Iris said, hopping off the stool. "And maybe...ice cream?"

"I thought you didn't eat stuff like that anymore!"

"That was the old Iris. Iris Drake. I think I'd like to be Iris Winarski for a little while."

"You don't have to be either. Just be you." Gwen grinned and plucked two spoons from the drawer.

"Like old times," Iris said. "The good old days."

Gwen nodded, because as trying as those adolescent years had been, and as much as she'd yearned for something different and better, those days had been some of the sweetest of her life. Iris had made sure of it.

20

IRIS

IT DIDN'T TAKE long to discover that there was an AA meeting every day at eleven thirty at the First Presbyterian Church just off Main Street. Iris had an Uber bring her into town early so she could decide if she was going to attend or not. The church was walking distance from the town square; she'd have no problem making a last-minute decision.

The coffee shop was busy, full of thirty- and forty-something women in their typical uniforms: expensive yoga wear, clunky lace-up snow boots, fur-trimmed down parkas, and hats with oversized pom-poms. Back when she'd lived in Westlake she couldn't keep up with the fashion sense of her classmates; she couldn't afford to. Now, as her Rolex caught the light when she reached into her handbag to pull out her wallet, she couldn't help but feel empty. She had done it. Outdressed all of them. Had more money, too, even if she was currently low on cash.

She had everything. But she had nothing.

Except for Gwen.

She checked her watch now, remembering when Julian had given it to her, for her birthday, the first year they were married. He had three of them himself, and he felt it was time that she stopped wearing the watch she'd had all through her twenties, which she'd bought at Bloomingdale's for two hundred dollars—a serious splurge at the time.

At first the watch, like the engagement ring, like the apartment, all felt special, and she couldn't stop staring at her wrist, her hand, walking from room to room, soaking it all in, the euphoric relief that she had actually done it, landed right where she always wanted to be.

At some point in time, the novelty had worn off, along with the high that was associated with her new lifestyle. She couldn't pinpoint the time any more than she could determine the exact moment when her novelty had worn off for Julian.

"Iris?"

Iris set down her coffee and turned to see Gwen's tedious neighbor staring back at her, her smile frozen, her ponytail perky, her eyes downright crazy. Did the woman ever blink?

Her gaze roamed over Iris, from the earrings to the wedding ring to the handbag she had just hooked over the back of a chair.

Iris was going to say that she was surprised Susan would remember her name, but then she thought the better of it. Of course Susan would remember her name. Women like her were very transparent. She knew plenty of them back in New York.

In many ways, she was one of them herself.

Rising to her best friend's defense, she tipped her head and said, "I'm sorry, do we know each other?"

"Susan Sharp! Gwen's neighbor? We met at the nail salon a couple of weeks ago." Her eyes widened a notch. Still, the woman did not blink.

"Oh, yes. Nice to see you again," Iris managed a smile she hoped was just dismissive enough and turned back to her coffee.

"I heard through the grapevine that you're joining Forevermore Beauty!"

Oh, Jesus. Joining Forevermore Beauty permanently was never part of the plan. But earning some much-needed cash and helping out Gwen were high on her list. Besides, what else did she have going for herself? If she and Julian divorced, she would need to do something to bridge the gap in her resume.

"How did you find that out?" she asked, genuinely interested. It was one of the things she hated about Westlake. The gossip. The talk. The speculation. She'd thought in a big city she could be anyone she wanted.

How wrong she'd been. About a lot of things.

"Oh, I'm in the know, as you might say." Susan gave Iris a wink, and Iris felt her upper lip curl. "And if you *are* interested in Forevermore Beauty, let me give you my card. I pretty much have the Westlake market covered, but I'm always looking for a new recruit who might add a certain level of sophistication to the brand. And I always choose one special member of my team to join me at the annual conference in New York each year."

Iris stared blankly at the card that was thrust into her hand.

"Oh! There's my coffee date. Call me if you have any questions. Love that bag, by the way!" She smiled so big that Iris had to pull back an inch, and then ran off to the other side of the café.

Women like Susan were the reason that Iris had left this town all those years ago, back when they were kids, but in many ways, Susan was just like her, filling the emptiness the only ways she knew how.

Iris looked down at the card and then tossed it into the recycling bin on her way out. If there was one thing Iris knew, it was how to take on a social climber. And how to take one down.

Unlike the meetings back in New York, there were no donuts in the basement of the First Presbyterian Church. There was no coffee either. There were twelve folding chairs, all empty, and either Iris was the first to arrive or she had the time wrong.

Or maybe she was the only resident of Westlake with a problem.

Was it the reason her marriage was crumbling? No. But it was a symptom. Of unhappiness. Of a realization that finally getting everything she ever wanted might not be what she wanted after all.

She took a seat close to the door, having flashbacks of sitting in a similar circle with Hilda. She managed a smile, something she couldn't have done just two weeks ago. She'd told Gwen all about Hilda. They'd had a good laugh. Had a good cry, too.

A man walked into the room, and Iris felt her heart speed up. It was a small town; she was bound to see someone she recognized or someone who recognized her. But this group was also anonymous. Safe.

The man was older: early seventies, maybe younger. Hard to tell when it came to this kind of crowd. He was thin and wore a plaid shirt tucked into his jeans. Clearly a regular, he took a seat two to her left, gave her a nod, and hooked his right ankle over his left knee.

Iris checked the clock. The meeting was scheduled to start in five minutes. She wanted to ask if they would be the only ones, if she had the time right, but she didn't get the impression the man wanted to talk. He stayed quiet, reserved, a pleasant enough expression on his face until he glanced at the door, a smile crinkling his eyes, and Iris, curious, looked over to see who could transform him in such a way.

It was her mother.

"Ma?" Her voice croaked, and she looked around the room hurriedly, even though she knew she couldn't run. Excuses formed in her mind—she had found the wrong building, she was waiting for a friend—but then it dawned on her that she wasn't the one with the secret.

Lois stood in the doorway to the room, her arms hanging at the sides of her purple coat—the same quilted purple coat she'd worn since Iris was a kid. It broke Iris's heart to realize that. Why hadn't she thought to send her mother a nice coat? She had so many. A few new ones each season. She'd sent her money each month instead. Because she cared. Because it made her feel better. But it hadn't been enough.

Lois stared at Iris, and Iris stared back, and then, because Lois probably didn't know how to react any more than Iris did in that moment, she burst out laughing, a low, gravelly laugh that came right from the gut.

"Well, I suppose there's no use trying to hide. I take it that we're here for the same reason. Like mother, like daughter." She sighed, looking displeased, and Iris opened her mouth to protest. She wasn't an addict. Addicts couldn't stop themselves. She just popped in for the routine. To find a few moments to clear her head. To ground herself.

But that would be lying, wouldn't it?

"We'll talk after," her mother said, giving her a wink. She sat down in the seat between Iris and the man in the plaid shirt, chuckling to herself as a few others flowed in, people Iris had never seen, mostly older than she was, except for the rough-looking kid in his twenties who sat with his long legs splayed in front of him, his arms crossed, his head down.

Iris knew that look. It was the look of denial.

The meeting started, led by a woman who briefly introduced herself and then told her story. A few people spoke. Slip-ups. Temptations. Shame. Iris had never participated in any of these meetings, but today, sitting next to her mother, she didn't want to hide anymore.

"I'm Iris," she said, her voice loud and clear, filling the silence. She looked around the room. Blank faces stared back. They were kind. They were interested. They didn't judge. They didn't care that she was holding a six-thousand-dollar handbag. They weren't impressed. And neither was she.

She pulled in a breath and looked at her mother, who gave her one nod of encouragement, but there was steel in her eyes, just as there had been the time that the electric bill didn't get paid and Iris had gone outside with an ax to chop up some firewood from the trees that had fallen in the previous winter's storm. They'd survived that much. They'd survived a lot. And they'd survive this too.

When the meeting was over, Iris hovered outside the church while her mother said her goodbyes to everyone in the group. It seemed that she was a regular, or at least that she'd been here before, and more than once.

"Well, well," Lois said when she finally stepped outside. Iris could see her breath.

It was cold. But she couldn't walk away. Not just yet. "I wish you had told me."

"Oh, come on. It's no surprise I like my cocktails. Surely you know that?"

Iris winced. She did. Of course she did. She'd known when she was younger that her mother was different than the others. That while they were drinking iced tea or lemonade in the summer, Lois was pouring gin into her coffee mug. "I didn't realize that you were trying to stop."

"Off and on for years. It's part of why I decided to move. I need a change. A lot of change. But then, you understand that." Lois lifted an eyebrow.

Iris did. And she was still seeking it, wasn't she?

"So? What has you here?"

"Oh, I…" Iris pulled in a breath, looked out across the town square. They had a festival there every summer. She'd save up her recycled can money for ride tickets. She'd loved that carnival. Loved the lights. The music. The excitement. She and Gwen had gone every year.

She longed for those times. Life was simpler then. In some ways, it was even better.

She looked at her mother. There was so much she could say, and so much that she hadn't. "I like wine. Too much, maybe. Julian...Julian thinks I'm at rehab right now."

"He doesn't know you're in Westlake?"

"No." Iris shook her head, and said quietly, "He doesn't know I'm in Westlake. We're...we're having a lot of problems."

Lois didn't look surprised to hear this. She pulled out a pack of cigarettes, offered one to Iris.

Iris shook her head. She wished Lois would quit, but everyone had their vices.

"You still love him?" she asked.

"I don't know," Iris replied. The response confused her, surprised her, but it was the first thing that came out of her mouth. And it was the truth, she realized.

"You're a strong girl, Iris. Always were. And you always come out on top."

"I'm not so sure I came out on top this time, Ma," Iris said, shaking her head. It was cold, and she shivered into her coat, but she wasn't ready to leave just yet.

"Maybe not. But maybe your story's not finished yet. Maybe this is just part of your path. Not where you end up."

Not where she would end up. Iris liked the sound of that.

"Things will get better. They don't always stay the same. That's the funny thing about life. You can't get too comfortable, Iris. In any situation. But I think you know that already."

She supposed she did, even if she'd broken that rule.

"And you?" She smiled at her mother, watched her drag on her cigarette and then blow it out in three perfect rings. "What do you really want from life, Ma?"

"That's just the thing, Iris," Lois said wryly. "I don't want for much, not like you. I know how people see me around here, but that's not why I'm leaving. I like the sun. I'm sick of this weather. I'm ready to try something new. But I'm not running away."

"And you think I did?" Iris knew the answer already.

"Well, you never came back," Lois pointed out. She said it frankly, without accusation. Without judgment. "This wasn't where you wanted to be back then. I understand that. The question is, where do you want to be now?"

Iris looked at the pavement under her feet, salted to melt the snow. She hadn't thought that far ahead, she supposed. Hadn't dared to. Now she looked up at the town square again, imagining it filled with lights and music, the smell of cotton candy, and Gwen's hand on hers, pulling her through the crowd. A breeze blew, cold on her face, and she closed her eyes, pretending for a moment that she was back on the Ferris wheel, still just a fourteen-year-old girl, struggling, scared, but so happy for that split second of time.

And for the first time in a long time, the future felt wide open, without an assurance or security. But instead of seeing it as scary, she saw it as full of possibility.

21

GWEN

THIRTY-THREE PEOPLE were coming to their party, at least by Iris's last count. They'd spent most of the last two days shopping and preparing the house. The kitchen island would serve as the buffet for the food, and the dining room table would display all the Forevermore Beauty items, both for sale and for order. Extra chairs were brought into the living room, where Iris and Gwen would take turns giving demonstrations and makeovers, and the mudroom off the kitchen would be closed off for order taking and cash collection.

Walking through the rooms of her house, Gwen could almost feel the possibility that they might sell a good portion of her shipment tonight. At best, they might even get some orders. As for a recruit, well, you never knew. At least one out of the bunch, maybe two?

"This display is really impressive," Gwen said, not daring to touch her dining table for fear of knocking over something that Iris had carefully put into place. She'd grouped everything by color rather than by product, creating a visual that would have brought tears of rage to Susan's eyes. "I almost wish Susan was here to see it."

"Just seeing thirty cars parked on the street will have her calling all her friends and eating her emotions for hours," Iris said with a sly grin. "She won't know what you're doing over here. And that alone will kill her."

The thought should have thrilled Gwen, she knew, but right now, it didn't. She was too overwhelmed with how much they'd accomplished in such a short period, and too nervous for what the night would bring—or wouldn't—to think about anything else.

"The flowers were a nice touch," she said, looking at the cheerful arrangements that Iris had set up throughout the first floor of the house.

"Don't wait for the next party then," Iris said. She gave her a pointed look. "Sometimes you need to buy yourself flowers, Gwen."

Gwen released a steadying breath and nodded her head. Iris was right. And sometimes it was the smallest things that could turn an entire house—or night—around and make everything feel a little better.

"You want to borrow my fur-trimmed poncho again?" Iris suggested, and Gwen opened her mouth to say yes, thank you, but she shook her head. Iris had given enough. Without her help, there was no way that Gwen could have put this all together, or even thought to host a party at all.

"I'm good, but thanks. I might have you do my makeup though," she said, looking at Iris hopefully.

"Just like when we were kids! I'll meet you back here in a half an hour then?" Iris called over her shoulder as she headed toward the back door.

Gwen ran up the stairs, Bailey at her heels. He'd stay in the bedroom for the party. Michael was taking the kids to a movie. It had taken all of last evening for them to agree on one, but the decision was made. They'd leave in twenty minutes.

She walked into her closet, pulled out the outfit she'd worn for brunch with her mother, and put it on. She wouldn't be as fashionable as Iris, but then, she never would be, and that was okay.

"You look nice," Michael came into the bedroom as she was fastening the back of her earrings.

She was so surprised to see him there that she didn't bother to cover her shock. "I didn't realize you were still using this room."

He narrowed his eyes. "What's that supposed to mean?"

She gave him a long look. Did he really not know what she meant? She waited, huffing out a breath when she realized she would have to now say what she'd been avoiding. On the night of her party. When she didn't want to get into this.

"I mean that you usually sleep on the sofa." She didn't mention the office. She didn't need to explain that Iris was staying another week.

"Well, I'm tired."

"We're both tired. We have three kids." She walked past him to the closet and then came back out again. "I still come to bed every day. I still make an effort."

"I make an effort!" An edge of hurt crept into his tone, and oh, Gwen didn't need this tonight. Tonight was her big night. It was what she had been working toward.

But Michael, and this family, that had always been her number one goal, hadn't it? It was all she'd ever wanted.

"You look nice," he said again.

She rolled her eyes. "You have to say that." As soon as the words slipped, she realized she'd heard them before. From Norah.

"You never accept one of my compliments." Michael sounded exasperated as he walked into the closet and came back with his fleece.

Gwen frowned at her reflection in the mirror. "I do too."

But Michael shook his head. "No. You don't. You just put yourself down. I tell you you're pretty, you're beautiful, and you just say that you aren't. I tell you that you look nice. You tell me that I don't have to say that. But I want to say it. Because that's what I think. And you don't believe me. Sometimes I wonder why I bother."

Gwen turned to stare at him. Was it true? But it was, and she knew it.

"You don't like it when I touch you," Michael went on.

"Michael!" Gwen started to argue but the hurt in his eyes told her something she'd already known but she hadn't pieced together. How many times had she pushed Michael away since they'd come back to Westlake? She'd felt weary, tired with three kids, and she'd struggled to lose the baby weight after Bea. She'd known they were growing distant, that there wasn't as much affection, that they were spread thin, that they had other things to think about, like an endless list of responsibilities. But now she thought of the times he used to reach over and put a hand around her waist, and she'd scoot away, afraid he'd feel her muffin top. Afraid of what he'd think.

She had been one size smaller then, too. But she still hadn't felt good enough. For her husband. For the man who told her she was beautiful and believed it too.

She'd been waiting to hear that her whole life. And when she finally did, she didn't believe it.

"God, Michael, I'm sorry," she said, blinking back the tears that filled her eyes.

"I can't make you feel good about yourself, Gwen," he said. "But sometimes, well, sometimes it's made me wonder if you just aren't attracted to me anymore."

The thought had never crossed her mind. She could still picture the way he looked, that day he'd come into her office, gave her his sales pitch, his brown eyes earnest, his smile boyish and a little crooked. She'd never dared to make a move on a guy before. Never dared to flirt. She'd been too scared. Too fearful of rejection.

But Michael. She couldn't let him get away without trying. She still couldn't.

"I'm the one living the life we agreed to. I'm the one coming to this room every night. I'm not the one sleeping on the sofa every night. You say you fall asleep watching television, but that's a choice, Michael."

"And you have a choice, too," Michael said, almost angrily. "Things don't just happen to you. Susan. Iris. Your mother. You have choices."

Choices. For so much of her life, she felt out of control, like she was just reacting to other people, keeping the peace, not making things worse for herself. Now she considered the possibility that maybe she could have found a way to make them better. To not judge herself on other people's opinions of her. To decide whose opinion mattered at all.

And Michael's mattered most.

"You wouldn't even tell your mother that I lost my job," he said. "It's like you're ashamed."

"I'm not ashamed," she said quietly. "I was never ashamed. I was worried. And scared. And I feel...out of the loop. I don't know where you go. And I don't want to ask because I don't want you to, I don't know, feel worse if you don't have a meeting or an interview."

"I do have an interview," he said, giving her a small smile. "Next week. I wasn't going to tell you about it because it might not turn into anything, but I'm hopeful. It's a great opportunity, and it never would have come about if I hadn't gone through what I did."

A silver lining then, Gwen thought. Life had a funny way of presenting those when you most needed them. If you were willing to look.

She stepped toward him, setting her hands on his arms. "Oh, that's wonderful, Michael. It's what you needed. What you deserve. And if they don't hire you, the next person will."

He shrugged, but she could tell he was pleased. "We can talk about it more later. I should get the kids out of the house."

Reluctantly, she nodded.

"If you need more time, I can also sneak the kids into another show," he said from the doorway.

Gwen's eyes flew open, and she almost knocked the necklace she was about to put on off her dresser. "Don't you dare!"

Michael laughed and kissed the top of her head. "Oh, Gwen. You haven't changed one bit."

But she had, she thought, as she studied her reflection in the mirror, watching Michael leave the room, closing the door behind him. And she wanted to.

In the distance, she could hear the muffled chatter of the kids, Bea's voice the most animated, and Michael ushering them out the door. It took forever, at least five times as long as it would have taken her, but then, that was her job, wasn't it? She was a mom. It was the role she'd always wanted. Sometimes she was winning. Sometimes…Well, she was far from perfect.

But to Michael, she was beautiful. She let that soak in for a minute.

A moment later there was a knock at the door, and Iris was standing there, looking elegant as ever in an outfit that Gwen never could have pulled off, and for once didn't wish she could. A cream cashmere sweater dress with a gold chain belt and matching stilettos. Her flaxen hair was draped down her back, her makeup perfectly applied, her earrings sparkling.

Iris was beautiful, yes, but she didn't need blush or lipstick or even expensive clothes to make Gwen see that. Gwen knew her heart. Her secrets and dreams, her fears. Iris might look like a woman who had it all, but only Gwen knew what she had done to get to this moment. And that it wasn't all as wonderful as it appeared.

"Ready for your makeover?" Iris waggled her eyebrows and followed Gwen into her bathroom.

Like she had when they were kids, Gwen sat on the toilet seat, closed her eyes, and tipped her head back. She could hear

Iris rustling through her top drawer, and just like all those years ago, she didn't feel the need to give her friend any direction. She trusted her.

Iris went to work quickly and efficiently, with that confidence she'd always held, until she finally blotted Gwen's lips and said, "All done."

Gwen opened her eyes and stood to look in the mirror, grinning at what she saw. Two friends, side by side. No longer young girls, wondering what bright plans the world held for them, but two thirty-nine-year-old women who had realized that life would never quite be everything they'd hoped it would be, and that was okay.

The doorbell rang and Bailey let out a bark from where he was lying on the bed, watching her get ready with passive interest. She checked her watch in panic, wondering if someone was early. Seeing no choice but to let them in from the cold, she hurried down the stairs to see her mother standing on the front stoop.

"Going somewhere?" Eileen frowned as she stepped inside. Her eyes roamed over Gwen's outfit. "I just saw Michael pull out of the driveway."

"I have plans with Iris tonight," she said, glancing at the oversized wall clock over the console table.

"I see." Eileen's lips pinched. "So you have time for friends but not your mother."

Gwen felt her shoulders sink. She had a decision to make, and a week ago it wouldn't have been a decision at all. A week ago she would have apologized to her mother, promised to make it up to her, offered to do something with her at the earliest date possible, even if it wasn't convenient, and then she would have felt guilty for hours, and her party, the event that she and Iris had worked so hard for, would be ruined.

But tonight she felt bold. Tonight she felt...beautiful. And tonight she had someone waiting for her upstairs. Someone who was always on her side.

"It's healthy for me to have friends," Gwen said. "Why don't you see if the women from your card group are free tonight?"

"So this is how you treat me?" Her mother scowled. "I gave you life. I took care of you when you were sick. I paid for your education. But I see, this is how you choose to spend your time."

Gwen pulled in a breath. Her mind was racing, and she didn't know what to say next. Didn't know what she could say. It didn't matter. It never would. Never had.

"My family is at the movie theater right now so that Iris and I can have a few hours. This has been planned."

"Your family?" Eileen blinked.

"Michael and the kids. They're my family, Mom, just like Dad and I were your family. You're still my family, but right now, I need to take some time to give my attention to my husband and my children."

"What are you saying?"

"I'm saying that I need to have some space to focus on my family."

"Some space? But I never see you!"

Gwen bit back a response. They would never agree on this statement. She had long ago reached the conclusion that she could see her mother six days a week and only be reminded that she hadn't seen her seven.

"Well, I shouldn't be surprised. Your husband is sleeping on the sofa. You remember what I said about that." But before Gwen could respond, Eileen just tossed up her hands. "The way I see it, Michael's just had it."

Gwen ground her teeth. "Why would he have *had* it?"

Eileen looked at her as if she was crazy. "All these kids! I always put my *marriage* first. Bea's a sweetheart, of course," she added. "This house is cluttered, and I know you won't admit it, but you've put on weight. I tried to help you, but you've let yourself go."

"And that gives my husband a reason to have *had* it?" Gwen had heard enough. And *she* had *had* it. There would be no convincing her mother of anything. She'd only upset herself more by trying.

Eileen just shrugged. Her smile was satisfied.

"And Bea is sweet," Gwen said. "But she's not perfect."

"What do you mean?" Her mother looked appropriately affronted.

"She's been in trouble at school. She took things from the classroom."

Eileen put a hand to her heart. "You spoil those children too much! What children need is discipline and to respect their parents! You've ruined them!"

"Oh, so now Bea is ruined? And Norah is ruined because she has struggled with adjusting to high school? And Declan is ruined because…because…" She couldn't even find an answer to that one. "They're not perfect. And I'm okay with that."

And I'm okay with not being perfect either, she thought, smiling.

Her mother's brow pinched and she took a step forward. "What is that?" She jabbed at Gwen's mouth, forcing her to take a step backward. "What is that on your tooth? Did you *chip* it?"

Fury built up in Gwen's chest, making her feel like she could burst into tears. But she wouldn't. Not tonight. Not when Iris had just applied her makeup, not when she was supposed to be having fun, not when her friend was somewhere in this house, standing behind her.

She'd assumed that the chip wasn't noticeable anymore. No one else had mentioned it, and she no longer felt self-conscious about it. Until now.

Eileen's lip curled. "So now you're walking around with a chipped tooth? What will people think of how I raised you?"

"I have to go, Mom," she said with a sigh.

"Well, I can see that I'm not wanted here." Eileen pushed toward the door. "Have fun with your friends tonight. I won't live forever, you know," she added bitterly.

Gwen should have let it drop. Should have known that her mother would need the last word and that nothing she could say would make this conversation shift in a direction she wanted it to go. But she was tired of the threats. She was tired of pretending that nothing was wrong.

"What's that supposed to mean?" she asked calmly.

"It means that you'll be sorry when I'm no longer around." Eileen lifted her chin and sniffed, giving a long, lingering look, but Gwen said nothing.

Eventually, Eileen opened the door and closed it behind her with more force than needed. She took her time backing out of the driveway. Maybe she was expecting Gwen to come running out after her. To tell her that she would cancel her plans. To tell her that she was sorry.

Or maybe she just wanted to ruin her night.

Gwen turned her back to the door and took in her house. From this viewpoint, the back rooms of the house where the party would be held weren't visible, but still, the entire house seemed to shine in a new light. Nothing she ever did or said would ever be enough for her mother; she knew that now. But all this, from the framed prints to the throw pillows to the color of paint she'd obsessed over for weeks, was her future. It was the life she always wanted, and she intended to enjoy it, starting tonight.

Keeping with her promise, Iris didn't pour a single drink the entire duration of the party. And she wouldn't have had time, anyway. Caroline from next door was surprisingly the first person to volunteer for a makeover. "I don't know how to choose the right color," she admitted sheepishly. "I saw all those women going to Susan's house, and I thought, no one even tried to ask me!"

"I'm sorry," Gwen said. "I assumed you wouldn't want to go. I didn't think you liked Susan."

"Of course I don't like Susan!" Caroline hooted. "Who does? That woman is, well, frankly, she's a real bitch."

Gwen laughed. "She's certainly not the nicest neighbor on the block."

"Then why did you go?"

Gwen stared at Caroline for a moment, feeling the shame at her reason. "Honestly? I guess it just felt good to be invited."

Caroline nodded. "Well, hopefully you give that bitch a run for it tonight."

Gwen laughed at the pet name Caroline seemed to have adopted for Susan and tossed an extra tube of Beautiful Burgundy lip liner in Caroline's goodie bag for that. They could help each other out, they decided. Caroline's son could practice piano with Declan in exchange for cosmetic tips from Gwen.

"But I have other advice I need too," Caroline said. "Are you a decorator? I never invite anyone over because my house is a mess. I bought curtains, but they're too short and not wide enough! I bought pillows for the sofa? My husband says they look like something that would belong to an old lady. I could never host a party like this."

But, Gwen realized, maybe she wanted to.

The old Gwen would have been modest, would have put herself down, would have said that it was nothing, she just looked at some catalogs, anyone could pull this together, and had they seen Susan's house? Because that was way nicer.

But this house was her pride and joy. And she hadn't let enough people inside it.

She practically sailed into the kitchen, looking for Iris, who was standing in the laundry room, scribbling on an order sheet. All at once, the warm glow seemed to leave her and the old apprehension seeped in again. "How'd we do?"

Iris glanced up at her. "You ready to know?"

"That bad?"

"We've sold out all our inventory and I already have an order sheet filled." Iris beamed. "And you need to stop being such a pessimist."

"We sold out?" Gwen snatched the order sheets from Iris's hand. Sure enough, it was full to the bottom. "We'll have to place an order from corporate," she whispered.

"I told you this would work," Iris said. "When have I ever let you down?" They exchanged a look, and Iris winced. "Bad question."

Not a bad question, just the wrong one.

"You know what I always admired about you, Iris? You always knew what you wanted, and you believed in yourself to go after it."

Iris raised her eyebrows. "Funny. I could say the same about you."

"As fun as this was, I don't think that selling cosmetics and giving Susan a cut of my profits is the right job for me. I think..." Gwen bit her lip. "I think I could do better."

Iris grinned at her. "I was waiting for you to say that."

That night, after the party, just as she was drifting off to sleep, the bedroom door opened, eliciting a bark from Bailey that was loud enough to wake the entire household.

Gwen shot up, her heart thundering, until she saw Michael, shushing the dog.

He walked over to his side of the bed, which was still perfectly made. She'd learned a long time ago to sleep on only half the bed, and she still did, as if she had been subconsciously waiting for his return. For this moment.

He slipped under the duvet and, without a word, reached out and held her hand. It felt good. It felt right. It felt like what had been missing, and what might have been there all along.

22

IRIS

THE FLIGHT TO New York was scheduled to land at one, giving them just enough time to drop their bags off at the hotel and make it to the apartment before Julian went out for the night. She knew his schedule. On Friday he stayed at work until five, came home, poured a drink, and changed for dinner. Reservations would have been made, probably at his favorite steakhouse. Whom, she wondered, was he dining with tonight? After all, he wasn't expecting his wife back until tomorrow…

Iris had booked a suite at the Essex House, with a sweeping view of the park and an ideal central location. She charged it to Julian's credit card, because technically, her time at rehab had come to an end, not that it mattered anymore. She was a free woman, or she would be, soon enough.

"This hotel is gorgeous!" Gwen's eyes were round as she walked through the space and straight to the windows. Iris tried to feel the same rush that she once felt when she walked into hotels and restaurants that once felt so far out of reach, like a part of another world, but the oversized sofas and polished wood no longer elicited that spark.

She came to stand next to Gwen at the window, and there, looking down at the city sprawled out below her, was that feeling. That excitement. The little kick in her pulse that had never gone away in all the years she had lived here.

"It never gets old," she whispered, and it didn't. Here, right now, anything felt possible.

And maybe it was.

She stepped away from the window and went into the bedroom to unpack her clothes. They were here for two nights, and she'd packed light, knowing that the majority of her clothes were still in the apartment, so close that if she went back to the window and searched the sea of buildings that stretched over each side of the park, she would surely spot it. High in the sky, with views as grand as this. Once this sight had made her feel a sense of accomplishment, of closure. Now, it made her think of everything that was yet to come, and all the life that was left to be had.

And staying in that apartment with a man who didn't love her was no way to live at all, was it?

"I don't think I'll be very long," she said to Gwen when she came back into the living area half an hour later.

Gwen was flicking through the hotel's amenities brochure. "No rush. I think I'll go for a walk. Take in the sights."

"Let's go to dinner after," Iris said. She was craving carbs, lots of them, and she knew just the place. She hadn't been there in ages. It wasn't Julian's scene. Or Stephanie's. Really, they belonged together.

And they certainly deserved each other.

Gwen looked pleased, but concern lined her face as she watched Iris take a long look in the mirror above the minibar. It was tempting to reach for a drink. Just one, for liquid courage, but that wouldn't exactly put her in a position of strength with Julian. And today, she intended to show him that she was in control. Of her life. And her future.

"I could come with you, if you want, for moral support. Sit in the cab?"

Iris considered the gesture, knowing that half of her wanted the comfort of having Gwen there, someone on her side, but also knowing that this was something she had to handle on her own. This was her husband. Her marriage. The life that she had always wanted but didn't want in the end. It wasn't a life at all.

"Thanks, but I'll be okay." And she would be, she thought, as she pulled in a breath and walked out the door to the elevator bank. Somehow she would be okay. She'd gotten this far on her own, after all.

The cabs were lined up outside the hotel, and the doorman opened the door to the first. She slid in, inhaling the scent of tobacco and leather mixed with pine-scented air freshener, and gave the address to her house. To her apartment. To Julian's apartment.

Traffic was bad, and after only being gone for a few weeks, she was reminded of the noise of the city, the stress of congestion, and for once it didn't make her feel like a part of something bigger. It made her feel lost. Insignificant. Like she could fade into the distance and no one would notice. She didn't have people here, at least not ones who cared.

"Hello, Ernie," she said to the doorman when the cab finally arrived at the building.

If he seemed surprised to see her, he was too professional to make note of it. Instead, he walked to the trunk and said, "Bags, Mrs. Drake?"

She shook her head. None coming in, at least.

"It's good to have you back, Mrs. Drake," he said, opening the door for her. "Mr. Drake just arrived a few minutes ago."

Alone? She refrained from asking. She'd find out soon enough.

A ripple of nerves shot through her, but she pushed them back again. She walked through the marble lobby, her heels clicking past the oversized floral arrangement that was changed each week, to the elevators, and pressed the button for her floor.

The doors slid open sooner than she recalled. Time felt distorted. Everything felt just as strange as it did familiar.

She had her keys in her bag, and she opened the door to the front hall, which opened into the living room at the far end. It was dark outside the wall of windows. The apartment was quiet. If Ernie hadn't told her that Julian was home, she might have thought otherwise.

His study door was closed. Was he in there? She could knock, find out. Or she could open the door. See what was going on behind it.

She supposed it didn't matter anymore.

She put her hand on the solid brass knob, pulled in a breath, and, before she lost her nerve, pushed it open.

Julian was in his favorite leather armchair. He shot up when he saw her.

"Iris!" His expression changed from surprise to confusion. "I wasn't expecting you until tomorrow."

"I know," she said, giving him a tight smile. He looked good, she thought. Too good. No one could ever say that Julian Drake wasn't a good-looking man, with his slicked-back hair and piercing blue eyes and a smile that still made her heart roll over. Made her overlook his transgressions. Made her want him to want her.

But he didn't want her. Not anymore. And she didn't want him.

"Don't mind me," she said. "I'm not here to interrupt your plans. Because I know you have them, of course. You have your secret plans."

He sighed, looking annoyed. "Have you been drinking again?"

"That's a convenient excuse, isn't it? Make me look like the crazy one instead of admitting your secrets? I know all about you and Stephanie. I found her red thong right here in this chair."

Now she had his full attention. "Iris—"

"I've been wondering what your end game was. How long you would drag this out. When you would finally just let me out of this misery."

"It was nothing," Julian said, growing a little red in the face. "Stephanie is a client. I've represented her in two of her divorces. We have history. She's fun, but she's not…marriage material."

Iris cocked an eyebrow. She walked farther into the room and picked up a framed photo of their wedding. It had been beautiful, but she couldn't let herself get swept away by fantasy. Setting it back on the shelf, she turned to face him. "The thing is, Julian, that I have a little secret of my own," she said. "I didn't stay at Andover these past twenty-eight days. I've been in Westlake for the past three and a half weeks. And it was a better cure than any formal program might have been."

He frowned. "Westlake?"

He didn't even connect the name.

"My hometown, Julian," she said. "Westlake, Wisconsin. That's where I was raised. In a three-bedroom, one-bathroom house that used to belong to my grandparents. It was twelve hundred square feet, and sometimes we didn't have money to keep the lights on. So you see, Julian, maybe I was never marriage material for you, either."

"But you…" He stared at her, and for a moment she felt bad for the part she had played in all this. She'd let him see what he wanted to see. A beautiful, smart, confident woman with a nice enough apartment and a good education. She was all those things. But she was so much more.

"I wasn't completely honest, Julian. But then, neither were you," she said sadly.

"Iris, I can explain," he said, holding up a hand.

"No, I don't think you can," she said. "But that's okay. I have accepted one truth, Julian, and that is that you don't love me. Maybe you never did. Maybe I was just a younger version of Nance. Maybe I was more glamorous, or maybe I at least tried to be. But we started our relationship being dishonest, and it would seem that we're finishing it that way, too."

"Finishing it? It's not what you think. Stephanie was just a onetime thing. It was wrong. I want you here. I want you in our home."

For a moment, she almost believed him, and it would have been so easy to accept his words. To keep living this life. To walk into her bedroom, her closet, to wake up tomorrow in her California king with the soft sheets and cloud-like mattress and eventually pretend that none of this, not even her trip to Westlake, had ever happened.

But she couldn't pretend anymore.

Iris shook her head. "No, Julian. This is *your* home. Once it was Nance's. Then it was mine. Maybe soon it will be Stephanie's, despite what you say. But it was always yours. I was just passing through, and I think you knew that."

He had the decency to look ashamed.

"I loved you, Julian, but I wasn't happy. This life...well, it's not for me after all."

"Where will you go?" he asked.

She shrugged. She knew just where she would go, but there was no need to tell him that. "This was just a chapter in my life," she said. "I don't know where my story ends, but I'm excited to find out."

She walked to the door, her head held high, but she wasn't finished, not yet. "Oh, and you'll be hearing from my attorney, of course. Monday."

Sofia was standing in the foyer when Iris emerged from Julian's study, clutching a dust rag, her eyes wide. "You're leaving, Mrs. Drake?"

Iris didn't have anything left in her to come up with a witty response. Sofia had won. She'd gotten her way. They'd all gotten their way. "Yes, Sofia. I'm sure Delilah and Katrina will be just as thrilled as you are."

But then, they already knew, didn't they? They'd marked her time from the moment she'd first unpacked her suitcase in the walk-in master closet. There was no reason to invest in her. She wasn't a permanent fixture.

"That Stephanie is no good, Mrs. Drake," Sofia said, following her into the bedroom. "I wanted to tell you that she is not a true friend."

"I would have appreciated that, Sofia," Iris said, turning to look her square in the eye. "A true friend. We all need a few of those, don't we?"

Sofia twisted the rag in her hands until Iris decided she couldn't be bothered. She didn't need her maid's approval. Or Delilah and Kat's. Or the strangers in the restaurants. Or anyone's.

"Don't worry," she said as she began emptying her drawers. "I've got people in my corner."

They'd been there all along. And they were infinitely more loyal than anyone under this roof.

Gwen was waiting for her in the hotel lobby when Iris returned. It was late and her stomach was rumbling. Of all nights, this would be the one to pour a drink, but she strangely didn't feel the need for it. The life she'd said goodbye to tonight wasn't much of a life at all.

"There's one more place I want to go before we head out of town," Iris said. "Will you come with me?"

They took a cab across town, pulling to a stop outside the church off Broadway on the city's Upper West Side. It felt like months since she had been standing outside these doors, sunglasses covering her face, her eyes darting in case she ran into anyone that she knew.

"I thought you were going to pay a visit to Stephanie," Gwen said. She was shivering in the cold.

"I have nothing to say to her. She won. Maybe she and Julian will live a long, happy life together. It's weird, but I almost don't care anymore."

Iris had missed the Friday meeting, of course. She might never see Nick and the others again. But she didn't want them talking about her, she didn't want them speculating. And not because she was concerned what they might think, but because she knew they cared, and she didn't want them to worry.

She had a note, brief but honest, tucked into a hotel stationery envelope. She slipped it into the mailbox of the church, knowing Nick would get to it soon. That he'd know she was okay, or would be, soon.

"Dinner?"

Gwen nodded eagerly, and they went back to the cab that was waiting for them, the meter still running. In typical Gwen fashion, she buckled her seat belt and gave Iris a little smile. "You sure you're okay? You can talk about it, you know."

Iris knew she could tell Gwen every detail, but not tonight. Tonight she wanted to enjoy New York the way she had when she'd first come here, wide-eyed and full of hope and determination. She hadn't felt like that girl in a long time. Until recently.

"Julian and I are over. Maybe we've been over for a long time. Maybe we never stood a chance." She sighed.

"You loved him," Gwen said quietly.

Iris nodded. "I did." But she didn't anymore. At some point, she had stopped loving the man and started clinging to the life they had instead. And she was tired of hustling and scraping by, pretending that everything was fine when it wasn't. Pretending that she was someone she wasn't and would never be.

Gwen's phone pinged, and she glanced down at the screen, unable to suppress her smile as she typed something and then slipped the device back into her handbag.

"Everything okay?" Iris knew how much importance Gwen had placed on this trip. What a big deal it was for her to leave her kids and Michael, even for a few days. She'd been checking in since they arrived at the airport, fielding calls from Bea, who couldn't stop asking when Gwen would be home.

"Better than okay." Gwen grinned as if she had been suppressing something big. "Michael's interview on Wednesday went well, but I didn't want to jinx it but…well, he just got a call from the human resources department. He got the job!"

"Oh, Gwen, that's great!" Iris could see the relief in her friend's eyes.

Gwen nodded thoughtfully. "I can relax now, honestly. Enjoy this trip. I feel guilty saying that I needed a break from the people I love most."

"It's a weekend getaway, and how often do you ever do anything for yourself?"

Gwen nodded. "I've been thinking about that. I don't want to go back to Forevermore Beauty—"

Iris snorted. "Good!"

Gwen leaned forward as the cab pushed through traffic. "But it was sort of fun to have something of my own. I think that I'd still like to work. Bea's in full-time school now."

Iris suppressed her smile now. "You'd still need something flexible, for the kids."

Gwen looked thoughtful. "And I want to do something meaningful, something that I care about, not just something to get me out of the house."

Iris nodded. "Something that helps other women, perhaps? Something that makes you feel good about yourself by making other women feel good too?"

Gwen stared at her, excited. "Yes! How'd you know?"

"Because I know exactly what I want to do next." She couldn't yet bring herself to say *after the divorce*; it was still too fresh. And as she looked out the window and took in the lights and buildings and people that had once made her feel like her entire life was about to begin, she had a strange sense of déjà vu, even though this time she was leaving it all behind, starting over again, in the place she'd sworn she'd never return to again.

She thought about it a lot, at the party, when Gwen had been so confident, and Iris hadn't thought of Julian or Stephanie or anything about her life in Manhattan even once. She was in her element, drawing on a part of herself that she'd honed in New York but had always been there, since she was ten years old and having sleepovers at Gwen's house, transforming each other with Gwen's mother's makeup, trying to make themselves better versions of themselves.

She wanted to be a better version of herself. Starting right now.

She described it all to Gwen as the cab wove through traffic: a boutique cosmetics company, all their own, in the heart of Westlake. By the time they'd reached Little Italy, they were talking over each other with ideas.

"Of course it makes sense for you to do this, with your corporate background!"

"Actually, it was the party that made me think of it, and once I did, it all just made so much sense," Iris said. "So, really, it's all thanks to you."

Gwen still didn't look convinced. "You're really going to be happy living in Westlake?"

Iris couldn't deny her trepidations, but she gave a firm nod. "There's nothing left for me here. But in Westlake…"

Gwen raised an eyebrow. "Joe?"

Iris shrugged, but she couldn't fight off the smile. Besides, this was Gwen she was talking to. She could see right through her. Always could.

"And you."

The cab pulled to a stop at the address Iris had given, and she pulled out her wallet to pay him.

"What's the plan for tonight?" Gwen asked, looking out the window.

Iris jutted her chin toward the place on the corner, with its harsh overhead lighting and neon signs. Iris hadn't had a slice of New York pizza since her early college days, and she wasn't leaving here without one more taste.

It wasn't fancy, but Gwen didn't mind. She'd never needed that side of Iris. She'd liked her just as she was.

ACKNOWLEDGEMENTS

Special thanks to Paige Wheeler, Lori Paximadis, and Diana Cox, whose contributions and expertise helped make this book what it is today.

Working with all of you has been, and continues to be, an honor and a pleasure.

ABOUT THE AUTHOR

Megan Leavell is a full-time writer and part-time dreamer. She enjoys writing about the relationships that define our lives, and her books are sprinkled with her signature warmth and humor. She is also the author of several bestselling novels under the name Olivia Miles. She lives on the North Shore of Chicago with her husband, daughter, and an adorable pair of dogs.

Visit www.meganleavell.com for more.

CPSIA information can be obtained
at www.ICGtesting.com
Printed in the USA
LVHW041910180521
687816LV00002B/7